P9-DNU-089

PRAISE FOR *WE LIE HERE*

"*We Lie Here* is another fast and surprisingly funny thriller from Rachel Howzell Hall. I was on the edge of my seat through all the revelations, twists, and turns in a fast-paced third act. Get this book and relax with the knowledge that you are in the hands of a fantastic crime novelist."

—Adrian McKinty, Edgar Award–winning author of the Sean Duffy series

"In *We Lie Here*, Rachel Howzell Hall gives us a tight, lean, eye-level look at the Gibson family—flawed, normal, abnormal, and each affected by a deadly secret left buried for years—while weaving a page-turning tapestry of dread, cold-blooded murder, and nail-biting tension. What a ride. What a wonderful writer. More, please."

—Tracy Clark, author of the Chicago Mystery series

"Rachel Howzell Hall continues to shatter the boundaries of crime fiction through the sheer force of her indomitable talent."

—S. A. Cosby, author of *Blacktop Wasteland*

"*We Lie Here* is definitive proof that it's impossible to be disappointed by Rachel Howzell Hall, who just gets better and better with each book. She has tools and tricks to spare as she pulls you to the edge of your seat with her razor-sharp plotting and keen eye for the darker side of human behavior that's too easily obscured by the California sunshine."

—Ivy Pochoda, author of *These Women*, a *New York Times* Best Thriller of 2020

"Loaded with surprises and shocking secrets, and propelled by Rachel Howzell Hall's magnificent prose, *We Lie Here* is a captivating thriller that I couldn't put down. It's very clear to me that Hall is one of the best crime writers working today, and she keeps getting better. *We Lie Here* is a can't-miss book."

—Alex Segura, acclaimed author of *Secret Identity*, *Star Wars Poe Dameron: Free Fall*, and *Blackout*

"Rachel Howzell Hall continues to prove why she's one of crime fiction's leading writers. *We Lie Here* is a psychological-suspense fan's dream with both a heroine you'll want to root for and a story you'll want to keep reading late into the night. A must read!"

—Kellye Garrett, Agatha, Anthony, and Lefty Award–winning author of *Like a Sister*

PRAISE FOR *THESE TOXIC THINGS*

An Amazon Best Book of the Month: Mystery, Thriller & Suspense

"This cleverly plotted, surprise-filled novel offers well-drawn and original characters, lively dialogue, and a refreshing take on the serial killer theme. Hall continues to impress."

—*Publishers Weekly* (starred review)

"A mystery/thriller/coming-of-age story you won't be able to put down till the final revelation."

—*Kirkus Reviews*

"Tense and pacey, with an appealing central character, this is a coming-of-age story as well as a gripping mystery."

—*The Guardian*

"The mystery plots are twisty and grabby, but also worth noting is the realistic rendering of a Black LA neighborhood locked in a battle over gentrification."

—*Los Angeles Times*

"Rachel Howzell Hall . . . just gets better and better with each book."

—CrimeReads

"Rachel Howzell Hall continues to shatter the boundaries of crime fiction through the sheer force of her indomitable talent. *These Toxic Things* is a master class in tension and suspense. You think you are ready for it. But. You. Are. Not."

—S. A. Cosby, author of *Blacktop Wasteland*

"*These Toxic Things* is taut and terrifying, packed with page-turning suspense and breathtaking reveals. But what I loved most is the mother-daughter relationship at the heart of this gripping thriller. Plan on reading it twice: once because you won't be able to stop, and the second time to savor the razor's edge balance of plot and poetry that only Rachel Howzell Hall can pull off."

—Jess Lourey, Amazon Charts bestselling author of *Unspeakable Things*

"The brilliant Rachel Howzell Hall becomes the queen of mind games with this twisty and thought-provoking cat-and-mouse thriller. Where memories are weaponized, keepsakes are deadly, and the past gets ugly when you disturb it. As original, compelling, and sinister as a story can be, with a message that will haunt you long after you race through the pages."

—Hank Phillippi Ryan, *USA Today* bestselling author of *Her Perfect Life*

PRAISE FOR *AND NOW SHE'S GONE*

"It's a feat to keep high humor and crushing sorrow in plausible equilibrium in a mystery novel, and few writers are as adept at it as Rachel Howzell Hall."

—*Washington Post*

"One of the best books of the year . . . whip-smart and emotionally deep, *And Now She's Gone* is a deceptively straightforward mystery, blending a fledgling PI's first 'woman is missing' case with underlying stories about racial identity, domestic abuse, and rank evil."

—*Los Angeles Times*

"Smart, razor-sharp . . . Full of wry, dark humor, this nuanced tale of two extraordinary women is un-put-downable."

—*Publishers Weekly* (starred review)

"Smart, packed with dialogue that sings on the page, Hall's novel turns the tables on our expectations at every turn, bringing us closer to truth than if it were forced on us in school."

—Walter Mosley

"A fierce PI running from her own dark past chases a missing woman around buzzy LA. Breathlessly suspenseful, as glamorous as the city itself, *And Now She's Gone* should be at the top of your must-read list."
    —Michele Campbell, bestselling author of *A Stranger on the Beach*

"One of crime fiction's leading writers at her very best. The final twist will make you want to immediately turn back to page one and read it all over again. *And Now She's Gone* is a perfect blend of PI novel and psychological suspense that will have readers wanting more."
    —Kellye Garrett, Anthony, Agatha, and Lefty Award–winning author of *Hollywood Homicide* and *Hollywood Ending*

"Sharp, witty, and perfectly paced, *And Now She's Gone* is one hell of a read!"
    —Wendy Walker, bestselling author of *The Night Before*

"Hall once again proves to be an accomplished maestro who has composed a symphony of increasing tension and near-unbearable suspense. Rachel brilliantly reveals the bone and soul of our shared humanity and the struggle to contain the nightmares of human faults and failings. I am a fan, pure and simple."
    —Stephen Mack Jones, award-winning author of the August Snow thrillers

"Heartfelt and gripping . . . I'm a perennial member of the Rachel Howzell Hall fan club, and her latest is a winning display of her wit and compassion and mastery of suspense."
    —Steph Cha, award-winning author of *Your House Will Pay*

"An entertainingly twisty plot, a rich and layered sense of place, and most of all a main character who pops off the page. Gray Sykes is hugely engaging and deeply complex, a descendant of Philip Marlowe and Easy Rawlings who is also definitely, absolutely her own woman."
—Lou Berney, award-winning author of *November Road*

"A deeply human protagonist, an intricate and twisty plot, and sentences that make me swoon with jealousy . . . Rachel Howzell Hall will flip every expectation you have—this is a magic trick of a book."
—Rob Hart, author of *The Warehouse*

"*And Now She's Gone* has all the mystery of a classic whodunit, with an undeniably fresh and clever voice. Hall exemplifies the best of the modern PI novel."
—Alafair Burke, *New York Times* bestselling author

PRAISE FOR RACHEL HOWZELL HALL

"A fresh voice in crime fiction."
—Lee Child

"Devilishly clever . . . Hall's writing sizzles and pops."
—Meg Gardiner

"Hall slips from funny to darkly frightening with elegant ease."
—*Publishers Weekly*

PRAISE FOR *THEY ALL FALL DOWN*

"A riotous and wild ride."
—Attica Locke

"Dramatic, thrilling, and even compulsive."

—James Patterson

"An intense, feverish novel with riveting plot twists."

—Sara Paretsky

"Hall is beyond able and ready to take her place among the ranks of contemporary crime fiction's best and brightest."

—*Strand Magazine*

WE
LIE
HERE

ALSO BY RACHEL HOWZELL HALL

These Toxic Things

And Now She's Gone

They All Fall Down

City of Saviors

Trail of Echoes

Skies of Ash

Land of Shadows

WE LIE HERE

RACHEL HOWZELL HALL

THOMAS & MERCER

This is a work of fiction. Names, characters, organizations, places, events, and incidents are either products of the author's imagination or are used fictitiously. Any resemblance to actual persons, living or dead, or actual events is purely coincidental.

Text copyright © 2022 by Rachel Howzell Hall
All rights reserved.

No part of this book may be reproduced, or stored in a retrieval system, or transmitted in any form or by any means, electronic, mechanical, photocopying, recording, or otherwise, without express written permission of the publisher.

Published by Thomas & Mercer, Seattle

www.apub.com

Amazon, the Amazon logo, and Thomas & Mercer are trademarks of Amazon.com, Inc., or its affiliates.

ISBN-13: 9781662500329 (hardcover)
ISBN-10: 1662500327 (hardcover)

ISBN-13: 9781542033695 (paperback)
ISBN-10: 1542033691 (paperback)

Cover design by Anna Laytham

Printed in the United States of America

First edition

To my mother, Jacqueline. I marvel at it all . . .

Three may keep a secret, if two of them are dead.

—Benjamin Franklin

Thursday, June 25, 1998

Every summer, the Afro-Americans came to hoot and holler at Lake Paz. Yes, every summer they arrived and talked loudly, and never kept private things private, and always spilled those secret things across the woods like cheap wine. And they always spilled those most-awful private things while good people, *quiet* people, tried to sleep.

Birdie glanced at the clock on her nightstand: almost an hour before midnight and those people in the cabin next door were doing this *now*. Of course they were. Their anger had slipped through the evergreens and rustled through the high grass to pull her from sleep.

They made the first Black family in these woods look flawless. Now, *that* family—the best of their people—would drive up, say hello as they moved from the car to their porch, bags of groceries already in hand and purchased from wherever they lived ten months out of the year.

The noise from *that* family would be laughter. A woman's. A girl's. His. Melodic. Harmonious. Pure. And he would play the piano, too. "Rhapsody in Blue" had been Birdie's favorite, and he'd play a few other songs she recognized from the movies or television shows. The girl played piano, too. Not as good as her father, but it was still nice to listen to. Not that Birdie would *ever* admit that to Bud. Oh no, not ever.

Any time *that* family sat lakeside, Birdie would hear them speak soft words. *I love you* and *You're beautiful* and *Yes, I'd like another*. And the way he looked at his woman and at his little one as he said those words . . . So soft. So dreamy.

What was that like? To hear soft words and silken declarations of love?

But that had been many summers ago. Tonight? Only hard words. *Stop* and *Let me go* and *Please don't*, with the little girl crying, screaming, shrieking even.

Birdie studied Bud, still sleeping in bed beside her. He was snoring with his mouth open. Lost to this world for the next seven hours. That was for the best, since Bud didn't much like the Blacks—not the ones who'd vacationed at that cabin summers before and definitely not the ones vacationing there now.

The girl shrieked again.

Birdie's pulse jumped, and she pushed away the heavy quilt. Mosquitoes lunged at her bare, pale legs. She slapped them away, then grabbed the bedside can of DEET and sprayed. After pulling on her robe and pushing her feet into slippers, she tiptoed toward the doorway.

The hardwood floor creaked.

Bud snuffled, then turned over in bed. "Where you going?"

"Fresh air," she said. "Can't sleep."

But he was already out again. Good. With Bud asleep, she wouldn't have to involve Karlton, Lake Paz's sole sheriff's deputy. He'd warned Bud and Birdie several times: *Leave them people alone, or I'll have to bring you in again.*

Let sleeping Buds lie.

Birdie grabbed the flashlight from the living room coffee table and the pistol from the empty sugar tub in the pantry. Just in case Bud was right.

The night air smelled of dying lake grass and still water and held the heat of the day. Croaking frogs and crickets vied to make the most noise. Tonight, the crickets were winning. Sometimes these were the only noises in the woods by the lake, and sometimes Birdie thought she was the only human surrounded by trees, water, and a sky as wide as forever.

Birdie now heard crying coming from the cabin.

These people.

This lakeside community had one restaurant, a general store, two churches, and a bar. No crime. No problems. Maybe not as fancy as Lake Arrowhead with all those movie stars and tycoons building mansions around its shores. Lake Paz was natural, created by the San Andreas Fault. Or, according to legend, created by the devil himself. Lake Arrowhead couldn't say *that*.

Beneath that moonless, forever sky, Birdie tromped through the crackling dry leaves and hard pine needles, past that gold Camaro (the only thing Bud actually liked about these people) with its god-awful thunderous muffler.

"Please, don't! Ohmigod, stop! Please."

All of this late-night hullabaloo made her underarms sticky with perspiration. What was he doing to her? And with their daughter right there? She'd heard that mental illness plagued the family. Every morning, she saw the woman, glassy-eyed and limp, wandering the shores of the lake. The child, wearing her Cookie Monster nightgown, trailing behind her mother, would stop to dip her hands into the water, but then call out *Mommy, wait!* because Mommy never stopped because she was drunk or whacked-out on drugs. The girl could've drowned a million times, and Mommy would've never known.

Maybe tonight he had tired of her spells, of searching for her *again* in the woods, of finding the little girl alone on the porch or playing by herself near the lake *again*.

Or maybe she cheated on him, and he found out and threatened to leave.

Or maybe he cheated on *her*, and the silly young thing had been enough of a fool to ask him about it.

"I'm begging you!"

Birdie's blood chilled. Crazy or not, any woman—white, Black, purple—knew desperation when she heard it. She slowed in her step as she came upon the kelly-green A-frame cabin, the nicest cabin at Lake Paz. It had a basement, a hot tub, and a deck that overlooked the lake. *They can't do anything without flash and noise,* Bud had complained, even though he'd wanted both a hot tub and a deck. Even though he owned the town's only general store, he still couldn't afford those fancy-pants things.

Hesitant, Birdie climbed the porch steps and pushed the doorbell. As she waited, worry flitted around her belly like fireflies.

No answer.

She ran her fingers through her short blonde hair, then banged her fist against the door. "It's Roberta Sumner from next door. I'm gonna call the sheriff's if you don't open up." She slapped at her neck—she'd forgotten to DEET there, and the skeetos were eating her alive.

The door cracked open. A smell wafted through that small slit. It wasn't alcohol. It wasn't drugs. Not even blood. Did terror have a scent?

Birdie stuck her hand into the robe pocket hiding the pistol.

All had quieted in the cabin. Even the girl had stopped crying.

The woman's eye, bloodshot and swollen from crying, peeked out at her. "Mrs. Sumner, how are you?" Always polite, she now sounded hoarse, tired.

"You all are too loud." These hard words made Birdie a little dizzy, a little nauseated. Because that wasn't what she'd meant to say, not right away. A Nebraskan, she'd been raised to offer pleasantries first—*how do you do, lovely evening isn't it, that's a lovely coat.* It was almost midnight, though. "You're gonna wake up the dead making all that noise."

"I'm so sorry," the young woman said.

Birdie tried to peer past her into the living room. The space was dark and quiet. Too dark. Too quiet. She gripped the pistol tighter. "Everything okay?" she asked. "Do you need the police? An ambulance?"

"I'm fine, thank you," the woman said. "Just a little disagreement. Nothing serious."

Birdie snorted. "More than a little disagreement, gal. And it sounds *very* serious. You woke me up, and you damn near woke Bud up, too, and you and me both know . . ."

The woman's eye widened.

What they both knew burned in the small space between them.

"We won't trouble you again, Mrs. Sumner. I'm so sorry."

Birdie squinted at the young mother on the other side of the door. She knew her entire face—tawny skin with freckles across the bridge of her nose, lips that usually curved into a smile but had broken tonight. Those brown eyes—or brown *eye*—weary, no longer merry. A flirt, she'd tried to soften Bud with those soft eyes and generous smile. The poor thing didn't understand that Bud would never, not ever . . . not even with a pretty thing like her.

"We've cooled off, I promise," the woman said. "We're leaving tomorrow. This will be the last fight you'll hear. I promise, absolutely *promise* you."

Birdie said, "Good. You take care, okay? Get some help." She leaned in closer and whispered, "You need anything, just leave me a note beneath my doormat. Nobody else has to know, okay? Just between us gals." She winked.

The woman nodded and whispered, "Thank you, Mrs. Sumner."

The front door gently closed, and Birdie started back to her own cabin. In the middle of her journey, she paused beneath the pine trees and cocked her head to hear . . .

Not a whimper. Not a word.

In the bathroom, Birdie grabbed the bottle of pink calamine lotion from the medicine cabinet and spread it across her neck, arms, and legs until she looked like a hot dog. Then she—

What was that? She closed her eyes to hear . . .

Bud snoring.

Mosquitoes buzzing.

No, it sounded like a small . . . *pop.*

Like a light bulb blowing out or . . .

Yes, she'd check under the doormat first thing tomorrow.

"Bird?" Bud shouted. "Come to bed. Can't sleep with you making all that noise."

"Coming, Bud." She placed the cap back on the lotion.

Yes, it sounded like a bulb blowing out.

A small . . . *pop.*

THE GOOD DAUGHTER

1.

The city of Palmdale takes my breath away. A vise, it squeezes air from my chest and leaves me wheezing with weak legs and a racing heart. I may die there, and yet here I am, sixty-three miles north of Los Angeles, behind the wheel of my Jeep and driving closer to that place. I sip air in anticipation, practicing how to breathe through a straw so that I can live.

I must be crazy going back.

"Yara, explain it to me. I really want to understand. Why throw the party there, then?" Shane's craggy voice booms over the Jeep's speakers.

I glance at my boyfriend, just a face now on my cell phone.

His bourbon-brown eyes narrow as his lips lift into a smirk. A native Angeleno, he has no clue why anyone would want to live anywhere other than LA, especially in the high-desert town where I lived for twenty-one of my twenty-four years.

"I'm hosting the party here cuz my family's here and most of my parents' friends are here. And since I'm paying for the whole thing, it's cheaper to throw a party in Palmdale than a party in LA. Make sense?"

Mom and Dad celebrated their twentieth wedding anniversary two days ago on May 15, and next Saturday night my sister, Dominique, and I will host the celebration they couldn't afford back in 1999. In my mind, I see family friends watching as Dad gazes down at Mom, his eyes filled with love, and I see my parents dancing to Etta James's "At

Last," feeding each other cake, and sipping a nice midrange champagne. I picture Mom later complaining about said midrange champagne and wishing, for once, that she'd sipped something decadent because if not now, then when? I see myself grinding my teeth but certainly understanding the desire to drink Moët. Later that night, I buy Mom a bottle of fancy champagne and then race back to Los Angeles as I ignore her *Is something wrong?* phone calls and eventually respond with *Sorry I missed your call* and *I'm fine* text messages.

So yeah. Instead of vacationing in Aruba, I've opted to spend nine nights and ten days in Palmdale planning this anniversary dinner party for seventy-five family members and friends at the Rancho Vista Golf Club.

Do I need a *real* vacation? Oh, *hell* yeah. But I also want to celebrate my parents' love and show Mom and Dad that they matter to me.

"I understand all of that," Shane says now, "but you also need a break, babe. To reset and see straight again."

I grind my teeth. "I *can* see straight . . . and I *did* give you back your credit card."

He says nothing, then: "Okay."

"I can see it in my mind. You were talking to your sister, and I said—"

"Okay, Yara. I've already canceled the card. Bank's sending me one overnight. And I wasn't talking about you losing—"

"I didn't lose—"

"I was talking about work and *that* . . . whole situation."

I grind my teeth again, this time to keep from crying.

It had been another long night toiling in the *Tough Cookie* writers' room. The team had broken down a future episode on index cards that spanned the length of three walls. I'd fully participated in the brainstorming session for the episode that focused on Cookie's grief over losing her only child to an asthma attack. Usually no one wants to hear the thoughts of a lower-level writer, but since I have chronic asthma, I knew firsthand the fear of not being able to breathe and the fear my parents experienced any time I wheezed. I'd finally been assigned to write the outline using the cards, which would be turned into the first draft of the script.

I don't know how I did it but . . . I misplaced the cards. They weren't in my bag. They weren't in the Jeep.

My ass was grass, and after my showrunner ran out of awful shit to say to me, I cried in my car for half an hour and used my inhaler more than once just to catch my breath. Then I pulled pieces of me together, shambled back to the office, and promised my boss that I'd find the cards. Later that night, I found them *on top of my refrigerator.*

How did the cards get there? No idea. But that was then. This is now, and now, my hands clench the steering wheel. "It's gonna be awesome. Everything's gonna work out. Nothing will go wrong. It will be perfect." My words taste like dust.

"You keep saying that, babe," Shane cracks. "But I'm hearing you freak out."

"It's being in my parents' *house* with all the cigarette smoke. That's what you're hearing."

And he's hearing low-key distress about future bickering with my mother and sister and having to listen to my parents' arguments over the next week and . . .

"I don't wanna go to Palmdale," I shout-whine to Shane. "Don't make me go!"

For the fifth time, my shaky hand ducks inside my satchel. And for the fifth time, I touch the inhaler's plastic actuator, the vial of Ativan (just in case), the box of Benadryl, and the bottle of eye drops—my battle gear against the dust storms that swirl over the city this time of year, against the mentholated clouds of smoke that burst from my sister's and mother's mouths from dusk to dawn.

"You should've invited me," Shane says now. "I would've made a great distraction from Gibson family madness. At least provided you some cover from the sniping."

I bristle—I was waiting for him to say that.

He chuckles. "Your line is: 'Oh, Shane. I should've invited you, too.'"

"Ha. You're the writer now?"

"I just figured . . . We've been together now . . . I just . . ."

I wanna grab the rose-gold cigarette case from the glove box. Mom gave me that case on my twenty-first birthday. The cigarettes inside are three months old, stale but never *not* smokable. *No.* I pluck the rubber band on my left wrist. The snap stings my skin, and beneath my wild curls, my scalp prickles.

I can stop smoking. I will stop smoking. I got this.

The desire passes. The wet-towel dread of going home has not.

"You really gonna try to write up there?" Shane asks.

"As Yoda says, 'Do or do not. There is no try.' So I will *do*, hence my stay at Ye Olde Holiday Inn." I pause, then add, "You're such a skeptic."

"I just know that sometimes . . ."

"Uh-huh?"

"You get a little . . ."

"Uh-huh?"

"Overwhelmed, especially when it comes to family stuff."

There's Palmdale in the distance. That's Lake Palmdale to my right . . . Pelona Vista Park to my left. Storage facility . . . ARCO gas station . . . Del Taco . . . May not be Pink's Hot Dogs, but Lee Esther's makes a mean gumbo ya-ya and shrimp po'boy.

"I'm good," I say. "I'm clear. I'm chill, and next week this time, I'll have a complete treatment for *Queen of Palmdale*. Maybe even a bad draft of the pilot script."

"Bet?"

"Bet," I say, "and it'll be grittier than my current engagement. I need to do this—*Tough Cookie* won't last forever. Talk to you later?"

"Yep," he says. "Promise me that you'll call if you find yourself going into 'that place.'"

"Promise," I say, then end our call.

Not that I hate writing for *Tough Cookie*—it's fun. After *Moonlighting*, it's actually my mother's favorite show, and not just because I'm one of its writers. A female private investigator named Cookie teams up with a washed-up action movie star to solve cases around the City of Angels. The title's a little . . . *eh*, but she survived years on the LAPD, faced the loss of a child, and continued to work in a traditionally male field. So yeah. She's tough. And her government name is Cookie. Therefore . . .

Writing for television pays well enough that I can afford to spend almost five grand for the party while helping my parents with my sister's college tuition.

The new drama I'm writing is inspired by my life growing up in this city. Palmdale living is different from Los Angeles living.

With its hot, dry desert summers and cold, windy winters, Palmdale (and its fast-food chains, meth farms, and GameStops) scars the Mojave Desert. With the Nazi Low Riders, Peckerwoods, Lancas 13, and Black Menace Mafia, there are way too many bored little boys living out here in the middle of nowhere. And there are way too many exhausted girls who clench into balls to take the hits or push out another baby, to become too small to see. Add dust storms and firestorms and heat waves . . .

There's no place like home.

My first sneeze comes the moment I open the Jeep's door in the Holiday Inn's parking lot. Grit swirls around the car. Not the cool-looking sci-fi grit in *Blade Runner* or *Dune*. It's the ugly grit that scratches eyes and clogs noses. By the time I reach the check-in desk, my lungs have tightened and my contact lenses have torn my corneas. My pink bra strap slips off my shoulder as I paw around my bag for the inhaler.

The redheaded clerk's name tag says HAYLEE. "Welcome. Last name?"

I'm still searching for the inhaler. It was just in here—I checked for it five times. I *know* that the inhaler is in the bag. Despite wearing faded blue jeans and a *Tough Cookie* crew tank top, I feel naked in the eyes of Haylee the hotel clerk.

And now two guests have appeared behind me with frowning red faces. The man shifts from foot to foot, and the woman pecks her blue eyes at my bare brown shoulders.

"I'm sorry, I'm . . ." I step out of line and roll my suitcases over to the seating area. I dump everything out of my smaller bag onto the coffee table. Pens, contact lens case and saline solution . . . prescription eyeglasses, sunglasses, lipsticks, three pairs of tangled earbuds . . .

No inhaler.

I cough and choke on my spit. My bra strap slips off my shoulder, and I wanna shove it in the lobby's water feature.

Over at the desk, more people check in. Over at the bar, guests sip cocktails. Everyone is hugging, slapping backs, and kissing cheeks.

And then there's me.

Back to the parking lot I go, my lungs tightening even more since I'm tromping through the swirling grit and kicking up more dust with the wheels of my suitcases.

The inhaler isn't on the driver's seat or on the passenger's.

Stop. Breathe. Relax. I close my eyes and hold a breath . . . release . . . in . . . out . . . *Okay.*

The gold lightning bolt pendant around my neck dangles and circles like a dowsing rod, directing me to thrust my hand between the seats and center console and . . . *There!*

Shane's missing Visa card. My face burns and I say, "Crap," before shoving my hand back down between the . . . *There!* The plastic casing of the albuterol canister.

I take a picture of the credit card and send it to Shane.

I'm so freaking sorry!
I don't know how it got in my car!

He texts back, No problem.

But it *is* a problem because by now, I've lost his headphones, the key to his gun case, and his car's registration. Most times, too many times, I'm run-down from workdays that start at nine in the morning and end at four in the morning.

Gotta do better. Gotta be more mindful. Gotta check a *sixth* time, because five times *obviously* isn't enough.

I shake my inhaler and then take a puff. Strands of my hair pull and straighten as the drug penetrates and opens my lungs. Glory be, I can breathe again!

In less than fifteen minutes, my hometown has already tried to do me in.

⚡

Room 303 is . . . fine. There's a coffee maker and a fifty-inch flat-screen television. There's a desk by a window that looks out to the parking lot and swimming pool. The clean room smells like lavender, and the tan carpet looks new.

I glance out the window, past the parking lot and to the foothills that ring the city. The ground is dusted orange with California poppies. At sunset, the hills will turn blue before plunging into the darkest black, and the skies will come alive as shooting stars streak across that vast nothingness. That's when I think of moving back home. That's when I miss watching *Moonlighting* DVDs with Mom and going shopping with Dominique a few times a week. That's when I miss hiking the foothills with Dad to stargaze just like we did back when I was a kid.

But then I remember.

The dust storms.

The wildfires.

The white supremacists.

The meth, so much meth.

And Barbara Gibson, my mother.

After graduating from USC, I left this place for good. Couldn't stand the high temperatures, the commute time, the Confederate flags hanging over garage doors. Mom was *pissed* that I'd escaped her queendom, and she wouldn't talk to me for a month. Usually, I celebrated these silences. This time, though, I thought we'd finally agree on something for a change—that she would be just as happy as I was that I'd left Palmdale. I was wrong. Once I landed my first gig as a writer's assistant and deposited cash into her checking account, the sting of me defecting to Los Angeles diminished . . . but not completely.

My cell phone buzzes in my hand.

A text message from Unknown.

Is this Yara?

Who wants to know? I text back.

Strangers have pitched me—I got a show idea. That's when I immediately text back, Not interested. Then I block that number because I don't wanna end up in court, accused of stealing some hack's story idea about a chimpanzee who solves crime on Saturn. True story.

I have information that will change your life! Unknown texts.

Wrong number, I text back.

As I swipe to check email, another message from Unknown pops onto my screen.

Who do you think you are?

2.

Yara Marie of the House Gibson, First of Her Name. Eldest daughter of Robert and Barbara Gibson. Big sister to Dominique Gibson. Voter, lover, and writer on the hit television show *Tough Cookie.*

"*That's* who the hell I am," I say to the phone.

I fall back into the bosom of the soft bed and call Shane again. Cool, clean air from the vent washes over me. "I feel wonderful right now."

"Your mother doesn't know, does she?" Shane says.

"That I'm staying at a hotel?" I ask. "Nope. Not yet."

"When are you telling her?"

"She'll figure it out once I walk to the front door to leave," I say. "She'll figure it out when she notices that I haven't brought in my bags. She's a smart lady, that Bee Gibson."

He says nothing.

"I'm a grown-ass woman, Shane," I say. "I can stay in a hotel room if I want. I don't need my mommy's permission."

A chill crackles up my spine. My body is telling on itself, and now, the need to nervous smoke fills my mouth. I pluck the rubber band on my wrist.

"I'd love to join you," Shane says.

"You've told me that forty times already."

"Forty-two, but I'm not counting." His laugh sounds like whiskey and brown sugar, and this time, I *know* why I'm tingling.

"What's the point of you being here?" I ask.

I know his head is cocking, his eyes are squinting. Right now, his nonverbal *Are you serious?* oozes through the phone.

"So . . . that . . . I . . . can meet your family?" he says.

A serious step that I'm not ready to take right now. Not that I'm ashamed of how he looks—he's a tall man with broad shoulders and those boozy brown eyes. And I'm not ashamed of what he does for a living—a US Marshal and a consultant on the show. A gentleman and a scholar, a roughneck and a grunt, Shane Christopher is *all* the things, but he is not . . . I am not . . . *we* are not ready to absorb awkward silences with my father because he tuned out the conversation and didn't hear the question asked. *We* are not ready to weather Dominique's microaggressions about cops. *We* are not ready to survive Mom's broadsides about . . . *anything*.

Just thinking about all this makes the muscles in my shoulders tighten. Just like that, Room 303 feels odd and tiny, and that cheap single-cup coffee maker looks as ridiculous as the faded watercolor of trees standing in a field of tulips.

⚡

Downstairs at the hotel bar, I order a Dark and Stormy for me and a Coke with a skewer of olives for my nineteen-year-old sister. "This for Dom?" The prison-muscles bartender smiles and nods toward the patio.

I pause, then nod. "You know her?"

He winks. "Who doesn't? Tell her that Myles from the Auto Mall says 'hey.'"

Dominique sits at the farthest outside patio table. She takes a deep pull from her cigarette, then blows dragon smoke to the sky—Snapchatting the entire time. She peers at me from behind her nonprescription Cazals—ugly, boxy things that would look horrible on anyone else. With her perfect long braids and perfect burgundy lipstick, Dominique's beauty is too big for this town. Her mindset—finesse, flex, and Glo Up on somebody else's dime—totally fits, though, in the Antelope Valley. I fear she may never leave.

I set the Coke and olives before her. "Bartender Myles from Auto Mall says 'hey.'"

Dominique leans past me and waves to Myles, then returns to squinting through cigarette smoke to see the menu on her phone. "I'm looking at the food you chose for the party and . . . What the hell is ca-ber-net demi-glock?"

"Demi-*glass*. Basically, it's like a red wine glazy gravy, but . . . *not*. Trust, it's gonna be delicious with the filet mignon."

"Filet mignon?" She snorts, shakes her head. "Ohmigod, y'all."

"You skipped the tasting and so you get no input, nor do you get to criticize."

She yawns, smacks her lips. "I love her, but Mom is a hype beast."

"Since 1970," I say. "What does that have to do with cabernet demi-glace?"

Dominique picks at the ends of her braids. "This is all fake, fake, fakety-fake."

I cock an eyebrow. "Says the girl wearing sixty percent fake hair."

"It's one hundred percent real virgin hair from Malaysia. The girl who wore it before me is more real than ca-ber-net demi-glock."

"Watch me ignore your trash reaction. Here I go . . ." I whistle and smile at the sky.

She gives me a raspberry.

I shiver with the thought of eating an anniversary cake made of fresh berries and fresh whipped cream layered between moist white cake, every bite followed by a sip of rich Colombian coffee. Dominique can "keep it 100" with her bag of Takis and tall caramel frap in the golf club's parking lot.

I sip my cocktail, then ask, "Which Barbara am I meeting today?"

"Anxious Bee. There's a big track meet tomorrow."

"Her girls healthy?"

"Pepsi had a charley horse yesterday, which means Mom's number one sprinter may be riding the pine tomorrow. Which sucks for her since recruiters are coming out and she may miss her shot. Her ass will be running from her gig at Walmart to her gig at Chili's."

Dominique takes a Snap of her cigarette and soda, then says, "Between planning this party, coaching stupid-ass teenagers, and going through menopause, I think Mom's finally losing it. And every time she catches her breath, somebody else texts her about Saturday night."

I slam down my cocktail glass. "They're supposed to be contacting *me*. My name and number are on the invitation."

"Auntie Cece and Xenia ain't trying to call you," Dominique says. "And when Mom's not on the phone or blowing her stupid whistle, she's been cleaning up, but the wind keeps knocking dirt back in."

Worst. Chore. Ever. Sweeping grit, only to find more of it an hour later blowing through the cracks of the house. Pissed that I hadn't done a thorough job, Mom always snatched the broom from my hands and swept it out. But the wind blew it back in. The day would seesaw like this, with neither my mother nor Mother Nature surrendering. Eventually the dust storm would move on due to time or boredom, leaving my mother exhausted but triumphant. She *always* wins.

"And it's worse since monsoon is, what, a month away?" Dominique says. "She keeps pacing and looking out the windows like she's waiting for it to come home from the war. Is that why I'm supposed to go to college? To effing . . . find the best ways to combat freakin' . . . *dirt?*"

"Next week," I say, "she'll wear a ball gown and swan in to 'Crazy in Love.'"

Dominique points her cigarette at me. "Oh. So. She doesn't want Beyoncé now. She played me this old Heavy D & the Boyz song. Now that we found whatever."

I roll my eyes and text the DJ. "That's her fifth song change this week. Oh—I checked the temp for that day. A high of seventy-three at noon. Perfect weather."

Dominique grins. "*If* there isn't fire."

"There won't be, and Mom will look lovely, and Dad so handsome, and we'll all be on our best behavior."

"Sure, Jan," my sister says.

"Very. Best. *Behavior.* I said what I said." I flutter my eyelashes. "Can't you picture it? Mom wearing a faux Christian Dior Spring 2011 couture gown with long sleeves and a cowl neck with layers of blue-beaded lace tulle. With tears in her eyes and a hand over her heart, Mom will flush as guests toss rose petals at her and Dad, who will tower over her in his tuxedo. After Judge Alvin Bader renews their vows, Mom and Dad will enjoy a slideshow and champagne. A Maybach will drive them to Santa Barbara's wine country."

Dominique gapes at me. "Flexing, are we?"

"Overkill with the Maybach?"

"Will the queen of England present them with Greenland at brunch in Santa Barbara?"

"Finland." I knock back the last of my cocktail.

"You still won't be the favorite daughter," Dominique says with a playful smirk.

I shrug. "I'll find some way to make it through the rain. Seriously: I still want to honor her for, you know . . . giving up her dreams to be a mom. We're not each other's favorite people—and one day, I'll figure out why that is—but she deserves this, Dom. Daddy does, too, but Mom worked so hard for us in *this* place, so let's give her this one perfect night, okay?"

Dominique bites into an olive, then says, "Ugh. Fine." We pinkie-shake.

I order another Dark and Stormy for me and another Coke with olives for Dominique. And all is perfect. There's a breathtaking high-desert sky above us, blue with faint white plumes made by air force jets.

Dominique bites her straw. "I'm dating someone." She pulls up a picture on her phone.

The brown-skinned man in the picture is bare chested, and his tats—Old English lettering, *2211, 3-18-9-16*, and a bulldog—run wild across his torso. With bleached twists on top of his fade haircut, Ransom Andrepont's ears stick out just like they did when he was a schoolkid two years behind me. He's also the youngest son of LaRain Andrepont, Mom's best friend and assistant coach. LaRain must be thrilled that Ransom's dating *up* for a change.

Me, on the other hand . . . Bile burns my throat. "Ohmigod, why?" I ask.

Dominique smiles as she swipes from shot to shot. "I don't have to explain anything to you. We're magic together, and I'm rubbing off on him."

I hold up a hand. "I don't wanna know about that."

"*Meaning*, he's talking about going back to school. Getting a real job."

"No longer jumping school principals in the parking lot?"

She rolls her eyes. "That was a long time ago. And if she couldn't handle the job, she should've stayed her ass in Baltimore."

"What about the pediatrician?" I ask, eyebrow cocked. "All that lady wanted to do was check rashes under a baby's arm and *vaccinate* niggas."

Dominique fakes a shiver. "Ooh. Listen to you. The n-word. I thought you overcame. Thought you was 'woke'?" She stamps out her cigarette on the bottom of her Vans sneaker. "And Ransom didn't *kidnap* her, and they dropped those charges." She sits up straight and proper. "Yes, he *liberated* a few things—"

"Her Lexus, her Gucci wallet, her stash of St. Joseph's baby aspirin, and three bags of lollipops. He stole the *lollipops*, Dom. What kind of depraved shit is *that*?"

She gives a one-shouldered shrug and laughs. "You're so judgy. You from Palmdale."

I chuckle. "Oh, I'll never forget. Mom is fine with this?"

Dominique smirks. Of *course* Mom's fine. Everything Dominique does is *fine, just fine.*

"So which penal colony is hosting your beloved right now?" I ask.

"He's in a really nice apartment with a pool," she says.

"Legally?"

"Don't you wanna come alive with flavor, darling sister?" She pushes her yellow-gold cigarette case to my side of the table.

"Nope." I don't dare even touch the case.

"You too good for a cigarette now?"

"First of all, you're too young to be smoking," I point out. "Second of all, Mom buying you a case like mine is totally ridiculous. I should be able to have something that you don't. No matter because, finally, I've stopped smoking. It's an unhealthy habit, and we're more likely to die from it than white women, and I'm not going out like that. And finally, most importantly, I barely have one functional lung. No matter how fabulous Rihanna looks smoking—"

"Fuck, *who*?"

"I don't like smelling like tobacco."

"Bougie."

"Okay, Miss Pumpkin Spice Latte." I pluck my rubber band, and the ginger beer and dark rum gurgle in my stomach. I'm nauseated, not because I want to smoke but because Dominique is triggering me. Once upon a time, she also hated her clothes smelling like tobacco. Like me, she'd hide Mom's cigarettes in the backyard. And somehow, here she is, a menthol lights influencer.

"Some of us can't afford to see a shrink," she says, continuing to press.

"It's covered with health insurance." I check my purse for the inhaler and find it zipped in the pocket with my sixteen lipsticks. "I know for a fact that you have health insurance."

"Bougie."

"Call me something other than the word you learned back in seventh grade."

"Supercilious. Grandiloquent."

"Better," I say. "Seriously: Am I, an asthmatic, bougie for wanting to like . . . *breathe* without having additional crap clogging my lungs? And instead of worrying about me, you need to worry about a boyfriend named after payment for the release of a captive."

She drops her cigarette case into her bag. "First of all, his name means 'deliverance.' Second, we should head to the house and get past Mom being pissed that you're staying here."

Depending on her emotional state, Mom will either:

A. Clap her hands, happy (maybe not happy but . . . *fine, just fine*) that I'm here, and *fine* with me being productive.
B. Criticize my choice of hotel, the wash of my high-waist mom jeans, and the fact that my hair curls this way instead of the other way.
C. Flick her hand, shrug, and say, *Whatever. What gift did you bring me?* or
D. Threaten to abandon us like she's done a few times after we've upset her.

This last option usually results in Mom getting her way. It's tethered our father for twenty years, and like a family choke chain, Dominique, Dad, and I go only so far. As much as we loathe Mom being there sometimes, the thought of her abandoning us makes us behave.

24

So I hope for Barbara A or Barbara C.

Maybe I should pop an Ativan just in case Barbara B or D is waiting for me.

Dominique's eyes widen, and she points at something behind me. But I don't need to look.

The increased wind speed and the harried hotel workers rushing to cover the pool tell me everything I need to know.

A storm is coming.

3.

The horizon disappears behind the wall of brown dust. No sun. No top or bottom. But we can still see buildings and cars in the parking lot. Although this isn't the worst storm, the wind howls with gusts around forty miles per hour, and grains of sand pelt our eyes. The trees bend but they don't break.

Dominique and I hurry into the lobby. As she and Myles the bartender chat, I watch the dry ground meet the air, whittling cars and trucks down to mere glints of chrome and metal. Just ten minutes long, the storm dies down, allowing visitors to hurry inside or out, eyes squinted either way as one hand covers their face and the other swats dirt from their clothes and hair.

"Ready to go?" Dominique asks, tossing a final wave to her Auto Mall friend.

I nod, hearing mostly the last shrieks from the dying storm. Together we head to the parking lot, everything now weighed down by disturbed earth.

"Don't say anything to Mom about me staying here," I tell my sister. "But still back me up. I'm gonna explain that it's closer to the medical center and with the air quality—"

"Nuh-uh," Dominique says. "I'm *not* getting involved."

I look over my shoulder. "You hear that? Like somebody shouted . . ."

With the wind still whistling and dust still swirling, I can't hear much, but I do spot a middle-aged Black woman climbing out of a big-ass purple Mercedes-Benz sedan. Her long, flowing duster and scarf match the car. Her gelled black hair is pulled into an up-top bun, and her silver hoop earrings catch muted sunlight.

Dominique stops in her step. "Who dat?"

"No idea."

The woman runs to catch up with my sister and me, and I'd like to tell her to take her time, that she ain't gotta run, but she's already standing in front of us. She smells expensive, offering a perfect-teeth smile through her huffing and puffing. Her eyes are red from the grit, and her mascara is gummy. "You're Yara, right?"

I nod. "May I help you?"

She grins at my sister. "That means you're Dominique." Her smile broadens. "I'm Felicia, your cousin. Second cousin, to be exact, on your mother's side."

Dominique and I look at each other, then shrug.

"We met a long time ago," Felicia says to me. "When you were just a baby."

"Ah," I say.

She hands me a business card. "You know Cece."

My mother's first cousin. More like my aunt than my cousin, Cecilia McGuire Campbell is busty, bawdy, and brazen. Her short, precision-edged blonde haircut requires a razor blade. She's been the ghost singer for many popular vocalists that she will not name . . . *yet. But you have two of their albums,* Aunt Cece always says with a wink. For Christmas presents, she sends Dominique and me concert tour T-shirts and sweatshirts along with autographed pictures from the headliners she sings behind, her own signature beneath more famous names.

"I'm Cece's daughter," Felicia says now. "Your mom and I grew up together."

Cece is singing at the anniversary party, but this Felicia . . . I have no idea who she is.

Her eyebrows crumple. "I know that I'm not on the guest list, if that's what you're worrying about."

Cheeks burning, I clear my throat. "I, um, can check to see if we can add a guest. Always room for family."

Felicia shakes her head. "I don't care about that. Don't worry." Her voice is deep like Cece's, and it's smoother, a Rolls-Royce compared to her mother's Shelby Mustang.

"Wait—how did you find me here?" I ask.

"Ma told me that you suggested guests stay at the Holiday Inn because it's nicer than the other hotels *and* it has a bar. Then Ma told me that Bee told *her* that you were arriving today, and that Dom told *her*, your mother, that you were staying here and—"

Anger bursts over me and I glare at Dominique. "You *told* her already?"

Dominique stammers, "I-I-Yara—we were just talking and it slipped out."

"And I asked the front desk to call your room," Felicia continues, "but the phone kept ringing and so I waited in my car closest to the entrance until I saw you."

I glance at the business card. She works for Northrop Grumman down in El Segundo.

Dominique also looks at the card. "Strategic business analyst. What's that?"

Felicia grins. "I take a lot of information and make it make sense. And I've been doing that in my own life, making things make sense. It still doesn't, and it's been more than twenty years now."

Dominique slaps on a synthetic smile and salutes. "Good for you, Cousin Felicia. We really need to—"

Felicia squints at my neck, gasps, and covers her mouth with a hand. "Oh my . . ." She reaches for my lightning bolt pendant.

"Oh, hell no!" Dominique swats Felicia's hand.

Felicia makes a startled bark as my chain breaks from my neck and coils in her fist.

Eyes wide, I yelp and clutch my now-bare neck. A lump lodges in my throat, and I can't speak. My skin stings. Cousin Felicia has scratched me.

Dominique snatches my pendant from the woman's outstretched hand and slips it into her pocket. She says to me, "I'll get it fixed."

"Yara, I texted earlier," Felicia whispers. "Did you get my messages? They probably showed up as being from 'Unknown' since I've never contacted you before, but I'm hoping you read them."

Numb, I can only waggle my head. The air is filled with foreign particles, but my lungs are gobbling oxygen and forcing air back up my throat. I start coughing, coughing, choking.

Felicia clasps her hands before her lips, prayer-style. "I'm so sorry," she says between my hacking. "I didn't mean to . . . I . . . I saw it and I thought . . . and I . . . I haven't seen a pendant like that in decades . . ."

Dominique spins me around and pushes me toward my car. "We ain't gotta stand here and listen to this bull." She turns back to Felicia. "No, you can't come to the party. Now back off."

"Wait," Felicia cries out. "I don't have a lot of time. Just give me a minute—"

Dominique growls, "No!"

I climb into the Jeep and catch my breath. My mouth tastes like dirt and salt. A fine layer of dust has slipped into the car and settled across the dashboard.

I have information that will change your life.

Who do you think you are?

How will my life change?

Have I inherited a haunted mansion, but I'll have to sleep in it overnight to claim it?

Am I a princess but years ago Mom renounced her throne to marry a high school football coach because of love?

I don't have a lot of time—that's also what Felicia said.

I don't care. She ain't getting none of my ca-ber-net demi-glock. She broke my pendant, and she's lucky that Dominique kept her hands on my shoulders instead of letting them find their way around that middle-aged neck of hers.

As I try to cough up dirt lodged in my throat, I study my cousin's business card again.

I have information that will change your life.

Though the hair on my arms stands up, excited for this mystery, I say "No" aloud. Right now, I don't have time for side quests from a woman my mother never talked about.

So . . .

Bye, Felicia.

4.

What could possibly change my life?

Being out nearly five grand if this event doesn't hit right? Mom knowing that I'm staying at the Holiday Inn because Dominique has already told her?

And why did Felicia yank my chain?

Mom gave me that lightning bolt pendant two years ago, on the day I graduated from USC with a film degree. *Light up the sky,* she told me. I don't think Daddy ever stopped crying. Also a Trojan, he stared at that lightning bolt around my neck and kept saying, *My girl, my Yaya* over and over again. I've never taken off the pendant, a rare gift from my mother. My mysterious, sexy-witchy-woman talisman fills me with wonder-working power.

But Cousin Felicia broke my chain, and now it lives in Dominique's pocket. My neck feels bare and vulnerable without it, and I'm back to being the short-stack word nerd that I've always been, on the way to meet Good Witch Barbara (or Bad Bitch Bee) with my throat exposed.

⚡

I've stopped following Dominique's turquoise Jeep.

She's now chopping space between a Subaru and a minivan, and I'm not trying to be killed today. She drives like a nineteen-year-old, all short stops and last-minute pedal-to-the-metal runs, never believing that a truck could run a red light and plow into her. Unlike me, Dominique learned early that spending $200 in Antelope Valley to detail a car is a waste of money, and so her Jeep's bright-blue paint has dulled from the dust.

The road to Gibsonville rolls through the west side—the closer my destination, the more my stomach cramps. I worked one summer at that boutique over there. During my rising-junior-year summer, I fell in love with Cayden Decker at Amargosa Creek Natural Park over there. Once I drive past my high school, I'm surrounded by houses the color of desert stones. Because of the midday dust storm, a few neighbors sweep their porches and walkways. The *swish-swish-swish* of a broom against concrete is as natural a sound in the Antelope Valley as the chirps of crickets and howls of coyotes.

Mrs. Duncan's front yard tree is leaning even more to the right than last year this time. Mr. Abernathy's American flag has been moved to hang above his garage doors instead of his house's second-story balcony. Foothills roll on and on behind our cul-de-sac, and creatures that live in those hills—bobcats, coyotes, reptiles, and arachnids—often visit at night.

By the time I reach Edgewater Court, my stomach has twisted so much that I'm damn near hunched over the steering wheel.

Our home, a taupe two-story California/Spanish, sits at the end of the cul-de-sac. The second garage behind our house hosts Mom's classic 1970 gold Camaro, protected beneath a tarp against the elements. She doesn't drive it, but she won't get rid of it neither because, duh, it's a classic. Behind that garage, the land rolls on until it hits the Ritter Siphon, where rainbow trout and largemouth bass swim part of the year. Past that is the Angeles National Forest.

Dominique already stands in the driveway with Mom—the duo hover at five feet ten. At five feet four, I'm the runt of the family. Wearing a *Purple Rain* tank top and jeans, Mom looks younger than forty-nine years old. A cigarette burns in one hand, and she holds a soft pack of Newports in the other. She whispers something to Dominique, and my sister glances at me, then laughs. Mom throws me a smile and waves as I park.

Talking about me already.

"Yaya," Mom shouts. The diamond, onyx, and yellow sapphire honeybee pendant twinkles against her skin. She takes me into her arms. "Miss Yara's home."

She smells like Chanel No. 5 and cigarettes, and she feels thin but healthy. Today, she wears a long, high ponytail and baby hair whorls like fire around her face. She's been in the sun—freckles sprinkle like cinnamon across the bridge of her nose. She takes a long drag from her cigarette and appraises me through the smoke.

I hold my breath.

"Lemme get this right," she says.

Here we go.

"Dom told me that you've been *hypnotized.*"

I laugh. "Uh-huh. I told you I was gonna stop smoking. I'm doing hypnotherapy." I lift my wrist to show her the rubber band. "Behavior modification. It's working."

She pulls a pack of Nicorette from her back pocket. "I've been trying to quit, too. Chewing these all day, but"—she takes a puff from her Newport—"I don't think it's working."

I point to the cigarette between her fingers. "You're not supposed to smoke that as you chew those."

She gapes at me. "For real?"

I nod.

She appraises the gum box, reads the directions. Grunts. Shrugs. Sticks the box back into her pocket. "I'm over it already."

"No, don't stop trying," I say. "Do hypnotherapy, like me. It's just a ten-dollar copay."

She kills the cigarette on the sole of her flip-flop. "I don't want people messing around in my head, making me remember everything I'm trying to forget. Anyway . . ." She holds out her arms again for another hug. "You're home."

I tiptoe to kiss her cheek. "Where's Daddy?"

"School—football tryouts today," Dominique says.

"He'll be home soon. C'mon." Mom grabs my hand and leads me to the porch.

She throws open the door, pulls me across the threshold and into the bright foyer. Nothing's changed since my visit on Easter weekend. The white couches remain spotless. The high, vaulted ceilings are free from cobwebs. Dominique's trophies and awards from her days playing high school volleyball crowd the fireplace mantel and china cabinets.

Mom's Louis Vuitton duffel bag sits in the foyer's nook, its contents as mysterious to me today as they were fifteen years ago, when that bag first appeared after a vicious argument between my parents. Dad had canceled one of my doctor's appointments without first consulting Mom, telling her that the therapist was a quack who only wanted to pump me with drugs. Mom told Dad to keep throwing balls through the air and leave the big thinking to her. He called her a petty dictator, and after that, the house banged and burned with fire and spit. Dad apologized, Mom placed the duffel bag in the nook, and it's remained in this spot ever since, a reminder of that night's warning. *This petty dictator will leave your ass here with these girls, Robert, since you know so much. Try me. Dare me.*

He didn't try her.

He didn't dare her.

An hour after every argument, he clamps his mouth and drops his head.

Dominique does, too.

I've dared her only once—*Go, then,* thirteen-year-old Yara shouted back. She called me disrespectful and ungrateful, said that I'd cease to exist if she ever, *ever* left me. *Little girl who can't even* breathe, she spat. *You ready to go there with me?*

Frightened by the infinite darkness in her eyes, I clamped my mouth and dropped my head. All just to avoid being taken deep into the Mojave Desert and abandoned on the side of the road like an unwanted puppy.

Why hasn't she unpacked that bag? No clue. Maybe she no longer sees it. Maybe it's become a piece of furniture forever in its spot like the fireplace tools.

The house smells of comfort food drenched in butter, coated in flour, fried in canola oil (because it's healthier). I smell biscuits and sweet onions and gravy over smothered chicken bubbling in the slow cooker. My tastebuds tingle, ready for all that fat and salt.

Dominique plops on the couch in the den. She aims the remote at the large-screen television on the wall and finds *The Wendy Williams Show*. Nothing in here is different except for that television—a springtime gift from me after the old set died.

Mom walks toward the kitchen. "Turn that off and come eat."

I trail after her. "Oh, I'm not hungry yet."

"Nope," Mom says. "Over the next eight days, I'm not listening to that. You need to eat better, Yara. When you're hungry and skinny and drinking too much—"

"I don't drink too much." I pluck a biscuit from the basket.

"Cabo last year," she says, eyebrow cocked.

"Uncle Stoney's wedding," Dominique shouts from the den.

"Those were special occasions," I say, nauseated from recalling four nights of drinking too many all-inclusive Tequila Sunrises and Long Island Iced Teas.

"You're not some rail-thin chick who can get by on Diet Cokes and cocaine," Mom says. "Your meds can't fully absorb if you're only eating salads and drinking green shakes."

"Which meds?" Dominique snarks. "The 'I can't breathe' meds or the 'my brain isn't working' meds?" She nudges me and grabs a biscuit.

Mom squints at my sister and says nothing, but that well-placed moment of silence craters Dominique's cockiness and she blushes and slumps.

I've taken anxiety medication since third grade, after waking too many nights screaming, thrashing around in bed, and drenched with sweat. I never remembered my night terrors, but I do recall the worry in my parents' eyes the next day. I'm on Ativan and switch to Symbyax occasionally to control bouts of depression. For the last three months, I've been flying without them, and I've been . . . *good*.

Mom eases the casserole dish of bubbling macaroni and cheese out of the oven and hustles it to the sideboard in the dining room.

Through the dining room window, I spot Dad climbing out of his blue Suburban. His crimson Highland Bulldogs T-shirt is dark with sweat.

Dominique retrieves the dish of sweet potatoes from the kitchen counter. "Mom, you cooked like it's Thanksgiving."

"Well, I'm thankful that both of my daughters are home," she says.

I grab the basket of biscuits and container of black-eyed peas. I peer at the speckled bits of meat in the peas. "This pork?"

"Turkey," Mom says. "It's healthier."

Dad bangs into the foyer and shouts, "Is my girl home?"

I rush over to greet him in the entryway. At six feet three, he's a redwood of a man, and now he's sweaty from running drills with fifty high school boys.

"Kicking and throwing?" I ask.

"Blocking and sprinting," he says.

"Shower, Rob," Mom shouts from the kitchen. "Yara's hungry."

My ears tingle. I'm not hungry, but Happy Mom must stay happy, so I say nothing.

He kisses the top of my head and trudges up the stairs. "Showering right now."

Mom breaks out the holiday wineglasses she found on Home Shopping Network. She pulls out two bottles of Pinot Grigio from the fridge, as well as a can of Coke and the jar of olives for Dominique.

My sister settles on the chaise in the den. She makes a duck face and holds up her phone to take selfies.

Upstairs, Dad sings Steely Dan's "Dirty Work" in the shower. His voice drifts down the stairs along with scented steam.

My heart is full and I'm filled with light. I'm no fool, though—this feeling won't last.

Minutes later, we're all seated around the round dining room table. After I offer the blessing, I open my eyes and survey the feast Mom has prepared.

"Looks good, Bee." Dad helps himself to the smothered chicken.

I select sweet potatoes, now glistening with butter and brown sugar. "Are there any . . . ?"

Mom scoops macaroni onto her plate. "Any . . . *what?*"

Dominique grins at me from across the table. "Any *what*, Yara?"

My cheeks burn. "Any veggies?"

Mom points to the dish of macaroni and cheese. "Black-eyed peas. Sweet potatoes—"

"Not those kinds of vegetables," I say. "I mean . . . broccoli, green beans, veggies high in fiber. Like your collard greens."

Mom uses her fork to point at Dominique. "You were supposed to remind me."

Dominique says, "Oops," and bats her eyes at me. "But Yara doesn't mind. You've been cooking for her all day. A badass on the track, a culinary goddess in the kitchen. A devoted wife and a wonderful mother—"

"Is this an ad for tampons, Dom?" I ask, eyebrow cocked. "Or are you simply kissing up to Mom cuz you need something?"

Dominique and Mom say, "Need something," together.

We laugh.

All good.

Fool's gold.

Dominque plucks an olive from the jar. "Somebody wanted an invitation to the party."

Mom smiles, thrilled that she's the guest of honor for what will be the hottest event next weekend. "That's the third person today. Who was it?"

"Some woman from LA," Dominique says.

Dad chuckles. "A bit more specific?"

I drain my first glass of wine. "Not 'some woman.' It was Cece's daughter Felicia."

"*Felicia?*" Mom smirks at Dad.

He rolls his eyes.

"There's room," I say, "if you want to invite—"

"Nope," Mom says.

Dad focuses on his mound of sweet potatoes.

I drop it. If Mom wants Felicia Campbell to come, she'll extend the invitation herself.

Conversation turns to sports since my parents and sibling are all athletes. Their competitive dinnertime banter makes me smile—whose team had a better season, which team trains harder, which squad has more endurance. In other families, the way Dad reaches to squeeze Mom's hand could be a reassuring gesture, an expression sweeter than the honey coating my biscuit. Because yessir, they've lived their vows for twenty years, a feat that many of my friends can't say about their own parents.

Really: I picture them on next Saturday night, Barbara and Robert Gibson dancing to Luther Vandross. Then Dominique and I join them on the dance floor for Sister Sledge's "We Are Family," shimmery butterflies fluttering around the King and Queen of Palmdale. Then I picture them changing into their going-away clothes in one of the club's hotel rooms. Dominique and I hunker near the door listening to the Queen of Palmdale tell the King of Palmdale to go fuck himself before she races to a mysterious paradise in her classic Camaro, all because he didn't want to dance anymore. Yeah, I could write that episode in my sleep.

Would Shane fit into this treacherous family alchemy?

Mom made blackberry cobbler for dessert, and Dad takes his bowl to the den to watch the Lakers game. Mom and Dominique retreat to the backyard with their bowls of cobbler and cigarette cases. Back in the day, I would've joined them out there, and together, we'd watch the foothills turn slate blue as smoke mixed with the sugar on our tongues.

Loneliness ripples across my heart, and I'm tempted to light up just to be a part. But I can't go backward—I deserve to breathe . . . *right?* I pop the rubber band on my wrist to tamp down that desire, and I take my dessert to the den and plop in the armchair across from Dad to watch the game. We don't talk much, just . . . *LeBron is a badass* and *The Jeep's running good, DeShawn caught a twenty-pound tuna down in San Diego last Thursday,* and *I bought a doorbell security camera for my apartment.* Dad stares at the television, unblinking, waiting for me to say more. But I don't know, can't possibly know, anything else that needs to be said.

At halftime, my phone vibrates. A text from Unknown a.k.a. Cousin Felicia again.

Please Yara
Talk to me before it's too late!

5.

Right now, I don't wanna talk to *anyone*, especially to a strange woman who broke my pendant and scratched my neck. Right now, all I wanna do is take a nap and sleep off Mom's soul food. Then I wanna drive to my hotel room, find *Cheers* on cable, and zone out for three hours with Sam and Diane.

As Dad snores on the couch, and the sun melts across the valley, I text Felicia.

Eating dinner
I'll call you later

Pushy broad. She's like algae—barely there but too slick to ignore. Is that why she and Mom aren't tight? There can be only one alpha in a pack, and that must be Mom, *no exceptions.*

Anyway, I don't have time to chat.

I have work to do.

On the way to the attic, I grab my IDEAS-*QUEEN OF PALMDALE* journal from my purse and jot down the ballroom scene of the happy dancing family, the argument, the Camaro racing into the moonlight. Idea captured, I shove the journal back into my bag.

To make the ballroom more personal, I'm placing items that symbolize my parents' love journey as table centerpieces. Like . . . pictures of my parents at Inglewood High School back in 1985. A framed love letter Dad wrote Mom once they reunited after college. Their first Christmas ornament as a couple.

Two weeks ago, Dominique seemed excited with the centerpiece concept. But now that she's here in the attic with me, not so much. She paws through a box filled with souvenirs and itineraries from our Bahamas cruise ten years ago. "How long are we gonna keep looking through all this?" Dominique asks. "Mom will be back from Big 5 any minute now, and you're supposed to clean the kitchen."

The attic is tall enough to house a low-slung chair and a lamp. Boxes and plastic tubs line the whitewashed sloped walls.

Dominique lounges like a cat in that chair. My back aches from sitting cross-legged, cramped between the boxes and the lamp. With all the dust, I can't stop sneezing.

My sister grimaces. "For real, how long are we staying up here, cuz you're about to die."

I take a breath. Sounds like I'm whistling. My eyes sting and my chest itches. "I just need to . . ." I pull my inhaler from my pocket and take two puffs.

"You're gonna have another asthma attack," Dominique says, "just like the last time you came to Palmdale. And I don't know how to do the Heimlich thing."

"Heimlich is for choking, Einstein."

"Whatever. You sound like you're gargling Pop Rocks."

"What's a little labored breathing to make your parents happy." I take another breath, and now, I don't whistle or crackle. I pluck from the plastic tub a faded, fabric-covered journal and a salmon-colored conch shell with Bahamas branding. "Random question: Why does Mom still keep that bag downstairs in the foyer?"

"What bag?"

"The Louis Vuitton duffel bag."

"No idea what you're talking about—ooh!" Genuine delight breaks over Dominique's face as she reaches into the tub.

An underwater picture of her and Mom snorkeling in the Caribbean's turquoise waters.

"I love that," I say. "Want to include it?"

She sets the picture in the centerpieces pile. "And I want a copy of it, please."

I've added more to the pile than Dominique has. Everything I find has meaning.

Like the conch shell from the Bahamas: I learned to snorkel beside Mom on that trip.

Like the camping knife: Dad cooked the best hash browns and bacon using this single utensil on our trips to Yosemite.

Not fool's gold. These were twenty-four-karat perfect moments.

I reach to the bottom of the tub and—*ouch!*—something sharp jabs my finger. A drop of blood pearls on my fingertip. "What the hell?"

Dominique has stopped looking for items and now scrolls on her phone.

I peer into the container to search for the mess that cut me. I spot a silver key with a circular head and cylindrical shaft. That couldn't have cut me. "A handcuff key?" I wonder aloud.

Dominique winks at me. "Kinky."

Another peek into the tub. I spot a broken picture frame, its glass shattered beneath the weight of the past. But the picture there . . . Mom is wearing a simple white slip dress, and Dad is wearing a dark vest and long-sleeved shirt as they hug beside an infinity pool. Taken at dusk, the hills behind them are lost in shadow and the sky above them is streaked with clouds. The pool reflects the sky and hills and newlyweds.

"Goals," Dominique says, breathless.

I love the warmth rolling off the photograph, and I snap a picture of the picture. "Where is this? I wanna re-create this shot."

"No idea, but you need to clean the kitchen. Don't wanna mess with her mood." Dominique places the pile of memories into a newer plastic tub I brought along for this trip. "I'll go start the dishwasher."

No, she won't. The kitchen will stay a mess until I go down.

"And are you gonna get my necklace fixed?" I shout at her back. "Or do I need to . . . ?"

She's gone.

I flip through the pages of the journal. Sporadic entries when Mom felt reflective, I guess. A twice-folded piece of paper sits between November 3, 1997, and November 7, 1997. *Major Depressive Episode/ Disorder—DSM-5 Criteria.* All nine boxes have been checked, from "depressed mood" and "loss of interest in almost all activities" to "psychomotor changes" and "recurrent thoughts of death."

Had Mom been diagnosed with depression? She'd been a new mother who'd ended her running career, so . . . maybe?

I stick the page back into the journal, then drop the journal into the plastic tub. I dump the frame's broken glass into a brown paper bag and take out the picture of my parents on their wedding day. "You will be the centerpiece on Mom and Dad's table and . . ."

A smaller photograph is stuck to the back of the perfect shot. In the smaller picture, a woman with cashmere-brown skin wears her thick hair pulled into an up-top bun. Behind her, water glistens as sunlight bursts across its surface. Her smile is as wide as the sky.

Though there's *some* resemblance to my mother, she isn't Queen Bee.

I don't know this woman, yet sadness finds me. It's heavy, sticky, like burned caramel.

I flip over the picture. There's fading block handwriting on the back.

E. at the lake

How did her picture become stuck behind my parents'?

Is she Mom's friend?

Dad's ex-girlfriend?

The welt on my neck from Felicia's fingernails tingles, and I now have a strange desire to burn this picture. I will *not* ask Mom about "E. at the lake." In this instance, what's found in the attic *stays* in the attic.

I slip the picture back into the dusty tub.

Still . . . I wonder . . .

Who's "E"?

6.

Something is wrong with Felicia.

Watching her stumble around the Holiday Inn had been funny at first—there she was in the women's bathroom, and there she was stumbling to the bar, and now, here she is, trudging to the lobby. Look at her shaky hands. Loot at her sweaty face. She looks as brittle and unreliable as the wallpaper in the bathrooms and as creaky as the bathroom stall doors.

Trippin'. That's what we used to call it. Losing your mind.

There's a history of women *trippin'* in the Campbell family, but no formal diagnoses.

Beating a man with a shovel. That had been Cecilia Campbell.

Running a woman over with a car. That had been Felicia's twin, Alicia.

Stealing a baby from the hospital. A Campbell woman back in the 1950s.

Murder. Felicia's great-grandmother.

These are the kinds of stories you laugh at over cigarettes and slices of Thanksgiving sweet potato pie, right after the Cowboys beat the Lions.

But this . . . *thing* happening to Felicia right now. This is different. She's not too far gone. She knows someone is watching her.

And she's right—I'm watching your every move.

A quick glance at the hotel lobby's digital clock. Almost five o'clock.

Yara *will* come back to the hotel. Without Dominique buzzing around, Yara will listen to Felicia. That can't happen.

Felicia now plops in a lobby armchair and stares at the large platter of apples on the coffee table. She closes her eyes as her lips move.

Is she praying?

Too late.

Two teenage boys snag apples from the platter and drop onto the couch across from Felicia. They set their sneakers on the coffee table. Felicia squints at them, irritated, but they ignore her and crunch into their fruit.

The hotel manager spots Felicia sitting in the lobby. She lifts an envelope and makes her way over.

Just as planned.

The manager holds out the beige envelope.

Open it. Open the freaking . . .

Felicia tears open the flap, then pulls out the note. She gasps, bows her head, and holds her heart. She looks up to the sky, to God, thankful.

Poor thing.

God had nothing to do with what she's received.

That letter?

Courtesy of the snake in the garden.

7.

After cleaning the kitchen (alone), I follow the sound of theme music from some schmaltzy Hallmark movie. Mom has returned from the sporting goods store, and she's resting in the den with a blanket around her legs and a glass of white wine in her hand. She looks like she's watching late-night TV on a winter night in Vermont even though slats of desert sunlight brighten the carpet.

The front door mail slot creaks, and envelopes and catalogs scatter across the tiled floor.

I scoop it all up, hoping that this story ends soon so that Mom and I can watch *Moonlighting* before I leave for the hotel. I sift through catalogs, utility bills, and the mortgage statement before stopping at an envelope from Southland Collection Group.

My heart jumps in my chest. This envelope is addressed to me.

> RE: Account 78736A
>
> We have attempted several times to resolve the problem of your past-due account. However, we still haven't received payment of the outstanding amount, which is now significantly in arrears. Your account is overdue in the amount of $7,000.
>
> Description of services or products: tuition.
> CALIFORNIA INSTITUTE OF THE ARTS

Dominique attends Cal Arts, and every month, I help to pay some of her tuition. Mom sends me their share to cover the balance. I've *never* taken out a loan for Dominique.

I place a calming hand over my fluttery heart—this is just a misunderstanding, a mistake. Yes, that's what this is. I step out onto the porch to call Southland Collection Group.

After pressing one, and then three, and then holding and explaining why I was calling, I listen as customer service agent Priscilla taps her computer keyboard.

I pace the arc of the cul-de-sac. Over at the crooked-tree house, Mrs. Duncan sweeps dust from her entryway. Her front door faces the wind, and the same dust she's sweeping will be back in her house two hours from now.

"You still there, Miss Gibson?" Priscilla asks.

"I am."

"The loan is under your name," Priscilla says. "Meaning, you completed the papers, and you signed the documents for ten thousand dollars."

"Ten thousand—*when?*"

Priscilla taps more keys.

"And it's for how much again?"

"Original loan amount, ten thousand, with the balance now at seven thousand."

"That's a mistake."

I love my sister, but I would've never . . . *Ten grand?* For *Dominique?* A girl who's never finished a word search? Who thinks that reading books is akin to climbing Everest?

"I can send a PDF of the loan documents," Priscilla offers, "though you should already have a copy when the loan was approved back in October."

Where was I back in October?

Sure as hell not signing loan documents for my sister.

My phone beeps. The email from Southland Collection Group just landed in my in-box. There it is. My name. My social security number.

But that's not my signature.

⚡

Mom aims the remote at the television to pause the show. "I signed for you."

I pinch the bridge of my nose. "Why would you do that?"

"You need to get some of that bass outta your voice." Mom narrows her eyes, and her lips tighten into a slash. A warning that Bad Bee is about to climb into the cockpit.

My fingers pluck at the rubber band around my wrist. I don't want Bad Bee to visit, but I refuse to just . . . let her *freaking* forge my signature anytime she wants, *what the hell?* So I squeeze my eyes shut and inhale slowly . . . then slowly exhale. "I didn't—I wouldn't have . . ." I push out a loud breath. "It's in collections."

Mom flicks her hand. "Not yet. We got a month to pay before it hits your credit."

"And you know this because . . . ?"

"Because it's happened before. *Obviously* I pay the bill, because your credit is perfect."

I don't answer.

"Isn't it?" Her words are cold fingers on my very hot face.

"Yes. But you didn't tell—"

She kicks off the blanket. "You *told* me that we could take out the loan."

"That you could forge my *signature?*" I shriek.

"That I could sign on your *behalf,*" Mom corrects. "When Dom first enrolled, I told you that we couldn't pay up front for the first semester because we needed to do the roof and restucco the house."

I nod. "I remember that."

"And then," Mom says, "I told you that we couldn't take out any other loans because our debt-to-capital ratio or whatever wasn't good since the house depreciated."

I shake my head. "No."

"You said that you'd sign for the loan if we paid it off."

My memory gyroscopes and I'm dizzy—I certainly don't remember that. *"No."*

"You didn't drive up to sign the papers," Mom continues, "because you were in the writers' room for a week and couldn't get away."

That sounds familiar. I use that excuse any time Mom asks if I'm visiting soon. My clammy face now burns with shame from crying wolf one too many times.

"And so I signed your name," Mom says. "And I've kept my word, paying off the loan in bits and pieces, and you just *happened* to be snooping through my mail."

I square my shoulders and hold up the letter. "My name is on the envelope."

She squints at me and shakes her head. "You know what, Yara Marie? You do this all the time. You do shit, then say that you didn't do it. Lose shit and insist that you didn't."

Like Shane and his credit card.

"Sometimes," Mom says, "*most times*, you accuse others of doing the shit that you do."

"Mom," I shout, "what are you talking about? I didn't accuse you . . ." But I *did* accuse her, maybe not outright but by inference.

Like I *kinda* accused my coworker Steph of losing the *Tough Cookie* episode six index cards. *Do you remember what you were doing before you set them down?* I'd asked her.

Mom stalks the den, eyes on me. "I can't stand this, Yara. You're looking at me like I took your million dollars and brought back a handful of magic beans." Her gaze moves past me and out to the backyard.

At the rear garage, Dominique and Ransom Andrepont lean against the tarped Camaro.

"I took out the loan to ensure *she* got a degree," Mom says, pointing at her youngest daughter. "Not to be tied down to *that* asshole."

I squint at her. "I thought you liked them being together."

Mom tilts her head. "Oh yeah. I dream of my child getting knocked up by a thug."

Ransom and LaRain insist that he's not a Crip, though he may have Crip *sympathies*. His friends and a few ex-girlfriends *may* be members, but Ransom is just a confused young man caught up in a town of unsupervised children. Those numbers on his torso—3-18-9-16—don't correspond to C-R-I-P. That's just . . . Ransom being random. At least, that's what his attorney claimed after fourth-grade Ransom broke into a 99 Cents Only store and stole twenty bags of Flamin' Hot Cheetos.

A crime of opportunity, not pathology, Ransom's social worker said after thirteen-year-old Ransom stole a bicycle that belonged to a mall cop.

The college loan makes sense now, and I probably *did* hear Mom's frustrations and fears that day and say, *Sign my name and just pay the bill.*

"It's all good," I say to Mom now. "I'll make arrangements to pay off the seven thousand. We just got our wires crossed, that's all."

"My wires *never* cross. I have proof."

"It's okay. I believe you."

"No, you don't."

No, I don't.

Mom scrolls on her phone. "Ah." She holds out her phone for me to see.

Just confirming it's okay, Mom had texted.

Yeah. That's me.

It's a big loan.

I know

We can drive down and you can sign

I trust you Mom
And it's a crazy time right now

You sure?

MOM I APPROVE ILY

My tongue sits dumb as meat in my mouth.

The front door opens. It's the second time today that Dad trudges into the house dusty and dank with sweat, this time after his evening hike. The camera I gave him for Christmas hangs around his neck. He beams once he sees that I'm in the den. "You're still here!"

"Always home in the nick of time," Mom mutters. "Yara was about to lose her head."

Dad's eyes flick between Mom and me, and his smile dims. "What's wrong?"

I wave my hand. "Nothing's wrong," I say, my voice still shaky. "How were the trails?"

He pauses, then bends to take off his boots. "Crowded. People kept getting in my shot. You should've come with me—"

"Robert," Mom says, "don't even think about it. Take that dirt out to the porch."

"Thought you liked it dirty," he says.

She smiles and winks at him. "Outside."

He lifts his eyebrows. "Haven't done *that* in a long time, but I'm—"

"Shoes on the porch, Robert," Mom says. "Then shower. Again. Please."

"I'll go next time," I chirp, watching as he turns to the front door. Out back, Dominique and Ransom cup each other's faces and kiss. Though part of me celebrates love and my sister finding someone to spend time with, the larger part of me worries. I can see this story arc play out, and in every episode of *Queen of Palmdale*, their situation worsens.

In the pilot: Dominique Gibson, former student body president and voted Most Friendly, gapes at a positive pregnancy test as Bruno Mars sings about twenty-four-karat magic from her HomePod mini. The baby daddy: Ransom Andrepont, the neighborhood gangsta who she thinks has a heart of gold.

In episodes one through ten: Dominique drops out of college, thereby wasting thousands of dollars of her family's hard-earned money. She wanders from one low-paying job to another, her belly swelling until she can no longer work because of gestational diabetes. She has the baby, and I throw a party to celebrate little Deja's arrival. At the taco bar, Dominique grabs my hand and says, *I'm leaving him. For good this time. You were right.* Credits roll as we all do the Electric Slide to Cameo's "Candy."

Midseason finale: Dominique lands in jail for getting caught up in some hood shit.

Season finale: Dominique takes gunshots to her head and shoulder because bullets meant for Ransom don't have GPS.

Postcredits scene: Dominique's eyes open—she's alive and it was all a dream . . . but then she finds herself back in the bathroom, gaping at a positive pregnancy test, wearing the same sweatshirt and listening to the same Bruno Mars song playing from her HomePod mini.

Stuck. There. Forever.

If being stuck can happen to Mom with a good guy, it can certainly happen to Dominique with a lesser man who lacks Dad's integrity and dedication.

I think about this as my mother and I watch Maddie and David edge closer and closer to consummating the relationship that fans wanted. This evening, we laugh, and I place my head on her shoulder. She doesn't light up a cigarette, and after I announce that I'm staying at the Holiday Inn so that I can be there for our out-of-town guests and finish a big project, *the* Barbara Nicole McGuire Gibson says, "Okay. That makes sense. I'll let it slide this time."

Holding my breath, I kiss her good night, then head to the front door. I glare at the designer bag tucked inside the foyer nook and head out to the driveway.

Dad sits in the lawn chair beneath our silver maple tree. Though there's a notepad and pen on his lap, he's texting on his phone.

I say, "Hey."

He startles and fumbles the phone to the grass. "Leaving?"

I peck the top of his head. "Yep."

Who is he texting?

He scoops the phone from the lawn, then slips it into his pocket. "No arguments?"

"You're kidding, right? We argued, but I survived. What about you? Everything okay? You guys good?"

He says, "Yep," then stretches. His legs and arms are as long as a spider's.

I toe a dandelion in a small patch of weeds. "Why doesn't she unpack that thing?"

He knows that "thing" I'm referencing. "I don't think she even sees it anymore."

"Move it, then."

He runs his hands over his face.

"Ask her nicely to move it. She doesn't need it anymore."

His jaw clenches. "I'm not trying to have that argument."

"But it's . . . I don't . . ." I sigh.

"It bothers you."

I wring my damp hands. "She may not think about it. She probably didn't even mean it when she said it, probably didn't think it affected me as much as it did—but it does." I pause, then ask, "Do you know what's inside?"

Dad stares out into the darkening desert. "Nope." He finally meets my eyes. "It's her business, what's in that bag. You don't have to know everything all the time."

"Fine." My shoulders drop. "I won't say anything. Don't wanna ruin the week cuz she's pissed at me." I've already flirted with my beheading over stupid loan documents.

He chuckles with no hint of mirth. "I've said that—*don't wanna ruin the week cuz she's pissed at me*—probably more than I've said my name."

"And yet, you made twenty years," I say, eyebrow cocked.

"That's because Bee and I wanted to give you and Dom what neither of us had." He squeezes my hand, then pulls me closer. "We were right to stick it out, because look at you, Yaya. Your career, yeah, but just who you've become. You're thoughtful even when you don't wanna be, and your mother would've . . ." His lips clamp, and his phone chimes from his pocket.

"Mom would've what?"

He stands from the Adirondack chair. "Would've loved for you to stay. Me too. But I understand." His chin quivers as he hugs me. *He's* quivering as he hugs me.

His phone chimes again.

"Should you get that?" I ask.

He says, "Nah. Parents tripping over why their boy can't catch a ball."

That's a lie. Like my "stuck in the writers' room" lie, "unreasonable football parents" is Dad's. I've tried to move him from this, hoping that I'd become old enough that he'd trust me.

"Find anything good in the attic?" he asks, walking me to my Jeep.

My heart jumps in my chest. "I did! I found the wedding picture of you and Mom beside this gorgeous infinity pool."

"I wanna see that," he says, grinning.

I show him the picture I took of the picture. "Where was it taken?"

"My booster's house up in Bel Air," he says, zooming in on the shot. "He was like a dad to me. Passed a few years ago."

I make a sad face. "I wanted to re-create it."

"That's okay." He tugs my ear. "You're doing enough as is." He nods toward the house. "You should get out of here before she changes her mind about you not staying."

⚡

Why did Daddy lie about that text message?

If that wasn't a football parent, who could have been texting him?

His buddy Corbin?

His cousin and assistant coach, DeShawn, absolutely the worst influence ever?

Another woman?

My bladder feels heavy because I've seen firsthand that same cell phone fumble in my own love life before Shane, and it's always been because of another woman. And growing up, I've heard angry whispers between my parents. At least twice a year, I've seen my mother's folded arms and tight lips and Dad shaking his head.

Feels like Another Woman Drama.

As I turn left onto Lake Paz Road, my phone buzzes with a text.

You need to know the truth RIGHT NOW!!!

Ohmigod, this lady.

"What 'truth,' Felicia?" I ask.

56

That you're crazy, which is why no one invites you anywhere, which is why I've never even *met* you? Mom, Aunt Cece, Nana . . . no one has *ever* mentioned Felicia. I've never heard stories about Mom and Lee-Lee or Shay-Shay or whatever Felicia's Gen X nickname would've been while kickin' it at RadioShack back in the day.

And if the Felicia back then was anything like the Felicia *today*, I understand Mom's desire to keep this woman at arm's length.

A bell dings in my head. Now *that's* a helluva plot for *Queen of Palmdale*. Annoying Relative shows up out of nowhere bearing bad news right before the big party of the year. They barge into the party and proceed to be an asshole and spill the secrets about the handsome groom. Next morning, Annoying Relative is found beaten to death on the ninth hole at the country club's golf course. Everybody wanted them dead—and everyone's fingerprints are on a Big Bertha driver that was ditched in a sand trap. Whodunit?

Ha. Maybe I *should* invite Felicia. Not to have her killed by annoyed family members. But just to see the dynamics between her, Mom, and Aunt Cece. *Hoo boy!*

No, I'd never wish her dead.

8.

Not many cars driving around or pedestrians strolling the sidewalks. No one walks in this town, especially at night. Over on the 14, the red and white lights from cars and trucks zoom back and forth like fireflies or tracer rounds. Beyond the 14, there's only desert.

I spot the green glow of the hotel sign, and the promise of breathing cleaner air makes me smile. For the next ten hours, I won't have to watch my words or listen to Mom's cracks about Dominique's student loan.

Okay: I *kinda* remember a conversation with her about signing those papers. Knowing my schedule, though, I probably *was* preoccupied with outlines, beat sheets, and series bibles. I do forget things, lose things. And she *did* have receipts with those text messages. But what did she mean by, *You do this all the time*? Refuse to automatically roll over any time she accuses me of deception? Do *what* all the time?

I open the door to Room 303, and clean, crisp air rolls out to greet me. On the carpet, there's an envelope that has been slipped beneath the door. My name is handwritten on its face.

A bill so soon?

I toss my bag on the bed, then tear open the envelope.

Two keys. Nothing extraordinary about these keys—the gold hexagon can be found on any person's ring. The other key is a silver square. The keys come with a handwritten note that doesn't fill the entire page.

Yara, this is Felicia again.

What I must share with you is very important. Please meet me tomorrow morning at ten at your mother's favorite place. I have critical information that will change your life. Please keep this to yourself for now! Here's the address.

Mom's favorite place?

1224 Stardust Way, Lake Paz, California.

Mom's favorite place is the Atlantis resort in the Bahamas. Stateside, it's the Bellagio in Las Vegas. Closer to home, Target.

Also: hell no. As much as I enjoy writing forty-two-minute-long episodic mysteries for a living, I'm not into meeting strangers (and Felicia *is* a stranger) at random spots in the freakin' forest. Why? So that some Nazi Low Rider can follow me cuz he thinks I'm trying to steal his hidden stash of meth? So that some Black Guerilla asshole can jump me cuz he thinks I'm homeboy's girl who stole that bag of weed over at the Red Roof Inn?

I text Dad since he's probably still holding his phone.

Made it to the hotel

OK I love you

I grab the IDEAS journal from my purse and write down every thought I had for *Queen of Palmdale*—more on the ballroom scene and the distant cousin showing up.

Before taking a shower, I search for Cousin Felicia on the internet. Her LinkedIn page tells me that she *is* a big deal at Northrop Grumman.

She graduated from California Institute of Technology, majoring in information and data sciences with a minor in history.

She's also past president of the graduate chapter of Alpha Kappa Alpha—we're sorority sisters. A class-reunion page on Facebook says that she attended Inglewood High School from 1985 to 1988, same time as Mom.

I log on to www.kanga.com, the inspiration for the people-search website Cookie uses on the TV show, and I find more personal search results on Felicia Campbell. She has a home in El Segundo, two ex-husbands and a current one. The single divorce petition I find names Darius Montgomery. A peek onto his social media pages shows me a curly-haired, squinty-eyed man who favors loud suits and expensive cigars. I find an obituary for her first husband, Aiden Rivers, a white guy who resembles the director of *Twin Peaks*. He died of a heart attack.

No arrests. No criminal convictions.

Although she checks out as legit on the web, having three husbands suggests that Felicia Campbell may have a messy personal life.

I type *1224 Stardust Way* into the search bar. While there's no street view available, there is a satellite image of a house built on the banks of Lake Paz. It's a thirty-minute drive north from my parents' house.

Is it a B&B? A spa? And why does Felicia say "critical information"? I click on www.lakepaz.com/visitinglakepaz.

Lake Paz, 65 miles north of Los Angeles, sits atop the San Andreas Fault. Fed by an underwater aquifer, this lake—3,550 feet above sea level—cuts through the Angeles National Forest, making it a popular destination year-round. From hiking and camping, to cross-country skiing and water sports, Lake Paz has it all!

As promised, I call my cousin. Felicia's line rings . . . rings . . . No answer.

I don't leave a message, but she'll see in her call history that I called at nine o'clock.

Critical information . . .

I wonder about this as I shower, as I spray my hair with dry shampoo, as I Febreze my clothes to get rid of the smell of smoke. I sneeze and sneeze again, my eyes burning. My allergies, along with the quick tugs of anxiety, have returned.

I take two hits from my inhaler, pop a Benadryl, and crawl into bed. Right now, I can't even smell the clean, bleached sheets, one of the best things about hotel room beds. I skip the Ativan, because with the Benadryl in my system, I'd never open my eyes again. Since *Cheers* isn't on, I find *Iron Chef America* on the television just in time for the bacon battle. As the competing chefs prepare dishes featuring one hundred types of bacon, the little pink pill kicks in and . . .

⚡

My phone vibrates from the nightstand . . .

Bacon . . .

The phone . . .

Nightstand . . .

Whatever it is . . . can wait.

Whatever . . .

9.

The note that the hotel clerk handed Felicia had been the greatest thing ever written.

I miss you so much. And I couldn't stay away anymore. I heard about the party. They're ridiculous and I'm ready to fight back. But I need your help. Please, I'm asking you to make it up to me. I will forgive you for everything if you come and meet me. Call me and I'll text you the location. We'll meet there, and then we can talk.

Felicia had called that number, but only a fool would actually *answer*. She left a voice mail, and a minute later . . . Tap, tap, tap—text message sent.

And now, it is the darkest of night out here. The parking lot is empty, and nothing moves across the flat horizon. Not even the full moon can make this inky lake water beautiful.

There! A pair of headlights shines in the rearview mirror. Hopefully, Felicia's alone. Hopefully, she isn't armed. Felicia's not well, and so she's unpredictable. If she *is* armed, she won't be the only one.

The Benz careens into the parking lot and stops beneath a sherbet-colored safety light.

Here we go . . .

The smell of lake water is sickening. Cold out here. Fortunately, the walk over to Felicia's Benz is quick.

The sedan's passenger-side door is unlocked. The inside smells of rum and dead things.

Felicia presses her hand against her heart. "Oh my goodness, it's really you!" Tears stream down her cheeks. She moves in for a hug but stops short.

"Are you drunk right now?"

Felicia gasps. "What? No! I can't believe it—"

"Why are you here?"

Felicia's smile falters. Her lips tremble, and her breath hitches in her throat. "Because . . . I thought . . . You . . . The note, you left it for me."

"Did I ask you to do any of this?"

"No, but—"

"What did I ask you to do?"

"I'm sorry," Felicia says now. "I . . . just . . . want to be happy, once and for all."

"Always about what *you* want, right?"

Felicia blinks, then looks away. "I'm sorry. I didn't mean—"

Out comes the gun.

Felicia sees the weapon glint before it rests against her forehead.

"Start the car."

Giant tears spill down her cheeks. "Please don't, no, no, please, oh God, help me."

The gun nudges her sweaty forehead. "Start the *car*."

Felicia barks like a seal, then pushes the ignition button. "Where . . . ?" She can barely speak and wipes her face with the backs of her hands.

"To the other side of the lake."

The Benz's tires crackle against sand dumped by the afternoon dust storm.

"Money—is that what you want?" Felicia whispers with a side eye. "I'll give you anything you need. Whatever you want."

So dark out here. The parking lot on this side of the lake doesn't have many streetlights.

Felicia parks in the space closest to the water.

"Get out."

Felicia barks again, then exits the car.

So cold. Gotta be forty degrees . . .

"Walk."

Felicia refuses to move.

A push.

Felicia pushes back.

A slap. Another slap.

The gun raises, and reality sets in as Felicia clutches her stinging cheek.

"Walk."

The gun pushes into the space between Felicia's eyes, and she laughs.

"Turn around and walk."

"What did I do?" Looking straight ahead now, Felicia inches closer to the lake, the lapping water becoming louder with each step. "Why are you doing this?" she asks. "I'll give you anything. I'll give you everything. I'm not well. I have a brain tumor—glioblastoma. I'm dead anyway." Felicia stares back at the gun—she's thinking . . . thinking . . . Is she weighing death by gunshot against death by drowning?

"Don't even think about it. This gun? That'll bring certain death. At least out there"—a nod toward the dark waters—"you can try and hold your breath." A chuckle.

And if you do, I'll still be here with this gun, waiting to finish the job.

Felicia blinks, then looks out to the lake. She walks and yelps, the cold water shocking her. She clutches her elbows as the lake water hits her knees . . . her thighs . . .

Felicia throws one last look back at the shore.

No sanctuary here.

She takes deep breaths as the water hits the middle of her back . . . her neck . . .

And now, it's like she was never there at all.

10.

Spiders—big, small, hairy, thin—swarm my condo. They drift like commandos through the windows on silky parachutes. I lift my sneaker, and millions of spiders spill out of the shoe as my foot throbs from bites. I collapse onto the couch, but black spiders and red spiders erupt from the cracks between the cushions. I want to scream but can't. A hairy blue spider crawls up my arm, and a bigger, hairier spider crawls out of my mouth. Thunder rumbles . . . rumbles . . .

My eyes pop open. They feel weird, stretched out and achy from the spiders. My throat is sore. The dream was so real that I swallow to make sure any spiders in my mouth are now en route to my stomach.

My vibrating cell phone has pulled me from this nightmare.

I grab it from the nightstand. It's 10:50. I've been asleep for only an hour?

Dominique is calling.

"Dude," I growl at her. "I'm asleep." My eyelids weigh more than a turbine engine, and even as I talk, a snore tumbles from my mouth.

"Mom wants you to stay at the house." Dominique says this with no emotion or surprise. It's a done deal for her.

"Too late, I'm asleep." My head falls back onto the pillow. "It's easier to be here—"

"I know, you gave me the speech at the Holiday Inn."

"I took a Benadryl, Dom. I'm not driving over there."

She says nothing.

Nerves taut as a tightrope, I sit up in bed. "Shouldn't she be getting ready for the track meet tomorrow? Wrapping batons with tape? Polishing her whistle? She hates it when I'm home. *I* hate it when I'm home." On television, Iron Chefs have launched into a canned-tuna battle.

"She's upset," Dominique says. "She and Dad got into a huge fight about you staying at a hotel. Dad called her a bully and said he totally understood why you didn't want to stay here. She called him crazy, and you *know* that makes him lose his mind. He shut down, and she stormed out and drove off and won't come home. The end."

"Are you serious? Where is she?"

"Probably where she always goes when she leaves like this."

Your mother's favorite place. For a moment, I think about that address in Felicia's note. I wish we had talked earlier. I rub my face to coax life back into my skin.

Dominique gasps, whispers, "She's back. I hear her coming up the . . ." My sister clears her throat and says, louder now, "Because she doesn't see you anymore. And I think it's because she thinks that you didn't like dinner."

"I could've cooked more vegetables," Mom says in the background. She sounds wounded.

I squeeze the bridge of my nose. "Dom, you know she's trying to manipulate me. Trying to make me feel guilty, right? She knows that me staying here isn't about her cooking."

"How do you think it looks for you to be staying there and not with your family?" Mom shouts from wherever they are. "You'll look disloyal, and I'll look like I've failed—and I don't fail." Unlike her mother, Lolly, an alcoholic who drank herself to death just five years ago.

I groan. "Dom, I'm a freaking adult. I don't have to do what she—"

"Yara, stop. I'm tired. You need to get over it and come home." Dominique sounds scratchy and annoyed. As a child, anytime arguments broke out between our parents, my sister grabbed a loaf of bread from the kitchen and disappeared beneath the dining room table. She'd eat slice after slice, listening to our parents' angry words but never interrupting, never crying.

One tumultuous summer, we never had enough bread to make bologna sandwiches. Tonight sounds like it's been a "bread beneath the table" kind of night. Mom won't take no for an answer, and she'll make Dominique and Daddy miserable until she wins.

"Fine." I turn on the lamp and kick away the comforter. My mother doesn't care that I *literally* cannot breathe at that house. But whatever Queen Bee wants . . .

"She's leaving the hotel," Dominique tells Mom.

"Tell her don't come if she thinks I'm trying to kill her with my smoking," Mom says.

"Fuck you," I mutter.

Dominique chuckles but doesn't speak.

"What did she say?" Mom asks.

"I'll try not to suffocate in her presence," I shout, my mood like hot coals. "Don't want my death to get in the way of her image."

Dominique says to Mom: "She just said *okay*." To me: "See you soon."

It'll be just like the good old days. Mom will sigh every time I use my inhaler, since that's somehow a rebuke against her as a mother. That means I won't use my inhaler as much as I should because I don't want to annoy her. I no longer care about annoying her. Now, I will use my inhaler every time she lights up, and three days from now, she'll want me out of her house. I'll write—my version of therapy—and try to figure out how to survive a difficult mother.

And so, I will not surrender my hotel room. No. *Hell* no. When the week turns left—like it's turning already—I'll return to Room 303 and write the best pilot script of my life.

Nine days in Palmdale. Day Ten, I will take my ass back to LA and live happily ever after until Thanksgiving. Yes, for the next week, I will try my best to keep sweet and just *swallow* it. Then I'll purge it all on the page and in the Caribbean and become whole again.

I type *dream of spiders explanation* into my phone's search engine.

". . . associated with manipulation, either the dreamer is manipulated, or the dreamer is being manipulated."

A well-timed analysis. Another interpretation says that I may be feeling overwhelmed by a situation, that I'm feeling trapped by a lot of people or issues, that I'm feeling irritated. That I have an overbearing mother in my life. That I'm feeling like an outsider.

Yes, yes, and yes. Guess I'll be dreaming about spiders for the next eight nights.

Yippee.

Just tell her no, Shane responds after I text that I'm driving to my parents.

I sigh, then type, I know she's trying to handle her emotions better

That's why she didn't say anything when I left after dinner
But I can't expect a turtle to fly

Fair enough but
Explain to her that you love her but you need space
It's no knock against her or your love for her
She'll get mad but she's your mother
She wants the best for you

Does she? LOL

OF COURSE SHE DOES!!!

I shake my head as my fingers tap across the screen. I don't want
to fight

All fights aren't harmful babe

It's complicated
WE'RE complicated
It's easier for me to bend
She doesn't bend

I see where you're coming from but
This isn't healthy babe

Tell me about it.

I shove some of the clothes I unpacked back into one of my suitcases and dump some of my toiletries from the bathroom counter into
the overnight bag. I stow the envelope with Felicia's keys and the note
in my purse. Then I text Dominique that I'm on my way.

An unread text from Felicia's number came in while I slept and
dreamed of spiders.

Help
Lix uz

I squint at the unfinished text.

Lix uz . . .

What are you talking about Felicia? I text.

No ellipsis bubble on the screen.

No response to my text message.

It's nearly midnight. I should be asleep right now. I push out a breath and send my thumbs tapping across the keyboard.

DO NOT TEXT ME AGAIN!!
NO MORE!

Yes, I should be asleep by now. In my heart, I *am* asleep right now. Even as I stumble to the elevator bank, my mind spins, a rock tumbler polishing excuses for tomorrow night.

11.

Out here in Antelope Valley, the desert sky is big. Although there are now more than 155,000 people living in Palmdale alone, that big desert sky swallows the glare of the shopping mall's lights as well as the neon burn of Applebee's, Olive Garden, and McDonald's. Right now, Jupiter and even Saturn burn bright up in that sky. During the Perseid meteor showers, I always feel like I'm at the planetarium instead of at home on a Friday night. Every week, there are weird, chopped-up lights that streak this sky. Space debris, UFOs, meteors . . . Since Edwards Air Force Base and Northrop Grumman are less than fifty miles away, anything can be up there.

You can't find a sky like this in Los Angeles.

I shouldn't be looking at this sky right now. I should be focused on finding my car in the parking lot and not running into desperate coyotes or horny, violent drunks. So hard to do since my eyelids are drooping, and my body wants to collapse into a bed.

But whatever Queen Bee wants . . .

Barbara McGuire Gibson, the mother of all spiders.

Not entirely her fault. After my grandparents Lolly and Ezekiel divorced, Poppa moved twenty miles south to Long Beach, and Nana spent her days with a heavy crystal glass of Scotch in one hand and a television remote control in the other. She'd sometimes forget to pick

Mom up from school, often passing out before she'd finished cooking dinner.

Nana attended only three of Mom's track meets and lost her driver's license from too many DUIs. After that afternoon's episode of *General Hospital* ended and *Donahue* (and then *Oprah*) began, she'd throw that glass at a wall, leaving behind dents and holes that Mom hid with her certificates and ribbons. My father was Mom's rescuer (her word, not mine), and they had me before she could figure out all that she needed from this life without an alcoholic parent. She needed me with her at all times to control every move I made and to show the world that she was the anti-Lolly. My mother learned how to mother by watching the Quartermaines of Port Charles, TV talk shows—and now Hallmark movies. Today, she can point to the mostly positive results. I write for television. Dominique was a high school volleyball champion and is now a freshman in college. *Look at my successful, beautiful family. I did that!*

Mom's love for me is like this big desert sky: sometimes cold, sometimes unreachable, but also overwhelming and weirdly streaked with the most random colors. Her love is perplexing. Her love, like this city, takes my breath away. Despite how she treats me sometimes, I want her to succeed. I really do.

And now, I climb behind the wheel and make it one hundred yards before swirling red lights from emergency vehicles glow in my rearview mirror.

On my lap, my phone buzzes with text messages from my sister.

U almost here?
I'm tired

I text Dominique. Almost there
One day, I will do as Shane suggests and push past my aversion to conflict. I'll tell Mom, *Look, I love you, but my health suffers in this*

house. I need you to understand that. I've done it before, but my face still numbs with just the thought of telling Barbara McGuire Gibson no about *anything*. She's frozen me out the very few times I've done so, and there's nothing more miserable than being shunned by your family.

The fire engine and ambulance are now just a light behind me.

The whirs of sirens push through the Jeep's sound bubble, and I pull to the right side of the road along with the other idiots stupid enough to be driving in the desert at this time of night.

Like me, those first responders are traveling west, and although I may no longer hear those sirens, those swirling bright lights shine . . . and now, they're swallowed by that desert sky.

Nothing is west. Just mountains, lakes, valleys, and . . . the Twilight Zone.

What could've possibly happened at midnight in that direction?

Before I pull back onto the road, I notice a sheet of paper flapping in the middle of my windshield. I turn on the wipers, but the motion doesn't free it. After making sure I'm not about to be struck by a passing car, I climb out and grab the paper. The headlights of an approaching truck make me squint, and the lights illuminate this side of my—

In the truck's light, I see long white scratches against the Jeep door's paint. The gouges circle and spray, swerve and curlicue. Someone's keyed my car. Gutted, I climb back behind the steering wheel. With tears in my eyes, I open the sheet of paper I plucked from my windshield.

I can't wait to hug you and squeeze you to death.

HOME AGAIN

12.

Who did I piss off in the ten hours I've been in Palmdale?

My mind crunches . . . searches . . .

Can't think of anyone.

Maybe whoever it is thought my Jeep was their lover's. I see them now, swiping through pictures taken by their best friend, proof (finally!) of Joey's cheating. Pissed-off Lover hops in their starter BMW and races into the parking lot of the Holiday Inn. They spot the black Jeep, whip out their keys, and with tear-filled eyes, drag that metal across the black paint. Vindicated—*oh, wait, this isn't Joey's Jeep* . . . Makes sense. But the note—*I can't wait to hug you and squeeze you to death*—makes no sense, and so I crumple it and toss it in the back seat.

I want to cry, but I'm too tired to cry, and it takes all my energy to shamble up the walkway to my childhood home.

The murmur of people talking drifts from our backyard—those voices must belong to the drivers of the black Range Rover, the blue Chevy Impala, and the yellow Dodge Charger.

Dominique has guests.

My eyeglass lenses steam as I step into the house. The first thing I notice: the nook in the foyer is empty.

Mom's go bag is gone.

There are scrapes in the dust that surrounded it, and the single dried maple leaf that flew in during a 2018 dust storm has fallen from the nook and crumpled onto the floor. Tonight, Mom took the bag because she was *leaving*-leaving, and she needed whatever was in it. A fly-anywhere plane ticket? Bundles of cash? Sweatpants and running shoes?

I know Dad says it isn't any of my business, but one day, I *will* work up the courage to peek inside. First, though, I'll have to find it.

Cigarette between her fingers, my mother now smirks at me from the bottom of the staircase. "You didn't have to come back."

Dominique pushes out a breath, then gathers her phone and cup of tea from the living room coffee table. She rises from the couch. "I'm outside."

"Someone keyed my car," I blurt.

Dominique holds Mom's gaze and says, "I can't with the Yara drama tonight."

I glare at her. "What does *that* mean?"

She rolls her eyes and smirks at our mother.

"You don't believe me?" I shriek.

Dominique pivots and stomps to the kitchen.

Mom and I watch her disappear out the back door.

In the silence, the house clicks and groans as desert cold seeps into its joints and cracks.

"Why would I key my own car?" I ask.

Out in the backyard, the group laughs.

"Sounds like there's a hundred people out there," I say. "Did she tell them about my car? Are they laughing at me?"

Mom chuckles, then sighs. "I'll never understand you."

I wince—those words always shear pieces of my heart. "What am I missing now?"

Mom shrugs. "Nothing. Anyway . . . I made your room up nice." She comes to take my suitcase. Ashes from her cigarette drift onto the bag's handle.

I scowl at those wafting ashes and follow her up the stairs.

She natters about comforters and candles, tomorrow's track meet and Pepsi's hamstring as though this is all cool and she didn't just force me to come back home.

Dad is lying atop the blue comforter in their bedroom. He's yawning and rubbing the bridge of his nose as the theme music from *Frasier* plays on the television.

"G'night, Daddy," I say from the hallway.

He says, "G'night, Yaya. Don't worry about the scratches. I'll get 'em buffed out."

Mom whispers: "He's mad at me."

Right now, my anger burns like paper—I don't knock Dad for his rage.

I smell the shortbread-scented candle before I even enter my bedroom. The Justin Bieber posters and fairy lights have been replaced by yellow and gray paint and a framed poster of *Starry Night*, a new change since my springtime visit.

I point to the jar candle burning on the dresser. "This was my favorite scent."

Mom drops my bag at the foot of the bed. "I bought your first one the Christmas you were fifteen."

That holiday, I'd felt so grown-up. I could keep matches in my bedroom and burn a candle without supervision.

A humidifier sits on the nightstand, along with a box of essential oils and a bottled water, courtesy of Superhero Bee.

"Mom," I say, "you didn't have to do this."

"There's eucalyptus oil," she says. "When you were little, we used that and peppermint."

My asthma attacks and respiratory infections were legendary all-night affairs. Steam sometimes billowed nonstop from my penguin humidifier and from the shower in the Jack and Jill bathroom between my bedroom and Dominique's. Two inhalers—emergency and steroid—would sit on the nightstand, along with vials of prednisone and amoxicillin and a big box of tissues. Mom would climb in bed beside me, and together we'd watch *SpongeBob SquarePants* or *My Neighbor Totoro* until my breathing eased and the meds put me to sleep.

"And I bought the comforter set yesterday. Egyptian cotton." Mom pulls her hand across the green-and-mustard-yellow duvet. Printed with pheasants, orioles, and white flowers, the linens are fancier than the bedding at the Holiday Inn.

I shake eucalyptus oil into the humidifier. "Thank you." Still pissed, I try to smile, but it wrecks itself against my teeth and shambles into a grimace.

"I know," Mom says. "Guess I shouldn't have never let you go in the first place. Can't say that I didn't try." She throws me a smile, then stubs out the cigarette in a rainbow crystal ashtray she's carrying in her back pocket.

I pull back the comforter. "G'night. I'm exhausted."

Best Friend Bee leaves me and closes the door.

I open the Ativan vial, pop two pills in honor of the past and the future, then twist the cap off the water bottle. As I drink, something thuds above me. Some creature in the attic? Or did a box or picture I found earlier tip over?

My nerves zigzag, and I wonder how long it will take for the drugs to kick in. I turn to the humidifier now sending a stream of scented air across the bedroom. Nothing, though, chokes the ghosts of burned tobacco. It lingers forever in the carpet and in the paint, and it has soaked into the cedar of the bureau and nightstand.

Doesn't matter that I've kept my hotel room. Mom will not let me leave this house, no matter how valid or creative my excuse. And if I *do* confront her and tell her that I'm staying at the hotel, then she will make Daddy's and Dominique's lives miserable. I'd never hurt them like that just to stay at a freakin' Holiday Inn. Which means . . .

I'm right where Mom wants me: at home.

And I'm here to stay.

Point: Barbara.

She *always* wins.

I unpack, stuffing the bureau with clothes as I also search for pajamas. In one drawer, I find composition books and diaries. A book report on *Where the Red Fern Grows*. A self-portrait done in eighth grade art class. My third grade handwriting journals—my tortured *Q* and squirrelly *M*. *It's just print letters holding hands,* my teacher, Miss Karpinsky, had explained.

I place my cell phone and inhaler beside the humidifier. According to the dose counter, I have 130 puffs left. Enough to get me through the week. I search my closet for one of my old weighted blankets, just in case. No luck. Once I change into pajamas, I blow out the candle and settle beneath the sheets. Back in this room, I'm a child again.

In this scene of *Queen of Palmdale*, the moon glows past the bedroom's gauzy gray curtains, and shadows on the ceiling resemble long, tall aliens. That shadow has tentacles . . . That shadow blows bubbles . . .

Little Girl Yara has never slept well in this room, and now, as early-twenties Yara clutches her scratchy new comforter, there's too much moonlight and too many shadows. A coyote howls down the block. A shotgun booms and a hillbilly AK-47 goes *cak-cak-cak*. But gunshots don't scare her as much as—

CUT TO:

Barbara Gibson storming to that gold Camaro out back with her Louis Vuitton duffel bag slung over her shoulder.

Where had Mom fled tonight after her fight with Dad?

I want to grab Felicia's note with that address—*your mother's favorite place*—but I just got warm. I don't feel like climbing out of bed and searching through my purse.

My phone buzzes.

Shane's sent a good-night video. He's in bed, shirtless, and his finger traces the eagle tat above his heart. He smiles his wonderfully crooked smile and says, "I miss you. Dream of me."

I will, I text back. Promise.

Downstairs, the kitchen door slams.

Is that Dominique or . . . ?

"Where's the bathroom?" a young woman asks.

Who the hell . . . ?

"Behind the stairs." Dominique sounds far away. Is she not escorting her guest through our house?

Outside, a car door slams.

I slip out of bed and over to the window.

Dominique's Jeep backs out of the driveway.

Where the hell are u going??? I text her.

Taillights from the Jeep dim as she drives away from the house.

To get some drinks
We ran out

WTF?? Your friends are still here??

Chill they're people not werewolves
Ransom's still there

And is Ransom now a member of this household?

I glare at the phone, then glare out at Edgewater Court. Over at Mrs. Duncan's house, her cat, Nixon, slinks out from the shrubs. At Mr. Abernathy's, his son, Derrick, smokes a cigarette on the porch. I return to the bed, depositing my glasses on the crowded nightstand, then wrap the sheets and comforter around me, burrito-style. Confined by the sheets, my pulse slows, and I take deep breaths to tamp down my anger. My eyelids grow heavy, and my nerves feel fuzzy. The drugs are working!

Theme music from *Cheers* drifts past my closed door.

Dad chuckles.

Mom shrieks, laughs. "Rob, you are *crazy*."

Their bedroom door closes.

We have strangers at our gates. Strangers in our downstairs bathroom. Strangers occupying our backyard patio chairs.

Strangers . . .

⚡

Someone with dark skin stands over me. Their brown eyes shine in the dark.

Who are you?

The shadow doesn't speak.

Did I think those words? Did I speak those words? Did the phantom hear those words?

I reach out, but I touch only air. I bat my hand.

The phantom is too far away from me, and now, it's fading . . . Water all around me. Rocks poke the soles of my bare feet . . . I'm shivering. Frogs croak. So cold . . . Something cold presses against my forehead and . . . and I scream—

My eyes pop open.

Sunlight spills across the comforter. The carpet shines, and dust motes ride on the air blasting from the air conditioner.

A nightmare, not night terrors, because I remember.

I sit up in bed and wince from the twang in my neck. My blood feels like fizzy, shaken soda. I pull my arms out of the linens and press my eyes with the heels of my hands.

Ativan dreams.

Not of Shane. Not with spiders.

There was a person . . . here . . . but not *here*. There was a hand . . . A red splotch . . . Cold . . . There was a gun . . . A red splotch on a cold gun . . .

And the cold gun was pressing the space between my eyes.

13.

My mind sizzles like a cheap sparkler, and the dream breaks apart like foam.

I kick off the comforter, thankful that Mom keeps the house at seventy-three degrees. On this early Saturday morning, the sun bursts through my east-facing windowpane. The sky is grainy blue, and Mr. Abernathy's snapping and cracking American flag means that there's wind. An olive-green PT Cruiser is parked in the driveway. LaRain Andrepont is here.

Before going downstairs, I peek in the bathroom. The door to Dominique's bedroom is open. Her bed is made, and her hot-pink toothbrush isn't hanging in the toothbrush holder.

She must've slept over at Ransom's.

Both Mom and LaRain wear green-and-white Falcons High School tracksuits. Mom sits on a stool at the breakfast counter as LaRain brushes Mom's hair into a high ponytail. She's been doing our hair forever, in this kitchen and at her salon.

Mom smiles at me. "Hey, sweetie."

"Yaya-mama!" LaRain—full makeup, ponytail as long as Mom's, fake mole popping her lip—holds out her arm for a hug. If I didn't know her, I'd never believe that she was coaching at a track meet today. But glamming while running has always been her "thing" since competing together with Mom in high school and being crowned Miss Inglewood 1990.

"You sleep okay?" Mom asks, eyes narrowed.

I nod. "Why?"

"Just . . ." She lifts a shoulder, then offers me a wobbly smile.

"I'm good." Did I scream out last night? Did I wander through the house?

Mom points to the box of doughnuts on the counter. "LaRain brought you a cinnamon roll."

My favorite. "Thanks, Lala. Mom, where's Daddy?"

"With Paul, fixing your car," the former beauty queen says. "Whose man did *you* steal?"

I say, "Ha. Please tell Paul thank you."

"Dad has your keys," Mom says.

I give her a thumbs-up, then pluck the cinnamon roll from the box. "What time are you heading to Lancaster?"

"A little before noon," Mom says, looking at her hair in a compact mirror. She frowns at her reflection, then scowls at LaRain. "I said Beyoncé's high ponytail, not the head of the Alien Queen. Fix this."

LaRain says nothing as she unwinds Mom's ponytail to start again.

Mom grins at me. "I warned your father that we're gonna beat his school today."

I dump cream and sugar into my cup of coffee. "Is Pepsi's hamstring better?"

"Nope." LaRain spritzes hair spray around Mom's edges. "You know how she pulled it, right? Doing some upside-down twerking challenge on the internet."

"And I saw that you clicked 'Like' on her video," Mom says, smirking at her friend.

"Talent is talent," LaRain says. "If she doesn't land a scholarship, she can always land a job at Charlie's titty bar." She nudges my mother's shoulder. "I'm just *playing*, Bee."

"What's going on around Palmdale, Lala?" I ask.

LaRain's perfectly arched eyebrows lift. "I was just about to tell your mom that they found some dead woman floating in the lake."

Mom and I say, *"Again?"*

I grin. "Jinx."

Mom winks at me, then picks up her pack of cigarettes from the breakfast counter, catches me side-eyeing her, then tosses the Newports back on the bar. Instead, she plucks the packet of Nicorette from her back pocket and pops a piece in her mouth.

"Which lake?" I ask LaRain.

"Palmdale," LaRain says, finishing Mom's ponytail a second time.

Man-made and over a mile long, Lake Palmdale is part of the California Aqueduct. During fishing season, the Fish and Fly Club stocks it with trout and catfish.

Last week, a woman was found dead in her empty fishing boat. Investigators ruled her death a suicide.

A month ago, a woman was shot in the chest and dumped on the lake's bank.

That man-made lake has the worst man-made luck.

I hate this place.

This place hates women.

No love lost.

I unroll the pastry to eat one delicious segment at a time. "Who was last night's victim?"

LaRain shrugs. "Nobody knows." She takes a piece of gum from Mom's pack. "Police are running her car's license plate right now."

"Is Paul supposed to be telling you this?" Mom asks, eyebrows high.

LaRain snorts. "Nope. You think I'm only with him for his buck teeth and receding hairline? Nobody pays attention to the folks who keep the police station clean."

Paul knows *everything*, which means LaRain—and sometimes, Ransom—knows everything, too.

"The lady in the lake was driving this gorgeous Benz, too," LaRain continues.

My knees go weak and I stop in midchew.

"So, a rich bitch?" Mom asks.

"Uh-huh. The car has this custom purple paint job, like she's Prince."

Felicia Campbell drives a purple Benz. Could there be two rich bitches in Palmdale with the same tastes in cars?

"Was she Black? White? Old?" I ask, breathless.

LaRain's lip quirks. "Why you wanna know? You trying to write a new episode of *Tough Cookie*? You gonna pay me?"

The Andrepont family. Always hustling.

"Can we finish our damn breakfast, please?" Mom says. "We gotta get going soon."

"I'm serious, Yara," LaRain says, gathering her hair supplies. "Hundred dollars, and I'll get you whatever—"

"No, you won't," Mom interrupts. "Cuz you don't follow through."

LaRain frowns. "When haven't I followed through?"

"You been trying to leave Palmdale and move to Vegas since 2010," Mom says.

LaRain rolls her eyes. "All I gotta do is—"

"*Then* you always say *that*," Mom says. "Gurl, bye. Or hello, since you ain't leaving."

I turn away from them and find Felicia's last text message to me.

Help
Lix uz

I tap out a reply.

You there?

An ellipsis bubbles on the screen.

Who's this?

Yara
I was a little rude to you yesterday
Sorry about that

No response—she's pissed.

Fine. Whatever. I apologized even though *she* broke my necklace. Even though *she* came out of nowhere and tried to grab my arm, and told me all kinds of tinfoil, messy nonsense. How was I supposed to react?

But I *am* glad she wasn't dumped or drowned in Lake Palmdale.

Mom pulls out her phone and shows LaRain the seating arrangement chart for the anniversary party. Satisfied with her place in the ballroom, LaRain snaps her fingers and dances in place. "And where are you putting Sharla?" she asks.

"Near the kitchen door," Mom says.

LaRain throws her head back and cackles.

Mom points her pack of Newports at me. "Make a note of that, Yara." The gum has lasted all of three minutes before she tapped out a cigarette. And now, she blows smoke to the ceiling and watches her friend through the silvery veil.

LaRain runs her fingers through her ponytail. "Sharla shouldn't have gone to that dinner. Big mistake."

Mom shakes ashes into the ashtray. "They should've honored me. What more do I need to do to be recognized? I teach movement, and I coach those special needs kids at that school. I do makeup and hair for cancer patients. My daughter donated the walk-on from her TV show. But they're honoring *Candace's* basic ass?"

"And what happens thirty-six hours later?" LaRain asks.

"Busted on Al Gore's internet sucking some councilman's rancid dick," Mom says.

LaRain sucks her teeth. "And there goes Sharla, following behind her."

Like LaRain's always following behind *my* mother.

"So, Sharla's still invited?" I ask.

"Oh, hell yeah," Mom says, shooting smoke to the sky. "But her flat ass is now sitting by the kitchen, so make a note."

Rewarding one friend while sitting the other friend at the worst table. Not *disinviting* her because Mom wants a full ballroom. But punishing her for attending the gala honoring a rival. Classic Barbara McGuire.

I finish my pastry, then retreat up the stairs to take a shower.

Cousin Felicia—glad she answered my text. I wouldn't want *that* kind of drama this coming weekend. If anyone's gonna shenanigan, it should be my mother. She wouldn't have it any other way.

My phone buzzes from the counter as I lather in the shower.

I dry off and wrap the towel around me. My phone's screen shows that I've received three texts, each message from Cousin Felicia's number.

Yara hi
This isn't Felicia
Felicia is dead

⚡

LaRain has to run errands before the track meet, so she tells Mom that she'll meet her at the school. She leaves behind the box of doughnuts and retreats to her PT Cruiser. She and Ransom now stand in our driveway as she picks at the twists in his hair like a mama bird.

He peels off several hundred-dollar bills and hands them to her.

She shoves the money into her phone case, coos at him, pats his cheek, and, finally, waggles a stiff finger in his face.

He smirks and tosses his head, all *yeah, right.*

I turn from the den window. My cell phone bobs in my hand as I reread the message.

Felicia is dead

Eyes wide, Mom points at the phone. "If that's true . . . who's texting you back?"

Who is this??? I text. Then I pluck the rubber band around my wrist.

"What if Lee really *is* dead?" Mom whispers.

I shake my head. "But that wouldn't make sense."

Mom places her hand on my wrist to stop my nervous plucking. "Cece told me last night that Lee's having some kind of mental crisis."

My eyebrows lift. "I wasn't imagining it, then?"

Mom shakes her head. "I need to remember: This is what Felicia does. She cries wolf. She holds fire drills. Gets you worked up and freaked out." She pauses, then adds, "You kinda inherited that gene."

"She'd claim to be dead for *attention*, though?" I ask, even as her observation chafes.

"That's why, *to this day*, I don't fuck with Lee. I advise you to lose her number, or she'll pull you into her . . ." Mom wiggles her fingers at my phone. *"Thing."*

Too late. Felicia has already pulled me into her thing. The woman's given me a set of *keys*, for Pete's sake.

"And you didn't see her last night?" Mom asks.

"No."

"You sure? You're not forgetting like you do sometimes?"

"Positive."

Mom stares at me for several seconds, then pulls bottles of Gatorade from the freezer. She arranges them inside a zip-up insulated bag. "I haven't talked to her in years."

"But you talk to Cece all the time," I say.

She tears open a box of protein bars. "Cuz Cece is talented and entertaining. But Felicia . . . We went to high school together, and when she was running for senior class president, she made all these stupid promises that were impossible to keep. Like hamburger day every Friday, and no more detention. Of course she won the election. Of course everybody hated her when nasty-ass sloppy joes were served three Fridays after she'd won." Mom grunts. "Tell me the truth, Yara. You invited her to the party, didn't you? It's okay—I won't get mad."

"No, I didn't. I swear," I say. "She just *showed up* in the Holiday Inn parking lot. She didn't ask for an invitation, but she probably wanted one. This *is* the hottest party of the year."

Mom grins, huffs on her nails, and buffs them against her chest. But then she closes her eyes, her smile dimming. "What if Lee *is* the woman in the lake?"

I frown. "But who would've hurt her?"

Mom slips the protein bars into the insulated bag. "Girl, it's Palmdale. Take your pick: Crips or Nazis. Family, friends, strangers." She pauses, then sighs. "I can't stand her, but we're cousins. Once upon a time, we were friends. *Good* friends, but she was so smart and so *haughty*. She'd make it a point to show everybody just how much smarter she was than the rest of us. That her family had money and that Cece knew everybody in music.

"My family—we were the poor cousins, and Cece and Uncle Skip would host these big parties at their big house in Baldwin Hills where all the fancy Black people lived. Sometimes, I was invited. Most times . . ."

My mother slouches against the counter. "And then there were the boys. Lee ran through them like toilet paper, and honestly? I don't remember what happened that ended our friendship. Whatever it was, I took my girls, she took hers, and that was that." She zips, then unzips the insulated bag.

I touch her wrist, my own heart bobbing in sadness. "You okay?" She can be vindictive and controlling, but she *is* my mother.

Mom sucks in her cheeks, shrugging. "Haven't thought about any of this in a long time. And I'm low-key pissed that she's trying to suck all the oxygen out of the room again. Why the hell did she even drive up here? She doesn't belong in Palmdale."

I fake shout, "Wolf!"

"You are a *treasure*, Yara." Mom runs her knuckle along my cheekbone, then lifts my hand. "Promise me that you'll stay away from your drama-queen, wolf-crying second cousin."

I nod. "Cross my heart."

Together, Mom and I load all the track-meet supplies into the back of her SUV. Dust swirls across the asphalt, but nothing blocks the glare of the sun. No nuance up in that sky—it will be hot and bright today. By the time we're done packing, Dominique and Ransom are standing in the back garage, checking out Mom's gold Camaro.

Nothing useful is stored in that old shed—just rusted tools on pegs, a few old cans of paint, a giant deflated tire Dad uses as a part of his team's conditioning regimen.

Back in the kitchen, Mom and I both stop speaking to eavesdrop on my sister and her boyfriend—but we can't hear anything over the *brup-brup-brup* of a neighbor's motorcycle.

Mom's phone chimes from her back pocket. She says, "Hey, Lala. You're on speaker."

"*Girl,*" LaRain says. "The cops are sayin' that the woman in the lake is Felicia."

"No." Mom sinks against the breakfast bar, hand to her heart, eyes closed.

"And," LaRain says.

"And *what?*" I ask, because Mom is squeezing the bridge of her nose, unable to speak.

"And," LaRain continues, "they found a gun."

14.

Neither Mom nor I makes a sound. Beyond the kitchen, the desert crackles, restless with its cawing hawks, rustling shrubs, and barking dogs. My mother teeters between sharp breaths in and sharp gasps out, not wanting to cry but needing to expel *something*. She straightens the napkins in the holder. She rearranges the sugar jar with the flour jar. She holds her belly in between the keep-busy tasks.

Whose gun did the police find?

Where did investigators find that gun?

Did Felicia use that gun?

Paul hadn't known the answers to these questions, which meant LaRain didn't know the answers to these questions, either. More than that, Paul still couldn't absolutely confirm that Felicia was the lady in the lake.

And if Felicia is dead, who, then, texted me from her phone?

Have I been texting her *killer*?

I tear my eyes away from Mom and reread last night's messages from my cousin.

Help

Lix uz

The note she slid beneath my door is somewhere in my purse, but I remember those words. *What I must share with you is very important . . . I have critical information that will change your life . . .*

"She told me that she didn't have a lot of time," I whisper, tears in my eyes.

Mom comes over to hug me.

"I shouldn't have brushed her off," I say into her shoulder. "I should've listened to her and *then* . . . I don't know. Been *nicer* or . . . or . . ."

"Stop. No, Yara." She tweaks my nose. "Let's just wait to hear for sure, okay? Don't talk to anybody else about this. I'll call Cece after the track meet. And not to diminish any of this, but trust me when I say that Felicia was mean as hell. I'll show you some of the letters she sent me, okay? You'll see what I mean. I'm not being a hard-ass about her just because."

The front door opens.

Mom shouts, "Rob?"

He shouts back, "Yeah."

Mom clasps my hand. "Remember what I told you. Don't talk to *anybody*."

I nod, then dart to the foyer.

Sunlight shines at Dad's back, leaving his face in shadow.

"Did the scratches come out?" I ask.

"You okay?" he asks, head cocked. His eyes flick toward the kitchen. "What happened?"

I force my way into a smile. "I'm good. So everything's buffed out?"

His gaze lingers at the kitchen door, and then he beckons me to follow him out to the driveway. "There you go."

I run my fingers along the now-smooth paint. Like new again. I hop and wrap my arms around my father's neck. "Thank you! You made my day!"

He pecks my forehead, then hands me the keys. "Back to work." He tosses a weak wave to Mom, who's now standing on the porch, then ambles to his Suburban parked at the curb.

Mom, backpack and whistle in hand, pops down the porch steps and heads to her gold Cherokee. The dry desert air leaches the moisture out of my fingers as I take her bag and load it into the back passenger seat. Four pairs of sunglasses crowd the cup holders, along with unopened boxes of Nicorette gum. The interior smells of lemon and cigarettes. I learned to drive in this SUV, and back then, my things—notebooks, pens, and water bottles—mingled with hers.

I tilt my head to let the sun warm my face. "Felicia left me a key to some place . . . 1224 Stardust Way."

Mom tosses her jacket into the back seat. "Where's that?"

"According to her, it's your favorite place."

Mom smooths her ponytail. "And how would she know that? We ain't talked in years, and last time we did, I had *two* favorite places: Contempo Casuals and Orange Julius. Neither exists anymore."

I laugh. "Orange Julius is still around, Mom."

"Whatever." She points at me. "Don't *you* go off alone looking for a place you only know exists because someone with issues told you about it. I don't need you calling attention to yourself. You're not in La-La Land anymore."

I lift my chin and stick out my chest. "I'll have you remember that I traveled to Thailand *alone* after graduation."

"I'll have *you* remember that you caught dengue fever there, day three."

"Ha."

"And you have no time for field trips," Mom says, slipping behind the steering wheel. "We have a party to plan. Did you reseat Sharla?"

I flush and hold up my phone. "Doing that right now." I make a note on my phone, then beam at my mother.

She isn't smiling. "My schedule is crammed, and I don't have the bandwidth to save you because you fucked up while adventuring. Don't make me worry about you, too, little girl."

"Yep," I say and wave as she backs out of the driveway.

So . . . where is 1224 Stardust Way, and why did Felicia want to meet there?

15.

After I can no longer see my mother's car, I run back to my bedroom and change into a hoodie, leggings, and high-top Vans. I have no idea where Dominique and Ransom went. Twenty minutes later, I return to the driveway.

A dark-green Mazda that I don't recognize is parked across the street. A middle-aged Black man with close-cut curly hair and stingy eyes sits behind the steering wheel.

Something about him makes me stutter in my step.

I toss my bag into the Jeep and hop behind the wheel. I back out of the driveway and roll in the direction of the green Mazda.

The man ducks and turns his head.

Too late. I see him, and as I continue south, I squint at his license plate number in the rearview mirror and tap the sequence into my phone.

He doesn't U-turn to follow me.

Maybe he's . . . just a strange man being strange?

I punch *1224 Stardust Way Lake Paz* into the navigation system. It's only a thirty-minute drive north. How much trouble can I get in just a half hour away? I definitely don't want Mom joining me on this adventure. I have no desire to see the world through Bee Goggles, nor do I want to censor my thoughts. More than that, I know how to take care of myself.

The windshield rattles as dust and grit hit the glass. Sand sweeps across the highway, but the sky is still deep blue. Before the road winds between the mountains, my phone chimes with a text message.

From Felicia's phone number.

You there?
We need to talk

16.

Antelope Valley, the land of lakes and losers, spreads out before the car's hood.

Would've never thought . . . would've never *considered* . . . *living in this place*? With its constant wind, dogfighting, and meth? This was a place to *successfully* raise a family?

Also a surprise: having to follow this Jeep on a twisty road out of the valley. Sliding between cool mountains isn't as exciting as the promise of sliding the knife across her throat or watching those big brown eyes fill with fear and confusion. That will be the best part—that dumb look, the stuttered *Whuh-whuh-why?* That's when the knife will do the talking.

And that knife is snug now in a backpack. Its blade still shines, since there was no need to use it last night. Self-drowning had been a brilliant solution. No fingerprints, no blood, nothing to tie back to being with Felicia. Today, though, the knife will need to do its part.

Shoulda listened to me a long time ago.

There'd be no need to drive to who knows where.

Pretty simple becoming just another shadow in that house, sliding down the hall, that knife hidden beneath the jacket. First room on the left—that's where Yara slept. Even though the wick wasn't burning, the scent of the candle permeated the bedroom.

Yara had turned over in bed.

She thought I was a dream.

Not a dream. Very real. Yeah, it could've happened then, but there'd been too many people going in and out of the house. It had taken willpower to keep the knife stowed, to keep from grabbing a pillow, dropping it over Yara's head, and smothering her.

The plan, that voice had warned. *Stick to the plan.*

Plans were like tongues. Everyone had one and ignored the damn thing until it got bitten or burned.

Following Yara is part of the plan. Bringing the knife? An exciting detour.

Excitement swirls like confetti. Can't get this type of high with drugs, alcohol, or sex.

No new texts or voice mail messages brighten the phone. No interruptions now.

Only I can mess this up. By hesitating, by not knowing the lay of the land. Smart. Adaptable. A survivor. *That's who I am.*

And after this afternoon? After making the knife do its job? *I will make myself as small as a spider, and then, at the right time, I'll strike again and take the prize.*

17.

LaRain and Paul have been wrong before. Like the rumor they spread about our school superintendent. He was *not* having an affair with the hot young administrative assistant. The hot young assistant had been his *love* child. And the pastor at that Pentecostal church near the KFC hadn't been arrested. He'd been filming a "know your rights" video for his new community initiative on policing.

Felicia could be having bottomless mimosas right now at the Rancho Vista Golf Club—even though she's supposed to be at Lake Paz to meet with me.

I tap back a response to Felicia's last *we need to talk* text.

We'll talk when I get there

The phone rings—Felicia's number.

Irritated, I answer. "What?"

"Yara," a woman says. Then there's a canyon of silence followed by, "Hello?"

"Felicia," I say, "that you?"

Background noise, then silence.

"I'm losing you," I shout. "But I'm on my way to the cabin. I'm late but don't leave!"

The phone beeps twice and the call drops.

I try to call back, but the line rings and drops again. Bars for reception on my phone have dropped to just one. "I tried," I say, dumping the phone into the cup holder. I'll see her soon. And really, as twisty as this road has become, I need to focus on driving, not drama.

Behind me, the sky over the city is turning brown. Another dust storm may be brewing. The Jeep's steering wheel vibrates beneath my palms as the car pushes through swift, powerful winds. A mini disaster looms in the rearview mirror, but up ahead, nothing but blue sky.

Hawks circle high above treetops, sag ponds, and siphons. Twisty trails cut through forest that survived the last fires. Beneath blackened tree trunks and naked branches, superblooms of bright-white star lilies sweep the forest floor.

At Meditation Drive, I turn left and inch down the curvy-tight road to Stargazer Way. I make a right—more curvy-tight roads. Lake Paz winks at me through the evergreens.

There are rumors about this lake, like . . .

There's no bottom.

There's a monster that swims here named Angry Phoenix.

That the rich men who built these roads dumped dead workers into this lake and collected life insurance.

At Stardust Way, I turn left, and seconds later, I reach my destination: a kelly-green A-frame cabin tucked into a copse of evergreens overlooking the lake.

No purple Benz.

At the gingerbread-colored cabin next door, an old white man wearing a red baseball cap sits in a porch swing.

My shoulders hunch. I don't want no static, old man.

He stares into space as though neither of us exists.

Before leaving my Jeep, I try calling Felicia again.

The line rings once . . . then drops.

I climb out of my car and make my way up the porch stairs of the green cabin.

The cool air smells of pines and alkaline from the lake. Beetles buzz and whir from their hidden nests. It's much cooler up here than in Palmdale, and my hoodie protects me from the unexpected chill.

Even though I have a key, I still knock on the door. Don't wanna walk in on an unsuspecting family making ham-and-cheese sandwiches.

As I wait for someone to answer, I throw my eyes here and there. The old guy is still sitting in the porch swing. A woodpecker taps at the trunk of a pine tree. Two squirrels scamper across the power lines. Angry Phoenix lurks through the lake's unlimited depths, waiting for an unsuspecting swimmer.

The old man stands. He leaves the creaking swing and disappears into his cabin.

Here at 1224 Stardust Way, no one has come to the door.

And now, I look closer. No cars other than mine have recently disturbed the needle-thick driveway—but then a breeze slips across the concrete, and the needles spin into a new pattern. The marigold drapes in the windows look stiff, like they haven't been pulled back or washed in decades. The paint on the eaves is peeling, and the gutters are clogged with needles, leaves, and bird feathers.

I pull from my purse the envelope that Felicia slid beneath my hotel room door. Holding my breath, I slip one of the two keys she included into the lock.

Click.

With a heavy, shaky hand, I push the door open. Cool, pine-scented air rushes past me. Thank goodness. I anticipated the stink of rotting corpses. I squint into the dim space. "Hello?" I call out, then wait for a reply.

There's a wood-framed couch there. A standing fireplace there. A large floor-console television over there.

I close the door, making sure to turn the lock. I flick the light switch, and the lamp on a side table pops on.

Weak, golden light floods the room. There's . . .

Wood wall paneling. An upright piano. A quilt thrown across the back of an armchair. A layer of dust on the television screen. The logs next to the fireplace are cracked, and cobwebs hang from one piece to the next. The wood planks beneath my sneakers creak every other step I take, as though walking hurts them.

An old, framed photo sits on top of the piano. I tap the middle C key and stare at the couple in the picture. They're Black, they're attractive. But in the sixties, everyone was fly. He has wavy hair, wears plaid pants and a short-sleeved, button-down shirt. A cigarette hangs from his mouth. The woman wears a miniskirt and crop top. She wears her hair parted in the middle.

I don't know these people.

There's a frosted crystal lighthouse on top of the piano. I pick it up and turn it over in my hands. Just a frosted lighthouse—no switch to make it glow.

There is a small music box decorated with bars of a song. I turn the red-bead handle. It plays "La Vie en Rose."

The curtains smell of dust and mold and hang like dead skin.

This can't *possibly* be Mom's favorite place.

I open the patio door, greeted again by bright light and fresh, metallic-smelling air. Evergreen trees and boulders take up the most space on the islet just off the bank of the lake. What an awesome slip of land. Perfect for kids who wanna play castaway or pirates. The lake itself is so blue and so deep, its surface rippling with crests made by Angry Phoenix.

I plop into a dusty lounge chair and listen to birds and to water lapping against the shore.

Where is Felicia?

With the lake and trees, these dusty trinkets and the vintage photo, the out-of-tune piano and the old redneck next door? A great location for an episode of *Tough Cookie*.

I take a few pictures of the living room. Out here on the deck, I have two bars, maybe three. I send the shots to Shane.

My situation right now

You go back in time? Shane texts back.

Ha ha
Something like that
Long story
I'll tell you later

In this episode, Cookie receives an anonymous note telling her to
drive to this address. *The man you seek is HERE.* She creeps around the
deserted cabin, gun drawn, breath tight . . . and she finds the bloodied
and battered body of the man who may have killed her distant cousin.
Someone's killed the killer! But who? The door behind her creaks open
and . . . Next week on *Tough Cookie* . . .

Maybe I should keep this for *Queen of Palmdale.*

I return to the deck and settle into the lounge chair. I take more
pictures, then scribble notes into my IDEAS-*QUEEN OF PALMDALE*
journal.

I pull out Mom's fabric journal that I found in the attic and read
a few random entries from February 1998. Mom wrote about people
accusing her of smiling too much, of being unstable and erratic. *My*
uterus should not be tossed in a straw basket. Nana Audrey, my father's
mom, didn't like my mother much and absolutely hated Lolly. The words
"trapped" and "crazy" had spun crazily out of Nana's mouth anytime she
and Dad were together without Mom and figured that I wasn't listening.
My poor mother, Fighter Bee. She boxed against so many people.

I close my eyes. Free of debris, my lungs expand in my chest. I
could stay here forever. *This* could become *my* favorite place. Sit, write,
drink adult beverages while wrapped in a blanket. Shane mans the grill,
and then, together, we watch the sun travel across the sky and the moon
skip across the lake.

Yeah, it would be *sweet* to own a cabin by the lake. One day . . .

⚡

My eyes pop open.

What was that?

My brain moves like an Icee. Not a dream this time, but . . .

I glance at my phone. I've been asleep for almost forty minutes.

I slip the journal back into my bag, then dip back into the house. The front door is closed, but I remember the sound of the doorknob twisting, like someone was trying to get in.

A flare shoots in my heart, but I shake my head. "No. Don't. Climb off the ledge, Yara."

Outside, the lake water laps against the shore. Birds chirp from the trees. Too silent.

No Felicia.

I open the front door. A few dried leaves blow in from the porch, and I kick them back out. Leave the place as I found it—stuck in time.

At the cabin next door, the porch swing creaks, but there's no one sitting there.

I climb into the Jeep and push the ignition button. A cherry-red computerized graphic of my car brightens the dashboard. I blink at what I see, then stagger to the front driver's side tire.

The tire is flat, the rubber jagged.

The front passenger-side tire is flat, the rubber jagged.

The rear right tire . . . The rear left . . .

All four of my tires . . .

Flat. Jagged. Slashed.

18.

Click-clack.

I know that sound.

A hunting rifle getting ready to do what it does.

My hands shoot high in the air.

"What do you want?" The woman's voice comes from behind me. High-pitched and haughty, she sounds old, like she owns all of Angeles National Forest.

My throat closes and I want to cry, but I'm too scared to cry.

Feet crunch the gravel. It must be the other woman, because I haven't moved.

"You hear me, gal?" She creeps to the other side of the Jeep. Weathered skin, short gray hair, jowls. The rifle is nearly as tall as she is, and it's trained on my torso, not bobbing, not swaying. The old bird has done this before.

"I'm visiting. I was invited here. Someone slashed my tires." My voice sounds stronger than I feel.

She squints at me. "This your car?"

I nod but just barely. Sweat drips into my eye, but I dare not blink.

"What's the license plate number?" she demands.

I recite it.

Her eyes dart to the license plate. She confirms with a nod that I'm correct, uncocks the rifle, and lowers it to her side. She tugs at her red-and-black striped T-shirt, then pushes out a breath. "All right, then. Good luck with that." She nods toward the tires.

As tears slip down my face, I slowly lower my arms. I turn away from her to dry my cheeks with my sleeves.

"Didn't mean to scare you," she says, sounding sad now. "I heard whoever it was fiddling with your car. I peeked out, saw you in a black hoodie, and I thought . . ." She shrugs and comes to the front of the Jeep. "We don't have time to wait for the deputies to get here. And we only got one for Lake Paz, so we handle criminals ourselves."

I'm still crying, but I wanna say so much, including *you crazy old bitch*. She still holds that rifle, though.

The woman steps closer to me. "Come on now. Relax, gal."

I step back. "Don't call me 'gal.'"

Her smile crumples. "Well, I don't know your name, young lady."

"Cuz you didn't ask," I spit. "You decided to hold a gun on me, instead. Felicia Campbell invited me to come here."

The woman frowns. "I don't know any Felicia Campbell. Far as I know, this cabin still belongs to the Marshes."

I shake out the tension in my arms, then pluck my phone from my pocket to show her an internet picture of my cousin.

The old woman's face brightens. "Oh, I know *her*. Real polite. Big Mercedes. She's been here a lot lately, twice a month or so. She pays the bills, flushes the toilets, keeps the cabin alive. She rolled up here back on Wednesday and stayed overnight. Left yesterday morning."

Ready to confront me in the Holiday Inn parking lot.

"Where are the Marshes?" I ask. "I need to ask them a few questions."

She clucks her tongue. "That'll be hard to do. The parents are dead. The daughter disappeared maybe twenty years or so ago. Last time I saw her, there'd been some big fight over there. Sheriff's deputies came, asked me a bunch of questions, took some pictures. Wrapped that yellow tape around the trees, and then . . . I don't think anything happened after all that."

"Ah."

"I'm Birdie," the old woman says.

"I'm Yara, hi." My eyes don't smile, but my lips manage the task. My soul isn't interested in letting bygones be bygones.

Birdie smiles as well. "The Marshes didn't live here full-time, though. This was their second home, you see. He was a musician. Composed scores for a buncha films. A very handsome man. His wife, I can't remember her name, but she was a real beauty, too. She danced in a few of those race movies with Cab Calloway and the Nicholas Brothers, Dorothy Dandridge . . . Guess that's why they could afford this cabin."

"And their daughter?" I asked.

"She kept the cabin, brought her family here a bunch of times. They'd invite us over, but my husband, Donald . . . Well, he . . . umm . . . Anyway, they were good people. Quiet except for that last time. But we all have arguments that spin out of control sometimes. I asked them to keep it down, or else I'd have to call the deputy."

"And?"

"The noise stopped, but then she disappeared after that."

I place my hands on my hips. "So, my tires. You said you saw the person's back. Was it a man? A woman?" Maybe they were the same person who keyed my car?

Birdie scratches her temple. "No clue. Wore a black hoodie like yours—aren't you hot in that? It's a million degrees out—"

A girl shrieks.

I yelp and spin back to my car.

Birdie laughs. "It's just silly kids out on the lake. Sound travels out here—they're probably way down the shore. No kids around *here* in a long time."

More shrieks and some woo-hoos and lots of splashing. The smell of dying things—insects, plants, loose liquid earth—and the lightest breeze slip around the evergreens. For a moment, with that rifle in my life, I'd forgotten that I was less than twenty yards from the beautiful shores of Lake Paz, my someday place.

"You okay?" Birdie asks.

I chuckle. "No, ma'am. It's been a long twenty-four hours." I lift my face to the sky.

Breathe . . . Breathe . . .

"Well, I'm gonna head back in," Birdie says. "I was watching some *Forensic Files* when I heard the suspect killing your tires."

An old gray pickup truck rumbles up Stardust Way.

Birdie's gaze darts to the truck, then back to me. Worry bobbles in her eyes like tiny blue buoys. "My husband, Donald, he likes strangers less than I do. That can be a problem since we own the only store in town."

The Ford pulls into the driveway next door. The old man who'd sat in the swing now climbs from the driver's seat. The truck creaks and groans with relief.

"Hey, Bud," Birdie calls out with forced cheer.

"Why the hell you got the rifle?" Bud's beady blue eyes burn into me as he pulls the sweaty, short-sleeved shirt away from his chest. "Who are you," he asks me, "and why are you here?" He points at the Jeep's slashed tires. "You goin' around vandalizing the cars of hardworking, honest people?"

"It's her car, Donald," Birdie says.

"I'm the hardworking, honest people," I say, eyebrow high. "Sir, you were on the porch when I arrived."

He swipes his forehead, then swipes at the stars and bars tattoo on his leathery, liver-spotted forearm. "Gets dark out here. You better figure that out." He snatches the rifle from his wife, then turns to his cabin. "What's for dinner, Roberta?"

"Meatloaf and brussels sprouts," she shouts at his back.

I glare at him.

My reaction bounces off his shoulder, and he gives his wife a thumbs-up before trudging into the house.

Why is someone vandalizing *my* car?

My eyes skip around the forest. The tall trees, grass, and bushes are thick and high enough to hide behind. There is someone here watching me. I can feel it.

"Who knows that you're here?" Birdie asks. "We're well off the main road."

I shrug, shake my head.

Donald is the only person who cares that I'm here, and by the looks of his tattoo . . .

Oh—the shady-looking man in the green Mazda! Maybe he *did* follow me after all.

I push out a breath, then push the hair back from my forehead. "I don't know what to do."

Birdie ambles to her porch. "Stay right here. I'll make a call to a fella down the road."

"I'll let my family know that I'm here. They're expecting me." Just so that Birdie knows that folks will come looking if I were to disappear. Donald thinks life is awful with just *one* of me in the forest? He decides to fuck around, he's gonna find out how bad life can be with a bunch of pissed-off Black people in the woods without reliable 4G reception.

I tap a quick message to Mom.

Flat tires
Don't worry
Figuring it out now
And before you say it
Yes you told me so
And no I didn't piss anybody off!!

19.

The rifle-totin' senior citizen did a nice thing for me and called a tow truck company. Josh, the driver of said tow truck, arrived at the cabin forty minutes later with four new tires. It cost me $1,200, along with a lot of mumbled *thank you*s and *I appreciate it*s to the red-faced man with the strawberry-blond mullet and Odin forearm tattoo.

"They sure as hell didn't want you leaving," Josh says, kicking a new tire. "Couldn't have been old grand dragon Bud doin' the slashin' cuz you stayin' would be the *last* thing he'd want. Heh."

I say, "Heh," as Josh tries to cover his tat with his cap. "He seems . . . *particular*."

"Just stay away from him." Josh leans toward me and drops his voice. "Every summer, he was always messing around with the cars of the family that used to live here."

My mouth goes dry. "What do you mean, messing around?"

Josh colors, and his eyes dart over to Bud and Birdie's cabin. "Just rumors. You need a Coke or something? I got some Bacardi back at the shop."

Although rum and Coke would be lit right now, I say, "No, thank you." I continue to express my gratitude as I climb into the Jeep.

An hour later, I pull into my parents' empty driveway. No dust-storm sky. Just a bright, glossy blue crisscrossed with white plumes from jets. Also, no green Mazda parked at the curb.

A blue Crown Victoria is parked closest to our silver maple tree. The woman sitting on its hood is still too fair-skinned to live in the desert. Kayla Kozlowski, my former high school best friend, looks almost the same as she did when I last saw her six years ago. After high school graduation, Kayla told me that she needed space. I gave it to her. We haven't talked since.

Her face has filled out since graduation, and she's bulked up only because of the ballistics vest and shoulder holster she's wearing beneath a blazer with frayed seams. Kayla has chopped off her long auburn hair and now wears it in a boy cut.

Grinning wide, she slides off the car. "I *thought* I saw you drive away earlier today."

We hug.

"You've been waiting here that long?" I ask.

"Nope. I've been popping in and out all day. Remember, Palmdale is the size of a postage stamp compared to LA."

"Look at you," I say, waving my hand at her. "Miss LEO."

"That's *detective* law enforcement officer. And look at you, Miss Hollywood."

I snort because my nailbeds are caked with dirt and I smell like horse. "Yep, I'm as fancy as Mariah. What can I say?"

We cackle.

Kayla tells me that she's been with the Los Angeles County Sheriff's Department since earning her associate's degree. "Three years on patrol, and this year, I made detective."

We high-five.

"Married?" I ask.

"Nope," she says.

"Same. Kids?"

"Nope."

"Same."

She blushes. "Unlike you, though, I still live with my parents."

"And yet, the sheriff lets you carry a weapon," I say, eyes filled with wonder. "Wanna grab a drink? I know you need it."

Her smile fades. "I'm actually here on business."

I cock my head. "Oh! Is this about my tires? About someone keying my car last night? I didn't see who slashed—"

"Tires? Keying?"

I tell her about the scratches on my Jeep and my trip to Lake Paz. "And right before I left from *here*," I say, "there was a strange man parked right over there." I point to the spot across the street. "A green Mazda. I wrote down the license plate number . . ." I show her the note I tapped into my phone, and Kayla writes it down.

"The freaks are so after you," she says. "But I'm actually here about Felicia Campbell." She plucks a pad from her sports coat pocket. "She's dead, but I think you know that."

I squint into the sun. "Rumors only. My mom was gonna call and confirm with family this morning, but then . . ."

"Well," Kayla says, "I'm confirming. A patrol deputy spotted a purple Benz at Lake Palmdale early this morning. No one occupied the car, and because the lake has become a"—she clears her throat—"*destination* for final acts like this, he called it in. We got there and ran the plates. Car belonged to Felicia Campbell from El Segundo. We didn't see anyone on the surface of the lake, so we did a shore search and then sent in fire department lifeguards to swim around. Luckily, we found her not too far out."

My eyes bubble with hot tears. My sadness is like a cloud that comes out of nowhere, suddenly blocking the sun.

Poor lady. Poor Cece.

"You okay?" Kayla asks.

"I was hoping for the best." I shake my head and look back to the house. What will Mom's reaction be when she finds out? I clear my throat. "Autopsy?"

"Ongoing." Kayla waits a beat, then says, "You knew her."

"Not really. Just knew that she was our cousin. We met for the first time yesterday." I dab at my eyes with my knuckles. Dread eels through me and I shiver.

She flips pages in her pad. "She texted, *I have information that will change your life*, and you texted, *What are you talking about Felicia . . .* So you knew her?" She cocks an eyebrow.

"No. Well, she texted me, but I didn't *know* her. And when she texted me today—"

"That was *me* texting you earlier today. And then I tried to call, but—"

"The call kept dropping? That was *you*?"

"Yep, and Felicia was already dead by then. Those texts are why I knew to come here."

Oh.

Kayla's pen scratches across the pad. "The Holiday Inn's parking lot security cameras have video of you and Dom talking to Campbell yesterday. It looks like she confronted you. Dom looked like she was about to beat the crap out of her."

"Yeah," I say, and then I tell her about Felicia reaching for my necklace and breaking it. "That's gotta be on the security camera footage, too."

Kayla nods.

"After that, she kept trying to talk to me even after I'd asked her to stop. Like I said, she and my mom are cousins. They went to high school together, but she acted totally cringey and they were no longer friends by the time they graduated. Felicia sent me on some wild-goose chase to Lake Paz, I don't know why, and someone slashed my tires, and now, you're here."

Kayla writes all of this down. "So not only do you *know* her, not only are you *family*, there's contention there."

My eyes bug. "And if you do six degrees of separation, I'm also somehow related to the king of Sweden, and I'm pretty sure we'd piss him off during Christmas dinner, too."

Kayla looks up from her pad. She isn't smiling.

The air feels hot, crisp, close to combusting. Kayla's inferences are flints, searching, striking.

"C'mon, Kay," I say. "What's going on?"

"Just doing my job. *Detecting*, you could say."

"Is it because she didn't die by drowning but was actually shot first and *then* dumped?" When she blinks at me, I shrug. "Don't forget, I write for *Tough Cookie*."

She taps her pen against the pad. "Anything else I should know?"

"Nope." I lean against the police sedan. "How do you like being Da Man?"

"Drug overdoses, gang murder, and sexual assaults on Tuesdays. Meth-house explosions and wife beatings on Fridays. Juvenile crime in between." She gives me the up and down. "Nothing like *your* life. I see you on Instagram and Snap, living your best life. All those parties and interesting people who, like, do shit."

"It's not perfect," I say.

"Better than threatening some kid with taking away his mom's Section 8 vouchers if he doesn't give up his homie, wouldn't you say?"

I nod, laugh. "True. So, hey. One of the lady-cop consultants on the show—"

"Yes," she shouts. "I'll do it. Please let me do something cool!"

"You don't even know what I'm about to ask."

She takes a deep breath and holds it, and her eyes glitter as I tell her that one of our law enforcement consultants went out on maternity leave and that we need a replacement. "It's not full-time, nothing close to it, but you'd get to advise on set and enjoy craft services."

"I'd *love* to."

"I'll have to run it by the executive producer, but that shouldn't be a problem. You just have to remember that it won't be total reality. You're focusing on big things being right. Some small stuff, too, but . . ."

She's nodding and almost crying from joy. "I'm glad you're here."

"Y'all coming to the party next week?"

"Of course," she says. "Before then, though, my parents want you to come for brunch."

I screw up my face. "Are they off that raw food diet?"

She laughs. "Yes, but they're on macrobiotics now. So eat beforehand."

The front door bangs open and I yelp, caught off guard.

Mom bounces down the porch steps holding a tray of chips and guacamole. No longer in her tracksuit, she now wears faded blue jeans and a white tank top. Her honeybee pendant shines bright above her cleavage.

I clutch my chest as she brings the tray over to Kayla's car. "You scared me. I didn't see the Cherokee parked in the driveway, so I didn't think you were home."

Mom smirks. "We have a garage, you know. And I was taking a shower. Doing okay out here?"

"We are." Kayla snags a tortilla chip.

Mom ruffles my already-wild hair. "One day you'll listen to me."

I blush all the way down to my prickling scalp. "Yes, Mother."

"You done, Dora the Explorer?" she asks, her eyes weary, her tone brusque.

"I'm done."

She kisses my forehead, then clomps to the porch. "Glad you're safe. You stink, though."

"You're smelling strength and tenacity," I say.

She shouts over her shoulder, "That guac is fresh made." She disappears into the house.

"Does she know that Felicia . . . ?" I whisper.

Kayla nods. "She took it pretty hard."

My pulse jogs in my ears. What will be Mom's mood tonight? Will we postpone the party? Cece certainly won't be singing, with her daughter being found in Lake Palmdale.

Kayla dunks a chip into the green goop. "You're not gonna have any?"

I crunch on a dry tortilla strip. "I *hate* guacamole."

"Since when?"

"Since forever. It makes me gag."

Kayla frowns. "You tell her?"

"Uh-huh, but she demands that I like it since Dom likes it. And she says that her guac is different than other people's guac." I skim a chip over the top of the dip, then pop it in my mouth. The slick snot of avocado hits my tongue, and I shudder. "Yep. Still hate it. Just like I hate other people's."

"At least your mother lets you be you."

"Did you not hear what I just said?" I say, chuckling. "About her forcing me to eat this shit? Ugh." I scrape my tongue with my teeth. I can still feel the slime.

"At least she supported your dream of becoming a writer," Kayla says.

Did she, though? Mom told me that an English degree was a waste of time and that she wouldn't pay for it, that I had nothing interesting to write about anyway and that she saw me as an HR manager or a librarian. But I smile for Kayla because I'm supposed to.

Kayla saw the butterfly sunflower seed butter sandwiches and love notes Mom placed in my lunch box—but she didn't know that, before I'd caught on, Mom had secretly placed notes only in Dominique's lunch box and had also used cookie cutters on Dominique's sandwiches. I'd cried to Dad that Mom never wrote me or gifted me with a butterfly- or bunny-shaped sandwich. Dad must've said something to her, because after that, I'd sometimes find notes like *Do well today* and *Have a good day* in my lunch box, along with butterfly sandwiches that tasted gritty and clumpy from strawberry jam. Even as a child, I could tell that Mom's heart wasn't in it, and I told her that she no longer had to make special sandwiches or leave uninspired notes. She rolled her eyes and said, *You cried about it, so I'm gonna keep doing it.*

Same with this guacamole—I asked her to make it once for a sleepover. She did. I hated it and told her that she didn't have to make it again. And here we are, fifteen years later.

Sometimes, *most* times, what I want, what I like, doesn't matter much to Barbara McGuire Gibson. Unlike Nana Lolly, she won't throw heavy crystal glasses at the walls, but she *will* make you duck and run for cover with one perfectly placed moment of silence. She *will* have her way, and she *will* love you the way *she* wants to love you, and you *will* eat the crummy butterfly sandwiches and force down that slimy guacamole even if it's less than an ounce on a tortilla chip.

This is the way.

⚡

Kayla doesn't promise anything, but she'll check into the green Mazda and the vandalization that cost me $1,200. Honestly, though? My tires being slashed is so petty and stupid compared to Felicia's death.

Drowning.

Wow.

What was going on in Felicia's life that she felt the only solution would be walking into Lake Palmdale?

The sky turns copper as the sun descends behind the mountains. The neighborhood is coming alive again with the pop of beer cans and the clichéd lyrics of a Morgan Wallen song playing from Mr. Abernathy's open garage door.

As I wave to Kayla and watch the Crown Victoria slip down Edgewater Court, regret breaks over me like soft waves. Sentiments of *you should've done more* and *what would've been the harm just to talk* agitate me because, yes, I should've sat with Felicia and listened to all she needed to share and . . .

No.

I felt *threatened* around her. Just because someone shows up in your space, do you have to allow them to invade just to make them comfortable? Should I stay in the elevator alone with a strange man leering at me?

I mean, there's a reason Mom never introduced Felicia to Dominique and me . . . and I'm gonna find out why.

Back in the house, Mom has stopped chewing Nicorette, and cigarette smoke ghosts through the hallways. In the laundry room, she's on the phone with the athletic director sharing the good news that Pepsi's tight hamstring loosened and the team placed first, twelfth, and twenty-second in the cross-country meet.

Upstairs in the bathroom, I take out my contact lenses, pull my glasses from the pouch in my purse, and grab the small desk fan.

In the attic, the strange light makes me squint, and squinting brings on a headache. I listen to my breathing. My lungs sound different than they had at the lake. Hell, I couldn't even *hear* my lungs at Lake Paz. Up here in the attic, though, I sound like an accordion come to life, all reedy, huffy, and filled with the barest amount of air. It's hot, but at least the smell of tobacco has been filtered out by the insulation. I pluck the bottle of drops from my pocket. My eyes sizzle from the medication's instant cooling.

Mom's off the phone and now patrols the hallway below. Her flip-flops *pop-pop-pop* against her heels as she marches back and forth with loads of clothes in her arms.

I squeeze my inhaler twice, then renew my search through my family's memorabilia now living in plastic tubs and Martinelli's sparkling cider boxes. Some boxes have taped-down tops while others sag beneath the weight of Gibson family precious memories.

I find a small, corked bottle filled with black sand from our family trip to the Big Island of Hawaii. My retainers fell into the ocean that vacation, and Dad miraculously found them on a nearby rock.

I find a luggage tag from my parents' honeymoon cruise to the Mexican Riviera.

My nose itches and I open my mouth to avoid sneezing, but the sneeze gathers like a storm in my nose and—*choo-choo-choo*.

Even in Los Angeles, my allergies aren't this bad. But then my apartment is less than a mile from the Pacific Ocean. The cool air is pure and sweet, cleansed by HEPA filters, and I run the Roomba every other day. I don't smoke anymore, and I do laundry and change my sheets twice a week.

"It's the dust from being up there," Mom shouts from the hallway. My muscles tense and I growl. It's more than the dust. "I'm fine."

"Bring all the boxes down here," she shouts. "Better ventilation."

"I'm good—" *Choo-choo-choo.*

"Yara," she hollers, "it's not important to have fancy centerpieces at the damned dinner if you're gonna be sick. Cuz then you're gonna have an asthma attack and make everything worse. Please come down."

Anxiety may live in my head, but my asthma and hay fever are not psychosomatic. I grab one last tub of random things, then head down the fold-down steps.

"Can't you get hypnotized for that, too?" Mom takes the tub from me. "Your anxiety is making your breathing worse. That's what the doctor told us a long time ago."

Dr. Shana Feldman attributed my respiratory condition to pollutants. Including cigarette smoke. She wore her blonde hair in a short, nice-lady mohawk, and the insides of her lips were always cut from braces. After asking Mom to stop smoking, Dr. Feldman never saw me again.

Mom then found Dr. Hollie, a hard man who didn't know how to smile. He prescribed Cymbalta and psychological therapy. I attended one group session, and Mom yanked me after I described the Feelings Hot Potato Game. Pass the potato, the music stops, whoever's holding the potato must share a memory, a fear, a skill. "That sounds really stupid," Mom said. "He has no idea what he's doing. But you're keeping the Cymbalta prescription." Dad squinted at her before squinting at the sun burning over our backyard.

"What are you saying?" Mom spat.

"If you don't trust Hollie's approach for group session," Dad said, "then why—"

"You know what, Robert?" Mom said, hands on her hips. "Right now, there are a million things I can't stand, and every single one of them involves you."

"It's like you're trying to kill her," he said.

And then they fought.

Mom grabbed her go bag, then screamed, "Everyone in this house gets to be imperfect except for me. I'm trying to quit, but I guess that doesn't matter." Then she and Dominique left the house for two hours. Where did they go? No clue. Dominique wouldn't say.

Later that night, Dad and I returned home after a trip to the emergency room for my breathing treatment. He also picked up my Cymbalta from the pharmacy and whispered to me that I didn't have to take them. "It's your body," he said. "I'll never force you to take something that isn't helpful."

Ultimately, he lost that battle—but he said something that's stuck with me.

It's like she's trying to kill me. That feeling has never waned. It lives deep within me, gnawing at me like the slowest termite colony.

And now, I blow my nose and wince. The longer I stay in this house, the more my skin hurts. My brand-new comforter has already lost its fresh-out-of-the-bag smell, and a layer of fine dust from yesterday's storm already coats my vaporizer. Even after I scrub my skin tonight, the stink and grit will remain. I'm a living 1950s bowling alley.

Mom drops the tub on the bed, then studies me with tired eyes. "Long day."

"Sorry about Felicia," I say. "Did Kayla tell you anything more than 'she drowned'?"

"No." Mom fingers her bee pendant. "Cece is a wreck. She couldn't even talk."

"Should we postpone the party?"

Mom places a hand on her forehead, then narrows her eyes. "No idea. Let's move forward for the moment but give the club a heads-up." She waits a beat, then asks, "Are *you* okay? I don't want you to worry too much. You know how anxious you become."

I try to smile. "I just need Kayla to figure out what happened. This is way too close."

"I'll keep you posted," Mom says, "and you let me know if you hear anything, okay? Let me know, too, if you need to talk, take a walk, if you feel like you're losing control."

I nod.

"Do we need to buy you one of those heavy blankets?" she asks.

I shake my head.

"You're gonna be fine," Mom says. "I'll make sure of that."

I say, "Okay."

"Poor Lee," Mom whispers as she returns to the laundry room.

My phone rings—someone with a Las Vegas number—but I'm not interested in talking to a stranger. Instead, I turn my attention to the first beautiful object I've found in the attic: a hand-blown glass vase ribboned with orange, pink, purple, and lime-green dyes. The silver label on its base says Salviati & Co. made in Italy.

A forgotten wedding gift?

It must be worth thousands of dollars. This sure as hell won't be a table centerpiece. I can already see one of Mom's older friends wrapping it in loomanum foil and carrying it to her Chrysler 300 along with foil-covered plates of filet mignon and ca-ber-net demi-glock.

I set the vase aside.

What traces of my mother's life with Felicia Campbell will I find in these boxes? If I attend Felicia's funeral, will she simply become a memorial program stuffed into the Bible that Mom gave me after high school graduation?

Guilt pings at me like thrown pebbles. This Italian glass vase and that black sand in a bottle should not matter more to me than my cousin . . . but they do. These objects represent family, togetherness, joy, and relaxation, and that means more to me than someone I met on a random day in May.

I sneeze again and wince as I dab my nose. Mom witnesses my deterioration every time I come home. And each time, she tries to change—chewing nicotine gum this time and smoke-grabber ashtrays back in the spring.

You should tell her that you can, like, die, Shane always says. *One bad asthma attack and you're outta here.*

But I shouldn't have to tell her that.

Barbara Gibson ain't stupid. She *knows.*

And I'm up in that attic for *her.*

I'm in Palmdale for *her.*

My eyes and nose are dripping, and my lungs are straining for *her.*

But if I say something, we'll fight. And she'll say something that cuts me to my core like, *I'll care about your feelings when I'm paid to give a fuck.* And Dad will speak up in my defense and say something like, *Considerate people stop harmful behaviors, even if it's only for a week.* And then Mom's eyes will roll back like a shark's and she'll say something wild like, *Robert, you need to stop talking to me like I'm one of your bitches.* Dad will shake his head and whisper something equally wild, like, *Hamsters are better mothers than you.* Because sometimes hamster mommies eat their hamster babies, the house will explode with words and threats, causing Dominique to glare at me and mutter that she wishes that I'd just shut up since I get to return to Los Angeles while she's stuck here, picking up the pieces.

My phone vibrates. Whoever called left a message.

I tap the voice mail icon.

In the background, people are crying. The caller clears her throat. "Yara, you don't know me, but this is your cousin Alicia. What y'all do to my sister?"

20.

Alicia Campbell's voice sounds like the prickly burrs that stick to your socks every summer. "The police called, and told us the bad news, the awful news. My mama told me that Lee came up there to talk to you. Now, do I know why she went to Palmdale when we both know that you live over in Santa Monica? No, I do not, but you need to call me back as soon as you get this message. It's the least you can do."

I listen to Alicia Campbell's voice mail twice. Both times leave my face numb.

Who *are* these people?

My bedroom cramps around me. Alicia's astringent tone has made everything shrink and lose color. How the hell did I become a part of this drama?

I leave the Italian vase and head down to the kitchen. There is more sunshine down here than in my playpen-size bedroom.

Mom, earbuds in and phone on the kitchen counter, is running water over a pack of Newports. She glances back at me, makes a sad face, then whispers, "I'm gonna do better."

Doesn't matter if she means it or not. First, she has packs of Newports in her car and packs of Newports in her dresser. And then there are twelve cigarettes in her platinum case. So this "drowning my pack of smokes" is performative.

I step outside to the backyard. Hot and dead—that's how it feels beneath that dying, yet terribly effective, star in the sky. Some of the swirling dust isn't dust at all, but gnats and mosquitoes clouding over the dry grass.

Dominique, wearing a satin bandanna top and corduroy short-shorts, relaxes in the lounge chair beneath the pergola. Her fingers tap at her phone, but she stops long enough to look over the tops of her cat-eye sunglasses to say, "Yikes."

Ransom Andrepont, all sagging track pants and long white T-shirt, sits with his leg over the arm of the second lounge chair. He sips from a can of Mountain Dew, then tilts a bag of barbecue Corn Nuts into his mouth.

"You gon' say hi?" Dominique asks.

Since neither of us knows who she's talking to, Ransom and I blurt, "Hey."

"Yara rockin' the glasses," Ransom says, grinning. "Them thangs so thick, you can see the future." He laughs at the same joke I've heard since third grade.

"Don't talk about my sister," Dominique says, lip curled.

She sounds like Mom.

"Just playin'." Ransom holds out his fist to me for a pound.

I let him hang.

Dominique shakes her head. "You must be up in the attic again." To Ransom, she says, "Yara's doing this wonderfully stupid project—"

"Oh, it's stupid now?" I ask, settling on the deck railing.

"I also said 'wonderfully,'" she says, grinning.

I roll my eyes. "Weren't you all high-key less than twenty-four hours ago, saying that Mom and Dad were hashtag goals and whatnot?"

"Simmer down, Four Eyes." She returns to her phone.

"Ransom," I say, "you hear about Felicia?"

He scrunches his face. *"Who?"*

"Our tenth cousin or whatever," Dominique says. "The one who walked into the lake last night and never walked out."

"Oh, that lady?" Ransom nods. "Hell yeah, I heard. Don't nothing happen around this city without me knowing about it."

Dominique lifts her glasses to squint at me. "Did something else happen?"

I shrug. "They're investigating."

Dominique cocks her head. "I'm not gonna see this on some upcoming episode of *Tough Cookie*, am I?"

I grin. "No guarantee."

Ransom sits up in the chaise. "What else you wanna know?" The hint of anything Hollywood-related turns the most hardened thug into a puppy nipping at your heel.

"Why did she walk into the lake?" I ask.

He grins at me. "Did she wanna walk in, or did somebody force her to?"

"Is that a question or a clue?" I ask.

He drops his sunglasses over his eyes and settles back into the chaise. "You paying me now?" he asks, sounding just like his mother. "Am I a consultant?"

I peer at his ridiculous bleached twists and the misspelled tattoo of his mom's name—*LaRian*—on his forearm. He's had a crush on Dominique since fifth grade. Back then and up until last year, she'd deemed him gross, stupid, flagrantly delinquent, incurious, and *"Cringe."* What happened to change all of this, and when? Really, what does Dominique see in this asshole? Aren't kids supposed to look for someone who resembles their parents in some way?

"Everybody saw her roll in," Ransom says, head tilted my way. "That purple Benz put a target on her back."

"She *looked* rich," Dominique adds. "She didn't belong here."

"And someone took advantage of that," Ransom says.

"Someone?" I ask.

"Wasn't me, but I can probably find out who," he says. "Gonna cost you."

"Bye, Ransom." I hop off the deck railing and wander to the yard.

The sun is moments from dipping completely behind the mountains even as hawks continue to circle the sky in search of a last meal. Those clouds of gnats and mosquitoes follow me because I'm their evening supper.

Behind me, Ransom moseys past our gates. What does he know? Was Felicia *murdered*? Forced at gunpoint to enter the lake?

I don't have a lot of time.

That's what she told me. Did she know that she'd soon meet her end?

Dominique stands beside me. "So can Ransom—"

"No," I interrupt. "Ransom cannot come to the party."

"So Lala can come, but her son can't? You are so bougie."

I pick up a rock from the parched ground and throw it far into the desert. "My boyfriend isn't coming, either."

"Oh. So . . ." She picks up a rock and throws it. "I'm thinking of moving in with Ransom in the fall."

I place my hands on my hips. "No."

"No, what?"

I level my shoulders. "No, you're not moving in with Ransom. Why? So you can wind up pregnant and be crowned the fifth baby mama of a loser? You won't get your degree, and you'll end up living in some junky apartment on the east side, begging him for diaper money. So . . . no."

She glares at me. "Is this one of your weird visions? Are you gonna write about this like you write about everything else that goes on in this house?"

Probably.

I waggle my head. "That's not the point, and don't change the subject. If you move in with Ransom, I promise you, next year this time, you'll be begging Mom and Daddy for formula money. Or were you planning on breastfeeding?"

Dominique folds her arms. "Hollywood got you fooled. Got you thinking that you're all that. Like you're better than us."

"*Us?*" I throw my head back and laugh. "Dom, darling. You're not *us*. You're *we*. When you come to LA, you want to eat nothing but Thai food and sushi. You like Solange more than Beyoncé. You're a faux-ratchet cosplay hood rat, and you deserve better than Ransom Andrepont. If you think there's a future with him, go ahead and ask Katrice, Alizé, Chardonnay, and Vixen how that's working out for them and their sixteen children."

"Five children."

"Whatever." I push up my glasses. "I'm paying for you to be in school—"

"Mom and Daddy are paying—"

"No, *I'm* paying. The papers are in my name."

Tears build in Dominique's eyes, her nostrils flare, and a sob breaks from her chest. She hides her face in her hands. Sensing water, the gnats and mosquitoes bumble over to my sister. In between sobs, she swats at the insects.

I pluck the rubber band around my wrist. "I'm sorry, okay?" I look back at the house.

Mom's still in the kitchen. She's chopping something, but her earbuds are still in and she's still talking on the phone.

I squeeze Dominique's shoulder, then offer her a tissue from my pocket. "Stop crying before she hears you, and then we'll have to explain why you're crying."

The thought of explaining any of this to Mom makes my head hurt.

That calms Dominique down, though, and she quickly snatches the tissue from my hand to blow her nose. "You and me?" she says. "We're just different. I'm authentic. I'm not interested in *observing* someone's life like *you* do in your goofy TV show."

"Goofy?" I ask, fire in my eyes.

Dominique jabs her chest. "I *live* it."

"My *goofy* TV show paid for that Jeep you drive and degree you're throwing away."

"Whatever." She stomps back toward the house.

My phone vibrates.

A text from Ransom.

I accept Venmo and Cashapp

He's attached a PDF.

> At approximately 3:37 a.m., I spotted a dark-colored Mercedes Benz sedan parked in a lot adjacent to Lake Palmdale. I approached and observed the abovementioned adjacently parked vehicle in the lot, which could . . .

I gasp. This is the incident report on Felicia's case. Now, like every good investigator, I have my own informant!

> . . . knocked on the driver's side window and announced that I was with the sheriff's department. There was no answer. The door was unlocked, and there was no one in the cabin . . . Smelled alcohol . . . flashlight to determine if there was a purse left behind . . .

I read as much as I can on my phone's small screen.

One sentence stops me cold.

> I then observed a note on the passenger-side footwell of the vehicle.

A note? Written by whom? What did it say? Was it a suicide note or . . . ?

I reach the last two lines of the PDF that Ransom sent:

> At this time, I do not know with certainty the name of the deceased or if this MBZ sedan belongs to the victim.

My glasses slip down my nose, and I look up from the phone to push them back. With the sun dropping, the chaparral smells syrupy and the packed dirt skunkier.

Back to the PDF.

The crime scene investigators found six empty minibar bottes of rum in the footwell of the passenger seat.

Had Felicia been drinking alone, or was there someone with her? And if she'd been drunk and alone, would she have been in the mind to say, *Hey, this water is cold, maybe I should get back in the car?* Could she have passed out from drinking too much and accidentally drowned?

In one episode of *Tough Cookie*, Cookie investigated the death of a stuntman's wife. According to the husband, his beloved had taken too much of her antianxiety medication and had either slipped as she'd taken a bath or intentionally ended her life. Cops pulled the dead woman from the bathtub, not paying attention to the scene around them. Cookie noticed bruises forming across the woman's face . . . bruises in the shape of a man's hand.

What would Cookie do now?

AN OLD FRIEND

21.

Mom spins from the sink to the fridge to the pantry, a whirling dervish with *The Miseducation of Lauryn Hill* as her soundtrack, slapping at the air with her favorite knife, then slipping it across the soft throats of blood oranges and strawberries. The air around us is lush with the aroma of good cheese and ripe fruit. After the track, *this* is her favorite place. "Dom's sitting out front," she says. "What's she upset about now? What did Ransom do?"

I pluck a strawberry from the charcuterie board Mom's preparing. "She's pissed at me, not Random."

Mom snorts. "Random. What did you say to her?"

I select a chunk of smoked gouda from the pile. "'Stay in school. Don't let him wreck your life.' Y'know, the regular."

"That was a waste of time."

"I don't want her to be his life lesson, but she wasn't trying to hear me today." I pop the cheese into my mouth, then select a chunk of gruyère. "But I must give Random his props—he had some tea to share on Felicia's case."

I peek out the den window.

Dominique is sitting beneath the silver maple with her phone and a french baguette. Yeah, she's stressed.

Mom cocks her head. "He got info from Paul?"

"I don't think so."

Mom shifts her eyes to me. Blood-orange juice speckles her nose and cheeks. "And?"

"*And* he emailed me the sheriff's initial investigation report," I say. "They found Felicia's phone—we know that since Kayla texted me from it—and they found some empty rum bottles and a note in the car."

Color washes from Mom's face, and she blinks at me. "A *note*? What did it say?"

I shrug. "No clue."

"Who wrote it?" She leans forward and whispers, "Did *you* write it?"

"*Me?* Of course not. They don't know *who* wrote it."

She holds my eyes for a moment, then leans back. "And the gun?"

"The report didn't mention a gun."

"So where did LaRain . . . ?"

I shrug again. "What did Kayla say before I got here?"

"Just that Felicia had been found in the lake and that she was sorry for my family's loss."

I select a dried apricot from the board as Lauryn Hill tells us in her smoky alto that it hurts so bad. "And nothing from Aunt Cece?"

Mom nibbles a date. "No, I left a message but . . . I hope they don't show up before Thursday. I can't take her energy."

"Alicia left me a voice mail."

Mom gapes at me, but her shock turns to irritation and a scowl settles across her lips. "She didn't dare."

"Oh, but she did." I force myself to chuckle.

"You know she's Lee's twin, right?"

I shake my head. "I did *not* know that. Anyway, listen." I play the voice mail left by Felicia's twin sister.

"The least you can do?" Mom spits, curling her lip.

"Right?"

"I'll handle her."

I hold up my hands. "Nope. I got this. I'll channel my inner Bee and tell her to fuck off. It'll be a poor facsimile of your epic drags, but I'm sure she'll get the point."

Mom folds her arms and cants her head. "She doesn't even *know* you like that. Who the hell—" She snatches a breath and then another, then loudly exhales. "If she tries that again, let me know. She come for you again, she'll find her flat ass sleeping eternally beside her sister."

I nod and try to tamp down my nausea. Fancy cheese and dried fruit don't mix well with the talk of death.

"Please don't say anything about the report," I ask Mom. "Don't tell LaRain that Ransom sent it to me. I don't want Paul getting in trouble. Then we'll *never* learn anything."

Mom grabs the salami from the fridge and drops the roll onto the countertop. "Don't worry. I got your back. I'm not getting involved in a murder investigation, even if it's family."

I curl my arms to make biceps. "No, that's *my* superpower."

"You write for a TV show—that's *far* from reality." She taps the top of my head and then reaches to push the hair back from her forehead. But because she's wearing a ponytail, her hand flutters about her face like a lost bird.

This is her go-to stressed-out gesture. Anytime Dominique screws up, anytime Dominique's failing a class, Mom pushes back her hair. I stay out past curfew, I have an asthma attack, Mom pushes back her hair. Mom's hairline is prematurely receding from pushing back her hair since eighteen-month-old Dominique bit a boy who tried to steal her blanket at daycare.

Mom's head falls back. "Why, Felicia? You didn't need to bring your fancy ass to Palmdale, and now, here we are."

I nibble a grape and a candied walnut. "Seriously, what drove her to drive up here? Has Auntie said anything about why she came?"

Mom shakes her head, grabs the roll of salami, and points it at me. "Just . . . be careful, and let me know if you hear anything else. Hopefully Dom ain't caught up in this mess, too."

I, too, pray that Dominique isn't playing Bonnie Parker to Ransom's Clyde Barrow.

If so, Mom's gonna be pushing her hair back all summer.

Back in my bedroom, I pull up Ransom's PDF on my laptop.

The responding officer found the purple Benz abandoned in the Park N Ride lot beside Lake Palmdale at 3:37 a.m. Felicia had sent me the Help Lix uz text message hours before, at 11:01 p.m. Four and a half hours had passed between that text message and the deputy finding her car. No blood had been found initially at the scene—not in the car or on the asphalt around the car. If Felicia had a gun, dying by suicide would've been easier than walking into the lake to drown.

Why doesn't this report mention a gun? And who'd been drinking with the soon-to-be dead woman?

I stare at the Italian glass vase for the answer.

First rule of solving a woman's murder: statistically, it's almost always the spouse.

Felicia had three husbands.

I visit my favorite people-search website and type *William Harraway*, husband number three. He's several years younger than Felicia. Wide nose. Inked-up. A bare-chested personal trainer who takes selfies in bathroom mirrors. Most of his photos on Facebook show a shirtless man with his veins popping and his chin cocked. We have one mutual friend, Sierra Boone, who recently posted that Will and UPLIFT had helped her lose fifteen pounds. He studied at Xavier University and lives in El Segundo, about ten miles from my apartment in Santa Monica.

He could've easily followed Felicia up to Palmdale.

His wife, my cousin? She's nowhere on his page. No *married to Felicia Campbell* status. No pictures or selfies with Felicia skiing or sunning beside him. No tags, no likes, no Felicia.

This is the social media profile of a single man.

In the crime-writing business, this is what we call a "clue."

I send a friend request to William Harraway even though I don't use Facebook anymore.

Husband number one was Aiden Rivers, the older white man who worked at NASA Jet Propulsion Laboratory down in Pasadena. He invented something, patented it, made a lot of money, died of a heart attack, and left Felicia, his wife of twelve years, a fortune.

Can't be him.

Husband number two was Darius Montgomery, a man who doesn't seem to do one singular thing. "Businessman" is his catchall. He ran a Christian nonprofit whose status was revoked in 2018. He's now a "pastor" of a "church" in Tennessee.

Darius could've flown in. That hair. Those eyes . . . He's the man in the dark-green Mazda!

I text Kayla and tell her that I think the stranger who was watching our house was Felicia's ex-husband Darius Montgomery.

She texts back, Are you sure you saw that?

I snort and squint. Uhhhh YEAH. What kind of question . . . ?

Just need to be sure
You've always had an active imagination

Sure, I type, but I'm not a LIAR

The ellipsis bubbles, stops, then bubbles again. A thumbs-up pops beside my last text.

I'll check it out and get back to you.

Not five minutes pass before my old friend texts me.

Not him
Darius M. is in the hospital
Jet ski accident in Florida

Who was the man in the freakin' green Mazda?

It was dark green, right? Like the color of an old, cheap black leather jacket.

And anyway, what's the deal with Felicia's *third* husband? He looks like he'd never be caught driving a Mazda . . . unless he's trying to blend in.

I text Ransom.

Thanks for the report!!
You know everybody don't you?
Do you know anyone who drives a green Mazda?
He kinda looks like Jamie Foxx but with curly hair
BTW do you have a W9 form?
You'll need one to get paid as a formal consultant

Nothing else in the initial investigative report sticks out at me. I type *Lake Palmdale* into Google Maps and click on "Street View."

Where exactly did they find the Benz? The Park N Ride lot off Avenue S? Or the Fish and Fly Club's parking lot? Because the club is private and has gated parking, I'm thinking Felicia parked at the public lot off Avenue S. I click the east directional arrow on Avenue S. There's a shed business, the desert, parking lots . . . the glistening lake . . . At the intersection to turn into the Park N Ride, there are three traffic signals.

And atop each of those signals . . . three video cameras.

Did those license-plate-reader cameras record Felicia's car?

Since I only write about a private investigator, I have no access to the kinds of protected information Cookie would. I could bring up the cameras to Kayla and maybe she'd spill the beans, but gaining her confidence will take time.

I don't have a lot of time.

I need to know who killed Felicia before they strike again—and as a creator of drama, I know that killers *always* strike again.

Will Felicia's murderer show up at the anniversary celebration?

Will they come for my family next?

Am I in danger?

Yeah. I don't have a lot of time.

And neither did Felicia.

22.

Just as I'm about to return downstairs to watch television with Mom, my phone brightens with a Facebook message: Will Harraway accepted my friend request. I hold my breath and swipe into my mailbox.

Hey beautiful.

Ugh. Corny as hell already.
Hi Will, I write back.

I see we have a friend in common
She tell you how good I am?

No, Sierra didn't tell me about you
But she looks great

I chew on my cuticles and stare at the bubbles.

You looking fit and fine
Don't think you need those skills of mine
But I'd love to give you a free consult
Anytime anywhere

My stomach burns. This loser is trying to pick me up while his wife is literally chilling in the medical examiner's freezer.

Love to, I message back.

But I don't want any static from other—

Shall I type the word that I hate but guys like Will Harraway use? I close my eyes and finish the sentence.

females
Not sure if you know who I am or what I do
but I'm not one for a lot of "look at me," "look what I'm doing"

Outside, the wind whistles around the eaves of the house. Mr. Abernathy's flag flicks and pops like an air rifle. Downstairs, the Lakers game is a fusion of rubber-soled squeaks, crowd cheers, and pontificating ex-athletes analyzing Anthony Davis's free throws.

Yes, ma'am LOL, Will Harraway texts back.

You are a BEAST
Accomplished so much
#blackgirlmagic
You wouldn't catch static from other females
I'm fine and free
You caught me at the right moment

I glare at the screen. Why is that?
First, he writes, I'll be expanding

My client list is about to explode
There won't be enough of me to spread around

Second, an investment just paid off BIG TIME
I can take you to Rome, Paris, Milan
Wine you dine you LOL
Do all the things a woman like you deserves

My body hates me for playing this game, and all of me cramps. I drop the phone on my bed, then pick it up again.
And what is this investment, I type.

Tesla?
Amazon?
A divorce?

Ha, he types. I wish I had those stocks

As for divorce, she left me a lot
Didn't want to at first but she came to see my point of view

I click through his photo gallery.
Two Rolexes on each wrist. Him posing in front of a matte-black Porsche. Shirtless again while lying in a chaise at a swanky hotel in Tahiti. His connected Instagram account offers even more self-absorbed shots. None include my dead cousin, but there are no shots with other women, either. He's smart about that, at least.
Dude is a user. I don't know if he wants me for access to bigger Hollywood players or to write his "inspirational" story. No matter; his wife died less than twenty-four hours ago.
Investment just paid off?
Is that what Felicia was to him? A sugar mama? A walking ATM machine? Did he ever *love her?* Looking at his page, I'd say that he didn't.

So you're free, I ask.

Yep she's gone

Did he kill her?
Going by this conversation alone? Yes, he did.
And that's why I'll share this message string with Kayla.
U still there? he types.
Yes, I type.

I don't have to worry about dramatic confrontations with her?

My hands shake, and the skin around my knuckles feels thin, dry.

Dramatic confrontations?
Nope
She's gone
And I'm living my best life
Uplifted
Join me beautiful

⚡

I find my father in the front yard, sitting on the chair beneath the tree with his beer bottle, golf club (to fend off coyotes), and bag of Doritos. He gazes north to the desert and foothills now lost in shadow. A notepad and pen sit on his lap. It's cold out, but he's wearing shorts and has pushed up the sleeves of his sweatshirt.

I plop on the grass and wrap my arm around his leg. "Working on your toast?"

He kisses the top of my head. "My toast? For what?"

147

I snort. "You did *not* just say that."

He blinks at me with vacant eyes.

"For the anniversary party," I say, irritated. "I *know* you haven't forgotten—"

"No, I haven't forgotten. I'm just working on something else right now." He forces a smile to his lips. "I'm supposed to give a toast on top of everything else?"

I gulp cold air to calm the pounding in my ears. "What's 'everything else'? Showing up?"

"I didn't mean it like that." He swipes the pad, then shifts in his seat.

He says shit like this and never understands why we get so frustrated with him.

I lay my head against his knee. "If it's not a toast, what are you writing?"

He chuckles. "I'm not saying just yet. I've been stopping and starting drafts all week. I'm not good at this writing thing."

I take the pad. "But I am. Lemme help."

He reclaims the pad. "I want it to be a surprise, one hundred percent authentically me."

I squint at him. "Again, I put words in people's mouths for a living."

"I'll write the toast later, Yaya. *Damn.*"

"Fine." I draw my knees to my chest, anxious and burning and dreading the moment he blows it all up with something flippant and rote. *Words can't express the way I feel* or *Our love is forever* or *You're so perfect.*

The desert makes night sounds all around us. There's the soft roar of the distant highway. The skitter of lizards through dry brush and across sand. There's the birdsong of night wrens and ravens.

"You guys aren't arguing as much," I say. "Other than me staying at the hotel, right?"

He grunts, smiles, says nothing. He writes a few lines, then crosses them out.

"Did you know Felicia?" I ask my father.

"I did back in high school and a few years after that. We didn't talk much once your mom and I got married. A few times here and there."

"She seemed almost obsessed with me," I say.

"It's that ego of yours that makes you think that."

"Ha ha."

"It's as big as your head."

I smile and stick out my tongue. "What did you think about her?"

He shoves his hand inside the bag of Doritos. "I liked Lee, but we weren't close in school. I'm a few years older, so it wasn't like we saw each other every day. She was very smart, very organized, and extremely insecure."

I chomp a few tortilla chips. "Are we talking about the same lady? Our cousin from LA? The hot-stuff business analyst for Northrop Grumman?"

Dad laughs. "She was insecure because she knew more than everybody else and that people like your mom hated that. You remember being a teenager. Lee had to figure out how to balance her genius with wanting to be liked and invited to parties."

"Yeah," I say. "That part sucked. Doesn't sound like she and Mom made up."

Dad shrugs. "What's the term? Frenemies? I stayed out of it. Cuz not only was there girl drama, but there was also family drama. Felicia started writing mean things to your mother, so they stopped communicating." He pauses, then asks, "You hear more about what happened?"

"Not really," I say, grateful that he can't see my face, grateful that a raven's croaking disguises the quaver of my voice.

Unlike Mom, Dad doesn't share many memories. I've seen only a few pictures of him as an adult that don't include Mom. There are no LaRains flitting around him. For my father, he's about football, Barbara, Dominique, and me.

But here we are, talking about the past. And I don't want us to stop talking, so I give him a high-level version of Kayla's earlier visit. That they'd found Felicia in the lake, that there'd been empty rum bottles in her car, that my number had been found in her text message history.

He closes the bag of chips and chugs from the beer bottle. "I heard she got fired."

My eyes bug. "Really? Who told you that?"

"DeShawn—he dated Felicia's assistant's daughter." Dad takes another long pull of Heineken. "Felicia had complained about this racist, sexist asshole manager and *something-something* and boom, they revoked her security clearance. Of course, she can't do her job without clearance. She was gonna sue—she'd kept records and had all this evidence but . . . she's gone now."

A dead husband, an ex-husband, a current husband currently flirting with me on social media, and a fight with her manager.

Yeah, that lady was marked.

"Did Mom know you talked to DeShawn about Felicia sometimes?"

He smirks. "Do I need to report everything I do to your mother?"

"No. I just . . ." I shift on the ground to fully face my father. "May I ask another question?"

Dad doesn't respond at first, then says, "Sure."

"Where do you think Mom goes when she storms out of the house?"

He twirls the pen around his fingers. "In-N-Out or Barrel Springs Trail just to walk, just to get away." He nods to the desert beyond our property line. "Out there sometimes."

I frown. "I don't think that's where she goes."

"You ask her?"

"No."

"Then . . . true story. In-N-Out. Barrel Springs Trail. The desert behind our house." His gaze drops to the pad, and he scribbles a few lines.

"She took her bag last night," I say. "It's not in the little nook anymore."

He grunts, and his pen moves across the pad.

"Where do you think she went last night? In-N-Out? The trail? Back here?"

"Don't know, Yara. You'd go out there sometimes."

I cock an eyebrow. "Uh, *no*."

"Uh, *yeah*. When you were a kid, you'd sleepwalk, and after tearing up the house, looking for you, I'd find you out there."

I blink at him, near tears.

"I'd wrap you in blankets to keep you from moving." His eyes also glisten with tears. "I felt like shit doing that."

I shrug. "Wasn't your fault that I had sleep issues."

He takes a deep breath and looks out to the *out there*.

"Did you get Mom a good gift?" I ask.

"Haven't bought it yet." He picks up his pen to write.

I poke his calf with my foot. "Better be magnificent."

He says, "Uh-huh," and his smile dies as he writes.

My father is getting old, from the gray stubble on his jaw to the muscles that are still there but softening in his arms and gut.

I watch him for a minute and whisper, "Are you happy, Daddy?"

"With?"

"Everything."

His writing slows but doesn't stop. He focuses on the words now filling the page.

My heart wobbles. I don't know what to do with that reaction.

"You hear about my tires?" I ask.

"Dengue fever without the fever." He pushes out a breath, then lifts my chin. "You need to watch your back. What were you doing up there anyway?"

"No clue."

He returns his attention to the pad and starts writing again. His handwriting is a series of weird swoops, dips, and crags, and at this angle, I can't read a word that he's written. Definitely too many words for a toast.

I poke his thigh again. "May I write the toast for you?"

This makes him stop writing, and he frowns at me.

"I know what Mom wants to hear," I say, my underarms sticky now with flop sweat. "I know what the guests will want to hear. I know what Mom *wants* the guests to hear."

I was incomplete before I met you, or . . .

Life's road is long, glad you're by my side, or . . .

My very happiness is sharing my life with you.

"I think I can handle writing a toast to my wife, Yara Marie." He says this with a bite and a few flashes of irritation.

Right now, even though my eyes well up with tears and my heart still wobbles, I give my father a wide smile. "I just want this one night to be perfect. For the both of you. For all of us. Three hours is all I need. Okay?"

"Yep. Sorry for snapping at you." He guzzles the rest of his beer, then looks to the shadowy western Mojave Desert.

I lay my head back on his knee. My pulse revs and it's hard to breathe because . . .

Are you happy, Daddy?

Why didn't he say what I needed to hear?
Yes, Yara. I'm happy.
Why didn't he say that?
And why did I have to ask?
I already know the answer.

23.

Stinks out here. Dead fish and rotten eggs, wet dirt and skunks. No rainstorms lately, so the water in the siphon becomes stagnant. Just like this plan has become.

The world now knows that she's dead. But being dead can't always stop people from hurting you. A snake can still bite even with its head chopped off.

Watch your back. Now that's a credo to live by. More than "do unto others" and "live each day as a gift."

The cabin plot took a left turn. Wanted to do so much more, use that knife for something other than slashing those tires. But that old man had stumbled back and forth from his cabin to the porch to his truck. His eyes had pecked at the woods and had paused too long . . .

Had the old man seen?

Don't know, but it was time to move.

Out of fear, plain and simple.

You're a chicken.

A big chicken, but a smart chicken. It's not like there won't be any more chances.

I need a new plan.

A drive by the tiny post office helped. No ordinary mail in that PO box. No—the future can be found in that small metal cubby. Nothing will be the same next year this time. Hell, even two months from now. *I could've removed that obstacle today, but I chickened out.*

Bloody desire niggles at a place that's been abandoned for years. But after taking out Felicia, that . . . *urge* has returned. Like mold on bread. But mold never just *starts*. There's an invisible spore on that slice days before. And now, a craving to take out another swells and surges.

That need grows watching Rob sit there on the lawn with Yara at his knee.

Desire shifts to hatred, and it burns, scours, and sours.

Nothing more will happen tonight and so, back to the task at hand.

But something *will* happen, and sooner than planned. *There is a horizon.*

24.

I leave my father to whatever he's writing on that pad. My heart still aches that he couldn't answer my simple question. Even if he and Mom had argued all yesterday, even if he's been eyeing the door all this time (and I know in my gut that he has), part of me wishes that he'd just said his lines as written: *Yes, I'm happy, Yara. There's no other woman I'd rather be with than your mother. Sure, we have our bumps, and your mother's broken in ways that I can't fix, that she refuses to fix, but there's no other family that I'd ever want except this one.*

Dad's an idealist, and he's caring, and he never says anything he doesn't truly mean. Which is why he doesn't talk much. But for this anniversary party, I need him to come out of his psychological trailer, channel his inner Denzel Washington, say the freakin' lines, and make us all believe that *he believes* in this cast of actors known as the Gibson family.

Mom buzzes around my bedroom. Best Friend Bee is cute in her yoga pants and cutoff Aerosmith T-shirt. She's changed the linens and lit the candle. Now the room smells like shortbread cookies and the vapor from my asthma inhaler. She karate chops the middle of my pillows and says, "I know I just put them on yesterday, but there were leaves and dirt . . . I guess you were wandering around outside, barefoot."

I cock my head. "Bare . . . ?" *When did I climb into bed with . . . ? Sleepwalking again?*

"Doesn't matter," she says. "I was gonna change them anyway because of the cigarette smoke. No worries."

I hop onto the bed. "Did you use my inhaler after your workout? I smell it."

"Okay, so I'm almost fifty, not eighty. I don't need your inhaler." She throws up her biceps and grins at me. "I have something for you. Well, a few things."

I sit up on my knees, eager as a ten-year-old. "A pony? A Barbie townhouse?"

She reaches to the small of her back and produces a batch of old envelopes. "Remember when I told you that Felicia had written me awful things?"

My eyes widen, and I pluck the cache from her hands. "You *kept* them?"

She chuckles. "Read them and you'll see why I did."

"And the second thing?" I say.

"I've been holding on to this and planned to give it to you once you became a mother, but I can't wait anymore." She reaches behind her again, and this time, she produces a book.

I recognize the red cover of *Beloved* by Toni Morrison.

"And yes," Mom says, "I know you have your copy from school. Just open the cover."

There's writing on the title page. *For Yara, the magnificent . . .* Toni Morrison's signature sits beneath the inscription along with the date. Signed a month after I was born.

Mom's hands clench at her chest. "I know this is your favorite of hers."

Tears burn in my eyes now. "You've held on to it all this time?"

"Every time you reached a milestone, I thought, *Give it to her now*, but . . ." She dips her head. "I didn't want this lost in the grandeur of graduations and TV deals."

I turn to the first chapter and read the first line: "124 was spiteful."

Mom strokes my hair. "This way, you can appreciate it and enjoy it as its own thing."

We hug again. "I love it, Mom. And I love you."

She knocks my forehead with her knuckles. "We still bingeing *The Terminator*?"

"Yep. I say we don't wait for Dom. Where is she anyway?"

She frowns. "With OG Lucifer probably."

"Does your best friend know your nickname for her son?"

Mom rolls her eyes. "She's the one who started calling him that back in second grade."

I cackle. Then I read aloud a passage about thin love not being love.

Mom waggles her head. "I don't understand what the hell any of that means."

With a crazy smile, I lean forward and whisper, "It's about—"

"Slavery, love, haunting, yeah, sure, got it. Way too dense for me. Give me *The Bluest Eye* or give me death."

"Your skin's really irritated," I say, pointing to Mom's face.

She taps at her tender cheeks. "Being outside all day."

"Lemme do your sunburn mask!" I scramble off the bed.

She follows me into the bathroom. I grab from my toiletries bag my tub of goop that contains aloe vera, cucumber extract, and hyaluronic acid and slather it over Mom's delicate skin. "Now let this sit for fifteen minutes."

She examines herself in the mirror, tilts her head this way and that. "And I'm still fly."

"Yes, ma'am."

"I'll pick up dinner once this comes off." She leaves me, closing the bedroom door behind her.

How romantic! My mother waiting in line to have a book signed by my future favorite author before I could even sit up by myself. And *Beloved* was more than just a ghost story. Morrison wrote about mothers and daughters, relationships, freedom . . . In *Tough Cookie*,

Cookie's dead daughter (named Denver) haunts her mother like Toni Morrison's Denver haunts her mother, Sethe, in *Beloved*. In Cookie's worst moments, memories of Denver slowly cripple her momentum. She's trapped in the past—how can she help other people when she couldn't hear her daughter's ragged breaths until it was too late? How can she save lives when she couldn't save her own child? My showrunner had no awareness of the mother-daughter relationships in *Beloved*. Clueless, she blinked at me each time I told her how I'd threaded scenes with themes from the Pulitzer Prize–winning novel.

My ringing cell phone distracts me from *Beloved* and Felicia's letters. I don't recognize the number, but the 702 area code tells me that it's coming from Vegas.

"Is this Yara?" a woman asks.

"This is . . . ?"

"Your cousin Alicia, Felicia's twin."

A weight presses my lungs, and I gulp air that smells like my inhaler. She says, "Hello?"

"Hi." With a shaky hand, I pull the first letter from the rubber band. The envelope is typewritten, the stamp postmarked August 6, 1998.

"I called you," Alicia says, "and I left a message."

"There's nothing I can tell you," I say. "Sorry about everything, though. We're all shocked and confused."

"Why did she come up there to talk to you?"

"No idea."

"You know we're blood, right? You know we went to school with your mother, right?"

"I do."

"And you know Bee made life hell for my sister," she asks, prickly and certain that, yes, I know this.

This is what I've been avoiding. *This mess.*

"Bee was just like Lolly in that, making people choose," Alicia says. "And she always did that to Felicia. There were a bunch of us at

Inglewood High, and we crisscrossed in our little groups, know what I mean? Some girls went to church together. Some of us were in Jack and Jill. Some of us did sports, and some of us danced. You know, ballet, modern, jazz dance."

She sucks her teeth. "Lee was gifted, and so she participated in most things. Rotary, honor society, and track and field like your mother. She knew *everybody*. Lee did cotillion with a few of them girls and school government with some other ones. Got along with *everybody*. Bee, though, hated the dancers with the heat of a thousand suns. Ohmigod, for some reason, she was so jealous of them."

I could picture my mother back in the day with that sexy sneer of hers, whispering to coconspirators like LaRain, making fun of a dancer's calloused feet and crooked toes. Christmas would be especially hard for Mom with all those special holiday programs and the prettiest dancer starring as Clara in *The Nutcracker.*

"Lee and Bee were supposed to go to the mall one night," Alicia says, "but the Alvin Ailey company was performing downtown, and Felicia wanted to go to that instead. Bee lost it and demanded that Lee choose between being her friend or not."

"Let me guess," I say. "Felicia chose the dancers."

Alicia chuckles. "Yup. Bee told Felicia that if she didn't come to the mall, she wouldn't invite her to Bee's annual pajama jammie-jam."

"The *what?*"

"A party where you have to wear your pajamas. And Lolly didn't mind—she'd be the one making people drinks."

"And?"

"Lee didn't show up at the mall. Bee invited *everybody* to the party, including the dancers she hated. LaRain was there being a kiss-ass. Everybody was there *except* Felicia."

I fall back into the pillows. "Ouch."

"I left for the party from my girlfriend's house," Alicia says, "and I didn't realize until later that Lee wasn't there, that she didn't even get invited. That broke her heart, and she cried all night. Bee got her back good. Nothing that Felicia did or said to her afterward would ever top what Bee did."

I scrunch my face. "Okay, I get the teenage drama, but all of this tension till now because Felicia didn't go to the mall and my mother didn't invite her to a party?"

Alicia sucks her teeth. "I know it sounds petty, but you ain't got stupid grudges that grow larger every time you think about them?"

Sadness kicks around my heart. I tap the cache of letters written by Felicia to my mother. "I'm sorry that happened."

"You ain't gotta apologize," Alicia says. "Felicia was sweet, but she didn't let anybody decide her destiny."

"They went their separate ways after that?" I ask.

"Not really," Alicia says. "Bee popped in and out, calling Lee whenever it looked like she was having too much of a life."

I purse my lips. "My mother can be a handful. And yes, she embraces loyalty, but you're describing someone—"

"Bee was toxic," Alicia interrupts. "She probably still is."

"Nope," I say, chin cocked. "She has tons of friends, and obviously Felicia missed her because she wanted to come to the party next weekend."

Alicia sucks her teeth again. "I doubt that."

"Believe whatever you wanna believe."

"Felicia drove up there for a reason," Alicia says, "and it wasn't to toast Bee and Rob. We're gonna come out there once they let us take her body back to LA. If I were you—"

"But you're not me." I squeeze the bridge of my nose, and then I touch the still-hot welt that Felicia made on my neck. "I'm sorry about your sister. I really am, but I'm not gonna sit here and listen to you drag my mother."

Alicia bursts into tears.

I listen to her cry, and the queasy, anxious, tender parts of me want to join her until I'm lightheaded and free of weird guilt. Eventually, though, all things—including this call—must end. I apologize again for her loss and end the call even as she continues to cry. I wish I had answers, for her and for me.

My phone chimes. A text from Alicia.

Ask Bobby about Liz
WHERE IS LIZ???

25.

Bobby?

It's so weird to hear people call Dad by another nickname. He's always been Rob to me—that's a grown-up nickname for a man with two daughters, a wife, and a retirement account. That's the nickname of a high school football coach who always stays above the mess and drama created by his wife and her cast of *The Real Housewives of Antelope Valley.* And because of that, I sure as hell will not ask him about some chick named Liz.

Where is Liz?

Who cares?

I'm not scuttling my parents' five-grand shindig for some *High School Musical–Drag Race–Survivor* bullshit-a-thon.

Mom's face is still hidden beneath the now-cracking sunburn mask, which means she still hasn't gone to pick up dinner from Lee Esther's. Now on the phone with LaRain, she whispers to me, "Five minutes and I'll leave," before returning to her discussion about the bastard coach on that wack-ass-they-call-themselves-a-track-team.

"I can go get it," I whisper back.

"Yara, bye," she says, louder now. "May I handle my business, please?"

I leave the house by the kitchen door and wander out to the back garage.

The gnats find me and swirl around my head. The siphon stinks tonight more than usual. I look north. That strip of water lies out there somewhere in the dark, smelling of sulfur and still water until the next rain A soft breeze cools my face. It feels faint, like someone's eyelashes fluttering against my cheeks. Like someone is watching me out there in the dark.

I am alone, though, and I push away the tarp protecting the Camaro from the desert.

"This car just *feels cooler* than everything else in the town," I tell Shane minutes later, phone to my face. "How much would it take to restore it?"

"No idea," he says. "Probably closer to ten grand than five. Does it run?"

"Dunno. She's never taken us anywhere in it. Not to a practice, not on a road trip."

The land beyond ours crunches, pants, and clicks. I pause, having forgotten the snap of dry brush and the squiggly breaths of field mice. I shiver and then shush it all.

"Who are you hushing?" Shane asks.

"The desert. It's freaking me out." I grab the door handle and squeeze. It's unlocked. Surprised, I cough and taste the metallic saltiness that comes with wheezing.

Why is the car unlocked? First, the car cover is unlocked, and now . . .

Dominique and Ransom were looking at the Camaro yesterday. Uh-oh. Not too long ago, he and his crew ran a chop shop off Rancho Vista Boulevard. He stole a Dodge Caravan, a Kia Forte, an Acura Integra, and a few Honda Civics. A sheriff's deputy was a part of the operation, prowling in his patrol unit for cars with in-demand parts.

Is Ransom Andrepont planning to steal Mom's car?

A *pop-pop-pop* echoes from far away.

I pause, then poke my head into the car.

"How's the interior?" Shane asks.

The inside of the Camaro takes my breath away. The black bucket seats look almost new, and it's like the gods trapped my mother in this car's leather upholstery. From the smoky mint of menthol cigarettes to Clinique Happy, the citrusy, upbeat perfume she used to wear.

Behind me, the kitchen door creaks.

Mom's standing there. She's rinsed off the mask. "Gonna pick up the food," she shouts.

I toss her a thumbs-up.

She lingers there for a moment, probably sick of people loitering around her car, but she dips back into the house without comment.

"My mom just came out," I tell Shane, grinning into the phone. "I know she wanted to tell me to get my grimy little hands off her car. If you haven't noticed, I sometimes break things, and sometimes, a lot of times, I lose things, too."

"You? No way."

"Yes way, I do."

"You have a lot happening in that head of yours," he says. "Murder, death, Symbyax . . ."

"Albuterol, Ativan . . ." I send him pictures of the Camaro's interior. "I was always scared she was gonna leave us in this car. That she'd throw that bag she keeps near the front door into the trunk and disappear in a cloud of dust."

Shane chuckles. "I'd like to subscribe to your newsletter, Ms. Gibson. So, what song's playing as she races down the dirt road?"

"Hmm . . . don't know a title, but it's definitely country western. Dolly Parton."

Mom may have tried to leave last night, but she needs us as much as we need her. It's easier to manipulate people up close and personal.

Pop-pop. My breathing quickens. Those shots sound closer. A nighttime hunter?

My eyes flick at the rearview mirror just in case the hunter decided to hop our fence. But no one's there. *Of course* no one is there. Tell that to my lungs, now tight as knots in my chest.

Boom! Wood splinters maybe fifty yards away instead of a hundred.

"Someone's out here shooting," I say.

"With what?"

I close my eyes and call up the weapons training Shane offered the *Tough Cookie* writers. We learned how to load, shoot, and clean guns. We learned the sound of shots made by pistols, semiautomatics, rifles, and shotguns.

"Two separate shooters," I say now, "cuz I hear a *pop-pop* and then a shotgun *boom*. Both are making me nervous."

"Maybe you should go back in the house."

I laugh. "If I'd gone into the house every time a gun blasted out here, we would've never met. It's what they do in Palmdale. I just have to get used to it again."

"Sure," Shane says, "I get that, but maybe you should—"

"I'm good," I say, firmer. "I'll talk to you later, okay?" When he doesn't respond, I sigh. "I'm good. For real."

After ending my call with an annoyed Shane, I fish my inhaler out of my pocket.

Boom!

I startle, and the inhaler pops out of my hand and tumbles into the gap between the driver's seat and the center console.

Just stupid, bored boys playing with their daddies' guns.

I reach into the tight space. Carpet . . . Silver foil gum wrapper . . .

Where the hell did my inhaler go?

My breathing now sounds high, like a train whistle. I push away from the steering column and thrust my hand beneath the seat.

What's this?

A piece of folded paper—it's faded even in the shadow of a hot, stuffy car trapped beneath a tarp. Words written in purple ink take up half the page.

Bee, you know EXACTLY what you did, and I will never forget it. Payback is forever, and since you obviously didn't learn, guess I'll have to keep teaching you. Do not ignore me, not EVER! I'm watching you, and I'll take everything and everyone you love. JUST. LIKE. THAT!! Try me. Smooches . . .

Hate throbs off the page. Gooseflesh covers every bare inch of my skin.

I take a breath but my lungs strain. I thrust my hand back into the crevice. There!

My inhaler's plastic case. I also pull out a thin chain and hold it up before me.

A gold nameplate dangles in the light.

IRINA.

26.

Smooches?

Who the hell sent this letter to my mother? Regine from *Living Single?*

How old is this note, and did Mom do something about it?

And!

Who the hell is Irina, and why is her nameplate in my mother's car?

The Camaro is now squeezing me with its tight black leather and low roof. If someone's still blasting their shotgun, I wouldn't be able to hear it over the blood banging in my ears.

My cup of aggravation has completely runneth over.

Daddy, are you happy?

He never answered my question because he couldn't honestly answer my question.

Ask Bobby about Liz.

WHERE IS LIZ???

My question isn't *where*. My question is *who*.

My scalp pulls so tight that I'm shaking. I grab the steering wheel to gain control.

Did Dad cheat on Mom with Liz? Or did he cheat on Mom with Irina? Hell, did he cheat on Mom with both women? Is *that* why Mom places a go bag by the front door? Is *that* the reason behind the arguments? Why he hasn't completely bounced from their marriage? Because his guilt has kept him in place all this time?

I squeeze the inhaler's pump twice, and the medicine rushes down my throat to open my lungs. I shove the chain into my hoodie pocket and return to the house.

Mom is still out on the food run, so I can't ask her about the note. I retreat to my bedroom. Nothing's changed here and order still reigns. My bed is made, the Van Gogh print still hangs on the wall, and the air still smells of shortbread cookies and medicine. I grab my laptop computer even though I don't have much to search on, just a single name.

Irina.

Results tell me that the most famous Irinas are a Russian ballerina and a sports star.

I refine my search: *Irina Antelope Valley.*

The Irina who lives on Stanridge Avenue is ninety-seven years old.

The Irina on Willowvale Road died ten years ago. She's survived by her son, Asher; daughter, Talia; and husband, Nolan. She worked as an actuary for an insurance company. Grew up in Akron, Ohio, and came to California as a teenager in 1983.

This Irina is a possibility.

Someone knocks on the door.

I shout, "Yeah?"

Dominique pops into my room. "Where's Mom?"

"Getting dinner from Lee Esther's." I look up from the computer. "Where you been?"

"Livin' my best life."

"With Ransom?"

"Church."

"Confession?"

"We aren't Catholic." She waits a beat, then: "Your eyes are red."

"Comes from not being able to, you know, *breathe.*"

She squeezes beside me on the bed. She smells like bubble gum and soap. "I'm sorry."

I click on the next result for Irina. Still too old.

"I shouldn't have gone off on you like that." Dominique slips her arm through mine. "I'm just *frustrated*. I hate this freaking place and you escaped and here I am, stuck."

"Comes from being the favorite daughter."

She glares at me. "I'm being serious."

"Me too. You *are* her favorite, and that's fine—I got over it a long time ago." When she sighs, I look up from the computer. "If you're stuck, Dominique, then unstick yourself. Do it before the dust and heat wear down the rest of your ambition."

"How? Mom doesn't want me to leave. She keeps telling me that I'm not ready, that I talk big, but I can't figure shit out. And you know she'll fight me if I even try."

I blink at her. "Are you officially asking me for advice? You won't get mad at me for saying, 'Let's talk about your long-term goals'?"

She lets her head fall back. "I'm so tired of this shit. I'm tired of Daddy staring at me like I ran over his favorite football. I'm tired of Mom saying, 'That's not how the world works, Dom. What kind of jackass are you?'"

I grunt. "Yeah. I'm exhausted just being here for a day." I pull one of Dominique's braids. "Mom said the same stuff to me about not being ready to leave, about being unprepared for living on my own, and I didn't believe her. Don't believe her, Dom."

She nuzzles my neck. "I appreciate everything you do, for real. I'm a bitch sometimes."

I disentangle my arms and lean away from her. "Yesterday wasn't the first time you've said shit like that to me."

Her cheeks color. "Facts, part two."

"And I'm not being crazy or mean or stuck-up for saying that Ransom is a shark and a thief," I say. "*He'll* tell you that. It's printed on his business card."

She picks her nails. "He's not as bad as you think. LaRain and Paul treat him like he's trash, and he acts like it sometimes. He actually has photographic memory like LeBron James."

"Really? Fine. Maybe I *am* a little biased, but that's because he only shows his greedy, violent side."

"On your stupid show, Cookie's sidekick, Dalton, is greedy and violent, and you're always talking about how you love writing scenes for him."

"Bruh, stupid show again?"

Dominique bites the inside of her cheek. "I won't call it 'stupid' anymore."

Tears come, and I bow my head.

She holds out her pinkie. "I won't. Promise."

We pinkie-shake.

I blow my nose into a tissue.

"Ohmigod, you are so *extra*." She waggles my hand. "Stop getting all emo."

"My point is, you like his ratchet ways," I say, dabbing at my eyes. "And he's gonna catch you up in some chaos, but guess what? He'll slip away because he's done this before, and you . . . your life will be destroyed, and you'll be screwed. People will talk about how he has this memory like LeBron, and *if* they remember you, they'll say that you were nothing but a ho with a baby and that you're bilking the system.

"Will they remember the way you wore the hell out of a T-shirt? Or that you were the captain of the volleyball team? No. But *that* asshole . . . Ugh." I shake my head. "You're more than his girl, Dom. You're more than Bee's daughter." I take a deep breath, an underwater cave dive breath, then say, "Please don't move in with Ransom. That's certain doom."

Dominique smirks. "Is that your PCP talking?"

"If you mean ESP and not drugs," I say, grinning, "then, yes, it's my ESP working."

Dominique hides her face in her lap, then rubs her chin against her knees. "I'm tired of living here. I want a grown-up life with my own space, with my own dishes."

"You can still go to Cal Arts and live closer there. Or you can transfer down to Cal State Northridge or Long Beach and live down in LA."

She curls her arm over her head. "Would you talk to Mom?"

I snort. "Only if you do what you're supposed to do. I will not bare my neck to Barb Wire for the hell of it."

Dominique opens the top letter from the Felicia cache Mom gave me and reads aloud.

> Bee, since you won't pick up the phone when I call now, I thought it best to write you.
>
> This has gone on too far. You've always been stubborn, but now you're being stupid. I thought better of you, always gave you the benefit of the doubt, but now? If she destroys you, it's your own fault. Just because you're right doesn't mean she's wrong. You ARE a bitch, and I will join her in making you pay. You will NEVER sleep sound again. You should question everything you eat and drink. Your neck will cramp from looking over your shoulder for the rest of your life.
>
> What goes around comes around, and this is one party you are not invited to.
>
> With all my hate and the illest of wills,
>
> Felicia

My eyes bug. "Whoa. Cousin Felicia was straight *triggered.*"

Dominique gapes at me and then the letter. "You find this in the attic?"

I shake my head. "Mom gave them to me. She wanted me to see for myself why she's not a weepy wreck over Felicia's death."

"Felicia was cuckoo for Cocoa Puffs," Dominique says, then opens another letter.

> We're not stupid. You can make all the cupcakes you want, be the best coach in the world, but we will never forget. I wouldn't leave your cigarettes just sitting out like that. You never know where they've been.

And another letter.

> Gained weight, huh? Moo, heifer. Riding a broomstick doesn't burn as many calories as you think. And put down the whistle and run with your girls sometimes. We eagerly look forward to your future heart attack.

Dominique's jaw tightens. She's ready to beat down a bitch, but one of them is already dead. "Who is 'we'?"

"No idea, although . . ." I turn my laptop so that she can see the screen.

"Who's Irina?"

I point to her. "You *cannot* say anything."

Dominique's eyebrows furrow as she plops back into the pillows.

I fish the gold chain from my pocket and let it dangle between us. She taps the nameplate. "Again with Irina. Who dat?"

"Dunno. Found it in the Camaro."

She blinks. "Okay. So?"

"I'm seeing if there's an Irina around Palmdale or Lancaster, and if she knows Daddy. Or if she's a friend of Felicia's. Maybe she's a part of the 'we,' the author of this one?" I hold up the note I found in the Camaro.

Dominique plucks the letter from my fingers and reads. "Is this Felicia or someone else?"

"Someone else."

Dominique snickers. "Bee would kill Daddy if he cheated again, first of all."

"*Again?* So there *was* someone? I just wasn't imagining it?"

My sister shakes her head. "Nope."

"When was the first time?"

She shrugs. "I just heard them arguing about some chick. You were at school."

"*Name?*"

She shrugs again. "But he's not dumb enough to screw around with chicks in the AV."

"So why was this"—I let the nameplate dangle again—"in the car, then?"

"Because you're seeing drama where there is none. Yara, that's *Mom's* car, not Dad's. It could've belonged to one of her friends from college. Or, knowing Mom, she probably snatched it off some girl's neck."

I blink, then nod. "Say less."

Dominique is right: the Camaro *is* Mom's car, and I've never seen Daddy drive it. I can't even picture him behind the wheel. I can't picture him hugged up with some bitch at a random La Quinta Inn . . . Well, I *can* but I don't *want to.* I needed him to prove me wrong, that my weird hunches had simply been that. But no . . .

My head hurts from this bowling-ball dump of information.

Dominique seizes my computer and places it on the nightstand. "Ugh. The vein in the middle of your forehead is freaking me out. No more Sherlock Holmes-ing. We're watching stupid *Terminator* and finally eating that damn shark-coochie board she's been working on all day. BTW, you're taking me shopping tomorrow."

I rub my temples and squeeze shut my eyes. "I am?"

"I need an outfit for the party, remember? And you explicitly told me to spend more than thirty dollars on it."

"How about thirty-one?"

"I'm back," Mom shouts from downstairs.

Dominique says, "Are we asking her about the Irina necklace? I say no."

I say, "Okay," then drop the necklace in my purse.

We tromp down the stairs. The house is cool and smells of wine, cured meats, and now Creole food. In the kitchen, Dad hugs Mom from behind as she unpacks dinner. She giggles.

Bee would kill Daddy if he cheated again . . .

Are you happy, Daddy?

He's not, and this slapdash display of affection is a trick.

With my mouth dry, I turn away from the gambit of affection and notice a postcard sitting beneath the front door's mail slot. There's a stock photo of a Strawberry Daiquiri and a Bahama Mama perched on two wooden posts. The blue printed words say US VIRGIN ISLANDS.

Who's the lucky person on vacation?

I turn the card over. It's addressed to me. No return address. No signer. Just words.

I'm back. From outer space. Run bitch, run!

STRANGE LADY

27.

And now, the siphon doesn't smell so bad. Not with the rain drifting from the clouds.

The houses glow in the dark, and windows shine like eyes with different shades of light—from canary-yellow lamplight and atomic-blue television light to arctic-white garage door light. There's no one wandering Edgewater Court except for the Gibson family.

Yara stands on the porch with her hands clasped around her elbows. She looks up the street and across the cul-de-sac. Her worry shines as bright as those lights around her.

Yeah, she *should* be worried. Felicia should've worried a little more, too, but she let her obsessions grow Godzilla-size. Coming to warn Yara . . . big mistake. Well, she should've kept that crazy down in El Segundo. No one ever believed Felicia back then, so why did she think this kid would? Felicia died thinking the rules had changed. Since the beginning of time, liars have won the flock.

Rob, all-American-wide-receiver tall, towers over Yara. He places his hands on her shoulder, then joins her in looking up and down the dead-end street. His search stops.

Feels like he's looking right at me.

But then his roving gaze continues.

He and Yara study the postcard she holds. She flaps the card, then says something that makes him shake his head and pat her shoulder. He's always been the one who says, *It's gonna be okay. It's gonna work itself out.* Standing there like a big dog, like he's in charge.

He hasn't protected anybody. Not really. No, not at all.

Dominique slips her arms around Yara's waist, then cranes her neck to read the postcard. She steps to the edge of the porch and shouts, "Say that to my face."

Yara yanks Dominique's arm and retreats into the house. Rob continues to gaze south. But he won't see a thing. He's been blind or stupid—or both—all this time.

And one day, I will *say that to their faces.* And oh, what a joyful day that will be.

28.

Overnight, rain fell, and now the world smells new and crisp. Some of the dust has washed off my car, and the black paint looks fashionably matte instead of flat-out filthy. Dominique slides into the front passenger seat of Mom's Cherokee, and I pop into the back seat with my purse and foil-wrapped bacon-and-egg breakfast sandwich. Like the Camaro, the SUV's interior smells of cigarettes smoked yesterday and one hundred years before, and instead of Clinique's Happy, there's a hint of rose and jasmine from Mom's current perfume as well as heavier notes of running shoes, discarded athletic tape, and sweat.

Dominique drops her traveling mug into a cup holder, then pops down the visor mirror to add more shine to her bright-red lips and tighten her two french braids. Mom looks like our older sister in her black Vans and Thrasher tank top. I wish I could've kept on my pajama bottoms and hoodie and stayed in bed.

My eyes skip around our neighborhood. Who could've sent that postcard? Where is the man in the green Mazda? Has this Nissan Pathfinder parked here before? Who's hiding behind that hedge?

Mom doesn't believe the sender is a rando with a grudge. "Only because you're *always* pissing someone off, intentionally or not."

I take a big bite out of my sandwich and say, "I don't move around the state *trying* to become the object of someone's scorn. I haven't transgressed enough to receive a hate card. I haven't killed off a beloved character. I haven't stolen a boyfriend." Shane's last girlfriend is now living happily in Washington, DC, with her lobbyist husband.

I pull that hate card from my purse. So innocent and fun loving on the front with those frozen cocktails, and so whacked-out and creepy on the flip side. *I'm back. From outer space. Run bitch, run!*

If it hadn't been addressed to me, I would appreciate the tribute to Gloria Gaynor and "I Will Survive."

But no. Not cool.

Mom backs out of the garage, and for a moment, she meets my eyes. "Who have you talked to recently that may not appreciate your *vibe?*"

I chew bacon, and I'm sad that I can't even taste the smoky richness of my favorite meat. "Umm . . . There was Felicia, of course . . . and there's Alicia now."

"Alicia?" Mom's head tilts, and she watches my reflection in the rearview mirror.

I nod. "I told you that she called me yesterday. Well, I ended up talking to her. If you wanna talk about someone not appreciating vibes . . . She tried to blame *you—*"

"Me? For *what?"*

"For being awful to Felicia. I didn't let her talk about you like that, and it kinda pissed her off. But if she's sending an out-of-pocket postcard, it would be to you, not me."

Dominique sips her tea, then adds, "It's gotta be her."

I stare at the postcard's message. "Alicia lives in Vegas."

"So?"

"There's no postmark. See?" My hands shake as I show my sister and mother the blank space where a postmark would be. "This card wasn't mailed," I say. "Whoever wrote it slipped it into our mail slot in the front door."

"Ohmigod," Dominique says.

Mom rubs her jaw. "We all need to watch our backs, okay? Always let someone know where you are. Understand?" She squeezes Dominique's hand, then pushes out a breath. "Al and Cece are taking Felicia back to LA, but I don't know if the medical examiner here is ready to release the body. Guess I'm saying . . . it still could be Alicia. She's coming to town. She may already be here and just hasn't told anyone yet."

I take another bite of my breakfast sandwich. Hard to enjoy bacon when you're the pig in the poke. As I eat, I search for more information about Alicia Campbell on the internet. Physically, she looks just like Felicia—the same big cow eyes and broad forehead. But instead of dusters and clunky jewelry, Alicia prefers jeggings and crop tops, low-cut tops, any kind of top that shows off her cleavage and curves. She has four kids—my cousins Zachariah, Lucas, Blake, and Kenzie. If she could wear jeggings and a halter top emblazoned with a sparkly US Postal Service logo, Alicia would be the hottest, on fleek mail carrier in the country.

So I need to look out for a woman who looks just like a woman I've met only once and who's now also dead.

No, not creepy at all.

Dad (who allegedly drove down to Los Angeles to see his friend's son play baseball) calls to check in on us. Is he really planning to watch a USC game, or is he at some Malibu love shack with some trick named Irina?

At the hobby store, we grab frames of different shapes. We grab purple tulle and white ribbon for the anniversary favors and two bubble machines to add to the ballroom magic. Mom and Dominique laugh about Mom's track team parents as I hang back and keep my eyes on the other shoppers. Dominique pushes the cart like she's on the runway while I stare at a curly-haired man who would look like the man in the green Mazda if he were Black and not Latinx. My head feels trapped in air bubble cushioning wrap and disconnected from the rest of me. But my family—they're singing along to Muzak "Dancing Queen" as though no one died, as though no one's left a mean postcard and our patriarch isn't nearly one hundred miles south with another woman.

As the day passes, Mom, Dominique, and I dip into air-conditioned spaces and return to dry, dusty winds. My allergies worsen, and soon I'm constantly blowing my nose. Mom watches me in the rearview mirror and sighs every time I fluff out a tissue or slip the inhaler between my lips. Miserable, I apologize for the racket and sink into the seat.

Finally, Mom drops Dominique and me off at home before she heads to school for track practice. I check the floor beneath the mail slot. No postcards.

"Where you headed?" I ask my sister, who's now walking over to her Jeep.

"School. Thanks for the outfit."

I pop antihistamines, then retreat to the porch with shopping bags filled with party favors. I scan the neighborhood, looking for someone now looking at me. But nothing moves, not even the leaves of our silver maple. The newness of last night's rain has faded; the siphon stinks again, and the sun leaches any lingering moisture.

My nose is raw and my eyes burn, but I need to work. These goody bags won't stuff themselves. Sure: my inhaler has lost its effectiveness against the constant barrage of irritants, and I'm now down to one hundred puffs, but who will stuff gold heart wine bottle stoppers, monogrammed packets of cocktail mixes, Hershey's Kisses, and custom matchbooks into pockets of purple tulle and ribbon? Dominique?

Kayla's blue Crown Vic rolls into our cul-de-sac and parks in front of our house. Today, her badge is clipped tight to her belt, and her red hair is gelled down to her skull. "Oh, wow," she says, eyes big as she climbs the porch steps. "What's all this?"

I lift a Rob and Bee matchbook and sing, "These are a few of Mom's favorite things."

"What about your dad?" Kayla asks. "The man who doesn't smoke."

"Umm . . ." Tulle and ribbon, chocolate candies and drink mixes. "Guess I forgot."

She clucks her tongue. "Must be nice to spend money on . . . bottle stoppers?"

"Keeps wine fresh."

"Who cares? It's a three-dollar bottle."

"Sometimes you want more than Two-Buck Chuck."

"You so fancy now," Kayla says, smirking.

Can I enjoy a ten-dollar bottle of wine and not be called "fancy"?

Whatever. Kayla's right about one thing, though. Dad *isn't* in these goody bags. He likes Skittles, football, hiking, and Doritos. Nothing on this porch reflects that.

Guilt weighs down my heart. I never think of things Dad likes. Christmas gifts, yeah, but everyday thinking about making him happy? Guess that's why he couldn't answer my very simple question, *Are you happy, Daddy?* He wouldn't be, seeing these Bee-themed goody bags. Guess that's just another reason why he's always sitting beneath the tree with an empty notepad in his lap.

And maybe having another affair.

Kayla leans against the banister. "Cayden Decker asked about you."

The first boy who kissed me.

I snort as I stuff. "He's still alive?"

I know he's still alive.

Kayla says, "Yeah. He manages the Fish and Fly."

The city's members-only fishing and hunting club. Its members are also the only ones allowed to put a boat onto Lake Palmdale.

"He went from being a runner to a hunter," I say. "The story of America right now."

"When your dad's the president of the club . . ." Kayla shrugs. "And he's not as bad as our other classmates. And it's not like we all have millions of men to choose from up here. Your standards are too high. He's a ten in Palmdale. There's still good corn in dented cans."

Cayden has more than dents in his can. The one social media search I did on him . . . Yeah, he *was* as bad as our other classmates with the questionable patches on his field coat and the worrisome slogans cut and pasted into his profile. The vast collection of guns doesn't bother me as much as the company he keeps.

Kayla takes a steno pad from her jacket pocket.

"I got a strange postcard last night," I say.

"Strange how?"

I pluck the card from my purse and show it to her.

She reads it, then shrugs. "Okay."

"You don't seem worried."

"You are?"

I laugh. "Dude. Yes. Run bitch, run?"

She holds out her arms and makes a 360-degree turn. "But you're sitting out in the open. I just walked up on the porch, and you didn't try to shoot me cuz you thought I was an intruder."

I blink at her. "So . . . I can't be worried, then?"

"You tend to be naturally anxious. Just remember that and take a breath." She grins, waggles her eyebrows, and hands back the postcard. "Seriously, you can always call me if you're being threatened, okay?" She pauses, then adds, "I drove to 1224 Stardust Way. Found your fingerprints inside the cabin."

I sneeze into the crook of my elbow. "I was supposed to meet Felicia there. I told you."

"*Supposed to.*" Kayla slides the tissue pack closer to me. "Since she obviously wasn't there, how did your fingerprints get *inside* the cabin?"

I blow my nose. "Don't know why, but she gave me a key to the place. I went inside, to see *something, anything* that would tell me the reason I was there. Nothing stuck out. I stayed for about an hour, took a nap, and then I came out to see my slashed tires."

Kayla scribbles into her little notepad.

"Maybe she'd planned to give me high school mementos or family pictures," I say.

"I don't understand," Kayla says. "Why would she have mementos?"

I throw up my hands. "No idea, Kayla. The woman died before she could tell me why she'd come. I've had all kinds of random family members reaching out to me lately. Everybody either wants to come to this party or has an idea for a TV show." I pause, then add, "Speaking of family, they're supposed to be coming up soon for her body."

"*Umhmm.*"

"Does that mean the autopsy is done?"

Kayla flips a page in her notebook. "That's the medical examiner's call."

"We're just trying to figure out funeral stuff and . . ." I let my voice trail. *We're* not figuring out jack when it comes to Felicia. At least not in *this* house.

"Has your mother visited the cabin?" Kayla asks. "Does *she* know what Felicia meant? Why she came to Palmdale?"

I return to stuffing goody bags. "Other than Felicia getting revenge after Mom disinvited her to a big party back in the twelfth grade? Nope. Cousin Felicia was ultracompetitive. Also, remember that she had three husbands, two of whom are still alive."

Kayla says, "Other than learning that Darius What's His Face broke his collarbone in Sarasota, I haven't done a deep dive on the husbands yet."

"*And* Felicia got fired from her job not too long ago, according to my father's cousin. Oh—Will Harraway, husband number three? The widower posting thirst trap pictures on socials? I sent him a friend request on Facebook, and he's been sliding into my DMs ever since." I show her the *Join me beautiful* string.

"Send me that?" Kayla then writes in the pad for a long time. "Sounds like you're saying that anybody could've killed her. Or . . . she had plenty of reasons to walk into Lake Palmdale and end it all."

I give a one-shouldered shrug. "I'm just saying that she seemed troubled, and that anything's possible." I sneeze again and blow my nose.

Kayla winces. "You look and sound like crap."

I pluck my inhaler from my pocket and take a hit.

Ninety-nine puffs left.

"Just like when we were kids," Kayla says. "You're allergic to this house."

My eyebrows lift. "You think?"

"One more thing," she says. "Those fingerprints . . ."

I dab at my eyes with tissue. "I touched some things as I roamed around."

Kayla consults her steno pad. "A lamp. A lighthouse. A Lego block. A jewelry box."

Mom's Cherokee pulls into the driveway. Music from Jill Scott pounds past the windows.

Kayla and I watch my mother grab her track bag from the back seat. The muscles in her bare, long legs flex as she slips the strap of the heavy bag onto her shoulder.

Mom smiles. Beneath the sheen of sweat, the freckles across the bridge of her nose have muddied. "Didn't I just see you, Kayla K.?"

Kayla flushes and closes the steno pad, then stands tall and straight. "Yes, Mrs. G. Gotta get in all my time with Yara before she jets back to her fabulous life in LA." She grabs a bottle stopper from the pile. "I'm excited. We get to dress up and be deluxe."

"Right?" Mom swivels to me. "Did you reseat Sharla?"

I nod and waggle my phone. "How was practice?"

"Didn't have them do much since the meet was yesterday." Mom peers at Kayla like a lioness watching a lost baby elephant. "You need help with something, Kayla K.?"

Kayla smiles, shakes her head. "Nope." To me, she says, "Oh! My parents said brunch tomorrow morning works. Mom's trying out a few new recipes."

A thumbs-up from me.

Kayla says her goodbyes, then climbs back into the Ford. The car's engine rumbles, and Kayla pulls away from the curb.

Mom keeps her eyes on the retreating car. "She trying to stir up shit?"

My breath locks in my chest. I don't know what to say because *stir up shit*?

And a jewelry box?

A Lego block?

I don't remember touching either of those objects at the cabin.

29.

Maybe during my visit to the cabin, I tossed aside a random Lego that had been stuck in the chaise longue out on the deck. I *must* have, since my prints were found on those things. And why were Kayla and crew searching the cabin anyway? Felicia didn't die at *that* lake.

"You're not eating."

Mom's voice is pointy, hard, and it pulls me out of my hazy head cloud. I'm back in our dining room with its round glass table and comfy chairs. Gipsy Kings plays softly on the stereo. I've moved spinach lasagna from a place on my plate to another place on my plate. I've nibbled roasted broccoli and I've nibbled salad.

"I can't taste—" I turn away from the table to sneeze—*choo-choo-choo*—then to blow my nose. My lungs creak as though someone's stepping on tired wooden planks.

Dad says, "I'll find the humidifier."

Mom drops her fork. "Welcome back to Earth, Robert. The humidifier's already *in* the room." She turns to me. "Yara, did you take your allergy meds?"

I wipe my nose and sip from my cup of tea. "Not the nighttime doses. It's too early."

"Try to eat a little something."

"Bee, she's triggered," Dad says.

"While you were down in LA, *Robert*," Mom growls, "I cooked all of this for her while dealing with my crazy-ass family. She can eat at least half."

"You're forcing her to—"

I pick up my fork. "It's okay. I'm eating."

Mom and Dad glare at each other.

I make a show of shoveling a lasagna noodle into my mouth. It tastes like slick nothing, but I nod anyway. "Tastes good, Mom."

Dad squeezes the bridge of his nose. "Yara, don't force yourself to—"

Mom leans forward, her eyes dangerous slits. "You know what, Robert?"

"So now I can't even talk to my daughter?" Dad asks.

"Please don't," I say. "I'm eating, okay? And I'll stop when I can't, all right?" My voice sounds craggy and hoarse.

Mom winces hearing me speak and sits back in her chair. "You need *food* to absorb the pills. They don't work well on an empty stomach. *That's* why I want you to eat." She taps her small hoop earring and squints at Dad. "Or am I wrong in my thinking, Dr. Gibson?"

Dad's clenched jaw twitches. "No one has the right to force people to do what they don't wanna do," he mutters. Then he picks up his knife and fork and saws at the food.

Mom simply stares at him and sips wine.

I really do need to include a few of his favorite things in the anniversary goody bags.

The kitchen door opens and slams shut. Dominique pops in the doorway. "Sorry I'm late." She grabs a plate from the kitchen cabinet and loads it with lasagna and broccoli. Before plopping into her seat, she gazes at Mom and Dad, then gives me a cocked brow.

I offer her the tiniest headshake and return to chewing lasagna.

"Did you pick up the exercise bands?" Mom asks my sister. "I texted you, and you said, 'okay,' that you'd be passing the store anyway."

Dominique freezes.

The charged air makes me dizzy. I focus on the broccoli florets that haven't moved from their spot on my plate.

"That's a 'no,' then?" Mom says.

Dad closes his eyes, then leans back in his chair. He drapes an arm over his head.

"She had a school thing," I say, weighing each word. "We can pick them up tomorrow. All good."

Mom rests her chin in her palm. "I thought you were helping out at the shelter?"

Dominique drops her brown eyes to the table and places her hands in her lap. Even when terrified, she's a *Vogue* model with those cheekbones and that perfect lip color.

Mom frowns. "Let me guess: You were hanging out with Ransom?"

Dominique glares at her.

"You can mad dog me all you want," Mom says sourly, "but *you're* the one not handling business. *You're* the one messing up." She pauses. "I know you better get your face straight, or I'll straighten it for you."

Dominique's shoulders sag.

My heart deflates before it pops.

"Buy the bands tomorrow," Dad says to my sister. To Mom, he says, "I have a few you can use tonight."

With blood pushing to her face, Dominique picks up her fork.

"Don't you know some nice boys she can date?" Mom asks me, her eyes bright, shiny. "Guys who don't know what the inside of a prison cell looks like?"

Ouch.

After dinner, I retreat to the attic. Dust floats in the shafts of light, but in this quiet, I can think and hear my pulse pounding in the confines of my stuffy head. My parents' wedding certificate should be in one of these tubs since it's not in the home office filing cabinet. Now that LaRain's here, Mom won't pull herself away to help me look for it.

Her exact words: *I'm not your file clerk right now.*

A pink blanket with a pink monogrammed YMG and frayed satin edges sits atop a box that holds old life insurance policies, bank statements, and job orientation folders. A battered manila envelope bulges with postcards, greeting cards, and letters.

Black-ink handwriting fills the back of a Greetings from Arizona postcard addressed to Barbara McGuire.

You will never find peace and happiness. You betrayed me and I will never forgive you.

Whoa. I scan the card for a signer.

No name.

A postcard of the Saint Peter's Basilica dome isn't any nicer.

If only you knew how much I hate you right now. If I had a knife, I would drive it through your eyes.

This one had been sent to Bobby Gibson.

Again, no signer.

These words sound like they were written by the same pissed-off woman who keyed my car.

I stick the postcards back into the envelope and drop it back in the plastic tub. Not that I plan to display hate mail at the party. I just want to read more later.

An accordion file holds daycare applications and college transcripts.

We Have It All . . . 1987–1988 Green and White Inglewood High School

Mom's twelfth grade yearbook!

The pages smell like smoke and Starbursts. The boys wear black tuxedos, and the girls wear those traditional black drapes. Ha! Look at all the teenage awkwardness that surpasses race and class. Zits, braces, tiny heads, and Coke-bottle glasses. Lots of weird hair.

There's Barbara McGuire, her hair flawlessly feathered. Cheekbones bronzed. Lip gloss popping. Who can look this fly in a floofy black drape?

I turn the pages to find Senior Favorites.

There's Mom again. Voted Ms. Loudmouth.

Favorite quote: *The first thing I do in the morning is brush my teeth and sharpen my tongue.* Dorothy Parker.

In a flashback scene of *Queen of Palmdale*, high school senior Barbie McGuire, mischief twinkling in her eyes, sits in the middle of her clique rating students as they pass. She would've made fun of me, the scrawny girl heavy breathing and crying as she tries to open her jammed locker. An earlier scene would've shown me envying perfect Barbie running on the track—so pretty, so popular, so outspoken. So . . . *mean.*

Several rows above my mother's, a picture has been scratched out, the entire box colored in with black marker. The name has also been crossed out.

I flip back a few pages to students whose last names start with *C*. It's not Felicia because she's right there. Senior class president and valedictorian. Most Likely to Succeed. Her favorite quote: *Great spirits have always encountered violent opposition from mediocre minds.* Albert Einstein.

"Oh, Felicia," I say, "why couldn't you just *shut up*, sometimes?"

I return to the *M* page, but I can't see past that black ink.

Whoever this is, they're a high enemy of Barbara McGuire.

Next, candid shots. There's Mom at a debate meet. There's Mom on her racing block, ready to run, ready to win. There's Mom, Winter Court Queen clutching a bouquet of flowers.

A slip of notebook paper lives between the staff photos and the page that introduces the class of 1989. Handwriting fills the page, and I can't make it out . . .

Someone—*Mom?*—has written a name over and over again, like they're trying out the name of the person they're crushing on. There's a *Q* or an *E* or . . . All swoops and flourishes.

I sneeze—*choo-choo-choo*—and my head rings. "I can't . . ." I stick the note back into the yearbook, grab my baby blanket, and close all the boxes.

Dad sits beneath the tree again with that legal pad still in his lap. LaRain is here, and she's with Mom in the backyard doing training exercises that Mom wants her team to do. Since high school, LaRain has acted as Mom's squire, and I wonder how she feels about obeying Queen Bee's every command, always coming in second. She's not as fast, not as smart, not as pretty. She didn't date the handsome football captain. She didn't give birth to a kid she could brag about.

But!

LaRain benefits from holding Mom's shield, from landing jobs to being invited to join community groups. She isn't lacking in respect or regard . . . or suspicion, thanks to Ransom.

I slip my baby blanket into one of the dresser drawers, then grab my IDEAS journal to capture the high school flashbacks. After dropping the journal back into my bag, I retreat to the bathroom I share with my sister to take a shower. Dominique's cosmetics cram the counter, and I can fit only my toothbrush in the soap dish. Her dirty clothes pile on top of the hamper, and thousands of towels of every size drape over the shower rod. I curl my lip and dump my clothes atop the closed toilet lid.

The steam from the hot water opens my lungs and nasal passages, and my mind drifts back to the attic and to that yearbook. Then my thoughts turn to Cayden Decker and my first kiss and how the sun shone on my face all afternoon because I thought I was about to have my first boyfriend and—

The shower curtain darkens and rustles.

I snap back into the present. "Somebody here?" I call out.

The water pounds against the porcelain and my body. Steam billows all around me.

"Hello?"

No answer.

I push aside the shower curtain.

No one. I'm alone. Just me and the steam.

I duck my head beneath the hot spray of the shower and let my mind wander again.

That Virgin Islands postcard is now stuck between the pages of my IDEAS-*QUEEN OF PALMDALE* journal. Kayla didn't seem too concerned about it. But I've never received an anonymous card before coming back home, before Felicia's death. Who would send me . . . ?

I'm back. From outer space.

Run bitch, run!

And Mom's high school yearbook . . .

Who did she scratch out so violently that pen impressions had been left behind on the next page? Not even Cousin Felicia the Betrayer had been relegated to a black box.

I shut off the water and grab two towels—one to wrap around my wet hair, the other to dry off. My head feels clear. All the medications I've taken today now have room to work.

Can I stay in a steamy shower for the next week? I sure as hell will try.

I push aside the shower curtain and step onto the bath rug. The fan is already sucking away the steam and—

My eyes land on the mirror. I blink, squeeze my eyes shut, then open them.

Steam has completely fogged over the mirror except for the single word written on its silver surface.

SURRENDER.

I clutch the towel wrapped tight around me and gape at that one word. I hurry into Dominique's bedroom.

Clothes in tiny piles everywhere. Makeup bags where there aren't clothes. Shopping bags from our trip earlier today shoved in between the piles. No Dominique.

No one's here.

In the backyard, Mom and LaRain train with resistance bands. Dominique and her girlfriends sit in patio chairs, phones to their faces. Dad washes his truck in the driveway.

I open the kitchen door and call Dominique.

My sister gapes at the towel on her way to the door. "Why you walkin' around naked?"

Her two friends snicker.

My temper flares and heat washes up my throat. "Are you playing some kind of joke? Cuz it's not funny."

Her eyebrows furrow. "What kind of crack did you just smoke?"

"The message on the mirror," I say. "Ha ha, very funny."

A smile plays at the edge of her mouth. "Yara, homie, speak-a de English."

I grab her hand and pull her up the stairs.

"Can you tell me what's going on?" she says.

The steam from my shower has evaporated.

So has the message on the mirror.

Dominique's reflection gapes at mine. "What am I supposed to be seeing right now?"

I motion toward the clear mirror. "I was taking a shower, right? And it was all steamy in here and I stepped out and . . ."

Dominique waits for me to continue. When I don't, she says, "And *what?*"

"You tell me."

"Tell you *what?*"

Hot tears lick the backs of my eyes. "I'm not crazy, Dom."

Dominique grins. "Debatable."

A teardrop tumbles down my cheek. "A message was right there. I swear it."

"Yara, I haven't done anything. I haven't written any message." She glances at the mirror. "What did it say?"

I whisper, "Surrender." I turn the knob of the hot water.

"What are you doing?" Dominique's earlier amusement drains from her face.

"If it was there before," I say, "it will still be there. And you'll see for yourself."

Dominique stares at me.

I stare at the mirror.

Steam billows from the shower and licks at the edge of the mirror but doesn't stick.

Dominique claps her hands once. "Okay, so I'm done standing here waiting for steamy Bloody Mary to appear."

"Wait!"

The steam tries to grab hold, but it evaporates a second after contact with the surface.

"Deuces." Dominique throws up two fingers and leaves the bathroom, closing the door behind her.

I don't move. I *did* see "surrender" written in steam . . . right? Maybe I didn't. Maybe it was my anxiety, my overactive imagination. Maybe I should return to therapy. I haven't popped an Ativan since . . . since . . .

The women on Mom's side of the family . . . All *touched.* All *extreme.* Manic. Violent. Not right in the head. And I am a member of the sorority. Anxious. Prone to sleepwalking and night terrors. Forgetful. *Delusional.*

Steam from the shower clouds all around me. Once again, my head clears. I take in the vaporized air, closing my eyes and breathing deeply.

It's okay, Yara. We all go a little mad sometimes.

I open my eyes.

There it is.

Surrender.

197

30.

Maybe this word has been on the mirror forever, and I've never noticed it until now.

I pluck and pluck the rubber band on my wrist.

SURRENDER.

Maybe it's a . . . a diet message that Mom wrote spontaneously days, months, *years* ago?

Maybe this message—is it even a message?—wasn't meant for me. And who's to say that it's threatening?

No one was in the house with me to sneak in and write it as I showered.

Dominique and her friends looked at me as though I were moments away from licking all the doorknobs at the Red Roof Inn. While my heart had lifted seeing that one word again, it sank knowing that my little sister thinks I've lost my mind. Again.

My mouth waters. I want a cigarette. I need a cigarette.

Pluck.

No, I don't.

I hate this place.

This place hates me.

Even though it's just minutes after six o'clock, I wobble over to the nightstand to pop an Ativan and then climb into bed. Reset—I need to reset.

I aim the remote control at the television and find *The Bachelorette*. Who will Hannah choose? The pilot, the air force vet, the douche canoe . . . ?

By the first break, the Ativan has kicked in and my eyelids flutter . . .

⚡

My eyes pop open.

LaRain is standing over me, her breath ripe with tobacco, her bug eyes lined with black kohl like Cleopatra.

I startle and shift away from her. "What's wrong?"

She clutches her neck and hops away from my bed.

The clock says that it's six forty-five. Shadows smudge the ceiling of my bedroom. *The Bachelorette* still plays on the television.

"I heard you screaming," LaRain says. Her many-ringed fingers shake and tug at her clingy fuchsia tank top. "I was going to the bathroom downstairs and . . . Are you okay?"

"Screaming?" I say. "I don't remember . . ." I shake my head.

She pats her moist cheeks. "Your mom used to tell me, back when I babysat you and Dom, to never wake you up if you're having one of them nightmare-things. So when I heard you . . ." She flaps her face. "That shit's scary."

I blink at her. My throat feels raw, the only indicator that my nap wasn't peaceful.

"You don't take medication for that?" She side-eyes me and wanders around my room.

I grab a water bottle. "I do, which is why I'm confused right now." I take a sip of water and watch her slink toward the door.

"What are you doing up here?" My mother's voice zings from down the hall.

LaRain straightens, turns to her. "Your girl was having one of her sleeping fits."

Mom pops into my doorway, a scowl on her face. "They're not *fits*."

"Terrors," LaRain says, hands up.

"You didn't wake her up, did you?" Mom asks, frown deepening.

"No," I say, a reminder that I, an adult woman, am still in the room. "I'm okay, Mom."

Mom peels her eyes from LaRain, then flicks them at me. "I think you should start back on your meds. Too much is happening, and I can't be everywhere to watch over you."

My pulse pops. "You don't need to . . . I don't need . . ." I blink and blink. "I'm okay. I'm fine when I'm down in LA."

Mom squints at me, then grunts.

LaRain snickers.

Mom glares at her.

LaRain's face flushes.

I gape at the duo. "What?"

Mom gives me doe eyes. "Nothing. You got it all under control. Go 'head on with your bad self." One last smirk, and she dips out of my room with LaRain behind her.

31.

On a Friday morning during my sophomore year of high school, I attended cross-country track practice at Tejon Park. With my janky lungs, I didn't run, but because my mother was the school's running coach, sometimes I joined her on these outdoor trainings. With all the forests and hillsides burning around Southern California, the trails weren't crowded. Even though it was early morning, the air already smelled of fire, burning brush, and horse sweat.

Tall and thin, Cayden Decker had dark, wavy hair and a strong jaw. In some pictures, he looked bright-eyed, wholesome, and totally over it. The older we got, though, the more stoned and out of it he looked, with scraggly face hair and a droopy, bloodshot gaze. But not on that morning in Tejon Park. That morning, I'd walked behind the runners, earbuds in, listening to Drake and Rihanna on my iPhone. Cayden had lingered on the trail until I caught up with him.

"You're gonna get in trouble," I said. "Coach Bee's gonna break your back."

He'd been the king of cross-country at our school. "I'll claim charley horse," he said, golden in that early-morning sunshine. "I had fun at the movies last night."

"Me too." We'd seen *Resident Evil: Afterlife* with a group of friends, and Cayden and I had held hands for half of the movie.

Mom's whistle sounded in the distance.

Cayden startled.

"You better get going," I said.

We grinned at each other. He leaned forward and pecked me on the lips. I giggled. He leaned forward again, and we kissed a second time. His lips parted. So did mine. So *très français*. All of me burned, and I thought I'd spontaneously combust.

And that was it.

We didn't kiss again.

We didn't go out on any other group dates or even a first date alone.

His parents shut us down immediately. They loved him being trained by a Black woman, but didn't want him holding hands with or kissing that Black woman's daughter. I'd heard them say those exact words in the school's parking lot.

I didn't kiss someone again until college.

And now, here I am, nine years later, watching Cayden Decker stroll from the trap range to the gated entrance. His dark, wavy hair now hits his collar, and he's clean-shaven. A runner's body still burbles beneath camo pants and a green T-shirt.

My phone vibrates with a text from Dominique.

Still out on your errand?
Bring me back a McFlurry

Cayden throws the lock and pushes open the gate. "Hey, stranger."

"What's up?"

We hug.

He smells of gunpowder and Skoal, and he probably tastes like Mountain Dew.

His eyes flick all around my body. "You look incredible."

"Thank you," I say, flushing. The catnap and the Ativan have smoothed me out. "Kayla told me that you asked about me. I saw on the website that y'all were open until nine, so I thought I'd drop by on this lovely Sunday night." I take his left hand and raise my eyebrows at his gold wedding band.

He smirks. "You live in the complete opposite direction. This ain't a drop by."

"The woman found in the lake yesterday?"

He shoves his hands in his pockets. "Yeah?"

"She was my cousin."

His jaw drops. "No way."

I give him a sad smile. "For real. So I came to the lake to, you know, see it for myself. And since it's gated most times, I thought maybe you or whoever's in charge could let me take a walk around the shore. Or you can join me. Let's catch up."

He pushes the hair back from his face. "Absolutely. I may not be able to walk all the way," he says. "I need to start shutting things down soon."

I move past him and watch as he locks the gate.

Mountains formed by the San Andreas Fault ring us. The air is cold and crisp, and my cheeks sting from the icy breeze coming off the water. With the quacking ducks, the water lapping against the shore, and the clicking fishing reels, Lake Palmdale is almost tranquil.

Cayden's happily married to a woman named Hailee. They have two boys and a girl—Keller, Bryce, and Reagan—and a yellow Lab named Nell. And now, he points at the lakeshore by the first parking lot. "They found your cousin around there."

Nothing to mark the spot. No flowers left in memoriam. Like nothing had been discovered in those waters other than trout, catfish, and bluegill.

"The detectives are trying to figure out how she got in," he says. "I'm thinking from the Park N Ride."

We crunch across the gravel and move closer to the shore. He points at the dirt. "They found her phone around here."

Nothing to mark this spot, either. Like Felicia Campbell was never here.

"And that second set of footprints," he says, "was here."

The Park N Ride is directly behind us.

Second set of footprints?

The fencing that separates the lot from the lake has been knocked down. By the wind or by people? Or a car? A purple Mercedes-Benz sedan perhaps?

"How do they know Felicia didn't make those prints?" I ask.

"The tread's bigger than your cousin's feet," he says. "At least that's what I was told."

I grin at him. "And who told you?"

He blushes, then clears his throat. "Just picked up snippets here and there."

I side-eye him and say nothing.

We move on, our feet tapping against packed earth.

"Have they looked at any video from the security cameras?" I ask.

He pauses in his step. "Umm . . . Hmm."

"There aren't cameras at the club or around the lake?"

He nods but looks perplexed. "There are, but they haven't asked."

"Why not?"

"Cuz they think it's a suicide."

"Even with that second set of prints?" I ask.

He gives a quick nod, then looks at his watch. "We should head back."

My eyes roam the landscape. Downed fencing. Tall grass, perfect circles trembling across the lake's surface. "Would you mind if I looked at the tape?"

"I gotta start shutting—"

"Just fifteen minutes. You won't even have to walk me back. Do it for a friend, for an almost-girlfriend who'd been the wrong color."

His blush turns a darker pink. "Sorry about all that."

I tense, and flickers of old anger light my scalp. "What could you do? You were a kid."

"Yeah." His head falls back. "Fifteen minutes."

His phone rings. No picture with that number, but it says "Palmdale Sheriff." I can guess who's calling. What an interesting brunch Kayla and I will have tomorrow.

Minutes later, Cayden leads me to the club office and provides a quick tutorial on keying up the video. He selects the camera closest to the lot where the Benz was found.

After Cayden leaves, I pull out my phone to record the recording. Cars go in and out. At 10:50, car headlights brighten the screen. That car is followed by a second set of headlights.

The Benz parks in a space closest to the lake.

My heart bangs in my chest.

This is Felicia's car.

The door opens on the driver's side.

The cabin brightens. There's someone sitting in the front passenger seat.

Felicia stumbles to the hood of the Benz.

The front passenger door opens. The passenger wears an oversize hoodie that hides their face and is holding something in their gloved hand. That passenger joins Felicia at the car hood.

Felicia's left duster pocket glows. Must be her cell phone.

Felicia steps forward, and the passenger follows her out of frame.

That second set of footprints.

I keep watching . . . watching . . . Nerves twist beneath my skin like fishing line.

No one leaves that second car, a lighter-colored compact.

The video's too blurry to see if it's a Toyota, a Honda, a Kia . . . or a Mazda. There are no other distinguishing marks.

The passenger is back on-screen, face still hidden by the hoodie. Alone now. Ten minutes have passed since Felicia left the frame.

The passenger hurries past the Benz and climbs into the back seat of the lighter-colored compact. Someone else was driving that light-colored car? There were *two* people with Felicia that night?

The light-colored car reverses and leaves the lot in the same direction it came.

My lungs pinch as I watch and wait . . . watch and wait . . . even though I know how this episode will end. Felicia never makes it out of that lake alive.

I still watch and wait, though . . . and hope for the best.

Could the passenger who followed Felicia to Lake Palmdale be Will Harraway? Could the driver be the man who watched our house from the green Mazda?

I can't tell, no matter how many times I watch my recording of a recording.

But I now know this: Felicia didn't walk into that lake because she *wanted* to.

She was forced.

Murdered.

And Kayla needs to know that.

32.

This morning, the sun plays peekaboo behind banks of clouds. There's bright-white sky one minute, shadow and wind the next. The kitchen is dark, too, and doesn't smell of brewed coffee. Everyone's busy except for me. I spend too much time choosing an outfit and putting on makeup, as though I'm meeting Omari Hardwick for breakfast at Terranea Resort instead of having brunch with the Kozlowskis in East Palmdale.

I've neglected to pre-eat before this brunch with the Kozlowski family, and my stomach growls. I find a random bag of peanut M&M's in the Jeep's console, but the seven candies in the fun-size pack can't take off the edge.

Lord, let them prepare something edible.

Elise and Randy Kozlowski live eighteen minutes east of my parents' home. Randy, a fan of the New Orleans Saints, has a man cave (and a MAN CAVE sign designates the left side of the house's second level as such). The walls are plastered with pennants, helmets, signed jerseys, and a large-screen television. The sports theme competes against the framed pictures of Kayla in every stage of her life hanging in every other piece of wall space.

Randy manages the town's Food 4 Less grocery store. Elise works as a massage therapist and yoga instructor and believes sugar is a sin against the body. Most times, she walks barefoot so that electrons from the earth can neutralize her free radicals. She believes that Jeb Bush would've made an awesome president. She also makes the best cauliflower Wellington.

Today, she's prepared that dish, along with a vegan frittata; this thing with cut bananas, cantaloupe, strawberries, and yogurt over bread; Green Goddess vegan grilled cheese sandwiches; and crispy tofu nuggets that are too big to be nuggets and too wet-looking to be crispy.

Compared to Elise and Randy, my parents haven't aged in the last ten years. A strand of gray hair here and there for Mom, those softening muscles for Dad. Kayla's parents, though, have pruned—they're over-tanned and withered from desert living and a fat-free diet.

"I don't know how we're gonna eat and digest all that fancy country club food on Saturday night." Randy hands me the fruity vegan-yogurt french bread, then runs his large hand over his balding head.

There's more fat in a pine cone than in this entire meal.

Elise winks at him with her crinkly blue eyes. "We'll drive down to Topanga and do a megacleanse."

"*I'm* looking forward to all that fancy food." Kayla piles tofu nuggets on her plate. With her filled-out face, she's not surviving solely on cauliflower Wellington.

Elise sprinkles salt across her food, then tosses salt over her shoulder. "Lemme tell ya: I bought a gown from Dress Barn and some strappy heels from DSW and I tried 'em on and it was like I'd been wearing camouflage. 'Who's that woman?' That's what I said to the mirror. 'Where'd she go?' Ha! Love it! So *exciting* to celebrate, especially since it has been *rough* for them. And now with her cousin dying . . . Please offer Barbie our condolences."

"I will. Thank you." My fork slows from the plate to my mouth. "And you know, every marriage has its rough patches."

Randy says, "Heh. Forgive me, Yara, for saying that being married to Barbie is more like a rough *planet*."

Elise slaps Randy's hands, then offers me an apologetic smile. "The old ball-and-chain routine. You both will hear it one day. Men complain about their wives, but let us leave 'em alone for a week without instructions. They'll be stuck in the house, not knowing where the hell they put their dicks. 'Where's my dick? I just put it right there!' Ha! Love it!"

Randy rolls his eyes. "Rob's no idiot. Barbie left a few times, and he was okay. Sometimes she took Dom cuz she was pretty young. When she didn't, Rob took care of both you girls like a champ." He points his fork at me. "Braided your hair, dropped you at school, helped you with your science fair project."

Elise covers her mouth with her hand. "You *do* know about that, right?" she asks me.

Randy sighs. "For Pete's sake, El. She was *there*, for crying out loud."

I nod, remembering that one time Mom *did* take Dominique and leave Dad and me. The memory comes alive and beats around my head like a stunned sparrow.

"Do you know where she went?" I ask.

Elise finishes chewing frittata, then dabs her mouth with a napkin. "To her quiet place."

Her quiet place? That *has* to be the cabin.

"Of course, Rob kept calling her and begging her to come back home." Elise wags her finger at Randy. "Do *not* rewrite history. Case of the Missing Dick, that's what I'm sayin'."

"Can we not?" Kayla says. "Yara's not here for gossip about her parents' marriage."

"But I thought you wanted us to share memories and all that?" Elise holds my eyes as she bites into the french toast. Bananas tumble all over her tank top.

"I do," I say, nodding enthusiastically.

She waves her hand. "And Barbie left because of stress. I mean, golly. She was trying to raise two girls in this place and have a career. I mean, getting pregnant with Dominique had caught both her and Rob off guard, you know? Especially since he was totally about to check out.

Who *wouldn't* flip?" She makes a finger gun, aims it at her temple, pulls the trigger. "Country road, take me home. Ha!"

Randy chuckles. "That Barbie, always quick on her toes. She beat him to the punch."

A surprise pregnancy? Dad had been planning to leave us? Mom left before he did? What the . . . *what?*

"*Your* mom left," Randy says to Kayla.

"Huh?" Kayla screeches.

"For an *hour,*" Elise says. "This place was just squeezing all the juice outta me. But then I missed my Kiki-boo and flew back like the Flash. And your daddy's penis was right where I left it. Ha!" She squeezes Kayla's cheeks, leaving glazed banana on my friend's face. "Let's all sit here twenty years from now, okay? I can't wait to hear how many times either of you thought of walking away and leaving it all behind."

"Barbie came back, too," Randy says, "and that's the best part of the story. And she and Rob lived happily ever after." He snags more tofu nuggets from the plate.

"How long was my mother gone?" I ask.

Elise's eyes roam the ceiling as she thinks. "About two weeks."

The spaces between my ears click and thud. *Two weeks. What the* hell?

"I gotta tell you," Elise continues, "all of us moms envied her. Golly, I mean, who *doesn't* want to take a vacation without having to worry about kids and a husband for two whole weeks? Not *this* gal! Ha!"

⚡

Kayla and I take our bowls of store-bought lemon sorbet to sit beside the swimming pool. She checks the sofa cushions for scorpions, tarantulas, and other venomous creatures. A pale-yellow scorpion the length of a crayon scrambles off the seat and drops onto the concrete. Kayla lifts her boot and stomps it.

I shudder. "Ugh. I don't miss this."

"You were a supreme scorpion killer." She takes her bowl and plops on the sofa.

Though the sun sits high above us, the slatted pergola protects us as we enjoy our dessert.

"You ask your boss about me coming on as a consultant?" she asks.

Oh. Yeah. "Yep, she's put a pin in it." My face burns from the acidic splash of lie. "I'll keep you posted, but let me nudge her . . ."

I text Stephanie, the executive producer of *Tough Cookie*.

I may have a consultant replacement for Gemma

Kayla smiles and shimmies her shoulders.

"I gotta be honest," I say. "I don't remember that time my mom left for two weeks. Nor did I know that Dominique hadn't been planned." *Or that my father planned to leave us.*

Kayla's smile dims. "My parents talk too much."

I roll my eyes. "Parents are weird."

"Mine were also swingers."

"No way."

"Way. Totally disgusting."

I move my tongue against my molar to free a piece of cauliflower. "Your mom said my mom went to her 'quiet place.' That's the same reason why I went to the cabin. Because Felicia told me it was Mom's favorite place, but Mom . . . she brushed that off. Like she had no idea what I was talking about."

"Maybe she wants to forget that part of her life," Kayla suggests. "My mother acts like she never got behind the wheel of our minivan ten years ago and intentionally drove the wrong way onto the 14."

My stomach twists. I remember that terrifying afternoon. Fortunately, a highway patrolman was leaving from that same exit and stopped what could've been devastating. Elise was hospitalized for a month afterward. There, the doctors pumped her full of the good stuff and, after a few weeks, wheeled her to Randy's Subaru.

"Mysteries abound," I say.

"Totally."

"Speaking of mysteries," I say. "Did Felicia die by suicide, or did someone force her into Lake Palmdale?"

Kayla clinks her spoon around the bowl.

"Was there a second set of footprints in the dirt by the shore?"

No reply.

"Any weapons?" I ask. "Like a gun? A knife?"

No reply.

"Cuz if so, that wouldn't say 'suicide' to me. It would say that she was forced."

She blinks at me. "Any reason why you're asking about weapons and footprints?"

I scrunch my face. "Yes—I'm trying to figure out who killed my cousin. Duh. And I've been really nice to my mother lately so that she keeps spilling the family tea." I waggle my head, then say, "Anyway, Felicia's third husband, Will? He's still DMing me."

Kayla exhales, then peeks over at me. "And?"

"He's bragging about how much money he has. He's nowhere near mourning."

Kayla grunts, *"Hunh."*

"Here." I screenshot the newer messages—his hunt for future investors in UPLIGHT and an offer to join the UPLIGHT family—and forward them to Kayla.

Kayla's mouth twists as she reads the string. "What the hell?"

"Right?"

"I *will* say that Felicia knew that he was a low-down dirty dog. I have access to her phone, and she kept records of every time he left the house, went to the doctor, bought something. He followed her *every-where*—and she thought he'd followed her up *here*."

"The man in the Mazda, maybe?"

She blinks at me, tamps down a smile, says, "Sure."

"Don't do that," I growl. "I'm not—" *Oh, but you are, aren't you?*

Kayla tugs at a string on the cuff of her cargo pants. "Anyway, it sounds like he'd been trying to gaslight her. Made her think that she'd misplaced her keys. Left the back door open. Took money. And then she followed him to the Pink Cloud Motel in Pacoima. The kind of place with 'No Prostitution Allowed' signs and used condoms everywhere and bedbugs and bolted-down TVs."

"Ew. Gross."

"Felicia took screenshots of this text message conversation with his girlfriend, Soshea, saying that he's gonna do it—"

"Do *what?*" I ask.

"That he's gonna follow the plan. There're a bunch of messages she saved like that."

"What do you need me to do?"

"What you're already doing," Kayla says. "And save *everything.*"

We click spoons.

"You check the video from the surveillance cameras at the lake?" I ask, having watched it repeatedly last night.

She says nothing.

"I'm sure Cayden can help you with that." I pause, then add, "There may have been a third person at the lake that night."

Her eyes widen, and her cheeks and neck color. "Like I said, we're looking at Miss Campbell's phone records right now. There are messages with you, with Will, people at Northrop Grumman . . . She and her sister, Alicia, had some beef about money. There are a few numbers that are mysteries, but we'll run 'em down."

"Sounds good."

"You called her around nine," Kayla says. "Your number's all over the place."

I nod. "She kept drunk-texting me, and I finally had a free moment to talk to her."

"But you didn't."

I shake my head.

"You use any other phone? Or Google Call or Skype or . . . ?"

"Nope," I say. "Had she been drinking?"

"Yes."

"Alone?" I ask.

Kayla nods. "We're fingerprinting minibar bottles of rum found in her car."

"Sounds like you're treating this as a homicide."

She squares her shoulders. "I'm treating this as an active investigation."

I eat more sorbet and take my shot in the dark. "How long have you and Cayden been sleeping together?"

Her eyes go big and brighten with tears.

A hit dog hollers.

"Did he tell you . . . ?" she asks.

I push her knee. "Relax. I'm not gonna tell anybody." I point my spoon at her. "Check out the surveillance cameras at the Fish and Fly Club, please."

She swallows, nods, slumps.

The sorbet melts against my tongue, soothing all my itchy places.

"We found a note in her car," Kayla offers.

I contain my gasp. *This* is the note I've been wondering about.

She finds it on her phone and reads.

I miss you so much . . . Please, I'm asking you to make it up to me . . . Call me and I'll text you the location . . .

"May I have a copy of that?" I ask.

"I . . ." Kayla shakes her head.

Fine. I'll ask Ransom to get it for me.

"Felicia kept saying she was running out of time," I say. "Any idea what that meant?"

Kayla's jawline tightens as she stares in the distance. "No idea."

The dessert is gone. Store-bought sorbet was the best dish of the morning.

"Good thing is . . . ," Kayla says, licking her spoon, "there was a scratch on Felicia's face and hands, which implied that there'd been some kind of struggle. So we swabbed beneath her fingernails in case she got in a few swipes at her murderer. Happy to say that we recovered some DNA that didn't belong to her, too. Whoever she fought in those last moments on land, they're caught." She winks at me. "It's just a matter of time."

33.

As soon as I hit the first red light after leaving the Kozlowskis', I text Ransom.

> I need a favor
> I need more info on my cousin
> You never answered me about dude in the green Mazda

All around me, cars and trucks bumble along, blaring horns and banging into potholes. People are minding their own business, just like Ransom is. Because he isn't responding.

By the time I pull into the driveway at home, he still hasn't responded.

Dominique isn't home. Instead of answering my texts, she's doing who knows what with her boyfriend. If he could snag that PDF of the initial investigation, what else could he find? And how much would I be willing to pay to read it?

The house hasn't changed since I left it hours ago—drawn blinds, the smells of stale cigarettes, dust, and the plug-in fake freshness of freesia.

I find myself back in the attic, my new away place filled with my family's yesterdays. I find myself holding that yearbook from Inglewood High School, 1987–1988, staring at young Felicia Campbell, young Barbara McGuire, and that blacked-out square. I consider Alicia's picture. She and her twin had a beef about money. No big thing, right? I mean . . . Dominique and I are beefing about something every day, including how she's always trying to spend my money.

Felicia struggled with both her sister and her third husband.

My stomach feels hollow, and sadness finds me again. It's still sticky, and it still presses against my lungs. The longer I stay here, the heavier it gets. But I can't leave, not yet.

Downstairs, the house comes alive with jangling keys and tapping footsteps.

Unable to find where she went those two weeks away from us, I leave the attic with Mom's high school yearbook in my hand.

In the den, Mom hasn't changed out of her "I won't sweat today" tracksuit. She rests on the chaise with a book of crossword puzzles as an episode of *Hoarders* plays on the television. She looks content sitting there, chomping Nicorette in her alone time. I almost regret that I'm about to disturb it.

"Mother-dear!" I plop on the couch and my stomach growls. "That's me."

"Didn't you eat?"

"I so-called ate at the Kozlowskis'."

She peers at me over her reading glasses. "Cauliflower Wellington?"

"Yes. Also, these tofu-nugget things, some goopy sandwiches with fake cheese, and french toast covered in vegan yogurt."

Her lip curls and she shivers. "Rob and I had dinner with them once. Never again."

"Elise was telling me about the old days when we were all kids."

Mom narrows her eyes. "Like?"

My mouth dries. I can't mention anything that involves her leaving us for two weeks—the way her mouth has tightened tells me this. If I *do* mention it, she'll disinvite Kayla and her family, and I don't want that.

I clear my throat. "I probably shouldn't repeat this . . . Elise and Randy were swingers."

Mom sucks her teeth. "I knew that."

"Ew? And that she was committed after the freeway incident."

"They 5150ed that bitch and put her in the socks."

"Yeah. I'd forgotten about that."

She reaches for the foil pack of gum on the coffee table. "Seven letter word for 'heating part of a kettle.'"

I rest my chin on my knees. "Element."

I want to ask about so much, but it's all one land mine after the next. The note found in Felicia's car. The nameplate I found in the Camaro. An old girlfriend of Dad's. And Dad having an affair and moments away from leaving us.

"I wanna show you something." I pluck my phone from my pocket and show her the recording of the recording of Felicia at Lake Palmdale.

Mom stares at the screen, barely breathing. "Where'd you get that?"

"From the security system at the Fish and Fly."

She points at my phone. "Do the police know who that is?"

I shake my head. "I think that her third husband and another person are in the second car."

"Will?" Mom cants her head. "You know what? Cece told me that Lee caught him trying to change beneficiary designations on her bank account."

"*What?*"

"Lee wasn't stupid. Will's gonna find out any minute now that he ain't getting one thin dime of hers, so if he killed her, he's wasted his life."

My mind whirls. "Has Cece told this to Kayla?"

Mom shrugs, pops her gum between her teeth, then writes a word into the white squares. "What else are you investigating?"

"Since you asked . . ." I open the yearbook to the blacked-out graduation picture. "Who *is* this, and why were you so extreme? Like this person killed your puppy."

Her hand claws at her bee pendant.

"It's not Felicia," I say.

"Have you read some of her letters?"

"I did. Yowza. But who is *this*?"

Mom squints at the blackened box. "Yara, sweetie. It's been over thirty years since I graduated from high school."

"Yeah, well, try to remember."

She groans once she realizes I'm not gonna move on. "Fine. Gimme a moment." Her shoulders droop and she pushes out a breath. "Okay, remember the really pretty girls who knew they were really pretty? The ones who always bragged that they didn't have many girlfriends?"

"Ugh. Yeah." Marley, that gray-eyed witch in high school. Eva, that blonde in college.

Mom taps the yearbook picture. "That was this chick. 'Just friends' with all the boys."

"Let me guess: she also *slept* with all the boys, including your boyfriend."

"Tale as old as time." She twirls the pen between her fingers. "To goad. Four letters."

I lean forward. "Mom, who did she steal from you?"

Mom's neck continues to redden. "Who knows? He probably wasn't worth much. I don't even remember his name. He wasn't the point, though. Her taking him from me made me do *that*." She taps the picture. "If you think I'm crazy competitive *now*, imagine how bad I was back when I was full of estrogen and Funyuns."

I grin and say, "Don't fuck with Bee McG."

"No, ma'am."

I point to her photo at the bottom of the page. "You were cute, though."

"*Cute?*"

"Stunning."

"You can do better."

"Your beauty transcended time . . . Spur."

"What?" She wraps the gum she's been chewing into a tissue.

"The clue," I say, tapping her crossword puzzle. "To goad? It's 'spur.'"

"Ah." She writes the word, then says, "Oh. Before I forget . . ." She pops up from the chaise and scurries out of the den.

On the television, the *Hoarders* team tries to wrangle over one thousand rats living in this poor guy's disgusting house.

Mom returns, holding out a white envelope. "For you."

Inside: the wedding certificate for Robert and Barbara Gibson, married on Saturday, May 15, 1999. Officiated by Reverend Timothy Bertram.

"I hate that Pastor Bertram is living down in Belize now," I say, sticking the certificate back into the envelope. "I'd wanted him to come and renew your vows."

Mom chuckles. "Once was enough." She freezes, holds out her hand. The nerve above her eye twitches. "I don't mean that in the negative sense. I'm glad Wolcott can do it, though. He can add a new blessing. Give your dad and me even more years on the books."

"Yep."

She settles back into the chaise with her puzzle and squints at the last unsolved clue. "Eight letters. Bird's egg-producing plant."

"No idea."

Mom studies the ceiling, then nods. "Larkspur."

LaRain calls, and Mom answers, and that's my cue. Instead of returning to the attic, I retreat to the tree in the front yard. Gasoline fumes hang thick in the air. Mr. Abernathy is fixing either his ATV or his truck. Mom's voice is a dull murmur until she gets up from the chaise and retreats to another place in the house.

Two weeks—*Mom left us for two weeks.*

Where did she go?

What sent her fleeing to her quiet place?

Ask Bobby about Liz. WHERE IS LIZ???

34.

Out here in the Antelope Valley, temperatures rise around three o'clock in the afternoon. The shadows offer no succor, and neither do porches or pergolas. The sky gleams but drains, and the dust kicks up with late-day wind. Heat and sun find their way beneath the brims of baseball caps, and like my neighbors right now, the top third of their faces pale and become three shades lighter than the sunburned part.

Truth hides in spaces like that swatch of pale skin beneath Derrick Abernathy's Green Bay Packers cap. It lives low in swampy places that need light for all things to find balance.

I sit, thinking about that and watching my neighbor work on his father's truck as I also think about my mother leaving, about Felicia dying, about Liz—*who's Liz?*—and my father. Mom knows the person beneath that ink. She just doesn't want to say her name. And it *is* a her. If I were a betting woman, I'd say that blacked-out box is Liz, the lady in the lakeside picture and Dad's ex-girlfriend. (I'm certain that she *is* Daddy's ex-girlfriend, and I'd bet on *that*, too.)

Back in the kitchen, Mom prepares dinner—shrimp scampi with crusty italian bread, roasted asparagus, and a delicious Chianti I brought back for her from Rome last year. Since Dad and Dominique won't be home until an hour or so from now, I retreat to my bedroom and grab my laptop from the bureau. The humidifier sends vaporized water into the air that now smells of oranges and albuterol. Maybe this is Pavlov's dog but with smells instead of bells. I'm associating the humidifier with what always came when Mom turned it on. I'm expecting her to step into the room any minute now with pediatric prednisone and a mug of warm tap water.

I didn't want to anger my mother when she presented me with the envelope earlier, but this is not the wedding certificate I've been seeking. The one in this envelope is the ceremonial one with the flounce and the church-lady calligraphy. I want the one from the State of California with the official watermark in its belly.

I click over to the Los Angeles County Registrar's website. Here, you can order the trajectory of a person's life—birth certificate to wedding certificate, divorce decree to death certificate. I plan to frame three copies of the wedding certificate—for Dominique, for my parents, and for me. Then, as an old lady, I will hand my copy down to my own child, just one more precious memento in our family tree.

My phone thumps.

What's up

Ransom!
You ever get that W9 form, I text.

Nope

You know a dude that drives a green Mazda?

Lot of dudes drive green Mazdas

I tap in the license plate number.

And send me whatever else you can please

Like what

Any reports
DNA
Maps
Sound files
Doesn't matter
If it's related to Felicia's case, I want it.

I turn back to the registrar's website. The marriage certificate won't make it to me by Saturday night, but I still order it. I'll make a temporary centerpiece using the ceremonial certificate. Then, once the real certificate arrives, I'll drive back, and over brunch, I'll present the framed, authentic certificates to Dominique and my parents.

You paying, Ransom asks.

Flat fee just like we pay consultants

10k

U crazy

5k

No

1000, I type.
The ellipsis bubbles, then stops. Bubbles, then . . .

BATCH 1 PHOTOS.;

Yes!

So many photos.

Aerial photos of Lake Palmdale, Felicia Campbell's purple Benz, the note on the passenger-side footwell, her wallet. Pictures of one shoe—a black flip-flop with a cluster of jewels on top—her purple duster, the gun in the driver's side door pocket, the phone washed ashore, and that second set of footprints in the wet soil. Surveillance camera stills of the German sedan pulling into and parking at the Park N Ride lot. Stills of the light-colored compact behind it. Hoop earrings and three rings. Pictures of the interior, including the seats and door handles. A receipt from Bucelli's Italian on Friday, May 17, at 9:43 p.m.

Her last meal was all-you-can-eat breadsticks?

After paying Ransom, I pace my bedroom, not sure what to do with this information. On one hand, shopping bags filled with empty frames and goody bag ingredients line the walls. I have stuff to stuff in purple tulle. I need to pick out a frame for my parents' wedding certificate.

On the other hand, there's a receipt from Bucelli's Italian.

Cooking complete, Mom is conked out in the chaise longue as *Hoarders* continues to play on TV.

I scribble a note on the back on an envelope—*out running errands*—and leave it on the coffee table.

Outside, the neighborhood smells of barbecued meat and marijuana, all being consumed to the music of Toby Keith. Down at Mr. Abernathy's, his driveway is crowded with pickup trucks, some decked with American flags, Confederate flags, and MAGA flags.

The tightness that lived in my chest throughout childhood returns.

I don't miss this part of Antelope Valley life. This place where Hollywood used to come to blow up movie sets for action scenes, this landlocked Methopolis whose claim to fame is one-hit wonder Afroman and the mysterious hilltop mansion that everyone dreams of owning but no one knows who actually owns it. Stay for the beautiful sunrises and beautiful sunsets. Hike, dirt bike, and four-wheel drive in between. That sound? Oh, that's just a sonic boom over at Edwards Air Force Base. That shaking? Oh, did you know the San Andreas Fault is *right there*? Oh, him? He's a Nazi Low Rider. Not him, the other guy? The one burning the cross? Ignore him. Here, have some delicious breadsticks. Take a few. They're all-you-can-eat.

From the driver's seat of my car, I see Bucelli's patrons noshing on those breadsticks and sipping beers and glasses of Chardonnay. Inside, the noise of the restaurant overwhelms me—the clank of dishes and utensils, the Italian music, and the loud voices. For a second, I think of backing out to the parking lot.

The hostess wearing a WELCOME-HAILEY name tag smiles at me, but her kohl-lined eyes stay flat. "Welcome to Bucelli's Italian. How many?"

"My mom should be seated already. May I try to find her?"

Hailey says, "Yeah sure," and returns to reprogramming the waiting-list pagers.

The receipt in the evidence batch photo says that Felicia sat at table 49.

A busboy passes by with a tray of waters.

"Where's table 49?" I ask him.

He points to an empty window booth.

I shiver as I creep closer to the table. A stand-up menu sits on the surface, and the booth benches are clear and clean. There's nothing special about this table. Why did I come here?

"May I help you?" The server—her name tag says KYLIE—aims her bright smile at me.

My mind spins and grabs a story. "My mother ate here back on Friday night. She thinks her phone slipped into the crack of the booth."

Kylie gasps. "Oh, wow. Let's see." She scooches into one side of the banquette, and I scooch into the other.

"Were you working that night?" I ask. "Around nine?"

"Yep." She ducks beneath the table. "This is my table, too."

I also duck and paw around for a phone that won't be there. "You probably served her. African American woman wearing a very dramatic purple jacket, diamonds, hoop earrings—"

"Oh yeah. A bun?"

I nod. "That's her."

Kylie sits up. "I don't see anything, sorry. How's she feeling?"

"Mom?" I sit up. "You know . . . Meh."

"Yeah, she was *literally* upset and—*now* I remember. Are you the person she was expecting? Cuz she kept asking if you'd arrived, if you'd called the restaurant. Especially after she got a text. That's probably when she dropped her phone. Her hands were *literally* shaking. I comped her a tiramisu just to make her feel better. So what happened?"

I cock my head. "Huh?"

"You didn't show up. She was *literally* waiting for you. Something must've happened, right?"

"Yeah, *totally*." My face warms. "I *literally* got caught up. We hadn't seen each other in a while, and I thought that we'd be able to have dinner, but . . . total shit show. And now I'm sad she was sad. Thanks for hooking her up, though. That was an *awesome* thing to do."

She taps the tabletop. "Well. Gotta get back to work. Hope you find her phone."

"Me too."

She waves at me, then smiles her bright-white smile again. "Have a good night, Liz."

35.

Liz?

She's *here*?

Or she was *supposed* to be here?

But Liz didn't show up.

Why didn't she show up?

I wonder about that as I roam the aisles of the hobby store grabbing frames in one lane, and fun-size packs of Skittles from another. Usually, any song by Wham! makes me dance, but right now "Wake Me Up Before You Go-Go" has no effect.

Were Felicia and Liz planning to attack my mother? Show up to the golf resort and knock plates to the ground and pull all the fire alarms?

Back in the car, I scroll through the pictures Ransom sent me. The still photos from the surveillance video . . . The hooded figure that follows Felicia . . . I zoom in as much as I can, but there's no extra detail. I swipe over to the still pictures of the compact car and zoom . . . zoom . . . A hand drapes over the steering wheel . . . zoom . . . zoom . . . A ring . . . jewels on that ring.

A woman driver? Will's girlfriend, Soshea?

Or is that Liz?

Or Alicia?

Buried in the files of photos, there's something I didn't notice before.

Autopsy Report

The autopsy is complete?

I look up from the phone. Feels like someone's watching me.

Dodges and Nissans, Toyotas and Hondas. Loud stereos, people shouting, horns honking, sirens screaming. There's a smell of burning plastic. Someone nearby is smoking meth.

Time to go.

I pull out of the parking lot.

A black Chevy Silverado with thick tires pulls out of its space. Tinted windows and rumbly, the double-cab truck *brup-brup-brups* as it creeps closer to my rear. The windows aren't rolled down, but I can still hear the screams and riffs of death metal.

On Rancho Vista, I turn left at the light.

The Chevy turns left.

My hands clutch the steering wheel. I peek in my rearview mirror.

Two of them. Acne flares. Sunken cheeks. Angry eyes.

Living in Palmdale Lesson No. 12: If some redneck's following you, lead 'em to the sheriff's station. Cuz if you lead 'em to your house? Calamity and ruin. *Literally.*

Someone followed my friend Kenisha home once. About twenty people drove out to protect her, then stopped the stalker in the middle of the intersection and beat his ass right there. My friend Triste didn't have family to save her, and we cried over her grave a week later.

I call Dad as I race eastbound on Rancho Vista.

He doesn't answer.

I call Dominique.

She answers on the first ring. "What?"

"I'm being followed." My voice sounds thin but controlled.

"You sure?"

"Yeah. Positive."

"Where you at?"

"I'm headed toward the sheriff's station." I stay on the main street, traveling south with the sun a gold ribbon just below the horizon. Not much traffic, so I switch lanes.

And so does the Silverado behind me.

I avoid side streets—too many of the tightly packed homes there display flags with stars and bars and iron crosses.

The Chevy speeds up.

I'm shaking, but I'm too scared to cry, too angry to cry. And then I see it. A convoy of El Caminos and Bimmers, Mustangs, and Chargers pulls out of the Louisiana Famous Fried Chicken parking lot with trap music on blast and chains and diamond earrings glinting in the orange neon light of the best fast-food chicken joint in Palmdale. Dominique sits behind the wheel of her turquoise Jeep, and Ransom slumps in the passenger seat. She pulls up beside me, and together we stop at a light. Ransom's boys in a tricked-out Range Rover pull up beside the Chevy.

"We got a problem here?" the driver of the Range Rover asks the fools in the Chevy.

Hands up, the fool in the Chevy's passenger seat shouts, "No problem," and the driver pulls from behind my Jeep and U-turns. The Silverado's tires spin and burn against the blacktop as it heads north. The Range Rover U-turns and follows the truck. The stink of hot rubber rides on the gritty air.

"You okay?" Dominique asks me.

I gulp back tears and nod. I've been holding it together so long that I have a side stitch.

She tosses a pack of cigarettes through the window. The pack lands on my lap.

I stare at the Newports, and just the *idea* of smoking eases my trembling. Before my hand reaches for the pack, I notice the rubber band on my wrist. I pull the band back as far as it will stretch and then release. *POP!* My skin stings but my vision clears.

Dominique takes a deep drag from her own cigarette, then blows smoke in the air.

"Thanks, again," I say. "I didn't wanna drive home. Didn't want trouble at the house."

Dominique taps ash out the open window, then smirks. "Yaya, we got beaucoup trouble at the house already. What's one more thing? We'll follow you."

I'M NOT OKAY

36.

I am sputtering water, kicking my legs, and thrashing my arms. Small stones roll beneath my bare feet. Frogs croak as water glistens all around me like dark glass. My muscles and lungs burn, and my head aches. Something is holding me beneath the surface. Icy water rushes into my mouth, and I taste blood and cold water and—

My eyes pop open.

A bang of bright-white light and then blurry darkness. The air smells of stale smoke and peppermint, medicine and . . .

⚡

I sit up in bed, breathing hard, burrs in my throat. Above me, the ceiling fan buzzes. The digital clock on the DVD/VCR reads 2:13 a.m.

Nightmare.

Clank.

That.

I yank at my damp T-shirt. Cool air from the fan kisses my neck. The sweat on my skin feels thick as pancake batter.

Clank.

That.

I cock my head, close my eyes, and listen.

Water filling the toilet tank.

The rhythmic buzz of the ceiling fan.

My booming pulse.

I reach over to the nightstand for my eyeglasses . . .

Where are my glasses?

Maybe I knocked them over during my—

Clank.

That.

Holding my breath, I paw around the shadowy floor.

No glasses.

Bleary-eyed, I slip on my flip-flops and creep to the door.

The hallway is dark.

The door to my parents' bedroom is closed.

I tiptoe to the staircase and wince as the top floorboard creaks.

One step . . . Another step . . .

The refrigerator hums.

The moon shines through the skylight and bathes the living room with silver light.

That!

That is not moonlight brightening the windows of our front door.

Burglar!

I back my way up the stairs, keeping my eyes trained on that beam of—

Wait!

That light isn't coming from the outside.

A footstep.

Breathing.

I rush down the hallway and burst into my parents' bedroom.

Mom snores.

Dad sleeps with a pillow over his head.

I shake him first.

He immediately tosses the pillow aside and says, "What's wrong?"

"Someone's in the house," I whisper.

He kicks off the comforter.

Mom sits up in bed. "You okay?"

I nod. "Yeah."

She reaches behind the headboard and grabs her machete.

Dad reaches beneath the bed for his wooden baseball bat.

Downstairs, glass breaks.

We freeze.

Mom hands me the machete, then grabs a hunting knife from beneath the mattress. All we need is Dominique and the saber she bought in Little Tokyo. Mom and I creep down the hall behind Dad. Slowly . . . slowly . . . we tiptoe down the stairs. I can't hear anything over the roar of blood pounding in my ears. At the base of the stairs, Dad goes right into the living room, and Mom turns left into the den. I stay at the stairs.

"*Stop!*" Dad shouts.

Feet pound against the floor, and a hooded figure runs to the foyer, throws open the front door, and jams out to the porch.

Where's Daddy?

I run out of the house. The frigid desert air slams into me and takes my breath away.

The prowler climbs over the hurricane fence that separates the planned neighborhood from undeveloped land and scrambles north to the desert.

I follow even as one of my flip-flops twists in the fence's diamond-shaped wires.

I'm quick.

The prowler is quicker.

"Yara!" Dad shouts from somewhere behind me.

The prowler runs toward the foothills, incentivized not to get caught.

I'm wielding a machete, and I've suffered mini–asthma attacks since Friday. After three minutes of running, I stop and try to catch my breath. I rest my hands on my knees.

Someone grabs my arm.

I spin away.

It's Mom. Her eyes are wild as a mustang's. "Are you crazy running outside like that?"

I try to catch my breath. "Is Daddy okay?" I ask between gasps.

She grabs my chin. "Don't *ever* do that again. Do you understand me?"

"Is Daddy okay?"

She gazes toward the desert. "He's fine. Come on."

We walk back to the house. Dominique, wide-eyed, walks from the kitchen to the den with a pen and pad in her hands.

"So?" Mom asks, pulling her into a hug.

"TV is here, computers and phones are here." She shrugs. "Nothing's missing."

"You okay?" Mom asks her, smoothing her braids.

Dominique nods, then catches my eye. "Is Yara—"

Mom glances back at me. "She'll be fine."

Sure.

Minutes later, a sheriff's deputy stands before us and scribbles into his tiny pad.

Our house is now filled with the sounds of police radio chatter and the heavy boots of four men wearing khaki and green. Edgewater Court glows with red and blue lights from the squad cars. Our neighbors stand on the sidewalk in clumps of two and three.

"Description?" Deputy Gordon asks me.

"He's—"

"A male, then."

I swallow. "I'm assuming."

"You didn't see a face?"

I shake my head. "The *person* wore a hoodie. Lean. About three inches taller than me."

He blinks at me, then writes in the pad.

"Black Air Jordans, black jeans, black hoodie," I add.

"You're describing everybody in AV," Dominique snarks.

"Dom," Dad says.

"She's right," Mom says.

"What about identifying marks?" Deputy Gordon asks. "Tattoos, scars . . ."

"It was dark," I say, "and my contact lenses weren't in, and I wasn't wearing my glasses."

The deputy stares at me, then closes his notepad. "We don't have a lot to go on, and if we *did*, the fact that your sight . . ."

My stomach twists, and I avoid the gaze of Deputy Gordon, who isn't so blurry that I can't see exasperation in his face.

He and his partner leave.

A few neighbors are holding up their phones to record. Some clumps have merged into one megaclump, and they throw suspicious glances at the only Black family on the block.

Dad closes the front door behind him.

Dominique paces the den.

I sit on the ottoman and pull my knees to my chest.

Mom settles at the dining room table. She lights a cigarette, blows smoke to the ceiling.

Dad sits beside me and wraps his arm around my shoulders. "You're shaking."

Because the intruder wore a hoodie. Just like the person who slashed my tires. Just like the monster who forced Felicia to walk into Lake Palmdale.

"I don't feel safe," I whisper.

Dad squeezes my upper arm, kisses my forehead.

I close my eyes. "What if it's the person who was with Felicia that night? The person who sent that postcard, keyed my car, or slashed my—"

I gasp, then point to the fireplace mantel, to the family portrait there, broken glass, one face scratched out. *My* face scratched out.

"What the *hell* . . . ?" Dad asks, wide-eyed.

Mom stands and squints at me. "What aren't you telling us, Yara? Who's so angry at you that they're breaking into our house?"

The world fizzes at its edges, and I shout, "There's nothing to tell. I don't know who this is, or what I've done. I don't know who came into our house or who did that!" I point to the shattered picture frame again.

Dad and Mom hold each other's gazes. Something passes between them. "Need to go to the hospital?" Dad asks, his attention back to me. "Can you breathe?"

Mom draws cigarette smoke into her lungs. "She's fine, Robert. You're fine, Yara. No one's hurt and that's what matters."

She's now smoking *and* pacing, just as tense and scared as me, but she's releasing her fear by smoking and pacing. She sees that I'm watching her. Smiling, she kneels before me and takes my hand. "Sweetie, there's no reason for you to feel unsafe. No one's gonna hurt you, not anymore. Whoever it was? They're not coming back. Okay? It's all gonna be okay."

I don't think I believe her.

This isn't Felicia—Felicia is dead.

Yep, she's gone.

WHERE IS LIZ???

I'm back. From outer space. Run bitch, run!

Surrender.

37.

I can't sleep.

The buzz of anxiety keeps me from closing my eyes, from catching my breath, from falling back asleep. Downstairs, the lights burn bright in the kitchen. The music of opening cupboards and the *clip-clop* of slippers assure me that everything's all right.

Mom is flipping through her tea bag collection.

"Hey," I say.

"I knew you were gonna come down." She tosses me a smile. "How about chamomile peppermint? That'll calm us a little."

"Sounds good." I settle in the breakfast nook and place my cheek against the table.

Mom's phone vibrates from the countertop.

"Who's up this late?" I ask.

"LaRain heard about the deputies coming." She hums as she fills the teakettle with water, then sets it on the burner. *Click-click-click. Whoosh.* Fire licks at the bottom of the pot.

The phone vibrates again.

Mom reads the message and rolls her eyes. "Anyway . . ." She reaches into her robe pocket and pulls out my glasses. "Look what I found."

"Where were they?" I slip them on. "I can see!"

Mom pats my head. "They were on the dining room table. You probably left them there after you got in from the hobby store."

I don't remember that.

Soon, the teakettle whistles, and the air smells of steam. Mom pours water into our mugs, sets the honey bear on the counter, then slides into the nook.

As we prepare our tea, Mom's eyes burn through me.

"What?" I ask.

She places her hands flat against the countertop. "What's going on with you?"

I search her face for a clue. "*Nothing's* going on with me."

She pours honey into her cup, giving time for words to form in her mind. Finally: "You seem *stressed*. A little on edge. More anxious than normal. You taking your meds like you should?"

I swallow too-hot tea, scalding my mouth and throat.

"You're scattered, Yara. Losing things, forgetting where you are. Something's on your mind, weighing you down." She squeezes my wrist. "Instead of writing everything down in your little journal, *talk* to people. Just spit it out so we can face it. Together."

I chew my bottom lip, then blurt, "I don't think I left my glasses on the dining room table." There. I said it.

Mom tilts her head. "You think the phantom prowler tried to steal your glasses?"

"*That.*" I point at her. "*That's* my problem. *You* don't believe anyone was in the house."

She drops her eyes to the cup. "I don't know, Yaya. I didn't see this person." She pauses, then adds, "And you didn't see this person, either."

My stomach drops and my head pops back. "So who vandalized the picture? Who was I chasing in the desert?"

She holds up her hand. "Stop. You left your glasses on the table. That's where I found them. As for the picture . . . who's to say? You sleepwalk and you could've—"

"No!" I shout. "That's ridiculous—"

"You've done things like that before," Mom whispers, "back when you were a child. It's okay if you don't remember. I'm not sure if I *want* you to remember how . . . *destructive* you can become when you're . . . not *doing well*. And I also know that all of this screws with your need to be perfect."

I snort. "I don't need to be perfect. Something strange is happening here and I . . ."

"You don't think you sleepwalk?" Mom asks.

I hesitate, just for a moment. "I guess I do."

"Do you forget where you put things? Do you lose your train of thought sometimes?"

I chew the inside of my cheek, then nod.

Mom grunts, then lifts her cup to her lips.

I sink in the seat. "What's wrong *now*?"

She shakes her head and drinks her tea, and her hard eyes glare at the honey bear.

I know what this look means: *this ungrateful heifer.*

The kitchen feels small, and I try to look anywhere but at my mother. My eyes find the light fixtures in the ceiling and the shadows of dead fly carcasses trapped there.

I clear my throat and say, "Thank you for finding my glasses."

She looks me in the eye and grunts again.

"And thanks for the tea." I slide out from the nook. "I just need rest. I just . . . I'm gonna take my wonderful hot beverage upstairs and try to go to sleep." I kiss the top of her head and shuffle out of the kitchen, not expecting her to say good night but still hoping that she does.

My mother offers nothing but silence as I leave.

⚡

124 was spiteful.
The first sentence in *Beloved.*

Earlier today, I'd read up to only page 20. One cannot read *Beloved* like one reads *The Da Vinci Code*. You must peel it like soft baby onions, handle it gently like the brattiest soufflé. Reading it will help me fall asleep.

But *Beloved* isn't on my nightstand.

I open the top drawer and paw past my underwear. It's not there, either. I open the second drawer and paw past my T-shirts.

"What's wrong?" Mom stands in the doorway.

"I . . ." I paw through my socks and bras again.

"Your book?"

"Yeah." My tongue feels like rubber on cheap sneakers, and it pushes at the film of scalded gums in the roof of my mouth.

"I saw it in the den last night," Mom says.

"That's right." I *do* remember reading after taking a shower. "Thank you, Mom." I zip past her and hurry down the steps. Now it makes sense that my glasses were on the dining room table.

She was right. I *am* being dramatic.

There's *Entertainment Weekly*. There's *Popular Science, Sports Illustrated*. There's nothing by Toni Morrison.

I search beneath the couch, then the chaise longue.

"Don't tell me you lost the book," Mom says from the staircase.

"You said you saw it . . . ?"

"Right there on the coffee table."

I check the credenza, the windowsill, and in between the couch cushions.

Mom searches with me, moving the couch, throwing cushions to the ground, sighing as she searches but still searching.

"Maybe the prowler took it," I say.

Mom gapes at me. "You serious?"

Wide-eyed, I nod. My eyes skip around the den, from the chaise longue and couch to the television and coffee table. Pillows lay scattered across the carpet. Cushions push against each other like toppling gravestones. The broken picture frame and vandalized picture no longer sit on the fireplace mantel.

Mom smiles. "We have over sixty pieces of good shit to steal in this house, but a crackhead takes a book no one understands?"

"It was *signed*." I sound manic, even to me.

Mom's mirth dies. "Yara, sweetheart." She runs a hand over her face, then shakes her head. "I'm gonna eventually find out what happened to the book. So you might as well—"

I yank my hair, confused. "I don't understand . . . Might as well *what?*"

Mom perches on the couch and pats a cushion for me to sit beside her.

But I don't sit. I pace and pluck my rubber band because I want to smoke.

"When you were a child," Mom says, then pauses.

When she doesn't continue, I say, "When I was a child, *what?*"

"Whenever you broke something or lost something, you always told us that some *girl* did it. *Where's your coat, Yara? This* girl *took it.* You always described her as tall with freckles. One time, we went up to the school to talk to the principal because this tall, freckled *girl* stole your calculator. We demanded that this *girl* be suspended."

I blink at her.

"You don't remember this?" Mom asks.

Glimpses of calculators and the girls' bathroom and torn shirts and tight lungs clutter my mind. I shake my head.

"Everything okay?" Dad now stands at the base of the staircase.

"Yara can't find the book I gave her," Mom explains. "And I was just reminding her about the mystery girl she always blamed for taking and breaking her stuff."

Dad chuckles. "Oh yeah. The tall girl with the freckles."

"Well, something would happen," Mom continues, eyes on me again, "and you couldn't handle it anymore. Not the original crime of you losing or breaking something, nor the lie you told me about this girl."

"And you wrote these confessions," Dad adds.

A flare pops in my head. "*What?* No."

Dad nods. "Oh yeah. I still have one. I'll go get it." He darts up the steps.

While he's gone, Mom tugs at her earlobe, nervous now. "It's gonna be okay, baby. It's anxiety, and we know now how to control your anxiety."

My legs give, and I plop on the ottoman. "But I don't remember any of this."

"I know. You never do."

I try to chuckle. "This is crazy."

Dad returns to the den with his wallet. He pulls a folded piece of yellowed pink paper from the billfold.

Mom says, "Wow, Rob. You kept one?"

"Yeah." He unfolds the note and shows it to me. "From you. Fifth grade."

A child's wobbly penciled cursive fills the page.

"Read it, Yaya," Mom says.

With a trembling hand, I take the paper.

Dear Mommy and Daddy. I am sorry that I told you that the girl stole my inhaler. I am lying. I sold my inhaler because I wanted more money for the book fair. Please forgive me. Your daughter, love forever, Yara Marie Gibson.

My eyes cloud with hot tears, and I can no longer see my writing. My mind fuzzes, and I try to call up the memory of the book fair and ten-year-old me composing this confession, but this happened so long ago, and I'm so tired, and . . .

"You okay?" Mom squeezes my shoulder.

I pinch the bridge of my nose. My head . . . it's filled with mucus, and my memory is trapped in it like dinosaurs in tar. *Beloved*, the book Mom kept for me since forever, is lost now. Fat tears roll down my cheeks. "Mom, I'm so sorry. I'll find the book, okay?"

And I will take my pills. I've been raw-dogging life without my antianxiety medication and experiencing negative results.

Mom takes my hands and holds them to her chest. "I got you, Yara," she whispers.

I can't remember.

I'm doing that thing that I've feared for so long.

I'm losing my mind.

38.

I'm losing control.

The hunter can't lose control. The hunter can't zigzag here. Ping-pong there. Break shit. Make carnival-level noise.

Losing control means the prey escapes.

Just like tonight.

Losing control means the hunter bleeds.

Just like tonight.

Losing control means pink water swirling in the bathroom sink, carrying blood and dirt down into the drain. From getting cut after pounding that picture frame. From running and falling in the desert and slate and dirt scraping skin that now needs to be hidden.

Eyes, heart, throat—they all burn.

I'm losing control.

The plan was supposed to work.

Enter the house. Find the photo. Scratch out her face. *Leave as quietly as I came.*

But the stupid frame with those stupid metal teeth to hold the backboard . . .

Punching the picture like it stole something meant the glass was gonna break.

Stick to the plan next time

Well, fuck you. Nothing always goes right, plan or no plan.

Why do I have to do all the hard work?

Are you doing the hard work, though?
Sure. Okay. Whatever. The so-called mastermind gets to sit back and be slick. Sit back and judge. Sit back and stay clean.

The water rolling off the hand injury runs clear now. The bleeding has stopped.

Back to the tiny stupid bedroom with its cheap tan carpet and thin walls, rattling windows, and lumpy mattress wedged into a stupid, cheap, wannabe Italian headboard . . .

I hate this place.

All this hard work demands better carpet, better windows, a headboard from Macy's, not some strip-mall furniture store with neon SALE tags hanging in the windows.

Patience, the mastermind texts. Only a matter of time.

I'm gonna be blamed.

Swallow it. *Like I always do.* But don't choke.

And come up with a new plan.

39.

It's been a long night. I find snatches of sleep here and there, claiming it like a bird hopping from worm to worm. The bed linens scratch against my skin, and the air that I breathe wears spurs and sickles. But I don't reach for my inhaler because there are only seventy puffs left. The hunting knife now lives beneath my mattress. Someone *was* here. I couldn't have imagined that, right . . . ?

I haven't completed a straight line of thinking since arriving in Palmdale, but then again, I was forgetting and losing things before leaving Los Angeles County. Maybe it was the anticipation of coming here that shorted my brain. Or maybe my genetics are taking over, and the madness is setting in like pointy ears or thick eyebrows, also inherited from your parents. This is bad, though, and I'm only twenty-four. How bad will it be ten years from now?

I close my eyes and focus on breathing . . . In through my nose . . . slowly . . . out through my lips . . . like blowing out a candle . . . in through my nose . . . slowly . . . In . . . out . . .

⚡

Tuesday greets me with a kick and a snap as sunshine bangs across my face. The intense light makes me blink and turn over in bed. The DVD/VCR clock says that it's ten after ten.

With the help of Pfizer, sleep came. But my stomach is now wobbly, and my limbs feel like slabs of concrete.

But!

Five uninterrupted hours of sleep.

On a Tuesday morning, the house should be empty.

Mom has a track meet down in Los Angeles today.

Dad's at school watching high school boys run with tires.

Dominique is allegedly taking notes in her Introduction to Feminism lecture.

I grab my glasses from the nightstand and roll out of bed. I can hear my breathing, but I won't use my inhaler. Today's first line of defense: yoga. I go through the motions. The bridge: on my back, knees bent, pelvis up, deep breath, pelvis down. Then the cobra: on my stomach, legs behind me, upper body up, roll shoulders back, hold lower upper body . . . hold . . . hold . . .

As my chest muscles expand, blood rushes through my veins like smooth water. The scratchiness eases some until I remember: I lost *Beloved*, and last night, my parents reminded me of my forgotten history of lying. According to that pink note, I sold my inhaler for book fair money. I don't remember this, but it's definitely on-brand.

I pop down the stairs. The cushions are perfect, the area rugs straight, the aromas of toast, bacon, and coffee mixing with the fleshy odor of Dad's football duffel bags. On the fireplace mantel, there's a new, framed picture of our family. A group selfie taken moments before ziplining in Kauai. All of this is so normal looking that I can almost forget that someone wearing a black hoodie broke into our house last night. I shiver just thinking about that flashlight beam reflecting off the front door.

Now, though, I pad to the kitchen. On the breakfast counter, there's a foil-covered plate and a yellow rosebud in a slender vase. A note written on a napkin sits atop the plate.

Eat, take your meds, BREATHE!!! You will be okay.

Best Friend Bee has made my favorite breakfast: a bacon, egg, and cheese sandwich.

I slip the plate into the microwave and pour coffee into a mug. I return to peek once more beneath the chaise, coffee table, and couch. No *Beloved*.

At the front door, the mail slot creaks, and envelopes and magazines scatter to the floor.

I'll eat breakfast outside—there's no wind, no dust—and then I'll write. I shuffle to the foyer, scoop the mail from the tile, and sift through . . .

Catalog from Cheryl's Gifts, statement from Chase Bank, direct mail from Smile Train . . .

The label on the envelope from State Farm Insurance is addressed to E. M. Gibson.

Who's E. M. Gibson?

Someone knocks on the door.

I peek into the peephole—Kayla—and open the door.

My friend smiles and says, "Morning!" Her auburn hair glows. She's wearing khakis and an LASD polo shirt. A sheriff's duffel bag is slung across her shoulder.

"You're still asleep?" She closes the door behind her and follows me back to the kitchen.

"Just got up," I say. "About to eat breakfast. Coffee?" I ask.

"Yes, thank you." She settles on a stool and sets her binder on the counter. "You doing okay? For real: you're hogging up all the crazies."

"AV has enough crazy for all of Southern California." I set coffee, cream, and sugar at her hands, then catch her up about the driver who tried to follow me home and the intruder who escaped to the desert. As I talk, she scribbles into her notepad.

"Maybe—" I gasp. "Maybe the intruder was the guy following me in the Silverado."

"I'll check with the deputy who took your statement this morning. Until then . . ." Kayla pulls a stack of pictures snapped in someone's home from her binder, then lays each shot in front of me.

A sapphire brooch. A gold Tiffany pocket watch. An etching of dancers signed by Marc Chagall. A multicolored glass vase . . .

I tap the Chagall print. "Is that real?"

She points at the pictures. "Have you seen any of these things around the house?"

I snort. "Why would a Chagall be in . . . ?" I wave my hands at the nothing-special fridge and range, those bug-filled kitchen lights, the Formica countertops you'd find in any suburban tract home built in the late eighties. "This is not a destination for a Chagall."

The glass vase looks familiar, though, because there's a similar vase in a box up in my room. The vase in this picture, though, is wider, with thicker colored bands.

"Have you heard Dom talking to Ransom about any of these things?" Kayla asks.

Her questions dig at me, mosquito bites leaving a red-hot trail along my arms.

Kayla taps my hand and smiles. "I'm not trying to insult you or your family. I'm asking a bunch of people strange-ass questions. So?"

"Nope, I haven't heard her talking about any of this." I take a big bite of breakfast sandwich. "Ransom into some hood shit?"

Kayla laughs. "Ransom is the *chairman* of hood shit. She really needs to stop hanging around with him. Nothing good comes from that guy."

Except for the case files on Felicia and his intervening last night with the rednecks who followed me. Remembering this—Ransom helping me—adds to my fizzy stomach.

"Do these pictures have anything to do with Felicia's death?" I ask. "Or is this related to some other scheme?"

Kayla bites her bottom lip. "Can't really say."

"You talk with Will Harraway yet?" I ask. "He's stopped DMing me."

"I *have* talked to Will Harraway, which is probably why he's stopped DMing you."

"And?"

She clicks her teeth. "Can't really share."

"You've looked at the recording from Park N Ride?"

She smiles, says nothing.

"You zoom in yet? You see the hand of the driver in the light-colored car?"

Kayla raises an eyebrow.

"Maybe you should."

"What would I see?"

I sip from my cup of coffee, then ask, "Why are you keeping our family in the dark?"

Kayla cants her head. "You consider Felicia Campbell family now?"

I nibble on a piece of bacon. "Always have, since the beginning of this thing."

"We're communicating with her mother, Cecilia, as much as we can."

"According to *my* mother," I say, "Aunt Cece strongly disagrees. She doesn't think that you're communicating with her at *all*."

"Of course, I can't share everything with her right now. It's not the easiest case, either. On that note . . ." She rummages around in her bag and finds a slender box. She opens the box and pulls out a packet of swabs, purple latex gloves, and an evidence envelope.

"A DNA kit," I say.

"Ah. So you recognize this. Interesting."

I point a strip of bacon at her. "I write for a crime show, remember? So *not* so interesting. Why is it in my kitchen, though?"

"The DNA taken from Felicia's body came in, and we need comparisons."

A fuse heats my chest. "You think that I—"

She holds up a hand. "Remember, you *did* physically interact with her on Friday."

That's right—Felicia grabbed my lightning bolt pendant that day and scratched my neck. Yeah, my DNA would be beneath her fingernails.

Wait. Where *is* my pendant? Dominique was supposed to fix it. Totally slipped my mind.

"Will you consent?" Kayla asks, pulling on the purple gloves.

I study my friend and then study the kit. Finally, I open my mouth wide enough for the Spruce Goose to fly through. Because I have nothing to hide.

I didn't kill Felicia Campbell . . .

Unless I've forgotten that, too.

40.

I try to remember Friday night.

*I read the note slipped beneath my hotel room door. Popped Benadryl.
The Iron Chef... Slept...* From what time to what time, though? If I'd
left the hotel in a daze, the security cameras would've caught that just
like the cameras caught the confrontation between Dominique, Felicia,
and me in the parking lot.

Once I can no longer see Kayla's car, I turn to the foothills that
surround the neighborhood. With all the gorges, jutting rocks, and
brush the same color as dirt, the mountains hide all the life they sustain.
Someone could be watching me right now.

Like the person who killed Felicia Campbell.

Because *I* didn't do it. I would've remembered that. Not that I have
any reason to kill someone I didn't even know until Friday.

I'm shaken by Kayla's visit, her DNA swab, and the words she
didn't say. *Of* course *I don't think you killed that lady.* And why is Kayla
searching the cabin at Lake Paz? Who owns that Chagall and the Tiffany
watch? Knowing what I know now about my cousin—her marriages
and her antipathy toward my mother—I want to look at the cabin with
new eyes. There's nothing much for me to do today except pick up the
anniversary party programs from the printer.

After picking up the anniversary programs, I find myself on Lake
Paz Road.

The highway is wide open, and the sky above me is the bluest blue. The air coming through the windows feels thin as I drive higher, but my lungs feel looser. The drive calms me some, and the farther Palmdale is behind me, the more my heart beats at a regular pace.

There is a keyhole on the cabin's garage door handle, and on the off chance that it may work, I slip the cabin's key into that lock.

Click.

I roll up the door.

The lights automatically pop on. No cars are parked, but the walls are lined with shovels, bags of salt, a child's pink mountain bike, and an adult's blue mountain bike.

Not trusting chance, I park the Jeep in the garage.

Inside the cabin, nothing's changed. The fireplace is there. The piano is there.

No. That isn't true. There *has* been a change.

Black fingerprinting dust dirties the light switch plates, doorknobs, and fridge handle.

What do investigators think happened here?

Kayla told me that they'd found my fingerprints on a lamp, a jewelry box, and a Lego block. I don't remember touching any of that, but in the last three minutes, I've touched a fireplace poker, a ceramic duck, and back in the garage, the doorknobs and the handlebars of the girl's bike.

I wander from the living room to the kitchen, scouting for something that would spark a memory of a tossed-off comment from Mom about her time here. This cabin, though, is like all cabins except for the piano and that spectacular view of the twinkling lake.

I tap a piano key. The tone from the middle C key is still off. The piano still needs tuning. In both bedrooms, faded quilts remain tucked and neat. The mattresses have probably become home to fleas and ticks.

A slate-gray runner in the hallway. Unremarkable. The brass fixture beneath it, though . . .

I roll away the carpet. A thick rectangular seam cut into the hardwood floor. And that brass fixture is actually a brass handle.

A hatch?

I pull the handle.

The hinges of the door creak, and cool air washes up from the square in the ground.

I shine my phone's flashlight to see a ladder descending into the gloom.

"Hello?" I shout.

No answer, thank goodness. Just dark, thick nothing.

Did Kayla discover this basement?

With the flashlight still on, I descend the stairs. The air becomes colder with each step.

Smells like old paper, cinnamon, and stale breath.

A light panel glows on the wall. I flip the switch, and round in-ceiling lights pop on.

There are wood walls, a slate floor, suede couches, and a television. There's a wine rack and a short beverage fridge beneath the stairs. It's posher down here than upstairs. In the far corner, a pair of french doors. Past those doors, an office with a desk covered in boxes and walls covered with photographs and area maps of Palmdale and Lake Paz.

What is *this place?*

A secret room. *A quiet place* where a frazzled mother can retreat after learning that her husband cheated with some woman named Irina.

The boxes in the office are a mix of new and saggy. The plastic tubs on top of the boxes are new—I purchased similar ones at Target last month.

Dread buzzes beneath my skin. I'm trespassing and shouldn't be here, except that I'm not trespassing. I have a key. Still, if this were an Airbnb home, I wouldn't be pawing through the hosts' personal boxes. But this isn't a rental. This is my mother's quiet place.

The Martinelli's apple cider box closest to the door is filled with blank music composition pages, a box of guitar picks, wires . . . half-melted candles . . . Another box holds pictures of Lake Paz, rubber-banded insurance statements, rubber-banded savings pass books, quilts, videocassettes labeled E's A.A. AUDITIONS . . . A postcard of a rainbow sent to Felicia.

They want me gone. I'll go. Stop looking for me.

No signer.

A sheath of documents—Los Angeles County Sheriff's Department property receipt. The "physical evidence box" is checked: a Gucci handbag and a map of the US Virgin Islands.

There's a funeral bulletin with the cover picture of a smiling, beautiful Black couple cutting their wedding cake. A CELEBRATION OF LIFE: MARYAM AND SHELDON MARSH. The Dorothy Dandridge doppelganger looks elegant in her lace gown. The groom reminds me of Sidney Poitier in professor glasses. It's the same couple from the photograph atop the piano.

I read the obituary. *". . . car crash in Lake Paz on July 4, 1989."*

Maryam and Sheldon died together on a road somewhere around here.

I'm looking through dead people's things.

I continue reading. *". . . session musician for Warner Brothers . . ."*

That explains the piano. The lady next door mentioned Sheldon's beautiful playing.

". . . a dancer, and her credits include Stormy Weather, Carmen Jones, *and* Cabin in the Sky. *They are survived by their only daughter, Elizabeth."*

A manila folder holds batches of photographs and a binder clip of papers. The title of each document: Los Angeles County Sheriff's Department Statement.

I quickly flip through the bundle and stop at:

INTERVIEW WITH MAGGIE DOUGLAS AND DETECTIVE STALL
DS: Can you describe what you saw?
MD: Lots of fog and endless trees. You could barely see the islet off the lake cuz of all that fog and all those trees.
DS: So what made you go in that direction?
MD: The singing.
DS: Singing?
MD: "Jesus loves me this I know . . ." [pause] I'm sorry.
DS: Take your time . . . Tissue . . .
MD: Thank you. I just get worked up . . . The singing . . . I still hear it. I still hear her.

I sift through photographs.

A close-up shot of a woman's hand—she's wearing an emerald-and-diamond ring. Looks like Mom's ring. A picture of a small red jewelry box with a lightning bolt pendant nestled in red velvet—looks just like mine. A picture of the chaise longue on the deck and a red-cover edition of *Beloved* by Toni Morrison left on the cushions. Just like my . . .

I step back from the box.

Who are Sheldon and Maryam Marsh?

And how does my mother know them?

The snapshots capture the lake and the cabin as well as the islet off the banks of the lake.

Did Felicia tape these maps to the wall?

What would she have done to me if I'd come here to see her?

Upstairs, someone knocks on the front door.

I hop away from the desk.

Upstairs, whoever it is knocks again.

Who knows that I'm here?

After I place everything back in the box, I hustle up the stairs. My sweaty underarms stick to my T-shirt.

Birdie, the woman from the cabin next door, is standing on the porch. She spins around, startled by the opening door. She pats her heart and turns as pink as the blouse she's wearing. "There you are. I was hoping you hadn't left yet."

I step out into the sunshine and nod to the garage. "I parked in there this time. Didn't want them breaking my windows."

"That's why I'm here." Birdie holds up her phone. "Got something for you. You can't see 'em, but we have security cameras posted all around our cabin. I looked for the video after you drove off on those four new tires." She taps play on a video.

The recording is low quality and hard to make out, but it shows a person wearing a dark hoodie stealing past Birdie's place and headed to this cabin. The person stops at my Jeep. Kneels and slashes my left back tire, then the right back tire, then the passenger front tire, and finally, the driver's side. The figure backs away and hustles back the way they came, head down. The person looks back at the Marsh cabin, and for a moment, the hoodie slips back, and I see . . .

41.

Nothing.

The video stops, and static fills Birdie's phone screen.

"It cuts off," the old woman says. "I thought maybe you recognized this creep?"

I shake my head, thank her for trying, and return to the basement. I take pictures of the maps on the wall, then glance at the clock on my phone. It's almost two o'clock. I should head back soon. Birdie's husband, Bud, is barely tolerating my presence at this very moment. Who's to say that *he* wasn't the one who slashed my tires?

Police reports I've found in this tub tell me that Bud Sumner has a history of terrorizing Black folks, specifically Sheldon and Maryam Marsh, wealthy movie people with enough money to buy a nicer cabin than the Sumners.

In this report taken by Deputy Angus Wagner, Sheldon Marsh had called the sheriff's department because Bud had thrown dead squirrels on their porch and rocks at their windows.

Another report by Deputy Wagner details an encounter between the two men. Sheldon had videotaped Bud poking beneath the Marshes' Mercedes. Bud had claimed that he'd dropped a tennis ball and it had rolled beneath the Benz; he was simply trying to retrieve it.

Maryam Marsh had reported that Birdie had let the air out of their tires and that Bud had assaulted her in his general store.

Not nice people, the Sumners.

These pictures of the pendant and *Beloved* that I'd just discovered in the manila folder . . .

Maybe back in the eighties, lightning bolt pendants were a "thing" for girls at Inglewood High School, like chokers and checkered Vans were for my friends and me. In our clique, Kayla, Cheyenne, Tiana, and I wore matching puka shell necklaces to Magic Mountain, and then we'd wear tie-dyed, torn halter tops to the mall.

And if the lightning bolt pendant was a clique thing, Felicia could no longer wear hers once she chose the Black Swans over Mom and the Fast Girls.

And *Beloved.* Along with Terry McMillan and Alice Walker, Toni Morrison had been one of the most popular Black writers back then. *Beloved* had been made into a movie, with Oprah Winfrey helping a new generation find the book. Mom may not have understood the story, but she knew it *must've* been good if Oprah championed it. Ms. Morrison had probably come to read at a bookstore, and Mom had probably bought a copy and asked for her to sign it.

Deeper into the box, I find more pictures. Sheldon and Maryam dressed to the nines, smiling with Sammy Davis Jr. Sheldon, Maryam, and a little girl out on the lake in a fishing boat. That growing little girl wearing a pink leotard and tutu *en pointe* at a ballet barre.

That pouty, full mouth.

I've seen this woman before. The only daughter mentioned in the Marshes' obituary:

Elizabeth.

There's a picture of a handsome young man wearing a green-and-white football jersey.

And this man—Robert Gibson, my father—holds a football in one hand and uses the other to do a three-point stance as the pretty girl with the pouty mouth stands in fourth position on his back. *She's* the dancer

I saw in the yearbook, the one in the picture from the attic. *E. at the lake.* She's Daddy's ex-girlfriend.

I think I know who's behind that scratched-out picture in Mom's yearbook.

When were the pictures in this folder taken?

Daddy's last year playing in a green-and-white jersey for Inglewood High School was 1986, his senior year. Did their love affair end once he graduated?

Did Dad cheat on Mom with Elizabeth? And did Felicia, pissed that she hadn't been invited to the anniversary party, drive here to disrupt our celebration? Did she plan to show me proof that Rob and Elizabeth had found each other again after he'd married Mom? Was he planning to leave Mom for Elizabeth, but Mom got pregnant with Dominique before he could bounce? Did Dad feel guilty for wanting to leave his growing family?

Possibly.

No wonder Mom and Felicia hated each other.

I'd scratch out Liz's picture, too.

And Dad: What the *hell?*

I understand why Mom keeps that go bag by the door.

No wonder Dad keeps his mouth shut most times and grinds his teeth almost all the time.

Does Mom know that there's a picture of Elizabeth Marsh in her attic?

I glare at another picture, this one of Dad wearing a tuxedo and Elizabeth Marsh wearing pink chiffon. The look in his eyes is worshipful, adoring, smitten. It must've happened like this: He'd been in love with Elizabeth Marsh, but then they'd broken up. He met Mom, fell hard for her, so much that I was born, and then they married. Elizabeth Marsh showed her ass, Dad turned his head, Mom caught on and got pregnant with Dominique. They've resented each other ever since.

Makes sense.

Ugh. This woman wearing pink chiffon . . .

Was Daddy texting her a few nights ago when he should've been writing a toast honoring his wife?

I can't stay here any longer. There's plenty of air moving through the room, but my lungs are working too hard to keep me from suffocating. I grab the plastic tub, and on shaky, weak legs, I hurry over to the stairs.

The hatch is closed.

I shift the box to my hip and use my free hand to push the door.

The door won't budge.

I use my head to push against the hatch.

No give. Like . . . *not at all.*

I back down the steps and place my hands on my cheeks to tamp down my waxing fear.

Breathe in . . . out . . . slowly . . . breathe . . . Okay. I climb the stairs and use my two free hands and my head to push.

The hatch doesn't move.

I'm trapped.

42.

Sweat trickles down my spine as I bang on the hatch door. "Anybody out there?"

I can picture them now: Bud Sumner wearing his denim overalls stands beside his tobacco-stained-teeth buddy Gomer, and they're laughing at me. Another friend—Skeet or Junior—is out on the deck splashing gasoline over the makeshift cross they're about to burn. In the cold opening of this episode of *Queen of Palmdale*, I *may* be tonight's victim.

"Please let me out," I shout, not sure if being let out and still being surrounded by angry good ol' boys is ever a good idea.

My calm is whittling down into splinters. I feel it poking at the undersides of my skin.

I pull my phone from my pocket to call 911 or Mom or . . .

No SERVICE.

I wander to the wine rack beneath the staircase. I think about grabbing a dusty bottle of Cabernet Sauvignon and guzzling from it like a can of Sprite. But I need a clear head.

I drift back toward the office.

One bar pops up on my phone's screen.

I tap Dominique's number.

Calling . . .

The phone beeps twice and the call drops.

That single bar disappears.

I shift north.

The bar returns.

I try Dominique's number again.

Calling . . . calling . . .

Two beeps and the call drops again.

With my heart banging down to my ankles, I float back to the stairs.

Dust drifts down from the floorboards.

I sneeze, and maybe this sneeze will remind whoever's up there that I'm a real person and that trapping me down here is cruel. This very real person wants to cry right now, but she won't. If she's still down here an hour from now, she will weep and open that bottle of wine.

"Okay, okay, okay," I say, waggling my arms, forcing nervous energy to bubble out through my fingertips.

I charge up the ladder and ram my head and shoulder against the hatch.

Bam!

Yellow circles swirl before me.

The scissor hinges squeak and lift.

I peek out.

No one's standing in the hallway.

I sniff. I don't smell men, tobacco, or burning wood. Just pine forest and old furniture.

The panel is slowly dropping . . . this hinge is giving. I push the hatch door as far back as it can go, then duck into the basement for the tub filled with papers, photos, and crime reports.

Yeah, it's time to get the hell out of here.

⚡

I'm almost happy to see Palmdale in the distance with its tract-home sameness, the brown air and the traffic.

Dominique has left me a voice mail. "Are you trying to call? Should I be worried?"

I text her: I'm good. No cell reception.

Should she be worried? Maybe.

Because how long had Mom and Dad been married when Elizabeth Marsh danced back into their lives? What could she and Dad possibly have in common today?

Yes, Rob Gibson was hot back in the day. He had that great smile and a wide receiver's long muscles. He laughed and liked road trips to anywhere. He'd been a poor kid at USC on a football scholarship and had enough talent to be drafted to play for the Raiders. But he got hurt and became a PE teacher and high school football coach. Elizabeth Marsh, on the other hand, came from a family of dancers and musicians. I've seen the pictures: Count Basie came over for Christmas dinner, and Lena Horne sang at her christening.

My mother can be a supreme bitch, but she worked hard for Robert Gibson. *She* smoothed his edges and kept others from exploiting his good nature. Mom had his babies and lived in the freaking desert for *him*. To be frank, *he* should be throwing this party for her, not me.

Feels like I'm overheating, like my heart is boiling in my chest and my mind is broiling beneath my scalp. I've done too much thinking, too much living.

I can't go home, not with all this . . . *madness*—Mom, Dad, Felicia, Liz—in my head. It's too much. Instead, I drive to the Holiday Inn. Returning to Room 303 feels like a violation even though I've paid to stay here. The bed is made, and the air is so clean, cool, and sweet that I want to scoop a dollop with my hand and eat it.

The noise in my head fades as I stare at the plastic tub on the table. It's filled with too much of my parents' origin story.

I could bust up their marriage by asking questions about high school loves and extramarital affairs, about blackmail attempts made by a distant (and now-dead) cousin.

But I don't want to do that. That's not my job.

So why did I bring the plastic tub back with me?

Because maybe the reasons for Felicia's death can be found in this container.

I find two videocassettes labeled E's A.A. AUDITIONS. Elizabeth's Alvin Ailey auditions? I grab the sheath of statements and flip through again. One from Alicia Campbell ("Nothing is real. Not her love. Not her hair.") and another from Corbin Jefferson ("They were headed in that direction before everything went fucking nuts.").

I know Uncle Corbin—he and Dad played ball together at USC.

An evidence sheet is clipped behind his statement. Investigators found a Cookie Monster house shoe, a Smith & Wesson revolver, a mountain bike three miles from the cabin, and . . . *blood* on the light switch plate and in the garage.

So . . . did Bud Sumner assault the Marsh family? Forcing them to run to their Benz with broken brakes? And then that car careened off a cliffside and they died?

With shaky hands, I look through more manila envelopes and folders stuffed with papers. The Marshes had a post office box near the Sumners' general store. A key is taped to this sheet of paper. Does Elizabeth Marsh also have a key? Has she received forwarded mail?

I take this PO box statement and place it in my bag, then rummage through more manila envelopes and folders stuffed with photographs. I find an old-fashioned answering machine.

Ha. I've seen these things on the *Tough Cookie* set.

A label has been taped to the machine's bottom: F. CAMPBELL. A few microcassette tapes fill a plastic bag, but there's already a tape in the Easa-Phone.

I plug in the answering machine.

The LED digital display shows the number eight.

How do I listen to those messages?

I open the lid. There's a label taped beside the cassette with instructions.

Okay. Awesome. Play.

"That crazy bitch is still harassing me."

The woman's recorded voice sounds warped. The technology is ancient.

"I went into town this morning. There she was. I went to lunch and she was in the parking lot. Y'all think I'm crazy, but she's crazier than me. Girl, I'm getting scared. Call me."

My mind ticks . . . ticks . . .

Who is this? When was this message left?

No time and date stamps.

"She's here. I don't know what to do. Where are you? Please pick up."

The recording sounds muffled and scratchy, like the woman's hiding beneath a blanket with the phone. She's whispering, "I called the police again. They say there's nothing they can do. They say she hasn't done anything illegal." She starts crying into the phone. "I don't know what to do. What does she want?" Her frustration and fear come through, even on warped tape.

My phone vibrates on the desk.

It's Shane yanking me back to the present.

"So?" he asks.

I'd called Shane ten minutes into my drive from Lake Paz—because I missed him, because I needed his touch and his brain. I may invite him to the dinner party, which would mean introducing him to my family.

And since I have this hotel room . . .

"You don't sound happy inviting me up," he says.

"No. Yes. I mean—I can't *wait* to see you, but . . ." I push out a breath and close my eyes.

"But?"

Tears rim my eyes. "I don't know me right now. For real, I'm losing my mind."

"What's going on?"

I tell Shane about the intruder, about Kayla's request for my DNA, about losing *Beloved*.

"Take a breath," he tells me.

I inhale. That breath catches in my throat. "I can't. All the family shenanigans."

"What did Teddy Roosevelt say about family shenanigans?"

A teardrop tumbles down my cheek. "That thing?"

"Exactly."

"He was so wise."

"Hell yeah. We'll figure it out in person, yeah?"

"Yeah. Oh: don't forget to pick up my inhaler from CVS."

I need to breathe, especially since I'm so tired. I cringe seeing my reflection in the mirror over the desk. My eyes are swollen and blood-shot behind my Coke-bottle glasses. My nose is red and dry from being constantly blown. I look brittle. Even my hair looks like curly black straw. Who *is* this chick?

Shane may see me and see this place and decide that he *does* have something better to do back at home, that he'll see me back in LA, that maybe we *are* rushing things.

I shower, shave, and pluck. In the bag that I left behind in this room, I find hair lotion and rub half the bottle into my dry mane. I find my contact lenses in my purse, but the thought of sticking them into my eyes . . . I skip the contacts.

The woman in the mirror *almost* resembles the one who arrived here last week. She's in there somewhere, Yara under glass, banging her fists, begging to be let out on La Cienega Boulevard, right in front of Versailles Cuban Restaurant.

Back to Ye Olde Answering Machine.

In this message, a child is shrieking in the background.

The woman is now shouting into the receiver. "She's here! She's outside! What am I supposed to do? I called the police, but it just rings and—" There's banging, and the child cries louder. The woman shushes her, but the child is too far gone to hush. "Where are you? I don't know where he is. I'm so scared . . ."

The woman starts to cry into the phone, but not as hysterically as the child. No, she mews like an injured kitten. "I just wanna live my life. I just wanna be left alone. She wins." Another whimper, and then: "Bye."

There's a click and a dial tone.

I take deep breaths until I stop seeing circles. I push aside the answering machine and open another folder stuffed with papers.

The first document is a slip of notebook paper with Detective M. Stall and a phone number written in red ink.

I dial the number.

No one answers, and the call rolls to voice mail. No one says if this is still M. Stall's number. Does M. Stall actively work, or has he retired? No clue. After the beep, I say, "Hi. I'm Yara Gibson, and I'm calling about a case you worked on a long time ago up in Lake Paz. I'd appreciate if you called me back. You can reach me at . . ." I leave my phone number.

Which case?

I don't know.

Who was the victim?

I don't know.

What do you want?

I don't know.

A part of me wants to listen to more cassettes, to learn if that crazy bitch went away, if the terrified woman survived the night. I'm shaking, though, and sipping air because the distress in these recordings . . . No, I can't listen to any more today.

I shove the answering machine and the bag of tapes back into the plastic tub.

As I slip the folder back into the container, a piece of paper falls out. The document has been touched so much that it's as thin as a snowflake.

STATE OF CALIFORNIA

MISSING PERSON REPORT

ELIZABETH MARIE MARSH

43.

Whoa.

Elizabeth Marsh was *missing*?

Most of the type on the report has faded, but I can make out a few things.

Marsh, Elizabeth Marie

Female, Black, 28 years old

5'8", 115 lbs.

Curly brown hair, brown eyes.

Last contact: June 25, 1998

Report Type: Voluntary Missing Adult

Last Known Location: Lake Paz, CA

Detectives from the Los Angeles County Sheriff's Department are seeking assistance in locating the above missing person. She suffers from depression, and the family is concerned for her well-being.

Boxes for "X-rays available" and "photo available" are checked yes. The page is covered in fading handwritten swoops and sticks.

Another evidence sheet documents a prescription medication bottle containing sixteen OxyContin tablets found on the floor in the cabin's kitchen.

Where is she now? Did she ever come back? Voluntary missing adult—does that mean that she just rolled out of bed one day and decided to leave without telling anyone?

I turn to the internet. There *must* be stories written about her disappearance. She was the daughter of a prominent musician and dancer. But results for *Elizabeth Marsh* include an Englishwoman who was held captive in the 1700s and another woman who teaches at Duke. Toward the end of my clicking around the web, I find an obituary for Sheldon and Maryam Marsh, a quick snippet on Elizabeth's disappearance, and a brief article about Elizabeth taking over the dance school her mother founded. This article had been written almost nine years before she disappeared.

Daughter of Famed Dancer Takes Reins of Marsh School of Dance—December 12, 1989

Elizabeth Marsh's promising career with Alvin Ailey American Dance Theater was cut short after just two months' training when she and her parents went for an Independence Day drive in Lake Paz, Calif., nearly 100 miles north of Los Angeles. The family's automobile, a blue Mercedes-Benz sedan, lost control on the winding roads of Angeles National Forest and swerved from the road and off a cliff.

Sheldon and his wife of 30 years, Maryam, did not survive.

Their 19-year-old only child did, albeit with substantial injuries that would end her dream of dancing with the famed dance company. "My parents always told me that nature finds a way," Marsh said, pointing at her still-healing wounds and scratches. "And since I can no longer dance, I'll teach and I'll carry on my mother's dream. And now, my dream, too."

With the help of her best friend, Felicia Campbell, and her boyfriend, Rob Gibson, Marsh learned to walk again. After the day's classes, she spends an hour at the barre, fighting to reclaim her strength and flexibility.

"I can do first and second positions," she said with a warm laugh. "I'll never grand jeté again, but I'm here. Nature always finds a way."

She's so beautiful in this picture, with her pink satin skirt and curly bun. She's so strong and . . . Wow. Felicia and Dad helped her walk again. I click on another article written after her disappearance.

Over 50 people arrived at Lake Paz to search for evidence related to the disappearance of a Los Angeles–area woman. After a daylong search, volunteers found a "suspicious item" that was immediately turned over to authorities. Los Angeles Sheriff's Department detective Matt Stall says he can't reveal the nature of this item but expects it will help shed light on the circumstances surrounding the case.

Did she tire of the pain? Her loss? Why did she leave? In 1989, my father was twenty-one years old and a junior in college. Who had he been dating then? Mom or Liz . . . or both? And Felicia—she'd been a true friend; but then, that friendship hadn't been enough to keep Elizabeth *there*. Because . . . "voluntary missing adult," just like the report indicated. Wait.

The server at Bucelli's Italian told me that Felicia had been waiting for Liz. And then, the server had called *me* Liz. Felicia knew that Liz was alive and that she was no longer missing. They'd come to Palmdale, again, to do *what*?

How long has Elizabeth Marsh been gone?

I glance at my phone just in case I didn't hear it ring over the manic beatboxing from my heart. I want Detective Stall to call me now more than ever.

There are text messages from Ransom.

Got the cash
Here's more stuff

My screen loads with files of PDFs.
How is he getting all of this?
A report from the DNA lab.

Please examine the following items for foreign DNA:

- Swabs from under the victim's right-hand nails
- Swabs from under the victim's left-hand nails
- Swabs from the victim's neck (exposed skin).

Please examine the victim's pantsuit for foreign DNA in areas that may have been touched by suspect during the attack.

Though the victim was found in water, several injuries were to the back of head. Please have foreign DNA uploaded into CODIS.

There's an inventory sheet listing logged-in DNA buccal swabs. I see my name there, along with Alicia Campbell, William Harraway, and Ransom Andrepont.

My stomach drops. *Ransom?* Why did Kayla take *his* DNA?

Additional swabs being analyzed come from Felicia's car as well as from the gun found in the car door pocket and the note found in the passenger footwell. Felicia's car has been impounded—there's a receipt for that.

The last document is a spreadsheet: a GPS log with columns for dates and times, activity, and location of data. So many numbers. My eyes glaze, but I'm able to pick out words.

1224 Stardust Way (N 34.6661569°, W -118.4018816°). This is the Marsh family's cabin. Felicia created this route on Wednesday, May 15, at 6:53 in the morning. So . . . last week.

54938 Edgewater Court—that's my parents' address. Felicia also created that route on May 15 at nine that night. Did Felicia drive to my parents'?

I take a breath, but my lungs sit like knots in my chest. Because the third address . . . 9033 Fourth Street, Santa Monica. Route created on Wednesday, May 15, at 5:15 p.m.

I live at 9033 Fourth Street.

A FAMILY AFFAIR

44.

Where the hell did she go?

Yara hasn't been home since early morning.

You're supposed to watch her, the mastermind texted.

There are more things to do in life than following some spoiled bitch around Palmdale. Working a nine-to-five, first of all. Gotta work. Not everybody has multiple streams of untaxed revenue rolling in.

Do I have to do everything myself?

Ugh. Tuck in your tail and just take it . . . for now. Then you fuck *everybody* up, including the mastermind. If it keeps going this way, if accusatory texts keep blowing up the phone . . .

Switch teams. Simple as that.

And who's out here looking for the needle in the haystack in a city full of needles?

Again, after being on my feet all damn . . .

What is that?

The car's acting up again. The steering wheel is vibrating a little more than it vibrated yesterday. The car is dying. Need more money, to either fix it or buy a new one.

One last sweep and I'm done.

No black Jeep at Target.

No black Jeep at In-N-Out.

There it is! The black Jeep is parked close to the entrance of the Holiday Inn!

A slow drive past the car to look at the license plate . . . Yep, that's Yara.

Even in a parking space two rows over, the Jeep is still easy to see.

Found her!!! Best text sent today.

An ellipsis bubbles on the phone's screen. **Stay and watch.**

Ummm . . . **For how long??** Again, people got jobs.

For as long as it takes!

That could be all night. If it *is* all night, there's a new plan to follow. Run Yara off the road and make it look like an accident. And then all of this will be over.

New car. New headboard. But in a different city. Leave everything and everyone behind. Live a whole new life. A *better* life.

Finally.

45.

Room 303 smells like burgers and fries and the red wine I sloshed onto the table. The moon and the hotel parking lot's orange sodium lights shine through the windows.

I turn in bed onto my stomach. "But *why* did Felicia go to my apartment?"

Shane, all shoulders and smog-colored eyes, lies beside me. "Did she actually get out of the car and use the intercom to call up? Or did she just drive by?"

"I don't know." That night, I'd stayed at his place in Culver City and driven to Palmdale from there. "I wish she would've come earlier. I'd know whatever it was she'd wanted to tell me."

And why did she drive to my parents'? Did *they* talk to her that night?

Shane runs his fingers through my dry hair, then kisses my shoulder. His lips against my bare skin make me tremble, and I stretch toward him, a plant starved for sunshine. It's been nearly a week since we've seen each other, and I keep hugging him as though he's crossed the Atlantic on the slowest steamer.

The left- and right-side nightstands hold our phones. The nightstand on my side has vibrated all evening. It vibrates now.

Shane hides his face in my hair. "Your family knows you're here tonight, right?"

"I texted them this afternoon." I pause, then add, "They're doing this on purpose—it's all about control, keeping me in place."

At first, I thought there'd been an emergency. That Mom had gotten into a car accident, or Dad had hurt himself at football practice.

My dress isn't ready, Mom had texted.

Didn't Tynisha say that it would be ready???
One more couple to the guest list
Orlando Flores and his wife
He's a reporter with the Antelope Valley Times!!!
Is it possible to add them?

Of course it is

Make it so!!
Cece called
She'll be here either Thursday or Friday
For the body

And now I grab the phone again from the nightstand to make sure that all is well in the House of Gibson.

There's a cascade of new text messages.

He allergic to anything? Mom asks.

Don't want to kill him
Yet
LOL

Shane reads the text and says, "Ha," then climbs out of bed. "I'm allergic to peaches."

I text Mom, then place the phone on the nightstand. "Just another fire drill," I say and grab my IDEAS journal from the nightstand. "They're really helping me write this show."

Shane's muscles shift around his body as he performs the simple act of pulling up his boxers. It's like I'm watching a beautiful, complex clock reporting that it's seven o'clock.

"I look forward to meeting them," he says.

I smile and toss the journal onto the carpet. "Famous last words."

He squints at me. "How bad could it be?"

I hug a pillow to my chest and knead it with my chin. "My mother's favorite pastime is making grown men cry. They're caught off guard because she's beautiful and so they don't realize that her tongue has slit their throats. Saw it happen to our high school vice principal, who thought he'd get to walk away after calling my mother a Black bitch."

Shane winces. "Was it the 'bitch' part?"

"No, she actually enjoys the 'bitch' part."

"What happened to him?"

"He got promoted to principal. But he has this rasp . . ."

He holds out his hands. "Well, I come in peace. Oh, is there a wine store close by? I can't meet them emptyhanded."

"A *wine* store?" I crawl to the bottom of the bed and run my hand along his neck. "Bruh, you in Palmdale. We got a grocery store, some liquor stores, and a BevMo."

He kisses me, then grabs bottled waters from the fridge. He points to the plastic tub I took from the cabin. "What's all that?"

"Information involving a mistress, dead parents, racists next door, and Lake Paz." I trace the eagle tattoo above his heart and tell him about the cabin, the basement, and the boxes. About Bud and Birdie possibly and probably cutting the brake lines on the Marsh family's Benz.

"And I found this answering machine with Felicia's name on it, I think, and these tiny little tapes . . ." I tell Shane that I listened to a few messages and found the number to the investigating detective in one of the folders. "But he hasn't called me back."

He hops back in bed. "Who's the victim?"

"No idea." I guzzle from the bottle, and cool water nurses my thick tongue and scratchy throat. "But my dad's ex-girlfriend was missing at one time. Wanna hear the messages? They may make more sense to you."

I grab the answering machine from the tub and press a button. There's a beep and a voice.

"Erased. To start a new greeting—"

I slap my forehead. "Well, golly, Yara. Way to go."

He laughs. "How'd you press the wrong button?"

"Dunno." I drop the machine back into the tub. "It's like driving a freaking Model T-Mobile or whatever. At least there are still more tapes in the bag."

"I'll call the detective. Use my badge number and all that. Brother to brother."

I crawl beside him in bed. "You will?"

"Anything for you."

My smile dies. "What if . . . ? Maybe I shouldn't . . ." I clench— the shakes are coming on and twisting inside me. "I'm scared that I'm gonna find out the worst about Dad . . . or just confirm what I always suspected."

"Which is?"

"That he has this whole other life that I don't know about." I jam my hands into my armpits. "You think I should stop?"

His eyebrows scrunch. "You won't stop, though."

"I *could* stop."

"Impossible."

"If he's cheated on Mom and I find out for sure . . . I won't feel like celebrating."

Shane swipes his knuckle against my cheek. "Welcome to the world of adulting, Yara Gibson. Keep your arms and legs close to you at all times."

"I don't think I'm ready to grow up," I say, shaking my head.

Here in Grown-Up Land, you work too much, you don't smile enough, and everything you thought you knew turns out to be the sweetest lie.

Let me off this wack-ass ride.

46.

The western Mojave Desert is at its prettiest right now at six thirty in the morning, with that new sun making jeweled light across the sand and stones. Jackrabbits spring across boulders, and birds blanket the sky to do whatever birds do together en masse. As the moon fades in the western sky and the sun turns the horizon the colors of berries and wines, my family welcomes Shane with hugs and handshakes. Mom and Dad thank him for the Dom Pérignon and her favorite Pinot Grigio.

Anxiety feels like heartburn this morning, but there's nothing I can do to stop the spread. We settle on the back deck with our plates filled with the buffet Mom has prepared—from frittata and crisp bacon to fruit (no peaches) and fresh-baked cinnamon rolls. Dad has lit the firepit, and the rich smell of applewood mixes with early-morning sage and bacon.

My mother tells witty stories about her running career and the bigoted vice principal that she filleted. "He hasn't uttered the word 'black' since then," she says, laughing. "Just 'dark' and 'darkest brown.'" Though charming and pleasant, she remains watchful, waiting for Shane to slip up.

Dominique shows off her intelligence, using "boondoggle," "capricious," and "kitsch" in one breath. Though she, too, is charming and pleasant, she hides her yawns behind the rim of her coffee cup. Either it's too early, or she's completely bored by my boyfriend.

Dad shares stories about football parents who think their sons are the next Tom Brady but these same sons are scared to get hit by the ball or the other team.

Shane, too, is polite and attentive. He shares stories of playing football at Culver City High School and Duke University. He holds my hand, but not so much that it looks controlling and creepy. He congratulates my parents on their anniversary but doesn't say nonsense like, *I hope Yara and I find that same joy.*

It's the most perfect Wednesday morning in Gibson family history.

"That was . . . *interesting*," Shane says now as we drive back to the Holiday Inn.

I toss him a look as I grip the steering wheel. "Meaning . . . ?"

"Lakes look so calm and peaceful but . . ." He squints as he thinks. "Lakes have these hidden dangers. Weeds that wrap around your ankles. They're cold, and they host weird bacteria that works itself into your brain and kills you. Your family's like a lake."

I throw back my head and laugh. "You call it a lake. I think it's more like those high-security areas with the crisscrossing laser beams and fragmentation mines."

He chuckles. "Your parents . . . There's some anger bubbling there. Dom is *definitely* your mother's favorite. And you're a Daddy's girl—he made sure that you ate, that you were hydrated, that you were . . . *okay.*"

I make a face. "Did he?"

Shane nods. "He kept you stocked with juice, tissues, and bacon."

"He did!"

"I caught your mother glaring at him a few times," Shane says. "Like *you're* actually the other woman. Families, right? I understand you better, though. Why you're constantly thinking and imagining. Why you don't like conflict. Why you're writing *Queen of Palmdale.*" He turns to me and smiles. "Makes me love you more."

I loosen my death grip on the steering wheel as relief veins through me.

From the cup holder, my phone vibrates.
A text from Mom. He's cute and smart!!

Good jobbbbbbb

I send her, Dominique, and Dad a thank-you text.

I know it was a lot to prepare a last-minute breakfast on a
workday
THANK YOU!!!!

My phone vibrates with a response from Dominique.

He's grown on me!

At the Holiday Inn, the ladies with the cleaning carts are working
two doors down from my room. A good thing they're close—a pile of
towels towers on my bathroom floor, and the table is still tacky from
spilled wine.

Today, I can hang out with Shane until he leaves at noon. My
family has school. Afterward, Dominique and Mom are heading to the
dress shop to deal with the seamstress.

I capture show ideas in my journal before those thoughts evapo-
rate—lakes, high-security area, breakfast at dawn—but the plastic tub
from the Marsh cabin is calling me. I grab the file on Elizabeth Marsh's
disappearance. Even as Shane rubs my shoulders and kisses my neck,
even as my heart makes ticking sounds like a love bomb ready to burst,
I can't tear my eyes away from this woman's picture. Shane continues
to vie for my attention as he nuzzles my hair.

I sigh. "Housekeeping is *right there*."

He doesn't have enough time to respond before my phone rings.

"Matt Stall here." The detective in charge of Elizabeth Marsh's missing person case.

"It's the detective," I whisper to Shane.

My boyfriend tosses me a pen and settles beside me at the foot of the bed.

I tap the speaker icon. "US Marshal Shane Christopher is also here."

"Thanks for returning our call," Shane says.

"It's not a problem," Detective Stall says.

I tell him that I'm calling about the missing person investigation for Elizabeth Marsh. "My cousin Felicia Campbell was recently . . . murdered," I add, my tongue thick, "and I'm currently in possession of the files she kept and I'm trying to figure out if Liz's disappearance is related to Felicia's death. You may have something useful . . ."

The detective grunts. "Condolences on your cousin. Doubt that I have anything to add. You have the Marsh files right there. Elizabeth Marsh was reported missing on June 25 by Miss Campbell. In fact, Miss Campbell was the only one who thought Marsh had disappeared under suspicious circumstances."

"You didn't think Elizabeth disappeared under suspicious circumstances?" Shane asks. "I know the report says voluntary missing adult."

Detective Stall says, "Not at all. She left the cabin on her bike, which we later found down the road."

"That could also mean someone snatched her off the bike," I say.

"Nah," the man says. "People wanted me to arrest the neighbor, Don Sumner. Arrest him for what, I kept asking. Just because he was a little racist didn't mean he had anything to do with this. And Maryam Marsh never pressed charges against him after the incident in the store. I guess he thought that her being nice meant more than just her being nice. She rejected old Bud, and he lost it. That had nothing to do with what happened to her kid."

"Maybe old Bud lost it again on Liz this time?" Shane says. "And instead of assaulting Elizabeth like he assaulted Maryam, he murdered her."

"Nope," Detective Stall says. "Elizabeth got tired of the family thing and decided to go. Adults have the right to leave, especially if they're under a lot of stress, and it sounds like this lady was. Stressed and bored. At least, that's what her husband said."

"She was married?" I ask.

"Yep. He . . . I can't remember his name, I'm retired now. Anyway, he said that she was on a break, that they were taking a moment. That she'd always do this, and that she had a history of mental illness—but that she was fine." He pauses. "She mailed him a letter about a week after she left, which was also the day she showed up at our substation in Lost Hills."

Shane and I both say, "What?"

"Yep. I wasn't there that night, but Marsh talked to one of the deputies on duty. She explained the situation and even signed an affidavit. Once she showed her ID, we called the family, but we couldn't tell them where she was, not without her consent. That isn't in the file?"

I shake my head. "I haven't seen it yet."

"I'll send it to you."

I give him my email address.

"There's no active case," he says. "Everyone overreacted. I stuck around for nearly a year, checking in every couple of months, adding to the files, jotting down notes, observations . . . We took every missing person investigation seriously. The circumstances surrounding them don't matter. And I resent that people thought race had something to do with this.

"I don't see color. She could've been Black, white, or purple, it didn't matter to me. The available evidence was inconclusive. We didn't give up. But you gotta remember what we were dealing with. It was obvious she needed help. Her family failed her."

Shane and I roll our eyes at each other.

"It was an interesting case," the ex-cop continues. "I was a fan of her father's music, y'know? Poor thing. She was simply an unbalanced young woman who let life get the best of her. Frankly, I get it. Sometimes, I wanna leave this place, too. Most of us swallow it. Elizabeth Marsh said, 'Forget it.'"

I close my eyes. "Yeah."

"Fortunately," the former detective says, "there ain't no mystery here. As much as I like cold cases, this ain't one of 'em."

After we end the call with Detective Stall, Shane digs through the tub, pausing at a videocassette rubber banded to a crumpled piece of paper. "You have a VCR?"

"At home. But what does this paper . . . ?"

I begin to read.

> Dear Detective Stall:
>
> I couldn't care less that they think I'm missing. I know where I am, and I'd appreciate it if everybody BACKS OFF and LEAVES ME ALONE! I'm leaving this city of poison and traitors and heading to a place of peace and soft water. If you want, I will come meet with YOU before I go. I will also sign an affidavit if that means being left alone. I don't want to see anyone else. They are trying to destroy what's left of me. Please don't let them!
>
> To my family and friends:
>
> It is June 30, and I am alive and well. How many times must I leave? How many times will you drag me back? After all that I've been through, I'm tired of trying. I just want to BE. I don't want anything, just the clothes on my back and some of the money my mother and father left me. You know I'm hard to

please. You always wanted me to be perfect. Perfect is exhausting. I want to blame you for not seeing that, but I won't. Doesn't matter now anyway. I miss us. Before . . . her. I'm still here for you. Are you here for me?

Please let me exist the way I want. I love you, but please leave me alone. Trust me: it's better this way.

Love,

EMM

If Elizabeth Marsh visited the police station in Malibu and provided this statement, why did Felicia keep looking for her?

And why did both women come to Palmdale?

And where is Elizabeth Marsh right now?

Wait . . .

Did *Elizabeth Marsh* kill Felicia Campbell?

47.

Our house sits at the end of a cul-de-sac. I heard someone say once that in lesser neighborhoods, a cul-de-sac is called a dead-end street. Behind our house on that cul-de-sac is desert that stretches until forever. In lesser worlds, that desert is called wasteland, barren nothingness baking beneath the sun. Here, though, the desert moves with sage and chaparral, lizards and coyotes, and it's interrupted by a forest that burns only to be revived by the very thing that killed it.

My house sits in the middle of a desert at the end of a cul-de-sac. As I pull up, it looks abandoned, as though hours ago the land didn't burble with the click of forks and spoons against midprice china and stemware. There are secrets here that are actively being kept, and I will keep tugging that line until the anchor sits in my lap.

Yes, Elizabeth Marsh could've killed Felicia Campbell. She was supposed to see my cousin on the night she walked into the lake.

Maybe they *did* meet, and life turned left.

Maybe Ransom can pull the phone records from that night.

Elizabeth Marsh may no longer be missing, and this case may be closed, but my fascination burns bright. And on Sunday, *after* the anniversary party, I will present my mother with a bulleted list of topics to discuss.

⚡

Today, the attic smells of smoke and cedar, and the air is thicker than usual. The wood-slatted walls seem closer, and I feel like I'm wedged between the ground and the grave. I flip through Mom's senior yearbook again to look at those pictures of Elizabeth Marsh that my mother neglected to scratch out.

There's Liz, on stage at the winter concert and dancing as Clara in *The Nutcracker*. There she is, Most Popular and Most Talented.

Back in my bedroom, I find the Alvin Ailey American Dance Theater audition tapes from the plastic tub and slip one into my DVD/ VCR.

Elizabeth Marsh, wearing a black unitard, poses in a dance studio. There's a long, mirrored wall behind her. The most beautiful song in the world plays—"Clair de Lune"—as she swoops and spins, her arms remaining perfect in her adagios and grand allegros. In her second piece, she moves to African tribal drums, thrashing and bent, her arms wild and wheeling, followed by her body slowing like she's nearly frozen and breaking through ice.

By the time her perfect bun comes undone, I've stopped breathing and my pulse is racing. Shaken, I stop the tape and turn away from the television.

Yeah, my mother would've loved Elizabeth Marsh up until Liz ascended over Mom's station at school. When she disappeared, Liz was twenty-eight years old. Over twenty years have passed since then, and she's had time to live a whole other life.

My hands and knees are still shaky, and I'm having a hard time catching my breath. My bedroom is too small, too gray. Although air thrums between the walls and windows, each molecule has been loaded with dust and tobacco. What's the true color of paint on these walls? What more could I see if I cleaned the windows with a bucket of hot water and vinegar?

I grab the videotape that was rubber-banded to Elizabeth Marsh's statement and slide it into my VCR.

Closed-circuit television video. The caption in the lower right says LASD LOST HILLS. A woman wearing a baseball cap and a hoodie enters the station close to midnight. For ten minutes, she talks to the officer at the desk, then sits in the small waiting area with a clipboard and pen. She returns to the officer, hands him the clipboard, and leaves.

And she leaves, I guess, for good.

I turn my attention to the latest box I brought down from the attic. It sits beside the plastic tub I took from the cabin.

I look through the contents: Mom's track meet ribbons, her honor society pin, the car key to her ancient VW Jetta.

I find another manila envelope. Inside, there's an itinerary for a flight to Saint Croix on October 12, 1998. There's a piece of notebook paper with an address scribbled in purple ink.

26 Mount Welcome Way Unit C

Christiansted, VI

Laptop open, I type *Elizabeth Marsh* again into a generic people-finding site. Sixteen results, like the last time I'd searched. She wouldn't be the Elizabeth Marsh with nearly ninety birthdays behind her. Since she left her friends and family in 1998, she wouldn't be the Elizabeth Marsh who died in 1997. The Liz Marsh in the Virgin Islands could be her.

Did any of her friends and family think she'd disappeared to the Virgin Islands?

Yearbook in hand again, I stare at the mystery woman's winter concert picture. In some ways, she and Mom resembled each other. The same sharp cheekbones. The same almond-brown eyes. Mom's beauty is serrated, though. She's red pepper and cinnamon. Liz Marsh is smoked paprika and brown sugar.

No wonder Daddy fell for her and then settled for Mom.

I gasp and hold my breath.

Settled.

Throat tight, my eyes flit from the box and the plastic tub to the cluttered bureau and the Jack and Jill bathroom.

Mom, I didn't mean that.

Guilt pulls me down for using that word—*settled*—and for thinking that my mother is somehow *less* than this wounded stranger. Elizabeth Marsh tried to come between my parents and then left behind loved ones who feared that she'd hurt herself and would come to hurt them, too. If anyone's less, it's her, the woman who didn't stick around.

I pick up a pen and aim it for the young woman dancing as Clara in *The Nutcracker*. I could complete the job Mom didn't finish. I could black out her face from the yearbook.

But my pen hovers over this picture and . . . *Crap.* I toss the pen to the other side of the room and toss the yearbook back into the box.

I may be Bee McG's daughter, but this act of obliteration feels . . . *yuck.* I'm a lot of things—obsessive, hyperanxious, a bit of a snob. But I am not . . .

Evil.

48.

Mom is waiting at the bottom of the staircase, and her face is tight as an oyster shell. A mummy's arms aren't crossed as tight as my mother's arms right now. Her lips have twisted into an impossible knot across her face, and her nostrils are so flared that she's stealing all the oxygen.

I'm in trouble.

In the den, Dominique stretches on the couch and sips from a glass tumbler of Coke and olives. On TV, a troop of *Naked and Afraid* teammates are trying to make shoes from the hide of a dead impala. My sister looks away from the show and curls her lips. "Look who's decided to show up."

The nerves in my temples twitch. "Y'all knew Shane was coming. I didn't skip the dress shop trip for the hell of it."

"Why didn't he stay here?" Mom asks. "Something wrong with our house?"

I hold up my hand. "Mom, it would've been weird for my boyfriend and me to sleep in my childhood bed. And we had work to do, and we needed to tape things on the wall, and I didn't want all of that here."

"What *kind* of work?" Dominique asks. "You missed helping with party stuff. I had to—"

"Actually *do* something for a change? Drive to get *your* dress altered?" I grit my teeth and place my hands on my hips. "Tell me, Dominique, what all have you done?"

She sucks her teeth, mutters, "Whatever," then stalks to the kitchen.

I drop into the chaise longue. Something pokes in my back. For a moment, my spirits lift, and I reach behind me, hoping that it's my lost *Beloved*. No, it's just the remote control.

Mom is still glaring at me. "You're not participating."

I frown at her. "You're actually serious?"

"You're more interested in dead-ass Felicia than your own mother." Her eyes well up and she shakes her head. "So hurtful."

I slap my thigh. "Can you not? You're putting on, and lately I've been giving in just to keep the peace, but as I look at all my effort— from my depleted bank account to the thousands of text messages and vendors contacting me, I *know* what I'm doing, and I have evidence of it. So just stop, Mom. Please?"

Her eyebrows lift and she gapes at me. Those manufactured tears return to their ducts and reset for another occasion.

"Your dress?" I ask.

"Upstairs in the closet," she says, twisting the honeybee pendant on its chain.

"And you said Cece's . . ."

Mom nods. "Arriving Thursday and meeting with Kayla about the case. She has a mortuary driving up on Sunday to take Felicia back to LA." She pauses, then adds, "Felicia had a brain tumor. Glioblastoma. Her doctors gave her eighteen months."

I gasp and hold my neck. "Who told you that?"

"Cece." Mom settles on the couch. "Shane's a nice guy. He complements you."

I blink, then waggle my head to focus on Mom's comment. "Yeah, he's wonderful." I tuck my leg beneath me. "Question . . ." My underarms dampen with swampy fear sweat. "Elizabeth Marsh . . ."

Her breath catches in her chest. Her face hardens again.

I say nothing and wait.

The air feels smoky, stale, and I want to open the windows. Back in the wilds of South Africa, the naked and afraid white people are roasting impala meat over an open fire.

I aim the remote at the television. *Poof!* Black screen.

Mom crosses, then uncrosses her legs. She feigns interest in the dark television screen, but she's too jittery to demand the remote control. Finally: "Liz used to be my best friend. We met in junior high school. She helped me in Spanish. I helped her in Algebra. I was fire, she was ice, and we got sweatshirts that said so. When we got to high school, everything changed."

"You became rivals," I said.

"Eventually." Mom plucks string and lint from her socks. The threads drift to the carpet. "Money started to matter. And then there was Felicia. Her parents had a lot of money, and my dad was just a regular guy who helped maintain the highways, and my mother . . . Well, you know about her. Anyway, we were solidly middle-class, but the Campbells . . . Cece was singing all around the world with Anita Baker and Peabo Bryson . . . And she knew Liz's father—he had been a composer and . . . Again, my father had a great job with Caltrans, but I mean . . . he smelled like tar most days."

Poppa had always brought us stray dogs he'd found on the highway, and once I was older, he'd shown me pictures he'd taken at the scenes of highway accidents. Those afternoons with him and those glossy snapshots of twisted, charred metal and broken windshields had been some of my favorite moments.

"Anyway," Mom says, "in junior high school, Felicia and I were more like sisters than cousins, but then she started with the cotillions and ski weekends, and Liz . . . Her parents could afford that stuff, too, and so she and Felicia started doing those things together. My own blood chose Liz over me. And then my best friend chose Felicia over me."

"Is that why you scratched her out of the yearbook?" I ask.

Mom nods. "And boys made it worse, because *we all* wanted to be the girl on the football captain's arm." She cocks an eyebrow. "Believe it or not, every girl wanted your father, including Liz. He and Liz dated for a moment, but then Rob got his mind right and chose *me*."

"And Liz?"

"She never stopped trying to steal him away, even when she got married and started her own family. She got a little *extreme* every now and then. She had these *spells*." Mom stares at the carpet. "Maybe I should show you . . ." She hops up from the couch and darts up the stairs.

As I wait for her to return, the den quiets, the walls crunching and closing around me.

"Found them." Mom returns with a sheath of papers. "Feels like I printed them out a hundred years ago." She also holds a miniature photo album and opens it to the first page.

There's Mom wearing her green-and-white track uniform, her long neck stretched, her chin cocked, hands on her hips, three medals on blue ribbons hanging from her neck.

There she is, in the middle of her clique of five girls—including Felicia and Elizabeth Marsh—wearing sweatshirts and the whitest sneakers in the world. A yellow roller coaster corkscrews behind them.

There they are, Mom and Elizabeth Marsh, wearing airbrushed tank tops—flames for Mom, snowflakes for Liz. Toned arms around the other's shoulders, their cheekbones bronzed, and their lips glossed.

"Good times," Mom says, "and then she left. I came up from LA to help search for her, even though she'd been nasty and bitter toward me. It was hurtful, but I reminded myself that she needed serious help, until she started sending me *this* stuff."

She hands me printed-out emails.

> Bee, you long-legged bitch. Rob will never love you like he loves me. I hope you have a heart attack while you're driving. That way, I know you'll die for sure.

And . . .

> I see you made lasagna using the tomatoes from your garden.

And . . .

> Rob felt soooo good inside of me last night.

"*And* she sent postcards," Mom says, offering me two. A Disneyland postcard:

You know what I've been doing lately? Standing outside your window and just staring at you.

A Knott's Berry Farm postcard:

Bee, you stupid bitch. You weren't good enough for him then, you're not good enough for him now. You should just kill yourself.

And on and on and on.

"And Felicia was mailing you, too?" I ask, my pulse drumming in my head.

She nods. "It felt like an invasion. Like a poltergeist in my home. Except that Liz wasn't supernatural. She was *demonic*, but she wasn't supernatural."

"So eventually, what happened?"

Mom grabs her lighter and a pack of cigarettes from the coffee table. "*Eventually*, Liz and I smoothed things out. She stopped harassing us, and Rob and I just let her be and didn't bother her anymore." Mom's eyes disappear behind all that cigarette smoke now curling around our heads and licking at the ceiling. "But that's when I started doing this." She lifts her cigarette.

"Why did Felicia still believe that she was missing?" I ask.

Mom rolls her eyes. "You know the answer to that. You saw it first-hand. Lee was not well, Yara. She was brilliant in so many ways, but that gift and her illness tore at parts of her sanity." She pulls a crushed pack of Nicorette from her back pocket and pops a piece.

"Do you think . . . ?" I say. "That Elizabeth Marsh . . . ?"

When I don't finish my thought, Mom looks over to me.

I take a deep breath, then push out, "Left that weird postcard and broke into our house?"

Her eyes glaze, and she turns away from me. Her jaws work that piece of gum. She doesn't say the words, but her actions say, *Yes, I do*.

I grip my elbows. "Is she the reason you always threatened to leave us?"

Mom laughs, a sudden, harsh sound. She waves a hand, then lights another cigarette. "You were a child. You misunderstood."

I bristle. "But you said those words. Once, you took Dom with you and left me behind. And another time, you left all of us for *weeks*."

She chuckles. "I probably did say those things, and those were bluffs to get your father to behave. I'd *never* desert something I fought so hard to win. And Dom was so young . . . We just drove down to LA, stopped at McDonald's, and drove right back. And that time I was away longer? Track meets with the team. For nationals. That's all. He just pissed me off at the right time, ha."

She chomps Nicorette and stares at the cigarette between her fingers. "Sorry that you heard all of that grown-up stuff back then. You must hate me."

A headache starts behind my right eye, because a little part of me *does* hate her. No child wants to believe she's a burden to her mother.

Mom's cigarette hovers inches from her lips. Her hand shakes and the cigarette bobs, and the smoke makes her eyes glisten. "I miss her. Sometimes, I wish I could see her again but . . ." She flushes. Mom lost this fight, a rare thing, and it makes us both uncomfortable.

I appreciate her candor. By the way her voice quavers and that cigarette wobbles, she loathes this part of her life and probably hates that I know she's been rejected by friends.

Every villain is a heroine in her own story. I want to call Elizabeth Marsh and hear her version of their beef. I want to tell her that Mom doesn't hate her anymore, that she doesn't have to skulk around in the shadows and send threatening postcards. That we can get her help if she needs it; if she *did* kill Felicia Campbell, she will need as much as possible. We're a family who took in stray dogs from the highway and loved Noodles, Cecily, and Jupiter until their deaths. Not that Elizabeth Marsh is a stray dog, but I'm just saying . . . We were flea-infested, scarred from random nips, and the stinkiest house on the block, but sometimes love bloomed at this house on a dead-end street in the wasteland.

Ooh! That would be a great surprise—Elizabeth coming to the anniversary celebration, bygones being bygones. If she came, I could also ask her about Felicia—why she came to Palmdale, if she and Felicia met back on Friday night, and if we could talk later about what happened next.

After I take medications to treat my irritated eyes and nose, I text Cousin Alicia.

Do you have a number for Liz Marsh?

The ellipsis bubbles beneath my text message.

Why??
Did something happen???

I just want to check something
I talked with the detective on her case
He says Liz voluntarily left

Right, Alicia answers, and that she came into the police station

She said that she was leaving the state
She wrote us a letter saying the same thing
Here's the last number I have

Alicia sends a phone number with a 213 area code.

Be careful
Something is seriously wrong with her

My stomach rolls, and I think about the nasty letters Liz sent my mother.

I love her but
THAT BITCH IS CRAZY!!!!!
I wouldn't call her if I were you

49.

The gardener is here, and the drone of his lawnmower makes me look away from the phone. The aroma of grass, dust, and gasoline slips past my bedroom window.

My phone vibrates again—a second text warning.

If you do call her, be prepared

I quickly save the 213 number in my contacts as Elizabeth Marsh.

I've seen glimpses of Liz's mental state from the police reports and the letters Mom shared with me. She'd been a little off, sure, but was she a sociopath? Doubt it. Women, especially Black women, are always mislabeled and judged harshly for expressing emotion. Still, I'll tread carefully even as I give her the benefit of the doubt.

If she moved to the Virgin Islands, that region is four hours ahead of California. It's ten o'clock there, not too late to call. I dial the number and the line rings . . . rings . . . rings . . . The automated voice mail tells me to leave a message.

I don't.

The chili powder and onions simmering for Mom's enchiladas beat back the scent of sticky-green cut grass, and my stomach growls.

Maybe I'll call Elizabeth Marsh again after breakfast tomorrow. If she's already here, we can meet for lunch. If the situation veers into nutso territory, Kayla will be close by.

Outside, Javier aims his Weedwacker at our shrubs. The cranberry-colored sky above him looks like the desert is on fire.

My phone vibrates in my hand—a text from the number I saved as Elizabeth Marsh.

Who is this??

A thrill spreads through me like new sunshine.

Hi!
You don't know me but I'm Yara Gibson
Daughter of two old friends of yours
Robert and Barbara Gibson

A pause.

How did you get my number?

Alicia Campbell gave it to me
She didn't know if you were still using it
Looks like you are!!!
Yay!

I just want to be left alone, Liz texts.

The energy I'm getting from Elizabeth Marsh is not one of excitement. It's more annoyance, irritation.

I take a deep breath and my lungs resist. The inhaler—I forgot to take it out of Shane's bag. I reach for my inhaler on the nightstand.

Twenty puffs left. I leave it on the nightstand since I can breathe okay for now.

Felicia and I haven't spoken in years, Liz texts.

She's a liar
She's a cheater
She's bad news
I should've kicked Felicia to the curb and stayed friends with Bee

Didn't you and my dad date?

Yes I did date Rob but I lost
I wish them the best

Does she still love Robert Gibson? Does she still think about him? They've been together for a long time now, Liz texts.

That's unexpected but whatever
Good for them
Good night Yara Gibson

But I have more questions! What can I say to keep her hooked?

Someone wants to give you something

Never lead off with what "something" is. Write a cliffhanger, my writing mentor advised, so that the audience tunes in next time. Humans are naturally curious, and they have to see what comes next— from Eve eating the apple to who gets knocked off next in *Game of Thrones*.

But there is no ellipsis, and no further texts come from Elizabeth Marsh. She doesn't bite. She doesn't care about a talking snake in the garden or who survives the red wedding.

It's been crazy here, I text.

I've found things that you'll want to see

My phone doesn't buzz. My head aches from willing her to text back.

Guess Elizabeth Marsh isn't the average woman.

Maybe, because of that tragic accident with her parents, she stays far enough away from *all* cliffs to avoid falling off.

But I'm not going away, not without a last shot.

Felicia told me EVERYTHING, I write.

Really, she texts.

Time for a reunion then
I can't wait to hug you and squeeze you to death!

I drop the phone.

Those words . . . *I can't wait to hug* . . . I dig in my purse and find the note left on my windshield on the night someone keyed my car.

I can't wait to hug you and squeeze you to death!

Did Elizabeth Marsh . . . ?

The crumpled note in my hand shudders as I look at the same words on my phone.

50.

Are you here in Palmdale right now?? I text Elizabeth Marsh.

No response.

Eventually my phone's screen fills with texts and emails from everyone in the world except Elizabeth Marsh. Megan, the event coordinator at Rancho Vista Golf Club, has sent up an early-morning flare. A brussels sprouts E. coli recall is in effect, and thus there'll be no brussels sprouts for Saturday night. She's offered to let me sample vegetable dishes, a rare thing since vegetables are the bridesmaids on a plate, never the bride. But Megan has also met my mother.

And now I sit at a table in the golf club's Desert Willows ballroom, staring past the full glass windows. Sprinklers shoot streams of silver water across impossibly green lawns. Old men wearing chinos and golf caps swing, stoop, and bullshit in the cool of the morning. On the table, three small plates sit at my hands.

Glazed carrots.

Sauteed spinach.

Steamed broccoli.

The broccoli tastes like boiled paper, so plain that I'm annoyed.

Though the spinach is delicious, Mom may not want to smell like garlic while wearing faux couture.

The carrots are delicious as well. They're also inoffensive, and the lovely orange will pop against the filet and shrimp scampi.

I text Mom, who's now putting girls through their paces on the track.

She immediately texts back her approval.

Megan, a round pink woman who kinda looks like the Megan I always sat next to on the bench during PE because of asthma (for me) and a tilted uterus (for her), claps her hands and apologizes for the last-minute change.

I flick away her apology. "If this is the worst thing that can happen, I'll take it."

A dust storm is brewing west of the city, and this one is the real deal. The golf course crew is scurrying to remove flagsticks, empty trash receptacles, and take down umbrellas. As I walk back to my car, I notice no birds are flying through the air. My phone vibrates with an alert.

DUST STORM WARNING TILL 11:00 A.M.

AVOID TRAVEL.

CHECK LOCAL MEDIA

My phone vibrates again, this time, with an email from VitalChek.

> Thank you for placing your order with VitalChek. We have received your request for a Public Marriage Authorized Copy: Barbara Nicole McGuire/Robert Louis Gibons. Unfortunately, there is no record of marriage.

"What?" I drop the phone onto my lap, then I immediately catch the megatypo: Gibons, not Gibson.

Did VitalChek make that mistake, or did I give them a misspelled surname?

I find my original request: Gibons.

Of *course* there wouldn't be a Robert Louis Gibons and Barbara Nicole McGuire. I hit the Jeep's steering wheel, pissed that I made such a dumb mistake and that I waited so long to request a certificate.

Mom will have her glazed carrots and framed ceremonial marriage certificate. Nothing else, Universe. Stop right there.

The sky is no longer a brilliant blue. A wall of dust that reaches the sun looms in the horizon. Time to find clean air. I'm closer to the Holiday Inn than the house, so I head there. The wind has already picked up by the time I rush across the parking lot toward the lobby. I throw a glance west—dust has burst like water from a dam and now rushes toward the Antelope Valley. Awestruck, I stand at the sliding entry doors with my jacket pressed against my mouth and watch as the storm billows and bulges just a mile away.

My phone vibrates with a text from Mom.

U okay??

I send a thumbs-up and hurry to the elevator.

Back in Room 303, I open the curtains. Sand pellets strike the glass. There's nothing to see except swirling brown nothingness. I plop on the bed and pull my laptop from my bag to resubmit my request for my parents' marriage certificate. This time, I check for errors. G-I-B-S-O-N. M-C-G-U-I-R-E. All good.

I toggle over to Google and search for *26 Mount Welcome Way, Christiansted, Virgin Islands*, the location of Elizabeth Marsh's condo. I see only overgrown trees, a single-lane road, and a dialysis center. A gated courtyard with stairs leads up to yellow condos on a hill.

I search Zillow for the same address, but this time, those yellow condos on the hill look out to a harbor. A unit in the same development is for sale. It's cute inside—glass-door cabinets, granite countertops, a hilltop pool, and a private balcony. It can be mine for only $298,000. There's no public tax history or data on the year it was built.

A search for *Elizabeth Marsh + Virgin Islands Saint Croix* doesn't yield anything, either. It's been twenty years since she *maybe* left the continental US, and there was a husband whose name I don't have. But she could've remarried three times by now and taken the last names of each spouse.

There is no way for me, a regular citizen, to know. Time to make a call.

Kayla answers on the first ring. "What's up? Got something for me?"

I pause, then ask, "Was I supposed to get you something?"

"I was just hoping you learned something new, or maybe Will had contacted you."

"Ah. No. I have a request, though. I'm looking for an old friend of my mother's. They had a huge girl fight back in high school, but over the years, they smoothed things out. I'd love to fly her here, but I don't have a reliable address. Could you look in your computers? She lives in the Virgin Islands."

Kayla laughs and laughs, then laughs some more.

"What's so funny?"

"Dude, I've been a low-level detective for less than a year. I can search LA County. I don't have computer programs that go east of Vegas."

"You sure?" I ask, skeptical.

"This isn't TV, Yara."

"What if I tell you . . . ?"

"Tell me . . . *what*?"

"Nothing. Never mind," I tease. "Because if I say anything, then you'll lock me out even more than you have and—"

"Does this 'friend' have anything to do with Felicia Campbell?" Her voice is hard. "If you're withholding information—"

"I'm trying to reach a mutual friend of Felicia's and my mother's. She may know more than what she's saying. I have her phone number and an address in Saint Croix, but . . ."

Kayla says nothing.

Outside, dust has dropped the earth into the dark of night, the end of times. The wind screams as this brown blizzard rages outside the hotel.

"What *aren't* you saying?" Kayla asks. "Yara—"

"She and Felicia were supposed to meet Friday night."

"Are we talking about Liz Marsh?"

"Yes," I say. "They were supposed to meet at Bucelli's Italian near Walmart. Your turn."

"You haven't told me anything new. The autopsy confirms that pasta was her last meal."

And a complimentary tiramisu. "You were gonna fingerprint the bottles in her car."

"Only her prints were found on the bottles," Kayla says. "Now, it's your turn."

I pinch the bridge of my nose. "Felicia thought Liz Marsh was dead." I bite my lip.

"Yara—"

"Your turn."

"I can arrest you for obstructing an investigation."

"Only I'm not obstructing," I say. "I don't know Liz Marsh. I didn't even know Felicia, remember? But I'm hearing lots of oral history." A lie. Kinda. Not only oral history. Written down and official police history, too.

"This is stupid," Kayla says, then sighs. "An anonymous caller tells me that they know who forced Felicia Campbell into that lake. I'm supposed to meet this person tonight, and it would be great to have an idea who it may be before I go traipsing into the Red Roof Inn an hour before midnight."

Red Roof Inn at eleven o'clock? That's *never* a good idea.

I push out a breath. "Fine. Felicia reported Elizabeth Marsh missing in 1998, but she wasn't missing. Even when presented with evidence,

Felicia continued to believe Liz was dead. That is, until Friday night, when Liz invited her to dinner at Bucelli's near the Walmart."

Kayla doesn't speak.

"Hello? You still there?"

"Yeah, I'm here." But she sounds hollow. "You *talked* to Liz?"

"We've texted."

"She say anything else?"

"Not really." I wait a beat. "Do you *want* her to say something?"

"How about, 'I forced that bitch into Lake Palmdale'? Mind if I take your—"

"No, you cannot."

"You don't even know what I'm about to ask—"

"You cannot have my phone right now." I snort. "Dude, I'm in the middle of party planning. On Sunday, if you still need it, I'll lend it to you, but right now—"

"We can look at cell phone—"

"No." I peek out my window to the Martian-red world we're in. Along with the howling winds, I hear shrieking car alarms.

"Is this Liz Marsh dangerous?" Kayla asks.

I cock my head. "She's a stalker type. A bit obsessive. Holds a grudge. She told Felicia to leave her alone and Felicia ignored her request and now look." I cock my head. "Your turn."

"The DNA from Will Harraway doesn't match the DNA found on his wife."

"Doesn't mean he wasn't involved," I point out. "Men hire other people to do it."

"True," Kayla says.

"You have Felicia's phone," I say. "She must've been texting Liz all this time."

"She was. All numbers go to various burner phones, though."

"Do those numbers to burner phones match the number of the anonymous tipper?"

Kayla doesn't respond. Either she hadn't thought of that, *or* she had and one of the numbers from the burner phones matches.

My hotel window rattles. Eventually, the dust will clear, but I'll find myself in another dimension, just like the characters in *The Tommyknockers*.

"I should get back to work," Kayla says. "Let me know if you learn anything else?"

"Sure," I say, fingers crossed. "Be careful tonight."

I'll be watching.

51.

In just forty minutes, everything has been covered in fine, reddish-brown dust. The skies are blue again as though nothing happened. For the rest of the week, the county will sound like one giant vacuum cleaner. As I make my way home, pebbles on the road pop against my windshield and the body of my Jeep, threatening to crack the glass and continue their mission of ruining my paint job. My sinuses have swollen, and pressure is building around my eyes. I know this feeling: I'll soon need more than an inhaler, but hopefully the sinus infection won't fully hit me until Sunday.

My phone vibrates from the Jeep's center console.

A text message from Elizabeth Marsh.

Yes! Maybe I can ask her—

What are you doing?? she texts.

You need to stop before I lose control!!!
I've worked hard to move on
You are forcing me to remember the worst time of my life
Are you selfish like your mother???

My heart drops with every whoosh of text that fills my phone. I don't mean to . . . I didn't aim to . . .

If you want to ruin my life
I will be happy to ruin yours
and Bee's
and Rob's
I will fuck you up!!!!!
You people took everything from me!!!!!

My hands shake. After I pull into the driveway, I grab my phone.
I'm so sorry!! I text back.

I apologize for hurting you
Please don't think my questions are out of disrespect
Felicia is dead
I'm just trying to make sense of everything

Breathless, I bite the cuticle around my thumb and stare at the
screen.
The last thing I want is to—

LEAVE ME ALONE!!!
If you don't
I know where you are
I know what car you drive
I know that you live in Santa Monica

My phone fills with pictures: the outside view of my apartment
building, my IMDb page of writing credits, and a picture of me *today*
with my jacket pressed against my face.
What have I done?
My face burns. I've opened the sarcophagus. I've said "Bloody
Mary" three times in front of a bathroom mirror. I've whispered
"Beetlejuice" and "Rumpelstiltskin" and now . . .

I text, I'm so sorry and sit in my Jeep, thinking about nothing and everything.

Why did I even *reach out* to this woman?

I'm warning you, Liz Marsh texts.

Lose my number TODAY!!!

⚡

No one's home. The mounds of dust from the driveway to the porch are undisturbed.

I plod up the stairs to my bedroom, numb, heavy-headed, thick-chested. My bag is weighed down with items taken from the plastic tub, including the answering machine and mini cassettes as well as the key to Elizabeth Marsh's post office box. I change into sweatpants and a tank top, and for a moment, I stand in the middle of my dull-colored bedroom, breathing in more polluted air, letting my eyes adjust to the weird-colored sunshine.

I climb into bed, wrap the comforter over my body, and listen to the rattle in my chest. I don't think I'll be able to sneak to the Red Roof Inn tonight.

Someone knocks on the door.

I shout, "Yeah?" from beneath the comforter.

Whoever it is peels the duvet from around my head.

The sudden light makes me blink.

Dominique stands over me. Her hair and makeup are flawless. "We need to sweep before Mom gets—wow. You look worse than you did yesterday."

I frown at her. "Thanks."

She holds up a large bag from the hobby store. "There was a sale on frames, and I got holders for all the little pieces of whatever you want people to look at. And I picked up the big picture of Mom and Dad since I was there."

"Thanks." I sit up in bed and nod toward the window. "I don't miss this at all."

She settles beside me. "Didn't use to be this bad. If they keep ripping up all the vegetation to build houses, it's gonna be just like the Dust Bowl out here."

"You sounded so smart just then."

"You must be proud." She rests her chin on my shoulder, and we stare out at the hawk circling the now-clear sky.

"Lemme see the canvas print," I ask.

She scrambles out of my room and through the bathroom. Seconds later, she returns with the large print of our parents wearing their wedding clothes. They're holding hands and facing each other as that cloudy sky above them reflects across the pool.

Dominique's face brightens as she traces their image in the water. "They look like two totally different people. They must've been totally happy once."

I chuckle. "That one day in September 2007?"

"Christmas morning 2012?" Dominique scrunches her eyebrows. "Nice while it lasted."

I peer at her. She's not being snarky or flippant. She's not even looking at me and expecting a response.

My phone rings.

"Is that your *boyfriend*?" Dominique teases.

"Ha. Yes, it is." I answer with, "Hey, you."

Dominique shouts, "Hi, Shane!"

He shouts back, "Hi, Dominique!" To me, he says, "I still have your inhaler."

"I know. I'll try to get one from the pharmacy here."

"If not," he says, "I'll drive up."

"An hour-and-a-half drive just for one inhaler?"

"I need you to breathe," he says. "But I'm not calling about that."

Dominique is slipping the print back into its protective sheet. She doesn't seem to be listening, but she probably is.

"Remember when you said that you didn't know if Elizabeth Marsh was still married to the guy she left, or if she'd had two more husbands after him?"

I nod. "Yeah."

"She was married only once," he says.

My eyebrows lift. "Awesome."

"Yara," Dominique whispers.

I look over my shoulder. She's saying something, pointing to something, but Shane's still talking. I give her a thumbs-up and say to Shane, "I missed that. What?"

"I found their marriage license."

I grab a pen and my notebook from the nightstand. "Okay."

"Yara," he says, "there's one license for Elizabeth Marsh and . . . Robert Gibson."

I've stopped writing.

"*Your* Robert Gibson," he says. "Your dad."

The pen cracks in my grip.

"So," Shane continues, "I searched for *Robert Louis Gibson* and *Barbara Nicole McGuire*, and I found a marriage license for them, too."

Dad married two women?

"Bigamy?" I ask.

"No," Shane says. "He divorced Marsh, so your parents' marriage is legal."

Dominique is staring at me with question marks in her eyes.

I force myself to smile. "Work," I whisper to her.

Shane says, "I'm sending you pictures of the licenses and certificates of marriage."

My phone bings, and I say, "Thanks. I'll call you back," before hanging up.

There's Elizabeth Marie Marsh, daughter of Sheldon Allen Marsh and Maryam Elizabeth Unger. There's Robert Louis Gibson Jr., son of Robert Louis Gibson Sr. and Audrey Soares. Date of marriage: August 16, 1992, in Bel Air, County of Los Angeles, State of California.

Why didn't Mom and Dad tell me this? Why didn't Mom tell me that she and Liz had been more than *frenemies*? One had been a first wife and the other . . .

"And the divorce?" I can barely talk because my heart is skidding around my chest.

My phone bings a second time.

Petitioner: Robert L. Gibson Jr.

Respondent: Elizabeth M. Marsh

Notice of Entry of Judgment

You are notified that the following judgment was entered on October 12, 1998.

The "DISSOLUTION" option is checked.

October 12, 1998 . . .

I was born on April 25, 1995.

Dad cheated on Elizabeth Marsh.

And Mom, *not Liz*, was the other woman.

52.

Dad married Elizabeth Marsh.

Dad divorced Elizabeth Marsh.

Dad married Mom.

What the *hell?*

Dominique cocks an eyebrow at me, but once her phone rings, she forgets that I'm here. She smiles, says, "Thinking about you, too," then slinks out of my bedroom to talk to Ransom.

I hide my face between my knees and squeeze my eyes shut. My heartbeat is like the roar and rumble of cannon fire.

Breathe . . . breathe . . . What would Cookie do?

I dare lift my head.

A good first step. She'd have a drink, go to the shooting range, call her ex and fall into bed with him, then slip into the darkness as he sleeps.

But I don't drink like that. I don't shoot guns. My boyfriend is a world away. This shit hurts, and no matter my talent with a pen, Cookie is not real.

Odd, mustard-colored light that always shines after dust storms glows across the carpet. The windows aren't rattling. No, that noise comes from the mucus in my lungs and the trapped sludge pooling in my head. It's just the manic pounding of my heart.

Mom and Dad lied to me.

He had a whole other wife?

They had a whole other *life*?

Did Dad and Liz divorce because of her desertion? Because of her illness? Or did all that happen because Mom and Dad were having an affair? Because Mom had *me*.

What did my mother have to do with their ending?

Now, Liz seems reasonable in her anger. Moving to the freaking Virgin Islands—as far away as you can get from Los Angeles while still being in the US—also seems reasonable.

I need a drink.

Wait.

I race out of my room and down the stairs to the mail basket near the front door. I flip through bills and grocery store circulars and . . .

This. The mailing label on this magazine. *Beth Gibson.*

We're still getting *mail* for her? Did she live here *in this house*?

"Ohmigod." The living room spins, and my knees give, and I land on the bottom step. My hands shake as I stare at *Crochet World.* Did she make blankets and teakettle cozies and . . . ?

Mom's Louis Vuitton duffel bag. It's back in the nook, collecting dust bunnies again and serving as a constant reminder to Dad. That Mom would leave him just like his first wife did.

I hide my face in my lap. "I can't stay here right now."

I wobble to the front door and step out to the porch.

Now I'm walking toward the foothills and the endless dirt and the round rocks, sage, and chapparal. It's so hot out here that my tears dry as soon as they fall down my cheeks. As I walk I taste salt and grit, and I cough because my feet kick up dirt, because out here in the untamed, uncultivated wasteland, there's still wind and dust devils and danger.

I trudge toward those foothills, not sure what I will do once I reach the first hill or the fourth. There are so many hills stacked one behind another that I could walk forever.

A scorpion scrambles across my path.

I stop in my step and watch as it slips beneath a boulder.

I don't wanna turn around and look behind me. Because then, I'll have to see our house of lies, this city of dirt, everything that I hate and have always fought against believing to be true. In my heart of hearts, in my darkest imaginations, though . . . I knew that our house was haunted.

That's why I never slept well there.

That's why I escaped (and hid those times I couldn't escape) by writing stories about heroines like Cookie who fought against boogeymen, real and imagined, heroines who constantly struggled to understand people's motivations and potential for evil.

The dark terrifies me. Being abandoned terrifies me. These fears didn't randomly spring from the earth. They were planted and cultivated by the people who were supposed to protect me and love me the most.

All this time, we were a lie.

My head falls back, and I scream, "Damn it!" to the sky.

The sun dips behind the western hills, and the sky turns persimmon and puce. Soon, coyotes and mountain lions will leave their dens and start the hunt for food. The desert is the last place I should be alone at night. I don't know what to do next except—

I yelp.

A stranger wearing a hoodie—the same black hoodie from the break-in—stands just a few feet away from me. A black gaiter covers the lower half of the stranger's face. Sunglasses hide their eyes.

I take a step back. "Please, don't—"

The stalker lunges at me.

I scream and run toward the setting sun. I wheeze as fire zigzags through my lungs, and although I slow down, I don't stop moving.

The stalker grabs my hair and pulls.

I fall back.

Crack.

My head hits the desert floor. Dust finds its way into my mouth, eyes, and nose. My right hand slaps at the intruder's face, neck, and gaiter as my left hand claws at the ground in search of a broken piece of glass, a rock, or *this*!

Jagged slate.

The stalker's hands press at my mouth and against my throat.

Not breathing for a short period of time?

I do this too many times a year.

In my head, I'm screaming, but there's no sound coming from my mouth.

The world around me grows dimmer . . . darker . . .

I swing my left hand across my attacker's face.

"Shit!" That voice . . . could be male, female, brown bear, I can't hear anything over the frantic chaos happening between my ears. The attacker rears back and clutches their face, then gapes at the glistening blood there.

I lunge at this monster, aiming that piece of slate at the eyes just how Shane showed all the *Tough Cookie* writers as we beat out a fight scene.

The stranger blocks my jab and kicks my thigh.

I fall but scramble to my feet. My hands shine with slick blood, but I don't drop my weapon. No, I carry it as I run the most raggedy run I've ever run. All of me hurts until none of me hurts. My home is a mirage, and even as I run toward it, the house doesn't get any closer.

I cry out. "Help!" maybe, or "Stop!" or . . .

Yes. I wanna stop.

Yes. I'm gonna stop.

And I stop.

And I fall.

Way up in heaven, Sirius burns in the sky, bright and blue.

My lungs are deflated accordions, and soon, I will suffocate.

Okay. I'm okay. Let whatever happens . . . *happen.* None of this is real anyway.

We lie here.

The rest of this . . .

It's just a mirage.

HOW TO LI(V)E

53.

I've failed.

The cheek gashes sting from the free-falling teardrops.

Maybe one day, Yara will suffocate to death out there in the desert.

Maybe one day, a coyote or bobcat will find her, and she'll die that way.

"Maybe." That's another word for failure.

Only losers are uncertain.

I'm a loser. Just like they always said.

Time to bail, to switch teams—for real, this time.

It's not too late.

Snitches get stitches.

But I won't be around long enough to get jumped.

Fuck Palmdale and everybody who lives in this dump.

54.

One eye opens.

The world . . . just a blur . . . can't see . . .

My second eye . . . stuck . . . dark, still dark . . .

Beep . . . beep . . . beep . . .

What *is* that . . . ?

My second eye pulls apart slightly . . . Something sticky holds my eyelashes together.

Beep . . . beep . . . beep . . .

No pain.

Light. Almost floaty.

Life's a blur.

"She's awake."

I know that voice.

I try to move my head, but sharp pain pushes at me, no more floaty feeling . . .

"Yaya, it's Dom."

My sister.

My lips crack open. In my head, I hear my question, but after those words travel from my brain to reach my mouth, all that I'm left with is: "Where . . . ?"

"Hospital." She inches closer to me, and her maroon-colored lips lift into a smile.

Another question forms in my head, but I can only say, "Why?"

"You were attacked." Her words wobble on the air.

I squint against the brightness of her tears. My head hurts, and I think about . . . about . . .

Palmdale did it.

This city killed me.

⚡

Beep . . . beep . . . beep . . .

Mom stands over me, frowning. "There she is." She forces herself to smile.

Dad's eyes flare with fear. "Yaya, we're here."

Are you?

⚡

Sunlight creeps across my blanket. I'm wake again with both eyes open this time. A machine connects to a network of tubes that end in the back of my left hand and the crook of my elbow. I take a deep breath and don't hear myself wheeze.

"Progress," Dominique says. "Happy Friday."

I clear my throat, and my mouth tastes like blood and rot, metal and mucus.

Dominique hands me a cup of water and watches as I take long sips through the straw. "I FaceTimed with Shane. He blows my phone up, like, every hour to check on you. He's in San Francisco for a court case, but he's gonna call me the moment he leaves the courtroom. He says you two are gonna work on your comic timing."

I chuckle and whisper, "Thanks."

She scooches her chair closer to me. "You have to stop digging around and asking people questions. Somebody really got pissed enough to—"

"Jump me in the desert? And who have I bothered with questions? You? Mom? Kayla?"

"Just stop, okay?" she says.

"You haven't asked what sent me running to the desert in the first place."

"Cuz I don't care, Yara. Did you see who jumped you?"

"No," I say. "They wore the same hoodie the prowler wore. A black gaiter. Sunglasses."

She releases a held breath. "Okay."

"Did you think I was gonna recognize him?" I ask.

"*Him?* What does *that* mean?"

"You just seem relieved," I say, eyebrow high. "Who do you think I may have seen?"

Dominique sits back in the chair and massages her temples. "No idea. This whole thing is just crazy. You come here, and all—"

"Dad was married before he married Mom."

She gawks at me. "*What?*"

I tell her about the marriage certificate and divorce decree for Dad and Elizabeth Marsh. "I think Liz jumped me. She texted that she'd hurt me if I didn't leave her alone."

Dominique holds up a hand and shakes her head. "Stop. No. I don't wanna hear."

"You need to know the truth."

She swipes at her tears with the back of her wrist. "I can't take any more truth."

I clutch a pillow to my chest. "I wanna cancel the party." The words taste slick as snot, but saying them leaves me light and almost refreshed. I should enjoy this feeling before Mom squeezes it out of me.

Dominique yanks tissues from the box on the nightstand. "Fine. I don't care anymore. It's your money." She blows her nose and pushes out of the chair. "I never really wanted this stupid party, but you had to work out your mommy issues and bribe her with a party to love you more, and see what happened? The Ghost of fucking Christmas Past is trying to take you out, and now, canceling this party that never should've happened anyway will make her like you even less. Good job. Hope you're happy."

The puff of air from the opening door washes over me, and I gape at the now-empty chair. Sunlight has moved from my thighs to my feet, but my prickling fright is managed by a cocktail of drugs.

A freckle-faced nurse wearing pink scrubs pops in to take my vitals. Her plastic name tag says MAITLYN, and I wonder if I knew her from high school. "We're gonna let you go in a few hours," she tells me. "Your father's picking you up. The doctor's already put in prescriptions for amoxicillin, prednisone, and Vicodin for your injuries. But wow, your respiratory system is really messed up. That dust storm didn't help *at all*. When you got here, your oxygenation level was at ninety percent."

"Geez," I say. "That's pretty bad."

"You should probably find a way to quit smoking. We have special programs—"

"I don't smoke. You smell my mother's cigarettes."

"Ah. That sucks for you, then." She chuckles. "Anyway, whoever it was really roughed you up, but those are all surface injuries. It's what inside that counts."

No truer words, Maitlyn.

As I flip from television show to television show, my door opens again.

It's Kayla. "Knock knock."

I say, "Who's there?"

"Owls go."

"Owls go who?"

"They certainly do." She hugs me, and her touch spikes my skin like millipede feet. "So is this, like, the special two-hour season finale with you? I mean, Yara. *Dude.*"

I laugh. "Tune in next time."

Kayla plops into the chair Dominique abandoned. She wears a brown sports coat that muddles her complexion and kills the sparks in her eyes. "We're pretty sure who jumped you. The same person who slashed your tires."

"Yeah?"

She nods. "The last time I visited the cabin at Lake Paz, I asked the neighbor lady a few questions, and she gave me this." Kayla cues up a video on her phone.

"She showed me that video," I say, shaking my head. "Couldn't see a face."

"Right," Kayla says. "But another one of their cameras had a better vantage point."

Like before, the stranger slashes my left back tire, then the right back, then the passenger front tire, and, finally, the driver's side. The stranger hustles away and looks back at the cabin. But this time, once the hoodie slips back, I see the face.

I know that face.

I know *her* face. I whisper, "LaRain?"

"Yep. And yesterday, after the attack, one of your neighbors saw her running away toward Ritter Siphon. We don't know where she is right now, but we'll find her." She squints at me. "Why is she targeting you like this?"

My throat is tight. I can only shake my head.

"Strange, right?"

I nod. "Did the anonymous caller show up at Red Roof Inn last night?"

She shakes her head. "Remember when I took your DNA to compare against the DNA found beneath Felicia's fingernails?"

"Yes."

"The results came back and . . . you are *not* the father." She grins.

I snort, not surprised.

"I asked Dom for her DNA."

336

"Why?"

"Because you both told me that she grabbed your necklace from Felicia's hand. So there was touching and a possible transfer of skin cells."

"But wouldn't our DNA be the same?"

"Not completely, but yes, you'd both share mitochondrial or maternal DNA. I know, I know, but if this case goes to court, I don't wanna be the Mark Fuhrman of the LA Sheriff's Department. I wanna say that I did everything and collected everything I was supposed to, and I didn't let my friendship with the Gibson family override my duty or judgment."

"What did Dom say to your request?" I ask.

Kayla smirks. "Take a guess."

"Did she give it?"

"Ultimately, she didn't have a choice. Especially after I told her that your parents had."

My eyes widen. "*What?* Why?"

Kayla bites her lip, then takes a deep breath. "Because that letter we found in Felicia's car? Their fingerprints were all over it."

55.

Kayla's words make no sense. "There has to be a good explanation," I say, near tears. The hospital room goes all wiggly. The television has doubled, and there's suddenly too much light.

Kayla's face flushes. "We talked about—"

"*We?*"

"Your parents. We talked all day today. About the letter, about some other stuff. That's why you haven't seen them."

I gape at her. "You *arrested my parents?*"

"No! No, no, no." Her green eyes bug. "Just asked them some questions." She pats my hand. "Calm down. They told me all that I needed to know. I'm totally caught up now."

"On?"

The bags beneath Kayla's eyes have darkened just in the minutes she's sat with me. "Family spectacle." She pauses, peers at the IV bag hanging from the pole, and stands. "Get some rest, Yara. I'll call and check on you later."

An hour later, Dad pushes me in a wheelchair to the Suburban. Women flick their eyes at the bald, tall man with the easy smile.

I carry my bags of meds and dirty, bloody clothes on my lap and squint against the still-bright day. Outside the hospital, the world smells like dust and Del Taco. I want to flip down the truck's visor to see the damage, but I wimp out. My skin feels busted and tight, my hair coarse, tangled. My tongue feels too fat and full of blood, and my muscles—my heart, too—feel like they're pumping too much of everything for me to just be sitting here.

"You good?" Dad asks.

I nod, lying. "Thank you for picking me up."

"No place I'd rather be than taking care of my girl." He smiles a true smile with light in his eyes.

The potholes we hit during our short drive make my stomach wobble and my head brighten with pain. Dad sings along with the Doobie Brothers, telling me in between the verse and chorus that the group guest starred in a very special episode of *What's Happening!!* back in the day.

The Suburban keeps hitting potholes. I keep wincing.

He glances at me each time the truck dips. "We'll be home in three minutes."

I clear my throat and say, "Maybe . . . Well . . . I don't think we should have the party. I don't think it's a good idea at this point."

He sends his eyes to the rearview mirror, then exhales. A hint of a smile plays on the edges of his lips. "To be honest, I don't wanna have this party, either. We're not in a good place right now, but that doesn't surprise you, right? Your mother, though. It's all she's talked about, and whatever Barbara wants, Barbara gets."

Trembling with anger, I grab hold of the door handle to calm myself.

He thinks this admission protects him from any heat I'm about to hurl his way. He doesn't know that *I* know that he's lied to me. He doesn't know that *I* know he's had another life prior to Mom. That he and Elizabeth Marsh hadn't even been *divorced* for a year before he and Mom married. That it was obvious he and Mom had an affair back then.

Dad follows the road that brings us closer to home. Every sound scrapes my nerves—from the retching whir of the tires against asphalt to the squeak of the back of my head rubbing against the headrest. Michael McDonald's singing makes me wanna cry.

"LaRain jumped me," I whisper.

His jaw tightens. "Yeah. Kayla told us. They can't find her."

"Who's Beth?"

His knuckles whiten as he squeezes the steering wheel. The spots at his temple and the scoop of his neck pulse.

"Beth Gibson," I say. "There's a magazine at home with her name on it. Who is she?"

He chews the inside of his cheek. "No clue. Probably just junk mail. Magazine companies sell lists of people's names. One year, we received a subscription for a whole year for someone named Allyne Stanley. I don't know anybody named—"

"You're a liar," I say. "And you know what? It's fine. I now understand Mom a little better than I did just a week ago. I see why she's been such an asshole to you."

"Yara—"

"I don't wanna hear anymore," I say. "My head hurts. My heart hurts. You didn't want this party after I've spent time, effort, and money putting it together, and I wish I'd just stayed in LA and not bothered with this place until Thanksgiving. I hate it here."

We don't talk for the rest of the trip. He comes to my side of the truck to open the door, take my bags of pills and clothes, and help me up the porch steps.

Mom waits for me at the front door. She brushes my hair away from my face and kisses my forehead. She wraps her arms around me. She's wearing the most "Mom" outfit she owns: a pink fluffy sweater and capri leggings. No makeup. Headband and ponytail. "You okay?"

My skin feels hot and feverish. Her touch hurts. I say, "No," then ease out of her grip.

As I work my way up the staircase, she asks Dad, "What happened?" I don't hear his answer. Doesn't matter. He'd be wrong anyway.

Mom has cleaned my bedroom and changed the linens to shades of yellow. The vaporizer sends plumes of steam into the air. The shortbread candle flickers from the bureau. A drinking glass and a pitcher of cold water sit on the nightstand. Beads of condensation make a puddle that now drips onto the carpet.

Such a lovely prison.

Mom joins me in the room and doesn't speak as she arranges my pill vials on the nightstand. She helps me out of my jacket and shoes, then helps me change into boxers and a pajama top. After I dip beneath the duvet, she hands me the television remote control. Once I settle on *The Office*, she opens one pill vial after the next. I'm on an intensive regimen to control my asthma and respiratory infection as well as painkillers for injuries that resulted from being assaulted by my mother's best friend. We haven't even unpacked *that* yet.

She retreats to the door. "Need anything else?"

What did Kayla ask you?

Why did LaRain try to kill me?

Why did you sleep with a married man?

Why were your fingerprints on that letter to Felicia?

Need anything else?

I need answers.

I say, "No."

She waits a beat, frowns, then says, "Fine."

Fine.

We are so far from fine.

56.

I open my eyes, and the bedroom smells medicinal again, with the added notes of infected mucus and healing cuts. Dominique finds me in bed, half-asleep and watching *That '70s Show*. She holds a cup of peppermint tea, probably an offering from our mother. She's stripped her face of makeup. Her nose is red, her eyes puffy. She's been crying.

I ask, "You okay?"

She gives a small shrug, then sets the tea mug on the nightstand.

"You wanna talk about it?"

She shakes her head. "You talk to Shane?"

I squint. "I think so."

Dominique tries to smile. "He said you were totally out of it."

Beneath the laugh track of the sitcom, I hear unfamiliar murmuring somewhere in the house. "Who's here?"

"Auntie Cece and Uncle Skip. She's gone platinum blonde again," Dominique says. "And it's buzzed close to the scalp. She looks good. Tired. Sad. But y'know: *hot.*"

I sit up in bed, and the bones in my neck and face creak. I take the mug. "She mad?"

Dominique shakes her head. "Just . . ." She sighs. "My words aren't working right now."

"I was wondering . . . why did LaRain jump me? Why would she slash my tires?"

Dominique takes a deep breath and releases it through clenched teeth. "Probably because she knows how you feel about Ransom. You think he's trash. And you think she's Mom's slave and guinea pig and not her own person. You always have. She hates you for that, for looking down on them. She's hated you since we were kids."

"I don't think she's trash," I whisper. "I don't spend my days thinking about LaRain."

"See? She's no one to you."

"Why do this *now*, though?"

Dominique cants her head. "Menopause?"

I point at her. "But *that's* what I'm talking about. I mean . . . I don't want you to be with someone whose mother would straight *kill* someone else because she's insulted or having a hot flash. Who will she come for next? Mom? Dad? *You?* Do you understand what I'm saying?"

Dominique pads to the other side of my bed and grabs pillows that fell to the carpet.

Downstairs, Cece laughs, and it's musical and light as a xylophone. Mom says something, but her words sound blurry.

"Do you feel like you *can't* leave him?" I ask.

Dominique throws up her hands. "Ohmigod, Yara!"

"It's a real thing, Dom. Women feel stuck, that he'll kill you if you try to—"

"Stop."

"I can help you. Shane knows people—"

"You are so *extra*." Dominique shakes her head. "Now you're getting the US freaking Marshals to free me? From *what?*"

I lean back in bed, one arm over my head, my dissatisfaction as heavy as the moon. "Okay. Do what you want. I'm leaving soon, and you and Ransom can continue to be ratchet together. When he beats your ass, or LaRain comes back and does it for him, I'll send a moving van to pick up your furniture and a few of your teeth."

She grabs a pillow from the carpet and tosses it to the foot of my bed. "Wow."

"Yeah. Wow. We don't have to talk about him or you anymore. I'm done."

"Oh," she says, lip curled. "So now, you won't pay for school?"

"No," I say. "I'll keep paying. Just so we'll be clear who's at fault when you drop out, have baby number three, and lose parts of yourself because Ransom's hands got away from him *again*. I want *you* to know and to remember that I was *never* the enemy, that I wanted better for you." I squint at her. "Go 'head on with your bad self. I know how this story ends."

"You have *completely* lost it." She laughs, but there's something in her tone that signals reluctance, that maybe I haven't *completely* lost it. She settles beside me in bed, another sign that she worries that I'm right. We sit in silence, until . . . "Mom says you're mad at her and Dad."

"I don't wanna deal with them, either."

"Because they lied?" Dominique chuckles and arranges her braids into a high bun. "Dude, you are so tender. No wonder you stay medicated."

"We don't have to talk, either, you know," I snarl. "And I was fine before I came *here*." Losing keys, credit cards, index cards, having nightmares, smoking, getting hypnotized, slowly feeling peeled away . . . Not fine.

I shake my head to clear it, then say, "And where's my pendant? You said you'd fix it."

"And I *did* fix it. I put it on the dresser."

I shake my head. "It isn't there."

"Maybe you lost it like you lost *Beloved*."

"Or maybe you just didn't put it there."

Her lips tighten. "So I'm lying now?"

"Why not? It's the Gibson family's honored tradition."

She rolls her eyes. "You're really shook that Mom and Dad lied to you?"

"They lied to you, too."

"They were young, Yara. Our age. And what the hell do either of us know right now about living? Clothes, cars, and dick—that's what I care about *today*. You're the one who promised to buy me a pony if I got my degree and didn't get married."

"Cuz you're young," I say. "You don't know who you are away from this house, away from the Antelope Valley."

She waggles her head. "I agree. That's what I'm saying about Mom and Dad. He obviously got caught up with the female equivalent of Ransom, but back in the olden days, they had to get married. It wasn't working out, so he was side dickin' this hot chick named Barbara, and she got pregnant with you. He divorced old gal and married Mom. Kids being stupid and playing grown-up games. They wouldn't be the first. Obviously."

Tears burn in my eyes because, intellectually, this makes sense and Dominique is right. Emotionally, though? Our house was built upon the sand and now—for me at least—our foundation is being washed away.

Dominique shakes out my next dose of antibiotics. "Does it suck that you planned all this for Saturday and now your face is swollen because Mom's ratchet BFF let her fists fly? Yes, and I'd be pissed at *that*." She waves her hand, then snaps her fingers. "The math around our parents, though? Let that go."

The pills slide down my throat as bitter as the truth I'm learning about my family.

Someone's crying in the room beneath me.

"Kayla told me she took your DNA," I say.

My sister sucks her teeth. "I barely touched Felicia that day."

I rest my head on her shoulder. "Same, but she's gotta do her job." I pause, then add, "Especially since our parents' fingerprints were on this letter they found in Felicia's car."

Dominique picks at her nails. "I really don't care about Felicia. She was messy and disturbed. Cece said the same thing, like twenty minutes ago. And by the way, I *did* fix the pendant. You were talking to Shane when I put it on the dresser."

I grunt, remembering, not remembering. My head pain turns from sharp to fuzzy, and my eyelids droop. I hear myself snore a few times, and I shift as Dominique eases out of my bed. She sets the remote control on the pillow and kisses my forehead.

The world dims . . . dims . . .

⚡

I awaken, breathless, gasping, pulse pounding.

My eyes skip around the room.

The world outside my window is dark now. The television screen brightens the room and makes shadows twist against the walls. Where am I?

Home.

Palmdale.

Bedroom.

I'd been underwater again. Sharp rocks poking my bare feet . . . Croaking frogs . . . Cold, so cold . . . I'd screamed and water had filled my mouth, my lungs . . .

The nightmare.

Feels like I'm trapped in solidifying gelatin and moving in slow motion. I rub my creaky face, then grab a bottle of water from the nightstand. The clock on the DVD/VCR says it's five minutes after nine. The murmuring has moved outside.

"All right now," Aunt Cece says from the driveway. I can barely make out her words. "You let me know."

Mom shouts back, "I will. Love you."

"Love you, too," Aunt Cece says.

Car doors slam. A car engine starts. The front door closes.

On broadcast television, local news anchor Pat Harvey queues up the next story. Something about a body found in a car a few miles northwest of Palmdale, near Rogers Creek. "Los Angeles County Sheriff's Deputy Detective Kayla Kozlowski says this vehicle may be connected to the murder of an aeronautics executive—"

Felicia?

The world is blurry, so I crawl to the foot of the bed to see those shots of the light-colored compact car. This car looks like the one that pulled into the parking lot behind Felicia's Benz. As I reach to the nightstand for my glasses, I knock over bottles of water, pill vials, eye drops . . .

Was I wearing glasses when LaRain jumped me?

If so, they could've fallen off and landed behind our house.

I close my eyes and try to remember.

Probably?

I search beneath my bed for my glasses as Pat Harvey says, "Detectives are still in the process of identifying the woman in the car and determining if her death is a matter of foul play."

Woman?

57.

Even at this time of night, the house makes noise. The refrigerator crunches and upchucks ice cubes into the freezer bucket. The toilets' water tanks hiss and fill. The thermostat clicks, and the vents send frigid air to cool the rooms.

But this noise isn't the reason why I can't sleep.

I can't sleep because there was a news story about a dead woman found in a car. I can't sleep because I can't find my glasses. Because I tried to sleep, and that nightmare kept seeping into my dreams, and I keep being pulled underwater only for my head to hit a rock and explode like dynamite. I can't sleep because . . .

Beth Gibson.

Dad really tried to pretend that he didn't know that name, but I saw the way his hands gripped the steering wheel, how his knuckles whitened and popped like ball bearings. How the vein in his throat pounded against his skin.

I steal over to the closet and reach into the darkness for the plastic tub I took from the cabin. I hid it beneath my suitcase and a blanket because I don't want Mom to know it exists. I grab the binder of statements and go through more papers only to find . . .

Partial transcript of 911 call
OPERATOR: 911. What is your emergency?

CALLER: I'm at my family's cabin—we're visiting from LA. I just drove up and my family . . . they're not here.

OPERATOR: Okay.

CALLER: I've been calling all morning but she's . . . she's not answering. And it looks like . . . There's blood here.

OPERATOR: What is the address of the cabin?

CALLER: 1224 Stardust Way, Lake Paz, the green cabin.

OPERATOR: Tell me what happened.

CALLER: They aren't here. Things are turned over. There's blood, not a lot of it, but there's blood, I don't know whose blood and . . . I freaked out and drove around in case there'd been an accident but our car—it's in the garage and there's a note from her, I think it's from her, and . . . she's . . . I don't know where . . .

OPERATOR: Stay on the line with me, sir. Okay?

CALLER: Are you on your way?

Had Daddy been the caller?

I push aside the folders, photographs, and all the other stuff that's already told me about Elizabeth Marsh, and I find a tan Kinney shoe-box, men's size 11.

Inside: title papers for 1224 Stardust Way. That's the cabin at Lake Paz owned by Sheldon and Maryam Marsh, my father's . . . former in-laws. There are insurance letters.

> Re: Policy AZ-3678-5002
>
> Dear Elizabeth Marsh:
>
> This letter is in response to a recent inquiry regard-
> ing the above-mentioned policy. The face amount of the
> policy is $2,500,000 with an issue date of July 14, 1989.

Also inside: a slick piece of paper with a baby's footprints at the bottom. But the type has faded, and the purple-ink footprints have ghosted. There's an infant's identification bracelet taped to this sheet of paper—it's the tag that newborns wear at the hospital. The print on the tiny identification band is also faded, and my eyes are too weak to read any remaining print.

Are these Elizabeth Marsh's footprints?

Or . . .

Elizabeth's daughter?

My spine sags because ohmigod . . .

She and Dad *did* have a child together.

Did Felicia know this, and that was yet one more reason she came to see me?

Is Felicia dead because . . . ?

Did my father . . . ?

He's not a murderer.

Right?

I need to talk to Elizabeth Marsh Gibson.

Daddy has already lied to me by omission, and if he's the one who . . . ? No, I can't ask him. Mom would freak out if there's even a *hint* of me knowing all that I know. Then again, what if she *doesn't* know all that I know?

And now, with trembling hands, I grab my phone from the nightstand and tap the number for Elizabeth Marsh. Yes, she told me that she didn't want to be bothered. Yes, she threatened to hug me to death if I did. She may choose to ignore me, unless she's just been found in a light-colored car miles away from here.

Outside my room, something thumps.

I hold the phone away from my ear and hear . . .

Thumping.

Has LaRain returned to end me for good?

The squinty-eyed mystery man in the green Mazda . . . could it be him?

Thump.

Someone's here.

Or maybe it's Dominique pacing out on the porch?

I grab the hunting knife from beneath my mattress and hold the phone in my other hand. I can make an emergency call at a moment's notice.

I take a deep breath and slowly . . . *slowly* . . . open my bedroom door.

The hallway is dark and empty. My parents' bedroom door is closed. Dominique's bedroom door is open. I creep to the staircase.

Downstairs, the water cooler hums. The thermostat clicks, and cool air whooshes through the ducts. My hair lifts with the chilled breeze, and new goose bumps join the old.

I whisper, "Dom, that you?"

The thermostat cuts off, and the house falls into silence again.

I hear . . .

My heartbeat.

My breathing . . .

Mrs. Duncan's faraway wind chimes . . .

I squint into the kitchen.

The light above the range shines bright in the night, but shadows lurk near the kitchen door and laundry room. Four wineglasses sit in the dish-drying rack. A filled ashtray sits on the bay window ledge with cigarette butts stained by two different shades of lipstick.

That's right. Auntie Cece stopped by.

I tiptoe through the empty dining room to the living room. The front door is locked. The powder room behind the staircase . . .

With my diminished vision, the prowler could be hiding behind the breakfast counter.

There's no one behind the breakfast counter.

I release the breath I've been holding, but I won't release the knife. If I could carry this knife forever, I would.

Sleepy now, I plop on the couch in the den and wipe my sweaty forehead with the tail of my T-shirt. For the second time, I dial Elizabeth Marsh's—

There it is again!

That thumping.

It's close.

I jerk as adrenaline spikes through me.

I slink toward the living room, then tap "End Call."

One thump, then . . . nothing.

It's finally happened. I've finally lost my mind. It feels like spinning and clanging pots and . . . Fighting tears, I let the knife fall to my side. There's no one here except me. Maybe I *will* return to therapy, and this time I'll tell Dr. Birch about my nightmares and ask her to prescribe some old-school remedies like ice baths and electroshock therapy. I'll do anything just to be *normal*. Just so that I won't see and hear shit that isn't there.

Queasy, I tap the number of a woman who may have been found dead tonight in a light-colored car. This time, I will ignore the phantom sounds. This time, I will ignore that *thump . . . thumpthump . . . Thump . . . thumpthump . . .* Since I'm crazy, it doesn't matter if I follow that sound or not, and phone to ear, I pretend that I'm not following that sound . . . that I'm leaving the den . . .

Elizabeth Marsh isn't answering.

Thump . . . thumpthump . . .

Not in the living room, but behind me . . . in the foyer . . . *thump . . . thumpthump . . .* It's here.

I stoop in front of the nook.

Thump . . . thumpthump . . .

The sound comes from inside Mom's go bag. I pull the zipper and the bag splits open.

Thump . . . thumpthump . . .

I push past sweats, socks, shirts to reach the bottom of the duffel.

Thump . . . thumpthump . . .

Though its ringer is off, the dark-red Nokia cell phone vibrates. Beneath the screen, the number keys glow. There's an incoming phone call . . .

My number fills its screen.

I'm calling this phone *right now.*

58.

No.

This . . .

I don't understand.

Why does Mom have Elizabeth Marsh's cell phone in her go bag?

And the phone's charged. Does she take it out and plug it into a charger each week?

I sit in that dim foyer, the phone light the only light in this little cubby.

I dial the number that Alicia Campbell gave me again, the number that I've texted belonging to a woman who responded with texts of her own.

The Nokia vibrates with my number on its screen.

I hunker beside the bag and call that number again.

The Nokia comes alive again and it *thump . . . thumpthumps* against the floor.

There are clothes in the bag. Baggy tan cargo pants. A white tank top. Platform flip-flops.

Fashion-wise, this bag has been here since the Middle Ages. I've never seen Mom wearing raised flip-flops because she *hates* raised flip-flops. *The devil's folly*, she calls them.

Also in the Louis Vuitton duffel, a matching Louis Vuitton phone book.

I flip through the pages of the book.

Dawn Gregory lives on Parkglen Avenue in Los Angeles.

Vanessa Lawrence lives in Marina del Rey.

Who are Dawn and Vanessa?

Alicia Campbell—I know that name.

Felicia Campbell—I know that name, too.

Audrey Gibson—my nana on Dad's side.

There's Daddy's information from back in the day, when he lived near USC.

There are loose snapshots of me that I've never seen before:

An infant me at the pumpkin patch, perched on a haystack.

An infant me eating ice cream, most of it on my face.

Toddler Yara banging the keys of a piano.

These pictures worry me, gnaw at my stomach.

Dust that coats the bag reaches my nose. I sneeze three times, and my head bursts from the pressure.

What should I do?

Say nothing about this or about everything I've learned in the last week?

Confront Mom about this phone?

What would be her excuse?

Liz left it when she abandoned Daddy, and I found it and held on to it all this time. Why is it any of your concern, Yara Marie?

Sounds like something Mom would say.

Cell phones came into regular use during the late nineties. This Nokia's face comes off. When did it come out? A quick Google search tells me that the Nokia 5110 featured changing fascia and debuted in 1998.

Elizabeth Marsh left Dad in June 1998, and they divorced in October 1998. She could've left her bag and phone, especially since she was in a hurry.

Except I texted Elizabeth Marsh using this phone number, and she'd texted me back.

How?

Could *my mother* be Liz Marsh?

No way. But my head swims, and I sneeze again; my skull rocks, and any deductions I've made are blown apart. The goop in my head has thickened as much as the goop pooled in my tight chest. My thoughts turn to sludge and lose all motion and momentum.

Nothing makes sense.

I shove the Nokia deep into the duffel bag and zip it up. I shove the bag into the cubby, then grab the knife from the floor. I can't figure out my next steps if I'm cloudy and in pain. Hot water always opens my lungs, and so I climb into the shower, setting the knife on the sink top just in case. The hot water needles my muscles like liquid acupuncture and I want to cry with relief, but I'm too tired to cry.

Steam covers the mirror completely—no SURRENDER, no words at all. As I wrap myself in a towel, I focus on that steamy glass and wait for a sick reveal. DIE BITCH or I'M COMING FOR YOU in dripping letters.

No words. No reveals.

Back in the bedroom, I put the shoebox and plastic tub back into the closet, then turn off the television. I pop two Vicodin and fall into bed, breathing hard, in pain. I wrap the linens and comforter tightly around my damp skin. Outside, dry leaves crunch and scrape across the wasteland. For a moment, I worry about my lost glasses but remember that I can always buy an emergency pair at the mall.

I reach to pull my rubber band.

Bare wrist.

My rubber band is gone.

My pulse revs and my mind loops . . . loops . . .

I can't . . .

59.

My vibrating cell phone eases me out of a medicated slumber. The late-night shower helped me sleep, and the barely there sunlight tells me that it's not time yet to abandon the warmth of this comforter. But the phone keeps buzzing, and so I wiggle out of my cocoon and reach for it as little blades stab at every part of my body. I wait for the ringing between my ears to stop and for the flare of pain roaring across my muscles to taper off.

Five minutes pass before I dare to slowly reach again for my phone. The screen is blurry.

Oh yeah. I don't have my glasses, nor can I find them.

Shane's left a voice mail. He tells me that he loves me, that he's trying his hardest to race back to Southern California to feed me wonton soup and fancy gelato. "And I'm just thinking about this case with Elizabeth Marsh. I found the number to the condo property manager over on Saint Croix. His name is Winston Rhymes. Nice, right? I'm sure he can tell you if she's been living there or not. I'll email everything, and when you feel up to it, we can talk it over."

I open Shane's email.

Winston Rhymes, Schooner Bay Condominiums, Saint Croix.

What if I flew to the Virgin Islands tomorrow? A treat after pretending for my parents that everything they've done together has been so freaking romantic? The Emmy, Oscar, and NAACP Image Awards go to . . . Yeah, I should fly to Saint Croix.

And maybe Shane will join me.

Since I now have the energy, I call him. "And now that you're done with the case," I say to him, "maybe we can stay there and live happily ever after."

"As much as I want to live in paradise with you . . . ," Shane says. "Tomorrow, though? You sound worse than when we talked yesterday."

"It's weird. I don't even remember talking to you yesterday."

"Yeah. See?" He clucks his tongue. "I'm gonna be an asshole and say that I don't find it funny that your family friend has been low-key trying to kill you."

I search the nightstand for my rubber band. No luck. "Guess you had to be there."

Now he laughs.

"You can take care of me when you fly down today," I say, searching the hospital bag full of my belongings. No rubber band.

"Ah. So you're *not* calling it off."

I squeeze my eyes shut and clench my teeth to keep from crying. "I can't tell my mother that and live to see another day. And that reporter from the paper is coming. And I spent a *lot* of money on this. Am I a coward?"

"Nope," he says. "You're doing the best you can, and that's why I love you."

"I love you, too. After we search for Liz Marsh, will you feed me pineapple on the island? I hear rum is therapeutic."

"Yeah."

"But?"

"I wanna make sure we're not running down blind alleys," he says.

"Excuse me?"

"Not you and me. I meant running down blind alleys with this Liz Marsh thing. We should call Winston Rhymes first."

"Let's." I sit up in bed.

Today, I was scheduled for a final walkthrough with Megan at the golf club. Yeah, I'm good. I'm not throwing any more time, effort, or money into this farce. It's past noon in the Virgin Islands, and so I call Winston Rhymes's number and merge that line with Shane's.

The phone rings . . . rings . . .

"Allo, Schooner Bay." The man sounds raspy, like he's been shouting all day. In this episode of *Queen of Palmdale*, he resembles Yaphet Kotto with his wide, dark, generous face.

"May I speak with Winston Rhymes, please?" I ask.

"This is him." In his world, a printer is spitting out pages. Beyond that spitting printer, a ship horn honks.

"My name's Yara Gibson, and I'm looking for my ex-stepmother." My cheeks warm at the wackiness of those words. "Her family owns a condo there, and no one's answering. Her best friend died, and I'm trying to reach her." I pause. "Not the dead woman, my ex-stepmother—"

"I understand," Winston Rhymes says. "She a Yankee or bahnya?" *Born here?*

"Yankee," I say. "Originally from Los Angeles."

"What's your muddah's name?"

"*Step*mother, and it's Elizabeth Marsh Gibson." That last name— *Gibson*—sticks in my throat and tastes how skunks smell.

"Lemme look."

In the background, the ship horn signals with another short honk. I type the condo's address into Google again. The results include images of cruise ships sitting in the harbor as puffy white clouds bumble in the sky. Lots of green hills and crystal-blue water.

"So," Winston Rhymes says, "whatcha asking me?"

"Does she still live there?" I ask.

"The unit is still owned by Marsh but rented by a tenant."

"For how long?"

"Oh . . ." He clicks his teeth. "Off and on since . . . 2001."

Eighteen *years?*

"Muddah and Fahdah Marsh passed a long time ago, and they had one girl, your *step*mother. She don't come hyah since '98. She a beauty—my boy fall in love with her just like that. But the girl was vexed, yuh check? Another woman come here a few years after that. Didn't like her much. A lyah, that one. She have me rent the place out. We've rented out ever since."

"What's the woman's name?"

"I'd have to find that and call you back."

I thank Winston Rhymes and end the call.

"So if she isn't living in Saint Croix . . . ?" Shane says.

"Where is she living?"

"And who was renting the condo?"

I shrug. "Felicia?"

After Shane and I end our call, I wonder . . . Maybe Dad had another girlfriend. *Irina!* Where the hell is *she?* I'd forgotten all about *that* chick.

Maybe there's something in one of those other boxes in the cabin, something that points me to the subletter's current address. Maybe this question—*where is Liz Marsh*—is exactly how Felicia's investigation started.

So where *is* Liz?

Dead and now chilling beside Felicia Campbell in the morgue?

I grab my phone and shoot off a text to Kayla. You identify the body found in the car yet?

No ellipsis—she's not answering. I grab my purse from the dresser. I haven't visited the cabin at Lake Paz since Tuesday, when I was momentarily trapped in the basement.

Where are the keys?

I dump the contents of my bag onto the bed.

My car keys are here, but the cabin key . . .

Not here. Not on the nightstand nor on the dresser.

Wait . . .

Where is my IDEAS journal for *Queen of Palmdale?*

Downstairs, the front door creaks open and slams so hard the entire house quakes.

It's almost nine o'clock. Everyone is supposed to be running last-minute errands for tonight's dinner.

Who's here?

60.

I creep down the hallway and down the stairs.

Mom's red handbag hangs from the staircase banister like a whale's heart. A pit craters my stomach. I've avoided her for almost forty-eight hours now, but we need to talk. After taking several deep breaths, I clomp down one step at a time as the shrill voice in my head whispers, *Don't!* and *Turn back!* and *There be monsters here!*

By the time I reach the bottom landing, I still don't know what I'm gonna say to her. I stand in the foyer, dumb and mute.

"I'm in here." Her voice drifts from the living room. Calm. Measured. Neither state of mind comforts me.

Mom, wearing a blue tracksuit, sits on the couch as upright as a steel rod. Her chin rests against the manila folder now clutched to her chest. Her eyes are cast to the Nikes on her feet.

I take tiny steps until I'm standing before her.

The cramped space smells like perfume and cigarettes. Too much light. Not enough air.

She looks at me with bloodshot eyes. Dried salt has left white trails down her cheeks.

The only sounds in the room are the wheezing from my lungs and the clattering breath from my mouth. I feel naked in my boxer shorts and tank top.

"You've been busy," she says. "Not just planning the anniversary celebration but also with . . ." She swallows and her chin quivers. "Yara . . ." My name crumples in her mouth.

"It's okay, Mom," I say, rescuing her, rescuing *us* from everything she's about to say.

"I'm so sorry." She swipes at new tears rolling down her cheeks. "I shouldn't have kept these big secrets from you, and believe me, I didn't want to."

She tries to smile and offers a one-shouldered shrug. "I'm many things, but most of all, I'm a mama bear when it comes to my girl."

"I know, Mom," I say, reaching for my rubber band but not finding it. "And I know you didn't plan . . ." I don't know what else to say.

"No one wants to be alone in life," she says. "We all have to compromise. We all have to tamp down those parts of ourselves that are raging monsters wanting to eat, burn, and destroy the people who invade our space." She sets the manila folder thick with papers flat against her lap. She smiles and her eyes shine. "Did you know that I've kept almost everything you and Dom wrote and gave me?"

I nod.

She opens the folder, then holds up a turkey made from brown construction paper. A Valentine's Day heart made from a painted paper plate. She finds a sheet of gray paper. No paint, glitter, or multicolored string on this piece. Mom's mouth tightens as she holds it out to me.

I don't move from my spot. Like my feet, my arms are frozen solid.

Her eyes meet mine. "Read this."

The paper—a pulpy lined sheet that children use to practice handwriting—flutters beneath the whoosh of the air conditioner.

The writing . . . It's my writing, although I haven't written like this in over fifteen years. But this writing . . . it's my writing.

And the words here terrify me.

"Read it aloud, please," Mom asks.

She wants me to *read*?

I don't know how to read, not anymore. I don't know how to breathe, not anymore. My lungs have died in my chest, and my brain swims from the lack of oxygen. I can only blink as the paper rattles in my hands.

Mom plucks the sheet from me and reads: "Dear Mommy . . ."

I saw something very bad and I don't know what to do. I am scared that I am going to Hell and that I won't be with you in Heaven. I saw something very bad and I did not say nothing and I am sorry. Daddy said she was a very bad lady. He did not want her to hurt me and you anymore. Mommy I am scared. I do not want to go to jail. Please do not tell Daddy that I told you. Please do not let me go to jail. Please do not let Daddy hurt me.

My mother's voice breaks, and she can't read the last sentences. But I already know those last sentences.

Liz is gone. Daddy made her go away with his gun.

All of me has turned cold and sharp as cut glass. My mouth moves, but no words . . .

"You wrote this confession," Mom says. "You thought you'd done something wrong, and I knew it had been an accident. Rob bought that gun for protection against those rednecks at Lake Paz, and Liz was unbalanced and lost control and . . ." She clamps her hand over her mouth.

I shake my head. "No. Daddy couldn't have."

"But he *did*, Yara. Elizabeth Marsh is dead. She's been dead for a while now, and you were there when it happened."

"No. I don't remember."

"Of course you don't remember," Mom says, clutching her bare neck. "You broke that night. All of you just *unraveled.* You couldn't sleep. Your health took a serious dive. You stopped talking. I didn't know *how* Liz died, not until you wrote this. And then it all made sense."

"But . . . *when?* When did I . . . ?"

The mail slot opens, letting in more light. Envelopes and catalogs whoosh to the floor.

Mom pushes back her hair. "Liz was staying up at the cabin and Rob invited you and me to stay at their house in LA for the week. Ratchet behavior, I know, but . . .

"Late that night, I'd gone out to pick up Burger King. You stayed at the house with Daddy. Liz drove down from Lake Paz and showed up at the house in LA. When I came back with dinner, you were crying. It was late at night, and so I figured you were just cranky. Your father was acting strange, but I thought that he'd just talked to—and had *lied* to—Liz over the phone. I didn't think anything else had happened. Just regular 'husband almost getting caught cheating on his wife' bullshit. But he told me that Liz came to the *house*, and that they argued but that she left *alive* and drove back up to Lake Paz.

"He told me that he'd demanded a divorce, and that he'd soon be free of her, but Liz . . . That wasn't her plan, and she wouldn't let go. She started sending me all the letters, postcards, AOL messages . . . I was terrified. How many messages did I need to get threatening my life before someone got hurt? And so, once we were a little family, *for real,* this time, we left Los Angeles and moved here."

She shakes her head and stares at the carpet. "It was bizarre to think that someone you thought you knew was sneaking around and doing all this stalker shit. She wrote Rob once and told him exactly what he was wearing. One time, she asked if he liked his beer—because she'd . . . I can't believe I'm about to say this. She said that she *urinated* in it. But that was a lie because it was a can, and the tab hadn't been pulled.

366

"Your dad thought that if he left us, that she'd leave us alone. We were willing to destroy our relationship to make her stop." Mom searches my eyes. "Yara, I've never been that scared in my *life*. For real, you know me. I'm not scared of nothing or no one. Except Liz."

Mom swallows, takes a deep breath, then pushes it out. "And then she sent you this." A postcard of butterflies dancing in the light.

Hey, sweetie pie! How are you?

"What did Daddy do?" I whisper, staring at the card.

"He lost it and said if she came within one hundred feet of you that he'd kill her."

A horrified, confused smile twists my lips. "He didn't actually *mean* that, did he?"

She sighs, shrugs. "But then you wrote this"—she holds up the confession—"years later when you knew how to use your words. You'd kept it bottled up all that time. That's when I knew it couldn't have been Liz who'd sent you that butterfly postcard. The timing was off—according to your confession, she was already dead before we left LA for Palmdale.

"As much as I was horrified that you'd experienced this *bullshit*, this *tragedy*, I was also so *proud* of you. But I needed to protect you from the police. I needed to protect *us*. They would've broken our family apart. The world would've found out, and I didn't want to traumatize you."

She takes a deep breath and releases it through clenched teeth. "Robert doesn't know that you wrote this confession. He doesn't think I know what he did to Liz."

"Who's been pretending to be Liz?" I whisper.

She cocks her head. "The same person who wants us to think she's alive."

Daddy.

HERE WE LIE

61.

My father killed Elizabeth Marsh Gibson.

He shot her to death.

I was there, but I don't remember.

Wait . . .

My mind drifts until something pulls and tugs at my belly button.

I *do* remember.

All this time, my nightmares have suggested that I experienced *something* a long time ago, that I was connected to something *traumatic*. The crying . . . the croaking frogs . . . the sensation of drowning . . . the screaming . . . the blast of a gunshot. All of this also explains my anxiety, the medication, going to therapy that sometimes worked but never stuck.

And now, there's my confession, written in careful loops . . .

I whisper, "I need a moment," to Mom. With my senses banging into each other, I shamble out of the house and sit on the porch. Saturday morning continues to happen all around me—from the drone of cars on the highway to the songs of desert birds. Sprinklers *tchecht-tchecht-tchecht* while down the block, car-stereo Toby Keith sings about the red, white, and blue.

How old was I when he killed her?

The case reports I found in the boxes from the cabin documented that Elizabeth Marsh went missing on June 25, 1998. I was three years old.

Birdie Sumner's witness statement said that she'd heard a fight that evening.

Was that what I heard on the answering machine tape?

Had that been Mom talking to Felicia? Liz confronting her? And then, afterward, Dad killed her to protect Mom and me?

On weak legs, I return to the foyer. Mom hasn't moved from her spot on the living room couch. Face hidden in her lap, her shoulders shudder as she cries. Her back should hurt—she's been carrying our family's secrets for so long. We've painted her as the villain, as the one ready to desert us on a whim. Little did I know. She'd been swallowing all of it to keep us together, to keep us from the law.

And then there's Dad. I knew there'd been something else out there. He's lied to me about his life with Elizabeth Marsh, with his other family. He's done something so *extreme* that my mind snags and tangles around the thought of him being someone else.

This isn't right.

I dash up the stairs and pull on sweats and a hoodie. I grit my teeth as I slip contact lenses into my eyes. They sting, but I can see clearly now, better than I have in days.

Mom, red-nosed and scratchy, haunts the foyer. "Are you okay?"

I run out the door without answering.

The stiff breeze moves the trees and bushes, but it isn't the hot and swollen wind that brings sandstorms. The sudden sunshine, so clear now with my contacts, makes me want to vomit. The rest of me . . . I'm too numb to feel the rest of me.

"Where are you going?" Mom shouts from the doorway. "Yara, stop! Wait!"

I climb into the Jeep's driver's seat. Somehow, the car turns on by itself and somehow, the Jeep navigates onto Lake Paz Road.

What am I doing?

Mom also texts me asking that same question.

To talk to Kayla, I text back.

About what? I don't know.

Cookie Monster house shoes.

Cookie Monster nightgown . . .

That answering machine tape—there's a child crying in the background.

Insurance policies . . . Music royalties . . .

I pull into the sheriff's station, a cream building with ceramic roof tiles and drop boxes on the sidewalk that can easily be mistaken for book drops. But this is no library, and those drop boxes hold needles and illegal drugs deposited by Joe and Jane Public.

Kayla's white Honda sits in the employee parking lot.

An older woman wearing raggedy sandals, her stringy blonde hair pulled into an updo, argues with a younger woman with the same meth face. *I can do what I want* and *You ain't had to come down here* and *I ain't bailing you out no more.*

Bile burns my throat. My life is about to change, I know it. Right now it's changing because I'm grabbing my cigarette case from the glove box. Three months since I last smoked. Three months wearing my rubber band, but that band is now missing. I roll down the windows, then pluck a Newport from the three left. I push in the Jeep's cigarette lighter and wait.

How long will Dad have to stay in jail?

Will Mom also be charged for the cover-up?

I stick the cigarette between my lips.

The unsmoked cigarette flies from my hand, hits the steering wheel, and lands on the passenger-side seat.

I shout, "Hey!"

"No!" Daddy stands at my window with his large hand too close to my face. "Your mother told me you were coming here."

I shove him away. "You're a liar."

He holds my arm. "Yara, calm down."

I bare my teeth, forgetting that the man on the other side of the window is my father.

"You lied to me," I shout, not too different from the mother and daughter moments ago. "You've lied to me about *everything*, and I'm tired of living with it."

Dad holds out his hands. "It's complicated."

"What did Kayla ask you and Mom yesterday?"

His mouth moves, but no words make it past his lips.

I roll my eyes and reach for that smacked-away cigarette.

Dad jogs to the other side of the Jeep and climbs into the passenger seat. In his practice sweats and cap, he smells like football.

"Get out!"

"I was married before," Dad shouts back. "I've wanted to tell you that for a long time."

I cross my arms and turn my head. I can't even *look* at him. His voice is raw liver and maggots squirming inside my ears, and I'm sickened by the sound.

He takes a deep breath and pushes it out. "I wanted to tell you, but it was complicated. Yes, that word again. And then there's the fact that she's missing. I don't know if you know that. She left, and I don't know where she is, and it broke me, and I looked for her for a very long time even though she'd *changed*. Even though she lost her mind and just . . . well . . .

"Your mother doesn't know this, but I'd been looking for Liz for about ten years, and I didn't have any luck. I still think about her a lot, and I still wonder about her, and that's what I'm doing beneath the tree." He squeezes his temples. "I'm out there trying to figure out where she could've gone."

He rubs his jaw. "Felicia was the only one who was more committed to finding her than me. She ping-ponged from thinking Liz was dead to Liz being alive, and we worked together to find the truth once and for all. But I slowed down in my searching because I had to start living."

Callous. Sociopathic. I've never thought of him like that until today.

"Sheldon Marsh," Dad continues. "He was one of the first Black composers for the movie studios. Maryam Marsh was absolutely stunning. She was a Dorothy Dandridge double for *Carmen Jones* and *Porgy and Bess*. And Liz was just as talented, just as beautiful.

"They were out for a drive around Lake Paz, and the brakes on their car went out. They careened off the mountainside. The accident killed Sheldon and Maryam instantly. Liz survived, but her injuries ended her dancing career."

I know this already, and I see the beautiful Clara in the Inglewood High School yearbook hobbled and broken.

Dad wraps his hand around my wrist. "Liz loved this Russian ballerina Irina Baranova. She was one of Balanchine's 'Baby Ballerinas,' and performed *Swan Lake* when she was just fourteen and all this stuff that—" He shrugs, shakes his head. "Anyway, Liz loved her and told me that we had to name our first daughter Irina. But when she looked at that beautiful little girl in her arms, she knew that Irina was too heavy and went with the nickname for Irina instead."

He squeezes my wrist and looks at me. "So we called her . . . Yara."

62.

"She even bought you a gold nameplate that spelled 'Irina,'" Dad says. "You weren't even born yet, but that never stopped her from buying you things."

I can't speak. I can only gape at the man in the passenger seat.

"Barbara isn't your biological mother, Yaya," he says. "Dominique is Barbara's biological daughter, but you're Liz's baby. From your uncontrollable hair to the shape and color of your eyes. You look just—"

"Get out of my car." I whisper this.

The smile that had spread across his face slowly dies on the vine. Confusion blooms in his eyes, all wild and silver-glisten. "We'd take you on long drives in the Camaro. That had been Sheldon's car before the—"

"Get out," I spit. "You're a liar."

"Why would I lie about—"

"You killed her."

His eyes bug. *"What?"*

"I saw you. I was there."

He shakes his head. "I don't know who told you that. No one knows where she is."

A light pops in my head. "You killed Felicia because she was gonna tell me everything!"

"Yara—"

I hit the steering wheel with the palm of my hand. "Get out of my car!"

Two red-faced cops stand in the employee parking lot, and they look over to us. *They* want us to keep going.

Dad realizes this, too, and runs a frantic hand beneath his cap and over his bald head. "I'm gonna find Dom—she's not answering. We'll talk about this at home."

"Get out!"

He launches from the car and hurries to his Suburban. My shoulders hunch, just like his, and the top of my ears point out like a bat's—just like his.

Dad has lied to me about Elizabeth Marsh's existence as a person, as his high school girlfriend, as his first wife. And now, this woman who didn't exist until last week has, suddenly, become my *mother*? And according to my *real* mother, Elizabeth Marsh is now dead because Robert Gibson, my father, shot her twenty years ago?

Of *course* he killed Felicia. She was the secret keeper all this time.

⚡

Mom's gold Cherokee is not in the driveway.

Neither is Dad's blue Suburban.

He said that he was gonna find Dominique. Did he decide to run away instead?

Did Mom decide to go with him?

I rush through the kitchen and out to the backyard. Small dust devils swirl behind the back fence. No one is perched on the lounge chairs beneath the pergola. No one sits in the chairs atop the small hill. Over in the garage, the tarp no longer covers the Camaro.

Liz's Camaro.

The car door is unlocked.

Felicia gave me a set of keys. One for the cabin . . . and maybe the other for a car?

Both keys are now missing.

I press the yellow trunk-release button inside the Camaro's cabin. *Pop.*

The trunk creaks open, and that smell of car leather and Juicy Fruit gum swirls past me. I sweep away the large CANCUN towel spread across the trunk space.

Beloved sits there, and my lightning bolt chain, now repaired, dangles like a bookmark between the red cover and the first page.

So Dominique wasn't lying. She *did* fix it, but it wasn't on the dresser like she'd said . . .

The plastic tub of reports I took from the cabin and hid in my bedroom closet, that I *just* rummaged through last night, is in this trunk. So are my eyeglasses, the keys to the cabin and to the Camaro, and . . . my IDEAS-*QUEEN OF PALMDALE* journal. There's a gun here, too, with a spot of red on its . . .

"Barrel," I whisper. Just like the gun in my dreams of drowning in a lake. This gun *does* exist. I *wasn't* imagining that. There's a baby book, and the bottom of the trunk is lined with cash wrapped with rubber bands and bundled together with binder clips and paper clips.

Whose money is this?

Who took all these things, *my things*, and hid them here?

I grab the revolver and, a moment later, set the gun back in its spot. I grab my journal, *Beloved*, and the lightning bolt pendant. These are mine. There's a copy of *The Monster at the End of This Book*. I flip through Grover's story—a dark-red splotch covers half of page four.

Blood?

I grab this, too.

I grab the baby book and open it to see *Yara Marie Gibson* on the title page.

The birth date—April 25, 1995—is correct. The family-tree page . . . Robert Louis Gibson Jr., father. Elizabeth Marie Marsh Gibson, mother.

There I am, page after page. I learned to walk in January 1996 at nine months old. I started swim school at two. Here's my yellow swim cap folded neatly in the page's crease. There are pictures of me wearing floaties on my arms while this *woman*—Elizabeth Marsh wearing a tankini—holds me close. Big smiles. There she is, lounging in a lakeside chaise, a picture similar to the photo I found in the attic. There I am, wearing a Cookie Monster beanie with a cookie puff ball atop it, standing in front of the green cabin at Lake Paz. And there *we* are, Elizabeth and Daddy, cheek to cheek, with me in between them, stealing all the focus.

We *were* happy once.

There's a folded transcription of an interview with Dad and Detective Stall.

MS: You were okay with leaving your wife and daughter alone?

RG: This is her family's cabin—she grew up here during the summers and holidays. She knows the people.

MS: The same people who'd been suspected of tampering with her parents' car?

RG: I was just going to be gone overnight. Liz isn't weak.

MS: Where did you stay back in Los Angeles?

RG: At our house in View Park.

MS: That would be 4255 Enoro Drive. *Her* house.

RG: She inherited the house. *We* live there.

MS: Were you alone that night?

RG: I had friends over.

MS: You had a party.

RG: No. Just a few friends.

MS: Any women?

RG: No.

MS: You sure?

RG: I know who was in my house.

MS: So if a woman has told us that she visited 4255 Enora Drive on the night of June 25, would she be lying?

RG: Okay, she dropped by—but she didn't stay.

MS: And who is "she"?

RG: Barbara McGuire.

MS: And what is your relationship with Barbara McGuire?

RG: What does that have to do with my missing family?

MS: It has *everything* to do with your missing family.

Missing family?

And there's another missing person bulletin.

MISSING PERSON AT RISK

Yara Marie Gibson

Female, Black, three years old

36″, 29 lbs., brown eyes, brown hair

Last seen with her mother, Elizabeth Marie Marsh, in a blue Cookie Monster nightgown at 10:00 a.m. on Thursday, June 25, 1998, near their residence at 1224 Stardust Way in Lake Paz, California. Elizabeth Marsh suffers from depression and anxiety. Any information, please contact the Sheriff's Homicide Bureau, Missing Persons.

What the *hell?*

I run back to the house with my arms filled with my things: *Beloved*, the pendant, the journal, the plastic tub, the children's book, the baby book with the transcript and bulletin, and the set of keys. Back in my bedroom, I drop everything on the comforter. I'm barely breathing as I search the tub's contents and everything relates to . . . *me*.

A witness named Earl saw me stumble out of the woods, crying. I ran from him.

According to Nana Audrey, I doggy-paddled over to the islet on Lake Paz and hid there.

And a statement from me: *The bad lady come. I scared.*

There's a transcript of Dad speaking to the county's child psychiatrist: *She's scared of water, and she has nightmares and night terrors. She sleepwalks and never remembers . . . She's in counseling every now and then, but we think that, over time, she'll, you know, snap out of it.*

I never remember.

A chill tears up my spine, and I wonder . . . *Did I put my things—* the pendant, the book, the tub, everything—*in the Camaro?* Was I sleepwalking while I did this, and I simply don't remember? What else have I done this past week that I don't remember?

Did *I* kill . . . ?

No. No. No.

The creak of the Camaro's trunk yanks me from my spiral, and I run across the hallway to stand in my parents' bedroom window. Mom is staring into the Camaro's trunk.

Where has she been all this time?

My phone rings.

It's Kayla.

I answer but keep my eyes on the woman at the Camaro. "Hey, I need to call you back."

"I have some news," she says. "Are you sitting down?"

63.

No, I'm standing and staring out the window as my mother rummages through the trunk of her—no, *Elizabeth Marsh's*—muscle car. What's she looking for?

Kayla is saying something else now. I'm more irritated than interested.

"Are you listening to me?"

"I'm sorry." I stumble back to my bedroom, a sad place with a crowded nightstand and bureau top, dingy walls, and the smell of sickness and smoke. "What's wrong?"

"The green Mazda—I found the guy."

"He exists?"

"You questioned that? You told me—"

"I know. It's"—*I'm*—"complicated. What about the guy?"

"You were right. Will Harraway hired him to follow Felicia, but he only had the address to your parents' house. When you saw him, he didn't know that his target was already dead."

I gasp. "Was he a hit man?"

"He says no, but of course, he won't admit it yet."

I close my eyes. "Can I call you back—"

"*And,*" Kayla says, "the light-colored car that was at Lake Palmdale when Felicia was killed? The one found near the creek back on Thursday?"

"The woman inside . . ." I cover my mouth with my hand. "You know who she was."

"LaRain Andrepont," Kayla says. "*She* was one of the people inside the white car."

My stomach drops. "But LaRain doesn't drive a white car."

"It was reported stolen a year ago. One of Ransom's when he ran that chop shop. LaRain was also the anonymous tipper. The phone she'd used to call me earlier this week belonged to her. We were supposed to meet that night at the Red Roof Inn, but she never showed up."

I bend over. My head swims with words and sounds.

"There's something else you should know," she says.

"Just *wait.*" Feels like I'm breathing through a straw. "I just need . . ." I thrust my hand at the nightstand and knock over the vials of antibiotics and steroids, old drinking straws, and near-empty tissue boxes. I need the inhalers just prescribed by my doctor, but they're not here.

I paw through the wastebasket in case I knocked them in, but they're not there, either.

I search my purse . . . no inhalers.

My lungs tighten as I drop to my knees to search beneath the bed, then beneath the comforter. No luck.

This city has taken my breath away. Just like I knew it would.

My parents have taken the life that I once knew, and they've broken its back.

Barbara—my mother—is not my mother.

Elizabeth Marsh is my mother.

And my father killed her.

Yoga-breathing poses will help, and I close my eyes and inhale. There aren't many free breaths left in me, and I release that precious breath already feeling stronger. I will conserve my words, and I will walk slow until I find my meds. If all else fails, I will drive back to the hospital and request another set. My doctor will certainly think that I'm either selling my drugs or that I'm getting high off Ventolin.

"I'm having a hard time," I whisper to Kayla.

"You need an ambulance?"

"Just . . . What else do you need to say?"

"The DNA that we found on Felicia? It definitively does not belong to you."

I didn't kill Felicia.

"But—"

"But?"

Kayla sighs. "It's a partial match to Dominique's."

I shiver. "Are you saying that my sister—"

"No," she interrupts. "Dominique has a solid alibi. We have security camera footage showing her and Ransom at BJ's and then at the Cinemark that night to see the new John Wick movie."

"Is there a complete DNA match?"

"Yes."

"My father?"

"When the medical examiner conducted LaRain's autopsy, he found something in her hand. He found a honeybee pendant."

"What?"

Kayla says nothing for a long time, then: "Where's your mother? In this instance, I mean . . . Where is Barbara Gibson?"

64.

Kayla's driving here right now, and I think she said the word "ambulance."

The world around me is worse than a blur. The world around me is soup and clouds and dragon's breath and breathing the world's air has broken my lungs and I can't even cry anymore because the world has broken my tear ducts, too.

With numb hands, I fumble for my bag and pull out the answering machine and the bag of tapes. I select the only tape that I haven't listened to and press "Play."

There's a woman's frantic voice and a child—me?—crying in the background.

"Where are you? I'm here alone and Rob's not calling me back." She hangs up.

Next call: "Felicia, it's Liz again. It's about three o'clock. Should I be worried? Bee wouldn't do anything in the middle of the day, would she? Anyway, call me." She hangs up.

Next call: "Felicia, ohmigod." She starts to weep, and the call ends a minute later.

Next call: "Barbara's gonna kill me, I know it. She's out there—I saw her Jetta. I think . . . I think I'm just gonna drive back to LA. Yaya's not feeling good, and Bee's crazy and unpredictable, and Rob thinks

I'm crazy, but I know she's the one who keeps calling and hanging up. I know she's the one who forged that letter to the parents at the dance school. I know she's the one who opened that credit card at Nordstrom. I know she's the one who spray-painted Rob's Bronco, but I'm just a hysterical female, right? I'm the crazy one. I'm not, and I told you and I told Rob, and no one listened to me. No one! I'll let you know when I'm leaving the lake."

Next call: "Yaya's sleeping, so I packed my bag and I'm just gonna load her up and get outta here. I can't call you on my cell phone—no reception up here. So I'm on my way."

Next call: "Ohmigod, Bee's outside. Where are you? Felicia, you there? Pick up."

The tape ends.

Packed my bag.

Is that the go bag now stowed in the foyer's nook?

Parts of me remember that night. The yelling, the crying, my shoulder hurting. All that water. I'd lived through something, but what?

Only one person would know.

Elizabeth Marsh wasn't the stalker. And Dad didn't kill Elizabeth Marsh.

Mom—Barbara McGuire—stalked and killed Elizabeth Marsh.

And somehow, she got me to write that confession . . . that is, if she didn't write it herself.

I know she's the one who forged that letter to the parents.

"Yara." Mom—no, *Barbara*—looms in my bedroom doorway. She holds my newest rescue inhaler in one hand and a revolver in the other. *The* revolver . . . the one I left behind in the Camaro, the one with the red mark on the barrel I've seen in my dreams.

I scramble to grab the hunting knife from beneath the mattress.

Her eyes narrow as she takes in the knife. "Where did you get that answering machine?"

My face crumples. "Does it matter? You did all of that because she was *prettier* than you? Because some people liked her more than they liked you? Because you wanted *Dad*?"

She snorts. "Your father ended up being just like that Camaro out there. Actually, he's more disappointing than the Camaro."

I shake my head. "You forced me to write that confession, and you've held on to it all these years."

"Forced?" She rolls her eyes. "You *loved* handwriting exercises. And if the police came and asked questions, well . . . better Robert than me."

I shake my head. "But all this time, you told me that I was . . ." *Dramatic, crazy, depressed, anxious, delusional.* But I was none of those things. I'd witnessed the murder of my mother and had been taken into the home of the woman who'd killed her.

"Yara," Barbara says, "I tried to love you like you were mine, and there were moments where I truly felt something like love, but then I'd remember . . . I wanted my happily ever after, and Felicia was gonna ruin it, just like she ruined high school. She really thought Liz was alive."

"You pretended to be Liz," I whisper. "You sent postcards, letters. Those text messages to me—*you* wrote those. You wrote those letters you claimed Felicia sent, didn't you? Made everyone think that *you* were the victim."

She says nothing.

"You wrote that note to Felicia on Friday night," I say.

The paper—Dad's legal pad. *That's* why their fingerprints were on that note.

"You killed Felicia," I whisper.

"Technically," she says, "LaRain and I worked together on that. I promised to give her some of your trust fund after helping me with you. Poor Lala had no patience."

"LaRain . . . She had your honeybee pendant."

Barbara pales. "Excuse me?"

"In her hand," I whisper. "The medical examiner found it." I pause, then cock my head. "What trust fund?"

She stares at me, reaches for her neck, thinking. Then: "You have a choice, Yara." Her shaky hands still reach for her missing bee pendant. "You can die from an asthma attack, which you've been doing slowly all week, or I'll handle it and afterward, I'll leave you in a spot in the forest that you used to love when you were a child. Lots of butterflies there. I picked it out for you a long time ago, that night at the cabin with Liz."

"You shot her," I whisper.

"You slipped out of the cabin," she says.

"You found me," I say, nodding.

"On the shore of the lake. You saw me and ran into the water." She chuckles, waggles her head. "I figured you swam out into the deepest part and drowned, which would've been perfect."

But I didn't drown. I rolled onto my back to breathe, just like I'd learned in swim class, and kicked over to that little island. I didn't freeze to death. I didn't starve to death. I survived. And now, I try to blink away my tears, but they roll down my cheeks, hot and free. I remember now. The cold water, the rocks, the frogs . . .

Hot tears fill my eyes. "Daddy?"

She rolls her eyes. "He'd always tell me, 'Maybe in another life,' and excuse me? *Maybe?* And when I made her disappear and I helped look for her, I took care of you and made sure that Rob ate and slept, and just like I planned, he fell in love with me. This time, *I* won. And beautiful Liz so nicely left behind all her bank accounts and fancy, sellable things. You can thank her when you see her on the other side."

Elizabeth Marsh had funded our lives. Her money had been used to buy this house, buy our cars . . . The Italian glass in the attic. The Chagall. The ring on Barbara's hand was the same ring I saw in pictures at the cabin. Those bundles of cash in the Camaro . . .

"And the cabin," I say.

"I went there that night, and I confronted her," Barbara says. "Rob was in LA and had left you two alone. She'd begged me to let you leave—there was a condo in the Virgin Islands—but we both knew that Rob wouldn't give up on her, not after being together since high school."

"The tapes," I whisper. "She recorded you coming that night. And the fight . . ."

Barbara nods. "We fought, and the neighbor heard and came over. But she left—Liz pretended that everything was okay. That was the first time she did what I asked. Guess seeing you with this"—she lifts the gun again—"pressed to your forehead convinced her to listen to me. But you surviving . . . You were worth more alive than dead. You *are* a treasure, Yara."

I twitch—she's always said this to me, and I thought she meant it out of love, not . . .

I gape at her. "You'll kill me, your daughter, for money?"

She cocks her head. "Would it be better if I killed you for love? For God? You're the writer. Tell me, what sounds better? And I've worked hard for this. All those postcards and letters and keeping Liz alive in everybody's head? Making it look like she'd completely lost it and abandoned y'all? Scared that the cops would realize that the woman showing up at the Lost Hills Station with the statement to leave her alone *wasn't* Liz, but that it was me?"

Barbara flaps her hands at her face and shivers. "I got gray hair that night. But it worked out." She sighs and shrugs. "I'm good and I'm smart as hell, but I still haven't figured out how to change my fingerprints to match a dead woman's. Give me time."

"You're fucking evil," I say, shaking my head.

"I'm the GOAT, my dear."

"Greatest of all time for *what*?" I ask. "Murder? Fraud? Theft? Gaslighting?"

She laughs. "I hadn't thought of gaslighting."

"Liz wasn't crazy."

Her eyes go hard. "She was for baiting me."

"Felicia wasn't crazy."

"Again," Barbara says, "she got in my way."

"And I didn't have an overactive imagination or lose things for no reason. I needed help, but you wouldn't get me the kind I needed. And you fought with Dad, who tried to help me."

She grins. "What else do you want me to say, Yara?"

My tears cloud the woman before me. "Does Dominique know?"

She sighs. "Why would I tell her anything? She'll be a very rich woman. And know this: I won't let Ransom anywhere *near* her money. We'll be very good stewards of your inheritance once you're resting on that hill with the butterflies."

"Barbara," I say. "*Mom.* They *know.* It's over. They know you killed LaRain. They know you killed Felicia. And they'll know that you tried to kill me."

"*Tried?*" She throws her head back and laughs. "You *still* don't know me. There is no try. There is only do. I *always* win."

I grip the knife and swallow the lump hardened in my throat. "*Actually*, it's, 'Do or do not. There is no try.' So go ahead: do it, *bitch*."

Her eyes are hard and dark as a shark's. She lifts the gun and pulls the trigger.

Click.

Click.

Click.

Nothing.

After discovering the gun in the trunk, I emptied the chamber and slipped the bullets into my pocket.

I use my last breaths to lunge at Barbara Gibson. I knock her to the hallway carpet and hold the hunting knife to her throat. A pearl of blood pebbles on the tip of the dark blade.

Her eyes bulge, but she doesn't beg. She smiles. "Go ahead. End it. *Do* something."

I want to whip this knife across her throat and glory in the spray of blood that would spurt from her arteries.

That's what she wants, too. And whatever Queen Bee wants, Queen Bee gets.

She *always* wins.

Not today.

Epilogue

July 12, 2019

There are over 2,200 mines near Palmdale—from aluminum and chromium to titanium, vanadium, and zirconium. Deputy Diego Castro has led his mine rescue team to search three of those, including the Tropico Gold Mine and Quartz Hill Mine, for the remains of Elizabeth Marsh Gibson. He hoped that either these mine searches or another dredge through Lake Paz would turn something—no, *someone*—up.

They haven't.

As I wait for a meeting invite to pitch *Queen of Palmdale* to a producer I met two weeks ago, I sit out on the deck of the cabin at Lake Paz examining the mail I found in Elizabeth Marsh's post office box: a bank statement with my name on it. Papers from another bank confirming my address on Edgewater Court. A letter from a lawyer "just checking in."

> As you come closer to reaching your twenty-fifth birthday and fulfilling all the requirements set forth by your mother, Elizabeth, we'll talk more about your trust—investments, philanthropy, and retirement.

The signature on other documents attesting that I understand is not my signature. The bank account receiving allowances does not belong to me. The names on those accounts are Elizabeth Marsh and Yara Gibson, but I've never received any money.

Of course.

My mother left me the cabin and required that I reach adulthood to inherit the full amount. If I'd died before then, Dad would've inherited half of the money, and the other half would have gone to a children's arts organization. Greedy Barbara McGuire Gibson decided to play the ultimate long game, waiting two decades to get her hands on the full amount. She probably tried to change the terms of the trust, but that would've required an in-person meeting with the trustee and fingerprints—*Elizabeth Marsh's fingerprints.*

I finish reading final witness statements from friends and family . . . including Felicia Campbell's.

STATEMENT FROM FELICIA CAMPBELL TO DETECTIVE MATT STALL:

I tried to tell you, but men always think women are hysterical, that we need psychiatric evaluations. I have two degrees from Caltech, and I'm working on a third. Does it look like I need psychiatric treatment?

Oh, Felicia.

You were right all along.

Dad offers me another bottle of water. His facial hair is now gray even though nearly two months have passed since Kayla arrested Barbara for the murders of Felicia Campbell and LaRain Andrepont.

Dad wept as I told him everything, as he listened to the answering machine tapes, as I showed him my coerced confession. He'd tried to leave Barbara, but then Dominique was born—just as Kayla's parents said. Dad gave Barbara an ultimatum: "Treat me better or else."

"She did," he told me, "until she didn't. I'd bring up divorce again, and she'd do better."

"Why didn't you just *leave?*" I asked.

"She would've never given me custody of Dom," he explained. "And I didn't want to separate my girls. So . . ." He swiped at the tears rolling down his cheeks.

He told me that he'd texted back and forth with Felicia on the night she died. He'd begged her for more time, said that he'd tell me everything and that he was writing it all that night, the same night I told him to write a toast for the party.

He had no idea that Barbara had killed Liz. "Why would I think that?" he asked me last night. "Especially knowing that Liz was struggling for so long after the accident. And then, when she started sending postcards and emails . . . To me, she was alive. And Felicia and I tried to find her—a body for Felicia, a living woman for me."

He shook his head. "I didn't cheat on Liz—with Barbara, with anyone. I really thought Liz left me. I mean . . . I *hated* her for going, but I'm not stupid: She *was* too good for me. She was Old Black Hollywood royalty, and I was an ex–football captain who tore his ACL on the third day at Raiders training camp. I never deserved her, but *she* loved me, too. I didn't think Barbara would've . . . How could she be so . . . *evil?*"

Held without bond, Barbara has nothing to say. For the first time in her life, she's gone mute. We will not allow her to use the money she stole from Elizabeth Marsh to pay for an attorney. There's a rumor that the DA won't seek the death penalty for the two murders if she tells us where she left Elizabeth Marsh so many years ago.

My phone rings.

It's Lukas, our contractor. "Hey, Miss Gibson. I hate bothering you again, but can you drive down right now? We got a problem."

Is it a news station wanting exterior shots of our house being torn down again?

Is it Dominique throwing herself in front of a bulldozer for the third time? She hasn't spoken to me these past weeks. She refuses to accept that Dad wants to rebuild and not sleep in a bedroom or roam a hallway that he shared with a murderer. She refuses to believe that her mother killed mine.

On the Saturday morning of the anniversary party, I canceled and forfeited all my money to the golf club. I spent hours texting friends and family, and my phone shuddered from all the texts of why and everything okay and tell me how I can help and who's paying for my hotel cancellation fee.

Lake Paz shimmers blue as the sky above us. Trees dance in the breeze and rain down dried leaves and needles. Once fire season starts, some of this will burn. For years, our lives have been ablaze and we didn't even know it.

Dad climbs into the Camaro's passenger seat. He just finished showering, but he still looks dusty and worn. He's always wanted to lose a few pounds, but not like this.

"Rib eyes for dinner?" I ask, revving the engine.

"Sounds good to me."

He's now renting a one-bedroom apartment four miles away from the house. I offered to let him stay at the cabin since it belongs to me, but he doesn't want to leave Palmdale. He doesn't want to leave his football team.

The farther we drive from the lake, the closer to the sun we get. By the time we reach the house on Edgewater Court, the thermostat on my watch hits 111 degrees. The main house, except for one wall, is gone. Little colored flags that mean different things—gas line, electric wiring—dot the ground. The contractor and his crew have started demolishing the rear garage, and now, they crowd around the spot where the Camaro used to sit.

Lukas, a man with a weathered face as square and red as a brick, shakes hands with Dad.

"What's up?" I ask.

"Sweet car," he says, nodding to the gold muscle car.

"It was my mother's," I say.

Lukas beckons us to follow him.

Last time, there'd been issues with the blueprints. *Cha-ching.* Another time, there'd been a suspected crack in the foundation. We had to pay for a structural engineer. *Cha-ching.* I hold my breath again as I parkour across the remains of my childhood home.

"We stopped cuz we found this." Lukas points to the spaces between chunks of concrete.

I lean in close. "What is it?"

Dad says, "What am I looking at?"

This is not concrete. It's too round and perfectly shaped to be concrete.

I turn on my phone's flashlight and move the light lower.

It's a skull.

Something gleams beneath the jaw cavity.

A lightning bolt.

And a gold nameplate.

Liz.

She's been with us this entire time.

⚡

I don't remember driving back to Lake Paz.

I don't remember falling into Shane's embrace on the cabin's porch.

I don't remember trudging to the bedroom that overlooks the lake.

My eyes open to a dusky room with shards of sunlight flickering across my hands.

Dominique slips in bed beside me.

I wipe away the tears rolling along the bridge of her nose.

Dominique does the same for me.

Without saying a word, we pinkie-shake.

She tucks her head beneath my chin and slowly lets out her breath.

And together we lie there, silent as secrets, as the sun dips beneath that forever-deep lake.

ACKNOWLEDGMENTS

I will never get tired of thanking those who continue to support this dream of mine. Thank you especially to those who choose to pick up my stories and attend events and buy books and engage and encourage me and my writing friends. Y'all are the best readers ever!

Jill Marsal, you've been my dream agent for almost ten years now—and somehow, I still feel like I'm your only client. Thank you for always looking out for me.

Thank you to my incredible team at Thomas and Mercer. Jessica Tribble, you are a dream editor, and I'm thrilled that we're working together, that you're so supportive and excited about the words I slap against the page. Clarence Haynes, you are still the best developmental editor in the world, and the more we work together, the stronger my stories become. Excelsior! Grace Doyle, Brittany Russell, Sarah Shaw, Nicole Burns-Ascue, all of editorial, all of production, all of marketing, Brilliance . . . Thank you so much for throwing your backs into it. I've never felt so supported in my publishing career—thank you for making me feel like I deserve any of this.

Thank you to my incredible team at BookSparks. Crystal Patriarche and Taylor Brightwell, I appreciate everything you do. I had some big hits this past year, and I have you to thank for that. Let's get some more!

Thank you, writing friends—too many to name. You continue to be sources of inspiration and writer envy. (How do some of y'all do those tricks?!) Thank you, especially, to Jess Lourey and Lee Goldberg for showing me around my new publishing home. The writing life is scary, and I'm blessed to have guides like you holding my hand.

Thank you to my family. These past pandemic years have meant fewer road trips to hang out, but the little time we've been able to spend means so much to me. Mom, you've always believed in me, in this dream of mine, and here I am. Gretchen, Jason, and Terry, your texts and our Sunday Zoom calls bring me joy . . . and great ideas. I love y'all.

Maya, you are the light of my life. I am so proud to be your mama and your friend. I can't wait to properly cowrite one of these with you. Thank you for your love and encouragement.

David, for twenty-seven years, you've been there for me. We've done a lot of living, and some of that winds up in my stories. You've never made me feel bad for that. Thank you for understanding and accepting me. I love you!

ABOUT THE AUTHOR

Photo © 2019 Andre Ellis

Rachel Howzell Hall is the *New York Times* bestselling author of *These Toxic Things*; *And Now She's Gone*; *They All Fall Down*; and, with James Patterson, *The Good Sister*, which was included in Patterson's collection *The Family Lawyer*. An Anthony, International Thriller Writers, and Lefty Award nominee, Rachel is also the author of *Land of Shadows*, *Skies of Ash*, *Trail of Echoes*, and *City of Saviors* in the Detective Elouise Norton series. A past member of the board of directors for Mystery Writers of America, Rachel has been a featured writer on NPR's acclaimed *Crime in the City* series and the National Endowment for the Arts weekly podcast; she has also served as a mentor in Pitch Wars and the Association of Writers Programs. Rachel lives in Los Angeles with her husband and daughter. For more information, visit www.rachelhowzell.com.